Praise for

THE FIRST ACTRESS

"A literal drama queen, the historical Bernhardt provides a great wealth of material—sleeping in a coffin, keeping pumas as pets, the circles in which she moved with the likes of Victor Hugo and Oscar Wilde—for the creation of a colorful melodrama, equal parts flamboyancy and pathos. Since Bernhardt loved to extravagantly mythologize her own story, she would doubtless delight in [C. W.] Gortner's first-person fictionalization of her extraordinary life."

—*Booklist*

"A compelling portrait that will certainly whet readers' appetites to learn more about this charismatic figure . . . recommended for fans of Melanie Benjamin and Allison Pataki."

—*Library Journal*

"Gortner captures the drama and pathos of legendary actor Sarah Bernhardt's life in this enchanting work. . . . Skillful first-person narration evokes Bernhardt's fierce energy and tempestuous liaisons, the vulnerability borne of her wounding childhood, and her struggles against misogyny and anti-Semitism. Gortner does justice to this trailblazing celebrity and her fascinating era."

—*Publishers Weekly*

"Gortner's fluid first-person prose paints a vivid portrait in an immersive, hard-to-put-down drama. . . . Highly recommended."

—*Historical Novels Review* (Editor's Choice)

"With his signature attention to detail and penchant for writing strong female characters, C. W. Gortner returns with *The First Actress*, the story of the inimitable Sarah Bernhardt, the world's first modern actress and international celebrity. . . . Without making his writing feel detail-heavy or overly absorbed in the history, [Gortner] is able to completely immerse his readers in the worlds that his characters inhabit. . . . Gortner's account of Sarah Bernhardt's life is deeply intimate and immersive, his characters richly written and wholly realized."

—*Bookreporter*

"C. W. Gortner's *The First Actress* is a sumptuous tale of a woman coming into her own. This novel about Sarah Bernhardt, the iconic French actress, is both a riveting portrait of the artist as a passionate young woman and a luscious historical novel full of period detail, a must-read for fans of the genre."

—MELANIE BENJAMIN, *New York Times* bestselling author of *Mistress of the Ritz* and *The Aviator's Wife*

"Sarah Bernhardt was a woman of fearless strength and awe-inspiring talent, both a living icon in her day and an unapologetic iconoclast. In his beautiful *The First Actress*, C. W. Gortner gives readers an intimate and rich portrait of Bernhardt's stunning career and tumultuous personal life. The Divine Sarah was a singular leading lady ahead of her time, winning devotees and breaking rules in order to demand more for artists and for women."

—ALLISON PATAKI, *New York Times* bestselling author of *The Queen's Fortune*

"C. W. Gortner has made his mark illuminating the private lives and untold stories of the world's greatest women. In *The First Actress*, he turns his talent to Sarah Bernhardt, the daughter of a Dutch Jewish courtesan who would rise over the late-nineteenth and early-twentieth centuries to become an icon of stage and screen. Readers will revel in the gloriously heady mix of love and war, and art and society. Combining immaculate research with scintillating prose and an unforgettable cast of larger-than-life characters, *The First Actress* stands tall among Gortner's remarkable body of work."

—PAM JENOFF, *New York Times* bestselling author of *The Lost Girls of Paris*

BY C. W. GORTNER

THE
FIRST ACTRESS

BALLANTINE BOOKS

NEW YORK

THE
FIRST ACTRESS

A NOVEL OF
SARAH BERNHARDT

C. W. Gortner

2021 Ballantine Books Trade Paperback Edition

Copyright © 2020 by C. W. Gortner
Book club guide copyright © 2021 by Penguin Random House LLC

Published in the United States by Ballantine Books,
an imprint of Random House, a division of
Penguin Random House LLC, New York.

BALLANTINE and the HOUSE colophon are registered
trademarks of Penguin Random House LLC.
RANDOM HOUSE BOOK CLUB & Design is a registered
trademark of Penguin Random House LLC.

Originally published in hardcover in the United States by
Ballantine Books, an imprint of Random House, a division of
Penguin Random House LLC, in 2020.

ISBN 978-0-525-62091-4
Ebook ISBN 978-0-525-62090-7

Printed in the United States of America on acid-free paper

randomhousebooks.com
randomhousebookclub.com

2 4 6 8 9 7 5 3 1

Title-page and part-title pattern: © iStockphoto.com

Book design by Dana Leigh Blanchette

IN MEMORY OF

my beloved aunt Meme

Legend remains victorious in spite of history.

—SARAH BERNHARDT

::

ACT I

1853–1859

▪▪

The Unwanted Child

One can almost always see in a little girl the threat of a woman.

—ALEXANDRE DUMAS

I

If great talent can rise from adversity, mine must have been forged in the cauldron of my childhood.

I was eight years old. The colors of my world were verdant and gray: windswept woodlands and mounds of ancient stones, washed by sea-lashed gusts across Brittany's fields; the sounds were the clangor of sheep bells as herds were led to pasture and the clucking of chickens in coops by the straw-thatched cottage with its vine-trellised terrace, where I lived. A rustic world marked by the rise and fall of the sun, by dawn-to-dusk chores and sodden gauze dampening fresh goat cheese; the warmth of crusty bread, fresh from the oven; and the sting of wild green onions, crushed under my bare feet.

Until the day my mother returned.

"Sarah? Sarah, where are you?"

Her querulous voice reached me from across the vegetable garden. I was perched on the bough of the old fig tree, among abandoned squirrel nests. My dog, Pitou, lolled at the base of the tree, panting in the summer heat, but the woman calling for me didn't seem to notice him, though to anyone else who knew me, he would have betrayed my whereabouts, as he was my loyal shadow.

Peering toward the terrace, I saw her like a distant figure in a painting, her white-gloved hand at her brow and her voice edged with impatience as she called out again.

"Sarah, where are you hiding? I haven't this entire day to waste. Come out this instant."

I knew who she was, though so much time had passed, I shouldn't have. When I first saw her carriage pull up to the house, a rush of anger overcame me, sending me racing out the back gate to this tree, my secret place. The last time she'd visited was over three years past. Like now, she'd arrived unannounced, bearing chocolate bon-bons and trinkets—a small, plump stranger with limpid blue eyes, in fancy ruffled skirts and a bonnet as wide as a platter, festooned with silk flowers. She'd stayed only long enough to sniff the air and issue her directives before disappearing again, back to wherever she came from. Seeing her again, after all this time, roused more than just anger in me; I didn't want to acknowledge her, even if her reappearance gave me a stab of comfort that she'd not forgotten me.

Pitou clambered to his feet, wagging his tail. The woman's irate calling of my name had alerted him. Fearing he'd give me away, I motioned at him to sit. As he dropped forlornly back onto his haunches, I looked again toward the house.

Nana Hubert emerged from the adjoining kitchen, wiping her doughy hands on her apron. As I saw my mother turn to her in con-sternation, Nana pointed directly at the tree and bellowed in her coarse Breton: "Milk Blossom! Come here and greet your mother."

Exasperated, I slid from the branch, catching the edge of my dress on a twig. It ripped. Thinking about how Nana would have to mend it later and chide me as she invariably did, citing her time-worn litany that dresses didn't grow like leaves on the trees I climbed, I padded unhappily to the terrace, Pitou at my heels.

As I approached, my mother scrutinized me.

Nana scowled. She wasn't unkind; she loved me as well as she could, when she had the time, but time was something she sorely lacked, with her husband in his grave and all the goats and chickens and vegetables to tend. Yet only this morning, she'd given me a blue ribbon for my hair—"Blue looks so pretty with your white skin and red curls," she said with one of her rare gap-toothed smiles—and as I now belatedly searched for it, I found the ribbon dangling from my disheveled braid. At least I hadn't left it on the tree with my clogs.

Meeting my mother's regard, I felt as soiled as my feet. She was . . . pristine. Immaculate. Like the statue of the Virgin in the town church, with the same marble pallor. I almost expected to see a single translucent tear on her cheek, like a drop of frozen sap.

"Well?" said Nana. "What do we say to Mademoiselle Bernhardt?"

I muttered, "Good day, mademoiselle."

My mother smiled. Or did she? It was hard to tell. Her pink lips, so bud-like they resembled an unfurled rose, twitched but didn't show any teeth. Still, I suspected her teeth must be as perfect as the rest of her, not like Nana's, who was forever complaining about her rotten molars and how even biting into a chunk of bread hurt.

"She doesn't recognize me." My mother's smooth forehead puckered. "And she's so thin. Has she been ill?"

Nana harrumphed. "She's not been sick a day in her life. You gave her over to me to suckle, Mademoiselle Bernhardt. And suckle she did. Like a starving runt. I've done as you asked. Nothing more, nothing less. She's thin, yes, but she eats more than a mule."

"And apparently bathes almost as often," replied my mother.

Nana shrugged. "Children get dirty. Why waste water? She takes a bath once a week."

"I see." My mother regarded me as if she wasn't quite sure what to do. "Does she speak any French?"

"When she has a mind to. We've not much occasion to use it here, as you can see. Cows don't care if you milk them in French or Breton." With a grimace, Nana said to me, "Say something to your mother in French."

I didn't want to say anything to her, in French or otherwise. Why should I indulge this woman's peevish requests, when in less than an hour, she'd be on her way back to wherever she'd come from? But

Nana gave me a stern nod and I found myself muttering, *"Pitou est ma chien."*

"See?" Nana planted her hands on her wide hips. "She's not stupid. Just stubborn. Girls like her need a firm hand."

She'd started to trudge back into the house when my mother said, "It's *mon chien*." She let out a sigh. "Perhaps this isn't the right time. I'm so occupied these days. . . . I can offer you more to keep her for another year—"

Nana came to a halt, glaring over her shoulder with a determination I knew all too well. "It is the right time for me. I'm getting old. I must sell this house and move into town with my son. You will take her today, as we agreed. Her bag is already packed."

I stood frozen, my hand on Pitou's ragged ears, hearing Nana's words but not believing my own ears. After all this time, my mother had returned to take me away? Before I could stop myself, I burst out, "I can't leave! What about my Pitou?"

My dog whimpered. My mother turned her blue eyes to me. I saw coldness surface in her gaze. "Your Pitou? Do you think I should take you *and* your cur with me to Paris?"

Paris?

My heart started to pound. "But I . . . I can't just leave him," I said, even as my mother turned back to Nana. A pained look crossed my nursemaid's face as my mother spoke to her in a low voice. Nana shook her head. "No," I heard her say. "It's impossible. My son's house has no room for her. His wife is expecting a child, and I must attend to her. Either you take her with you today or off to the orphanage she goes. She's not my responsibility anymore."

Sudden tears scalded my eyes. Just as I felt a wail hurtling up my throat, Nana looked past my mother and said quietly to me, "Milk Blossom, you must go live with your *maman* now. I'll see that Pitou finds a home, don't you fret. Now, wash up and fetch your bag. Mademoiselle Bernhardt is waiting and it's a long journey to Paris."

I couldn't move. This was my home, this cottage with its narrow smoke-stained rooms, thick with the smell of pottage and garlic, with my Nana and my Pitou. I didn't want to go to Paris and live with this overdressed stranger. I didn't know her at all.

"No," I said loudly, and as Nana's face darkened, I added, "I will *not*."

Nana jabbed her hand at me. "Shall I fetch the switch?"

The thin hawthorn strip that could raise welts on my thighs—it was one of the few things I feared. Nana had used it only once, when I forgot to mind the fences and went tromping with Pitou over her coriander. Afterwards, I couldn't sit down for a week.

"Go now," Nana ordered. "Wash up and fetch your things."

My mother stepped aside as I barreled past her into the house with Pitou. In my small room with its cot and sagging bureau, I found a cloth satchel stuffed with my few clothes and long-neglected cloth doll. Nana had set out my one nice dress on the cot. I only wore it on Sundays when we attended mass in town. I went still, staring at it. I wouldn't go. I couldn't leave my Pitou. I would run away, take my bag and him—

Nana's sharp whistle from the terrace sent Pitou bounding back outside. As I cried out and dashed after him, I found my mother in the doorway, blocking my escape.

"Never mind washing up," she said. "I cannot abide it here another instant."

"Maman, please." I struggled against a surge of panic. "Pitou. I can't leave him here if Nana sells the house and—"

She lifted her hand, silencing me. "You will do as you are told."

Pitou started barking as soon as I clambered into the carriage. Yanking aside the curtain on the carriage door, I was overwhelmed by a black tide of anguish as I stared toward the house. Nana stood on the threshold, holding my dog back by his scruff. He was trying to escape her to follow me; tears spilled from my eyes as the carriage jolted forward, the hiss of the coachman's whip over the team of horses sharp in my ears.

Within minutes, we'd left the cottage behind, the carriage rattling over the unpaved road. My mother sat across from me in
silence. She didn't speak for such a long time that my tears dried on
my cheeks as I waited, wilting under her brooding stare. Then she
finally said, "I'm not accustomed to having a child underfoot. I'm a
very busy woman, with no time or patience for antics. You must
respect my schedule at all times. Do you understand? *At all times.* If
you fail to obey, I shall find another arrangement for you."

"Yes, Maman," I whispered. A lump rose in my throat. I was too
frightened now for defiance. An orphanage had been mentioned; I
had no doubt she was perfectly capable of sending me to one.

"And you must never call me Maman in company," she added,
brushing her gloved fingers fastidiously over her dress. "My friends
call me Julie. You may address me by my name or as Mademoiselle
Julie, if you prefer."

"Yes, Mademoiselle Julie."

She gave me a glazed smile, passing her eyes again over my person. I'd barely squeezed into my one pair of good shoes and my little
cape and bonnet, all of which she'd brought the last time she'd visited and now barely fit. The shoes pinched my toes. I wriggled my
feet, wishing I could kick them off and wondering if I might also
manage to leap from the carriage and run back to the cottage. Yet
even as I imagined the shock on my mother's face, I knew she would
only fetch me back and be more cross with me than she already was.

"Stop fidgeting." Removing a fan from her bag, she waved it
about her. "Honestly. Did that peasant woman not teach you anything? You've the manners of a wild creature." She went quiet for a
moment. "I suppose you haven't learned to read or write yet?"

"No, Mademoiselle Julie." I was thoroughly miserable. Not only
had she forced me to leave my home and my dog, but she didn't
even like me. She didn't want me to live with her any more than I
wanted to live with her.

She sighed. "Then I suppose we must see to that, as well." She
returned her gaze to the window. "An illiterate," she mused, as if to

herself. "Without a single social grace to commend her. I daresay no one will even believe she is mine."

She sounded pleased by this assessment.

Three days later, we arrived in Paris. I'd cried into my sleeve every night in the inns where we stayed, while she turned her back on me. By the time we reached the city, I had no tears left to shed and I was certain I'd never know a moment of happiness again.

Paris bewildered me. So loud, full of rattling carriages and shouting people; it seemed colorless to me, a riot of smoky skies and stone-paved streets. It smelled like soggy laundry and animal ordure—like an old dragon, I thought, with the turgid river running through its talons. I almost started crying again as I recalled the green woodlands of Brittany, the fields and hiding places I'd made my own. Would I ever see a tree again?

As the carriage came to a halt, Julie said, "This is the rue de Provence," as if giving the street a name made any difference to me. I was sore from the long hours of sitting in the carriage, and ravenous, having eaten far less in the last few days than I was used to. When we disembarked, I found myself standing before a soot-stained building, tall and narrow, hemmed in by others just like it.

Then a pretty young woman with a startling resemblance to Julie swept out from the building's entrance. "Sarah, my child!" She kissed my cheeks, suffocating me in a rose attar that made me cough. She had bright eyes, only hers were a darker blue than Julie's, and her hair, tucked into a chignon at her nape, was reddish-gold. Like mine. She must be a relative, I thought, as she said softly, "Oh, my child. You don't remember who I am, do you?"

Behind us, where she was directing the coachman to unload her luggage—she'd brought two medium-sized trunks to fetch me; why did she need so much?—Julie said, "Don't be a goose, Rosine. She was just a babe when she last saw you."

"Yes, of course. Sarah, my dear: I'm your *Tante* Rosine. Your mother is my older sister." My aunt smiled. As she set her warm hand in mine, guiding me toward the building, I bit back another rush of tears. Kindness was the last thing I'd expected.

"Welcome to Paris," she said, and I leaned into her.

Perhaps living here wouldn't be so terrible after all.

II

The next year was one of lessons.

Rosine assumed charge of me; through her, I learned of my family's provenance.

Born in the Netherlands to Jewish parents, my mother and her two sisters had left their country as soon as they were of suitable age. The eldest of the three, Henriette, wed a cloth merchant in Ariège and had a family of her own, while Rosine and my mother traveled for a time before settling in Paris. What they did to earn a living was a mystery, however, as was our heritage. Julie didn't follow any of the strictures of our faith; there wasn't a mezuzah nailed to our doorway or a single item of Hebrew worship in the flat. As Nana had raised me Catholic, I assumed my mother's faith was of no particular importance.

Rosine soon set me to studying, tutoring me every day with a set of primers. I learned how to spell my name and recite the alphabet; I labored over basic letters until my fingers cramped and my eyes swam. But I proved an avid student, for I found words fascinating—a portal into a new world, where stories of swan princesses and frog princes, of witches in hovels and flying carriages made of pumpkins, helped relieve the strict schedule dictated by Julie that everyone in the flat had to adhere to.

The day when everything in my new life changed began like any other. The evening before had been tedious, with Julie entertaining her assortment of friends in her salon until all but one of the men departed. Since my arrival, I'd grown accustomed to seeing strange gentlemen come and go from the flat. All of Julie's friends were male; it was another mystery to me. Sometimes she had me serve these "suitors," as she called them, summoning me at the appointed hour with my tray of canapés, my unruly mass of red-gold hair plaited in a braid and an ingratiating smile on my lips. The men ignored me after a cursory glance; now and then, one reached out to pat my bottom and remark, "Such a bony child. Julie, do you not feed her?" to which my mother would reply with her falsetto laugh, "She eats without restraint and never gains an ounce. She was raised in Brittany, too; all that fresh country air . . . why, you'd think she'd be plump as a partridge, like me."

Despite the men's chuckles, I heard the petulant undertone in her voice. Julie clearly didn't like that I was thin as a whisper, my collarbones so incised that raindrops could collect in their hollows, as I once heard her say with disdain. Yet to my bewilderment, she never failed to chastise me if I dared to ask for a second helping at breakfast or dinner, remarking I hadn't yet learned that in Paris, food didn't just pop up out of the ground or fall ripe from the trees.

Yet her suitors always found her amusing, another baffling mystery to me. How could they not see she was pretending to be someone she wasn't? In the afternoons before her salon gatherings, she spent hours at her mirror, her maid helping her into her ornate dress as if she lacked the strength to do it on her own. But her angry reproofs if her stays weren't laced tightly enough or if her maid fetched her the wrong bracelet betrayed that she wasn't quite as helpless as she feigned, that everything she did was designed to an end.

Once her suitors arrived, however, she put on a constant smile, attentive to their every request, even as I felt her eyes boring into me as I served the canapés. The moment one of her guests paid me the slightest mind, she waved me back to my room, where I fell asleep to her laughter and the men's conversation.

She invariably slept until noon. Rosine saw to my breakfast and my lessons before sending me out to play in the building courtyard, so I wouldn't disturb.

"Your *maman*'s sleep is very important," said Rosine. "She needs to rest as much as possible"—yet another mystery, for it seemed to me that she did little else, languishing in either her bedroom or the salon, with only the occasional burst of activity when she pinned on a hat to go shopping or laded on jewels for an evening at the Opéra.

On this particular morning, I woke before Rosine. We shared a bedroom, the flat being cramped, but my aunt slept like a stone, exhausted from her oversight of the household's daily affairs. Through the crack of our door, I watched an elderly gentleman tiptoe from Julie's chamber. He was balding on top, but had very long mustachios that drooped about his mouth. In his gray frock coat with its shiny lapels, his black top hat and silver-tipped cane, to me, he resembled an overdressed grandfather.

I didn't think anything of his furtive departure. I'd seen him before. He'd been attending the salon ever since I arrived in Paris, favored above the others, for he often stayed overnight. He'd never given me more than a passing glance, either. Yet as he now paused to adjust his coat, he happened to glance up to catch me staring at him. I wasn't yet dressed. I stood in my shift in the open doorway, my braid unraveled in frizzy disarray that my aunt had sought in vain to subdue with hot irons and elderflower rinses.

His mild brown eyes took on an odd gleam. He crooked his finger at me. I felt heat creep into my cheeks when he whispered, "Come here, *ma petite*. Let me get a look at you."

Although I didn't know why these men filled our house almost every night except on Sunday, Rosine had drummed into my head that I must never ask. I must never question. They were my mother's "special friends" and I must show them proper respect.

"Children should be seen and never heard," admonished my aunt. "Sarah, do you understand? Julie would not wish to have her suitors subjected to inanities."

I had done my utmost to obey. I didn't even know this particular suitor's name, and as I grappled with the potential consequences of refusing what I sensed was not a proper request, he took a step toward me.

"*Ma petite,*" he said again. "Why do you hide from me? I only wish to see you."

He might tell Julie. He might mention that I'd been rude. Moving cautiously from behind the door, hearing my aunt snoring behind me in the narrow bed, I gave him a weak smile, bobbing a curtsy as I tugged at my rumpled shift, trying to cover my knobby knees.

A smile parted his mustachios, revealing yellowed teeth. "Ah, yes. Very pretty. *Très belle* like your *maman*. Come closer, child. Let old Morny give you a kiss."

I came to a halt. He said he'd wanted to see me, and now he wanted to give me a kiss? As his hand reached out between us— a knotted, liver-spotted hand, like a troll's in a fairy tale—I slapped his fingers aside before he could touch me.

He recoiled, his eyes flaring. "Do you know who I am?" he rumbled, and I heard Rosine gasp from behind me, her yanking aside the bedsheets as she came to her feet.

I glared at him. "Yes. You are Julie's special friend. Go kiss her instead."

Rosine rushed to me, her hands on my shoulders as she said haltingly, "Please forgive her, Monsieur. She's only a child, and—"

"A child?" He frowned at his hand, which of course had no visible mark. "She's an alley cat. Julie should do something about those claws."

A dreadful silence ensued. Then, from the opposite end of the painting-hung corridor, my mother lilted, "And so I shall, my dearest Morny. Please accept my apologies for her inexcusable behavior." Swathed in patterned blue *chinois* silk, her hair floating like an aureole about her shoulders, Julie glided forth to lead him to the front door, whispering and caressing as he shook his head and departed in a huff.

As soon as the door closed on him, she whirled around to me. I pressed against Rosine, who stammered, "You mustn't fault Sarah. Monsieur le duc was most inopportune. He wanted to give her a kiss and she—why, look at her. In her shift. It's not done."

"Not done?" echoed Julie. I'd never seen her like this; she'd gone rigid, one of her astonishingly milk-white hands clutching at her robe, strangling the embroidered storks. "She *insulted* him. He might forsake me, tell the others. How shall we exist then, eh? How will we survive when they hear I keep this feral creature, this *inconvenience*, in my house?"

Creature. She thought I was an animal. In a rush of rage I hadn't realized I still harbored, I tore myself from Tante Rosine and shouted, "If you don't want me, I will kill myself. Then you won't be inconvenienced anymore!"

Julie fixed her stare on me. Rosine let out a cry as I met my mother's cold blue eyes, marking their indifference, like a blade scraping down my spine. She did not care. She did not love me. She never had. I could die and it would mean nothing to her.

Reeling about, I fled into the salon. Rosine followed after me, catching me about my waist as I flailed, knocking over the little table with its clutter of porcelain figurines and vase of flowers. Shrieking like the wild animal my mother had called me, I threw myself at the window to grapple with the latch. I fully intended to throw myself onto the cobblestone avenue below. I could see it in my mind: my sliver of a body in my shift spiraling down to splatter before the early morning hansoms and servants going about their morning rounds.

Julie's voice slashed into the chaos. "Sarah Henriette Bernhardt. That is enough."

Half-caught in Rosine's grasp, my fingers clutching the windowsill, I watched my mother approach through the curtained archway and onto the Oriental-style carpet until she stood in the center of the salon—nearly overwhelmed by its excess, the fake Roman busts and overwrought landscape paintings, the stuffed horsehair couches and her upholstered settee, festooned with herb-scented cushions and lace shawls. So small. She was no bigger than I was. How could I be so afraid of her?

But in that instant, she seemed to loom over my entire world, her robe draping open to reveal the mound of her stomach under her nightdress. As she saw my eyes lower to this unexpected sight—she looked fat but only in an oddly specific place—she said, "You disgrace yourself. What is more, you disgrace me. I will not tolerate these outbursts another moment."

My fear congealed in my veins. The orphanage. It was always there, the threat behind every reprimand, behind every moment that I failed to please her. From behind me, I heard Rosine say, "Julie, she's but a child. How can she possibly understand?"

"Oh, I think she understands much more than she lets on," replied my mother.

"Maman," I whispered. The term I never used with her came out of me in desperation. "Forgive me. I promise it won't happen again."

She sniffed. "It most certainly will not. Go to your room and see that I do not hear a sound from you until you are called for."

I inched past her, treading over the shards of her broken vase. As I made my way to my room, Rosine began to murmur. Julie cut her off. "I'll not hear another word in her defense. This house is no place for a child; it never was. The time has come to seek other arrangements."

"I don't want to go. No! You cannot make me!" My shrieks resounded into the avenue, startling passersby as Rosine hauled me toward the waiting carriage. The team of horses snorted, jangling their harness as the coachman watched in wry amusement and I dug my heels against the pavement.

Ever since Julie had informed me that rather than slap her suitors, I must attend a proper establishment where I could learn much-needed manners, I'd mounted a series of ferocious protests. I refused to eat for an entire day. I refused to bathe or brush my hair, until Julie snapped her fingers as she departed in a cloud of perfume and organza for one of her evening soirées, and her maidservant thrust me into the bathroom with orders to strip and wash, or else. I refused to speak, biting my tongue when Julie arrived late the following morning, pausing to take one look at me, without saying a word, her fan tapping at her waist—which I noticed was so tightly cinched, I wondered how she could breathe—before she shrugged and went into her chamber to sleep away the afternoon. I refused to concede that I might be sent away again, bundled off to a remote place where I'd have to do whatever it was girls were supposed to do—all of it to no avail.

On the appointed morning, Rosine forced me into an uncomfortable dress with a matching black capelet, raked my hair into a knot with a ribbon, and told me we were going to the Tuileries to visit the menagerie, which she knew I loved, as I missed having animals about me since leaving Brittany. The moment I saw the waiting carriage—a fine equipage, which we never would have hired for the short trip to the Tuileries—I knew she was lying and I began to wail.

Rosine was near despair herself. "Sarah, please. It's not the end of the world. It's a boarding school. Don't you want to share lessons with other girls of your own age?"

"No!" I yanked against her, not caring that several ladies paused to frown at me from under their parasols. "I don't believe you. She's sending me away like she did before. You and she will abandon me, just as you did in Brittany."

"That's not true." Rosine paused, breathless from our struggle.

"Sarah, it was never my choice to send you away." She tried to cup my chin, even as I turned my face from her. "Sarah, listen to me. It's for your own good, until you're older. I swear it to you on my life."

My anguish waned at her anxious avowal. I loved my aunt, more so, in fact, than I'd believed I could, and certainly more than anything I felt for my mother. Rosine had been so kind, taking charge of me, crooning lullabies as we cuddled together in bed, taking me out on excursions to visit the city, and ensuring I never strayed too far into Julie's path.

"Then help me now." My voice cracked. "You've already taught me how to read and write. Can't you teach me whatever else I need to learn?"

She shook her head. "I cannot, my child. We must both do as we are told."

Another helpless wail clawed at my throat. I forced myself to swallow it. There was no escape, not unless I jumped before the horses and let them stomp over me—an idea that appealed, if only for the attention it would attract. But continuing to resist would just make Rosine more miserable and it would never dissuade Julie. She had made her decision. She hadn't even come outside with us to bid me goodbye.

"I'll visit as often as I can," Rosine went on, sensing my capitulation. "And on holidays, you can come visit us. You'll like your new school. You'll like it very much. It's a very fine establishment. Your mother has chosen the best for you."

"I doubt it," I retorted, boarding the carriage and sitting on the upholstered leather seat facing backward, scowling as my aunt arranged herself opposite me, my valise at her feet. The carriage lurched forward at a crack of the driver's whip.

As we entered the thoroughfare that would take me to my uncertain future, I stared out the window at the receding flat, up to the salon window with its lace curtains, where, it seemed a lifetime ago, I'd tried to throw myself out.

I thought I glimpsed a shadow there—the figure of my mother watching me depart.

Then I blinked and she was gone.

During the two-hour-long carriage ride, Rosine tried to reassure me again. "The Sacré Cœur at Grandchamp is one of the most esteemed boarding institutions for young ladies in France. It's in Versailles, not far from Paris. You'll be so happy there, taking your lessons with other privileged girls."

She kept repeating this refrain as the city melted away behind us, the vista opening onto fields of wheat and chestnut forests. I sat without speaking, my fists clenched in my lap. I imagined pulling open the door and leaping out. I'd run away and disappear, find refuge in a hamlet and beg in the streets until a kindly couple without children took me in. I'd grow up and herd goats; I'd get fat and rosy so no one would recognize me. Julie would search and search, overcome by guilt, Rosine would waste away in sorrow, but they'd never find me. I would become somebody else. Not the unwanted child anymore.

"We're here," said my aunt, surprising me as the carriage came to a stop. I'd expected a much longer journey, and as I stepped warily onto the unpaved country road, I saw nothing but high stone walls, lichen-stained, broken by a single, stout wooden gate.

My knees started to buckle. Though the day was warm, I felt cold as a tomb.

Rosine took my hand. "There's nothing to fear. You'll be safe here, Sarah. This is a convent of the highest order. And very expensive," she added, as if that made everything better. "Your mother has gone to considerable effort to secure you a place here."

I doubted this, too. I recalled the sour gentleman with the drooping mustachios, the Duc de Morny, whose hand I'd slapped. This was his fault. He must have suggested this prison for me. Hadn't Julie assured him that something would be done?

I stood clutching my suitcase as Rosine rang the bell rope by the gate. Only then did I whisper, "Please. I'll be good. I'll attend Maman's suitors in the salon. I'll learn to sing and recite poetry. To amuse them like she does. You can teach me how."

My aunt let out a sigh. "My child, you don't understand. That is not what Julie wants for you. She has struggled so much, sacrificed so many things to achieve what she has. She doesn't want you in her salon, enticing her suitors to kiss you. You may think her heartless, but she cares for you in her own way. She wants you to have a better life than she has."

I did not understand. All I saw was a flat in Paris on a fashionable boulevard, a well-appointed home; my mother in silk, glamorous and sought after, with suitors at her beck and call. What could possibly be wrong with her life? Why must her sacrifice require forsaking me? Then I remembered the bulge of her stomach, her shadowy figure at the window as she watched me leave, and whatever pleas I had left went unspoken.

Rosine rang the bell again. Moments later, bolts unlatched and the gate swung open. My heart lodged in my throat.

The figure before me was tall and plump, dressed entirely in black, a wimple framing her cherubic features. It took me by surprise, that childlike face with its keen brown eyes and warm smile, so at odds with her apparel, like an angel in a widow's garb.

"Welcome to Grandchamp. I am Mère Sophie, Reverend Mother of this blessed house of the Sisters of Zion." She lowered her gaze. "You must be little Sarah Bernhardt."

It was too much for me. With a desperate sob, I threw myself into the Reverend Mother's startled embrace, burying my face against her lilac-scented robes.

Although I did not know it yet, I had found my refuge.

III

The convent had a lovely garden with white-pebble pathways, lime trees, and birdbaths—a paradise of tranquility in a serene, efficient place. I was prepared to hate it, thinking it could never be like Paris, which I had come to love, with its deafening clatter of landaus, hansoms, and rickety omnibuses running up to the hill of Montmartre, its winding alleyways and bold new boulevards, its raucous brasseries, smoky cafés, and sumptuous emporiums. Rosine had claimed Paris was the most exciting place in the world, and, to accustom me to the city, had taken me to all the wonderful sites and shops where everything anyone could possibly want was available. I'd grown to see the city as my home, and now it had all been taken from me, just like my home in Brittany.

Nevertheless, after a few awkward months of adjustment, I began to realize that at Grandchamp, at last I could be myself. Or as much of myself as a convent would allow.

The unvaried routine proved oddly comforting: prayers in the chapel four times daily (my declaration that I was Jewish, made to evade the prayers, did not impress the nuns); lessons in arithmetic, grammar, history, and geography, followed by diction and deportment; and in the afternoons, sedate exercise. I wasn't an exemplary student, as I had no mind for facts or numbers. My sole interests were reading and the convent's old hound, César, who followed me everywhere, and creatures I collected in the garden from under rocks—lizards, spiders, and frogs that I kept in a perforated tin box and fed with flies.

And art. I soon proved to be the best artist in my class, perhaps in the entire school, able to assimilate the shape of almost anything I saw and reproduce it with charcoal on paper. I drew César many times, asleep at my feet. I drew lizards and flowers, the sparrows dipping in the birdbath. My drawings were so exceptional, the nuns pinned them on the board for others to emulate.

Mère Sophie was aware that I'd never been baptized. While Nana had raised me Catholic, the sum total of my religious education had entailed mass on Sunday and saying my prayers before bedtime, so my declaration of my Jewish blood exerted the opposite effect of what I'd intended. Rather than avoid extra lessons, I was obliged to study catechism in the hope that one day I might be deemed ready to receive Holy Communion. I thought I'd be bored. Instead, I found myself fascinated by the evil pharaoh and burning bush sent by God, by the ark filled with pairs of animals and the terrifying flood. I learned that the Jewish people had once been enslaved, important participants in this ageless tale of miracles and martyrs. It didn't feel like I was studying religion at all, but rather immersed in a fantastic, never-ending fable.

I shared a large dormitory room with the other girls of my age. Grandchamp was indeed exclusive, where wealthy families boarded their daughters. Some of the girls gave themselves airs because of their titles. But others, like Marie Colombier, whom I befriended after my arrival, were like me—of uncertain provenance, with mothers who toiled as—

"Demimondaines," Marie whispered one day after we'd been sent to the garden to study our roles for the upcoming annual Nativity play, performed in honor of the archbishop of Paris, who was one of the convent's benefactors. I had turned eleven; the last two years had passed swiftly, and I was now old enough to be assigned a supporting role in the play. I'd desperately wanted the lead as the archangel Raphael, memorizing every line, but the nuns allocated the part to Louise, an older girl with a family of status.

Now I looked up from the three lines I had as a shepherd in the play to meet Marie's mischievous gaze. She was dark-haired, with velvety brown eyes. I envied her beauty and her budding figure— I was still narrow as a twig—as well as her astonishing worldliness.

"Demimondaine?" I said in bewilderment. "Whatever is that?"

"Not what. *Who.*" Marie rolled her eyes. "A courtesan, silly. A cocotte. A *grande horizontale*. Remember? Like the Magdalene." As I went still, she added, "Surely you must know. How else could our mothers afford this place? We're not Rothschilds, Sarah."

"But that must mean our mothers are . . . whores?" I breathed out the unspeakable word in a hushed voice. I only knew it because of her. The story of Mary Magdalene had provoked many questions from me that the nuns refused to answer, so Marie had finally taken it upon herself to explain what Mary was. I thought it a very ugly word, but as she defined it for me, I realized it described my mother to perfection. Julie's salon and her suitors, that ghoul Morny tiptoeing from her chamber in the early morning hours—this surely was how she must earn her living.

Marie said, "It isn't how they would describe themselves; they don't sell themselves in the street. Demimondaines must be very sophisticated. They are . . ." She paused, searching for the right word. "Entertainers. Like actresses."

"Entertainers?" I felt a wave of revulsion, recalling my mother's insistence that I must learn proper manners, her chiding of me to respect her suitors. "How could any woman ever do such a thing with smelly old men?"

She giggled. "Well, if the smelly old man pays enough . . ."

I resisted a shudder. But even as I did, I lost my fear of my mother. I even felt a slight stir of pity for her, with the confidence of the very young that no matter what travails life might have in store for me, I would never stoop so low.

Marie told me that becoming a demimondaine was a coveted and difficult endeavor. Penniless girls from all over Europe flocked to Paris as my mother had, in the hope of transforming themselves into one of these scintillating creatures who never expressed in public what they were about. There was complex language involved, Marie said, made up of subtle gestures and expressions that conveyed what the lips could not. While every girl who entered the trade did so in the hope of success, only the most skilled ever achieved it.

"My mother told me of one who snared a prince's son," Marie said. "He was so in love with her, he gambled away his inheritance to win her favors. She fleeced him of every sou, then threw him aside for another. He challenged her lover to a duel and got himself shot. His father was so enraged, he threatened to see her run out of Paris, but she seduced the man instead. He made her so rich, she eventually retired to a château." Marie let out a sigh, as if she found this crude tale irresistible.

"My mother is nothing like that," I said, thinking of her crowded flat and overstuffed salon, of Julie's glazed fixture of a smile, as if a single misstep might cast her into ruin. "I don't think she's very successful or rich at all."

"Well, she must have something to place you here. Imagine it. To live as you please and make your own fortune: it's a freedom that of all women, only a courtesan enjoys."

I considered this. "Is it really freedom? Or another form of slavery, like the Hebrews in Egypt? Whatever these women possess can be taken away from them, can't it?"

"The Hebrews in Egypt?" Marie laughed. "Oh, Sarah, that was centuries ago! You don't understand. Wait until you are older."

I gave her a narrow-eyed look. Marie was a year older than me—a fact she often cited to assert her advantage—but I didn't think age was going to change my mind. Still, I also didn't go so far as to confide my suspicion that it was Morny, not Julie, who was financing my education here. Now that I knew the truth, that bump I'd seen at my mother's midriff must signal another child, perhaps one sired by the *duc* himself. Julie hadn't sent me away to safeguard me. She was preparing to bear another bastard; as she had said, I was indeed an inconvenience.

Believing I'd been sent away to make way for another child bolstered my determination that my time at Grandchamp mustn't be wasted. I must prove myself, and so I plunged into preparations for the play with renewed fervor. All the parents and guardians of the school's pupils would attend; Rosine's promise to visit me regularly had gone unfulfilled, though at least she sent a packet of fresh linens every month. But the presence of the archbishop of Paris might spur even my neglectful aunt and mother to make their long-overdue appearance, if only to ensure that I wasn't signaled out as the only girl at Grandchamp without any kin to support her performance.

I must shine on the stage, even as a shepherd with a few measly lines.

IV

On the day of the play, I was the first to rise. It was an icy morning in late November, as the annual Nativity play took place before the actual holiday. In the dull light filtering through the high windows above the orderly rows of cots, I hurried to smooth my tangled hair into a braid and make up my cot with the tucked blanket corners that the nuns insisted upon, while the other girls grumbled about how cold the flagstone floor was.

The nuns came to escort us to the chapel. During our prayers, I found myself begging God, not to make me more pious or virtuous or help me find a husband when the time came—as I suspected most of the girls did—but to make me extraordinary in my role. Then, lowering my eyes in a plea of forgiveness for my vanity, I asked that He, in His infinite wisdom, might strike Louise with a mild colic to impede her from performing that night.

"Blessed Lord, I don't ask this for myself," I whispered, "but for Your greater glory. She cannot play the role as I can. She eats too many sweets. Whoever heard of a fat archangel?"

When we went through the final rehearsal on the small stage with its hand-painted backdrop in the main hall, I noticed Louise was looking peaked. The thought that God had heeded me so promptly gave me a secret thrill, making me forgot my own entrance. Sœur Bernadette, who oversaw the production, chided,

"Sarah Henriette, you are late on your mark. Get your head out of the clouds and step to your place."

I babbled out my lines—"Hark! A star rises!"—and stepped aside, unable to restrain the impulse to jab Louise with my elbow. She stumbled as she moved forward to deliver her speech. I froze, thinking she'd tell Sœur Ana, who would forbid me from taking part in the play. To my surprise, Louise didn't say a word. She halted center stage with her mouth agape, as if she'd been struck dumb.

I went taut. I was prepared. As soon as she collapsed and was sent to the infirmary for a draft of anise and bed rest, I'd offer to assume her role. I knew every line; I could recite them in my sleep. What else could the nuns do? They needed an archangel, and it was too late for another haughty girl with a titled family to learn the part.

Then, to my horror, Louise croaked out her lines as if the archangel were asthmatic. As soon as she finished, she backed away in a rush, her entire face ashen.

"Well. That was . . ." Sœur Ana was at a loss for words.

From her seat in the empty rows of chairs set out for the audience, the Reverend Mother sighed. "You'll need to speak louder tonight, Louise. I could barely hear you. Do you think you can do that, my child?"

Louise gave a tremulous nod. Mère Sophie frowned. Though I didn't dare press my advantage, I caught the Reverend Mother's glance in my direction. Then she motioned to Sœur Bernadette; I couldn't overhear what they said as we were led out for an early supper, but as I looked over my shoulder, I saw Sœur Bernadette shaking her head.

I had no doubt the Reverend Mother had seen that Louise would be a disaster. If she could barely speak her lines now, how would she manage her entire speech before an audience? She'd shame us before everyone, including the Monseigneur of Paris.

While we sipped our consommé—we were given only light fare so as not to burden our digestion during the performance—I kept watch on Louise as she stared blankly into the air, her soup bowl untouched. Marie kept asking me whatever was the matter, until I confided to her my pact with God.

She regarded me skeptically. "You think God would smite her to suit you?"

"Why not? She's—"

"You're not baptized," interrupted Marie, in that spiteful tone she could take when she felt the need to assert her superiority. "God would never heed you over a Catholic."

"Just because my mother is Jewish doesn't mean God won't—"

"If your mother is Jewish, so are you," cut in Marie again, making me want to dump my soup over her head. "You're also the illegitimate child of a courtesan. That's four sins, in case you've forgotten to count."

I scowled at her as we were hustled into the area behind the stage, cordoned off by sheets on ropes to create a makeshift dressing room. I was crushed to see that though she hadn't eaten a bite, Louise didn't appear to be in the throes of an incapacitating colic.

As I dressed in my shepherd's tunic and turban, I could hear the guests arriving in the hall. I imagined the chairs occupied by fashionable women and men, come to see their pampered offspring perform brilliantly—

Without warning, a vise closed about my chest.

I didn't have a name for that paralyzing sensation, but it was powerful enough to make me think God was about to smite me, instead. I couldn't move. I could barely breathe. Icy sweat broke out under my costume and the chatter of the girls around me was a maelstrom, their shadows tossed upon the sheets in a nauseating mirage.

"To your places," called out Sœur Bernadette, as if from across a void. I stood rooted to my spot until Marie hissed, "Sarah, it's time. Or do you plan to wait for God to call you to the stage, as well?"

Turning in a daze, I tugged César by his leash and started up the steps to the back of the stage. The sound of last-minute whispers and muffled laughter as the audience settled into their seats washed over me like the roar of an ocean.

I was going to faint. I was going to make a complete fool of myself.

Sœurs Ana and Bernadette were at the curtain. All of a sudden, I felt someone grip my hand, and I looked around to find none other than Louise.

"I . . . I can't do it." Her voice quavered in panic.

Sœur Ana came to us. "What is the trouble? Louise, my child, are you ill?"

"I can't. I can't do it." Louise began yanking at the paper ruff of her angelic attire. "I'm suffocating."

"Nonsense," declared Sœur Ana. Mère Sophie was out front, greeting the guests and conducting them to their seats. "It's only nerves. A fear of performing. It's quite common; you'll be fine as soon as the play starts. There now. Breathe, my child."

Was this what I felt? Nerves? If so, mine were mild compared to Louise's, who appeared about to rip off her tinsel wings and robe as if she were on fire.

"*No!* I can't. I won't!" She burst into tears.

"Blessed Virgin save us." Sœur Ana enfolded Louise in her arms, exchanging a look with Sœur Bernadette, whose expression turned thunderous. "Whatever shall we do now?"

"I . . . I can do it," I whispered.

Silence fell, broken by Louise's sniffling. "I can do it," I repeated, louder this time. "I know her lines. I can play the archangel." As I spoke, that smothering sensation vanished, replaced by a sudden rush of vitality as Sœur Bernadette grumbled, "What choice do we have? Get Sarah into the costume. Quickly."

Removing my shepherd attire, I donned the robe and wings. The robe was fitted to Louise's ample proportions and too loose on me; I had to be careful not to trip on its hem. The wings sagged almost to my waist, obliging me to square my narrow shoulders to lift them up. As I went to take my place, Sœur Bernadette fixed me with her stare. "See that you don't bring us disgrace," she said, and I heard in her warning an echo of my mother on the day she'd decided to send me away.

Sœur Bernadette yanked the curtain aside, unveiling a vast darkness.

It felt as if I stood on the edge of a precipice. As the play began, Marie, dressed now as the shepherd, hastily spoke my lines and dragged César toward the girl playing the blind man Tobias, whom the angel would miraculously cure. I tried to decipher something in that anonymous mass beyond the stage, a familiar face—anything to anchor me. The robe, made of linen, felt like stone, while the wings precariously listed at my back like the sails of a storm-tossed galleon.

Then I caught sight of the archbishop in the front row, his signet ring gleaming on the hand curled at his chin. Beside him sat Mère Sophie, looking astonished.

I began to speak. "I come to you with a message of our Almighty's boundless love. . . ."

I did not hear myself. I didn't know if I spoke loud enough; if I sounded powerful as a celestial being should or scratchy and hoarse like a girl in a robe that overwhelmed her, acting a part she'd not been assigned. None of it mattered. As I spread my arms in the flowing sleeves that hung over my bony wrists, I *felt* divine light emanate from me when I blessed Tobias, and the townspeople fell to their knees. I moved across the stage as though my wings were ablaze, a blinding halo of feathers drenched in holy flame.

I was no longer little Sarah Bernhardt, illegitimate daughter and unbaptized Jew.

I had become God's divine messenger.

It was over in a minute. Or so it seemed to me. When the applause came crashing over us as we took our bows, I realized I was soaked in perspiration, pushing back my hair to find a damp, disheveled mass. I thought I must look anything but angelic.

Monseigneur was on his feet, clapping. So was Reverend Mother

Sophie, her smile beaming approval, obliging everyone else in the audience to follow suit.

Elation filled me. That applause . . . it was like music to me.

Until I gazed out over the sea of faces and upraised hands and caught sight, with a leaden blow to my stomach, of my mother and Rosine. My aunt was clapping with pride.

Julie was immobile, her gloved hands stiff at her sides.

V

"My dear child, you were marvelous!" exclaimed Mère Sophie. As the other girls shed their costumes for their uniforms, eager to go into the hall to greet their parents, I stood as if immured by invisible walls. I scarcely heard the Reverend Mother until she touched my shoulder.

"My mother and aunt . . . they are here," I said. I had wanted them to see me, to prove how accomplished I was, but in truth, I hadn't believed they would actually arrive.

"Naturally, they are," said Mère Sophie. "They're waiting for you." She set her palm on my forehead. "Oh, but you're sopping wet. Come, you must remove this robe and—"

I stepped back, not sharply, but enough to detain her. "Mère Sophie, if you please, I would like to kiss Monseigneur's ring."

Her face lightened. "And so you shall. As soon as you've dressed, I'll take you to him myself. But you must make haste. He prepares to depart as we speak."

"We must go at once." Without waiting for her response, I moved toward the hall. Behind me, she protested, "Sarah, you're still in your costume," but I wouldn't wait, so she had to hasten after me, catching me by the elbow as I entered the hall and saw the archbishop in his cloak, smiling benevolently at the people surrounding him.

"What is this?" asked Mère Sophie. "Why such urgent need to greet Monseigneur?"

"I must have his blessing," I replied, and the plea in my voice made her hesitate before she nodded.

"Very well. But just his blessing. We mustn't delay him."

As I walked to him, I was keenly aware of Julie and Rosine watching me from the edge of the crowd. I could feel my mother's eyes boring into my back when I stepped before the archbishop. He shifted his regard to me. I sank to my knees.

He chuckled. "Whom do we have here? Is this our fierce archangel?"

"Monseigneur," I said, with what I hoped was humble reverence. "I ask for your blessing. I was born a Jew, but I wish to be baptized and request that you be present to welcome me into our Holy Church."

The archbishop looked taken aback. He turned to the Reverend Mother. "Is the child sincere in her devotion?"

Somewhat flustered, Mère Sophie replied, "She studies her catechism daily and is very devout. Perhaps next year, upon her twelfth birthday, she will be ready."

Peeking up at him through my tangled hair, I found Monseigneur contemplating me. "Well, then. If she is ready, I shall give her my blessing and see her baptized."

I grasped his hand, kissing his ring. "God save you, Monseigneur," I whispered, and he smiled again, turning away. With a disconcerted glance at me, the Reverend Mother accompanied him out.

As I came to my feet, Julie and Tante Rosine walked up to me. My mother's indignation fell upon me like an ax. "Have you gone mad, to make such a spectacle?"

Her mouth was pinched. She looked paler than usual, but she was magnificently dressed in blue taffeta, a cameo affixing her fichu over her high-necked bodice. She was also svelte, the corset outlining her waist disguising any sign of her suspected pregnancy. It surprised me, until I remembered that over two years had passed and, of course, she would have given birth by now, if she'd been with child.

Rosine anxiously kissed my cheek. She, too, appeared well groomed in a mauve gown with canary satin trim, her dark blond hair upswept in contrived ringlets. My heart missed a beat. Had Rosine joined the family profession? In my naïveté, I'd failed to realize that my aunt was twenty-two, several years younger than my mother, and she must have been expected to earn her keep after I'd been removed from her charge.

Posed behind them, each with a sardonic smile, were two gentlemen in frock coats, with gloves and top hats in hand.

I ignored them as I returned my mother's stare. "Spectacle?" I said, pretending to misunderstand. "Monseigneur is our honored guest."

"Never mind that," snapped Julie. "Baptism is out of the question. I forbid it."

"But you sent me here, to a convent. Isn't this what you wanted?" I asked, taking satisfaction in the heated flush that spread across her face.

She looked about to explode in rage—a circumstance I found both frightening and curious—when footsteps hurrying toward us announced the return of Mère Sophie.

"You must forgive me," the Reverend Mother said. "I had to see Monseigneur to his coach, but I am so pleased you could come. As you can see, madame, Sarah is excelling in her time with us here."

"Yes," said Julie dryly. "I do see. Too much so, it would seem."

Mère Sophie patted my shoulder. "She can be overly enthusiastic, but she has such a generous heart. And significant artistic promise. You'll find she is—"

"Reverend Mother," cut in Julie, making me cringe. "Is there some place where we may speak in private?"

"Why, yes. My study. Only . . ." Mère Sophie glanced at the milling girls waiting to speak to her, most of whom, including Marie, were surrounded by their families.

"It is important," added Julie. "I'm due for an engagement."

Mère Sophie gave reluctant assent, leading Julie from the hall and leaving me with Rosine and the gentlemen. As the men leaned to each other to murmur, my aunt embraced me with such affection that I forgave her for breaking her promise to visit me.

"Oh, Sarah! You were splendid. Such presence. Not even Rachel herself could have done better. Who would have thought it? Have you ever considered that a career on the stage might be your calling in life?"

I regarded her in astonishment. Rachel Félix was the premier tragedienne of the Comédie-Française, a Jewish-born actress renowned for her virtuosity. Rosine had mentioned her to me before, once attempting to secure tickets for us to one of her performances only to find it had sold out weeks in advance. I knew I should bask in the comparison, even if it was ludicrous, my aunt's attempt to ease the sting of my encounter with my mother. Then I recalled Marie's words about courtesans—*They are entertainers, like actresses*—and I said sharply, "I've no wish to sell myself on the stage. Or anywhere else, for that matter. I think I want to be a nun."

My declaration was spontaneous, without any consideration of its implications, yet it exerted an immediate effect. My aunt trilled nervous laughter. "A nun? How like you to be so absurd!" She paused, her mirth fading as she took in my expression. "It is impossible. You do realize that? To enter a convent, a girl must have a dowry. Not even God's love is free. Moreover, you just heard Julie. She would never allow it."

"Why not? If I wish to serve God, why should she care? I'll be out of her way forever."

Rosine sighed. "You're speaking nonsense." She glanced at the gentlemen, who did not appear, as far as I could tell, to be paying us any mind. "You'll be twelve next year. Almost a woman. I told you why Julie sent you here, but I think you should also know . . ." She paused, an uneasy frown knitting her brow.

"Know what?" All of a sudden, I sensed something long with-held surface between us.

She looked down, twisting her soft leather gloves in her hands. "Sending you here was not entirely Julie's doing," she said at length. "Oh, she wanted you out of the house, that much is true. She had her reasons, but she'd never have chosen this particular place, had—" She reached up abruptly to caress my cheek. "What does it matter now?"

"Please." My voice quivered. "It matters to me." Although I wasn't certain I should hear anything else, I was growing increas-ingly worried over what Julie might be saying to Mère Sophie. I imagined my mother removing me from the convent for another, less hospitable, place, where I'd not find myself nearly as welcome. "I wasn't serious about the baptism," I added, as Rosine continued to hesitate. "I only asked for Monseigneur's blessing to annoy her."

She gave me a sad smile. "Yes, I thought as much. I do not blame you. But Julie takes our faith seriously. She dares not show it, but she is proud of our heritage and would not have any daughter of hers convert. And she did not choose this place for you."

I avoided the immediate question her words roused in me. Were there other daughters? Had my mother given birth as I suspected? Did I have a new sister, tucked away somewhere with a nursemaid, as I had been? Instead, I focused on the last part, asking warily, "If she didn't choose this place, who did?"

"Your father," said Rosine, with a pained look. "He insisted on it, in fact."

The revelation felt like a stab to my heart. I could scarcely be-lieve it. No one had ever mentioned my father to me before now; as a child, I'd come to accept that whoever he might be, he must want nothing to do with me. I'd fantasized about him, making up stories in my head that he was a prince in a distant land or a merchant sail-ing the high seas. Handsome as a pirate, bold and brave. I tried to convince myself he didn't know about me, just as I forgot at times when I'd lived in Brittany that I had a mother. Yet as the years went on, the idea of him grew so remote that he eventually was banished from my thoughts.

Now my aunt was telling me he actually existed.

"My father?" I whispered.

Rosine nodded. "Did you think you didn't have one? He's a notary in Le Havre. He sent sums for your maintenance after your birth. The situation with Julie . . . it was complicated. But he knows about you. He specifically requested that you be raised as a Catholic. He secured your place here. He paid for it in advance."

My throat closed in on itself. I could only stare at her in disbelief, not knowing if I should feel grateful or shriek at her for having kept such a momentous truth from me. Before I could find a way to express the emotions rioting inside me, Rosine turned around.

Mère Sophie and my mother had returned to the hall.

With a silken smile that implored a moment's patience from her companions, Julie stepped before me. "Mère Sophie assures me you are faring well here, so for the moment I will submit to her wisdom. But there's to be no more talk of baptism. Am I understood?"

Had I not been so aghast by what I'd just learned, I might have protested. Instead, I accepted my mother's tepid kiss and stern warning—"Do not disappoint me"—and I watched her walk away. Rosine hugged me and hastened to join her; Julie was laughing, a hand on her companion's arm as he escorted her to their carriage.

The hall had cleared of its occupants without my realizing it, the girls having said farewell to their parents and been hustled by the nuns back to the dormitory.

Reverend Mother Sophie regarded me in pained understanding.

"Come, child." She held out her hand. "You mustn't despair. God will see us through our trials if we have enough faith to surmount them."

VI

Marie wanted to know what was wrong with me. She declared I'd turned sullen and was no fun, trudging about as if I'd fallen off the stage instead of enchanting the audience.

"You were astonishing," she said, trying to entice me to smile. "Even Louise says you should have had the role from the start. She wants to be your friend now. All the girls do. It's all Sarah-this-or-Sarah-that. If I weren't so fond of you, I'd be jealous."

Not even her flattery could brighten my mood. In a fit of pique, I released my captive insects and lone reptile into the garden, my lizard wobbling forlornly under a bush, its tail mutilated after I inadvertently sliced it off when I snapped the lid on the can where I'd kept it. I refused to draw anything but mournful saints, copying works of art by old masters from books, and allowed only César to follow me about because he was so devoted I could have kicked him and he wouldn't have strayed.

At night, I lay awake, ruminating on this father I'd never met who lived in Le Havre with another family. I tried to picture him, wondering if I'd inherited his arched long nose—which seemed unlikely, since it resembled my mother's and was, according to Marie, undeniably Hebraic. Perhaps his eyes then, with their chameleon bluish-green hue that reflected my moods, though, again, Julie's were nearly the same color. Or his hair, my sole unique asset, so thick and frizzy and gold-red, even if it was only slightly redder than Rosine's. Nothing of me seemed a part of him. I closed my eyes to conjure his face, but all I saw was Julie, furious that I was a bony replica of her creamy perfection.

The only way I could grow closer to him, have a sliver of him to make him mine, was to embrace his faith. But how could I, when my mother forbade it? In my turmoil, I grew even thinner, barely eating and prompting the nuns to remonstrate that I'd fall ill if I insisted on subsisting on a sip of consommé and crust of bread. I pored over my catechism, despite the fact that Julie had refused my baptism, so there was no further need to study, hiding the primers in my satchel until the Reverend Mother asked me directly if I was disobeying my mother.

"I must become one with God," I told her, clasping my hands to my chest in imitation of the saints I painstakingly drew in my sketch-pads. "Lest I risk my immortal soul. My people crucified our Savior. I will be damned for eternity if I do not receive the chrism."

Oh, I knew exactly where to strike, how profound an impact my words would have on Mère Sophie. "Not all your people are to blame for our Savior's passion," she replied carefully, but I could see she was troubled, caught between my mother's demands and her own unshakable faith.

I dropped to my knees before her, as I had before Monseigneur. "I must be baptized, Reverend Mother. What if I die and my soul is condemned forever to purgatory?"

"My child, you are too fervent. How can you say such a thing?" Yet she eyed me as she spoke, marking my pallor and gaunt cheeks, my slip of a body under the convent uniform. Just in case, I un-sheathed my last weapon, held at bay for just such a moment.

"My father wants it," I said, and her eyes widened. "My aunt told me. She said he paid to have me educated here. He is a Catholic. He wants me to be baptized. He must."

"Your aunt told you this?" she said in dismay.

"Is it true?" I replied.

Mère Sophie couldn't lie. But she didn't answer at once, fidgeting with the rosary at her belt before she said, "I only know what your mother told me. Your father did ask for you to be sent here. As to who pays for it, I did not ask. And no," she added, holding up her hand, "I don't know anything about him. We've never so much as corresponded."

"But he is my father," I said. "We cannot disregard his wishes."

She let out a troubled sigh. "I dare not countermand your mother's, either. Sarah, you put me in an impossible position!" she exclaimed, and when I wilted, the tears that were so ready these days dampening my eyes, she said, "Unless you hear God's calling for yourself. If you possess a true vocation, no one can stand between you and the veil. You must be baptized and receive Holy Communion. It would be our Almighty's will."

"I do hear Him," I said eagerly. "God calls to me. I know He does."

She sighed. "A vocation isn't something one can decide upon in a minute. It requires much time and contemplation. Many girls who come to us think they want to stay, but as they grow older, the world beckons them. And the world, my child, can be irresistible."

"Not to me." I leapt to my feet. "I want to stay here forever."

"We shall see," she said, and I left her, determined to prove it. No girl at Grandchamp was more diligent. I didn't miss a single mass. I scrubbed the chapel floors and mended Our Lady's mantle, though I was hopeless with a needle. I arranged flowers in the urns before the altar and would have cut off my own hair to adorn the statues had Mère Sophie not prohibited it.

As spring softened the frost on the convent windows and marigolds peeped up in the garden, I watched as the Reverend Mother weakened, her joy at my sincere demonstrations of devotion wrestling with her reluctance to challenge my mother. Finally, shortly before October and my twelfth birthday, Mère Sophie informed me that Julie had granted permission for my baptism. She didn't explain why my mother had changed her mind, but I suspected Mère Sophie had worked her magic, her monthly progress reports so exulting of my virtues that she'd proven impossible to resist.

By then I was a wraith, floating about, as Sister Bernadette snorted, with my head in the heavens, having forsaken all but César. Marie abandoned me for Louise and her group of friends because, she declared, I spent every spare moment either on my knees in the chapel like a novitiate or with my nose buried in my Bible.

The night before my baptism, I couldn't eat. With my stomach gnawing at itself and my nerves strung taut, anticipation having built to a crescendo inside me, I found myself plagued by terrifying doubt. Was I doing the right thing, abandoning the faith of my mother and her parents? Was there only one God, who sent His Son to perish for our sins, or was there another, the God of Abraham, who promised my soon-to-be-forsaken people a promised land of refuge? Must I choose one over the other, if both existed? And if I did, would I risk the wrath of the one I betrayed?

I tossed and turned, hearing Julie's reproaches in my head and Mère Sophie advising me that faith could surmount every obstacle. Unable to sleep, I rose from my cot and tiptoed outside in my shift and bare feet, César snuffling behind me as I made my way through the dew-drenched gardens into the chapel. Collapsing to my knees on the flagstones, I implored God for guidance.

I did not receive any. By dawn, it was too late. Returning to my dormitory, shivering and with my teeth chattering, I donned the white robe for the ceremony, already dressed and waiting by the time the nuns and Mère Sophie came to fetch me.

In the chapel, I found my family assembled. I hadn't given any thought that they might attend, but even if I had, I would have forgotten because only days before, Monseigneur had been assassinated by a madman in Paris. The murder of such an important prelate of the Church convulsed the convent, compelling us to spend hours at the rosary, praying for the repose of his soul, though I secretly lamented his death more because he'd promised to baptize me, a privilege no other girl here had enjoyed.

Julie and Rosine stood by the font, draped in lace shawls. As I moved toward the officiating priest, I suddenly saw a small figure clutching Rosine's hand. As I lifted my eyes in bewilderment to Julie, I discovered a swaddled babe in her arms, whom I'd first mistaken for a muff of some sort. I went still. Mère Sophie whispered, "Your mother wishes to have both your sisters baptized with you."

I couldn't draw a breath for a moment. "Both?" I finally managed to utter, as stunned by the confirmation that I had siblings I'd known nothing about as by the unbelievable fact that my mother, who'd mounted such initial resistance, could have changed her mind so completely.

"Yes," said Mère Sophie. "Isn't it marvelous? You and your sisters shall be welcomed into our Holy Church together. God must indeed look over your family, my child."

I scarcely heard the ceremony, did not feel myself incline my head over the font to be sprinkled with holy water. I stood aside, dripping, as Julie brought her baby to the font, followed by Rosine with the struggling little girl, who couldn't have been more than two, and behaved as I had when I'd been dragged from the flat, kicking up a fuss.

Then it was over. I was now baptized as a Catholic. So were my two sisters.

By the time we departed the chapel, I was swaying with fatigue and a persistent chill. In the garden, Rosine urged the little girl forth. "Jeanne, give your sister Sarah a kiss."

The child stomped her foot. "She's not my sister. Régine is."

Julie clucked her tongue. "Now, Jeanne. We mustn't be rude. Sarah is your elder sister. Régine is your younger one." To emphasize her point, she leaned down to show Jeanne the babe, who'd not made a sound. I glimpsed a scrunched face, wisps of dark hair (*not* a Bernhardt trait, I thought), then looked up to Julie's terse smile. "Well," my mother said. "We are all saved now, yes?"

Only I detected the malice in her voice. "Sarah," she went on, "you're looking frail. Are you not eating again?" Her question was indifferent, as if she asked if I brushed my hair enough. "You mustn't let this newfound devotion of yours become an obsession. A communion wafer, however nourishing for the soul, cannot sustain the flesh."

I stared at her in disbelief. With her babe cradled in her arms and her eyes indulgent, while little Jeanne glared at me as if I were an imposter, Julie said, "Alas, we must return to Paris."

She walked away. Past the courtyard archway, I saw two gentlemen by the waiting carriage, the same ones I'd seen with her and my aunt at the play. At least my mother had had the foresight this time to leave her suitors outside.

Rosine gave me an uncomfortable embrace. "Sarah, dearest, please do take care. You're skin and bones. I'm so worried for you." But she hustled off as soon as she spoke, leaving me standing there.

Mère Sophie said, "That was . . . precipitous. But you must be so pleased. Not only did your mother agree to let you receive Holy Communion, but you shall also remain with us for several more terms, just as you wished. Isn't it wonderful, Sarah? Sarah . . . ?"

I opened my mouth to agree, but her voice came at me in fragments, echoing like a distant bell. Icy waves swept over me. As I reached out to her, everything darkened. I couldn't reassure her as Mère Sophie cried out, for I'd crumpled in delirium at her feet.

VII

I was sequestered in the infirmary with a high fever and severe congestion in my lungs that the nuns feared might be consumption. When I coughed up blood, Mère Sophie summoned a physician from Versailles, who pronounced me "not long for this earth," plunging the nuns into a frenzy. They tended to me day and night—and held me upright in their arms so I could receive my First Communion, for they were nothing if not diligent about the afterlife. I barely recalled any of it, drifting in and out of a dreamlike haze that I'd brought upon myself. All my deprivations, coupled with the night spent in the chapel, had done their work. In my brief moments of consciousness, I thought I was destined for an early grave.

One morning, I woke to find that while so weak I could barely sit up, I was no longer in the grip of fever. My shift under the sheets and blankets was dry; when Mère Sophie arrived to set her palm to my forehead, she let out a sigh of relief.

"The fever has broken at last." She regarded me, her face more weathered now, as if she'd aged years. "You gave us such a fright, my child."

"Am . . . am I going to die?" I said, in a thread of a voice.

"One day, yes, as all living things must. But not today. Nor, I should think, any time soon, despite your best efforts." She wagged her finger at me. "You go too far, Sarah. You must practice moderation henceforth. Your enthusiasm gets the better of you and you must learn to restrain it. You could have a magnificent future, if you choose to pursue it wisely."

I took her advice as a verdict; no one, much less the Reverend Mother, would ever say an aspiring nun had a magnificent future. Sagging against my pillows, I whispered, "I have failed."

She tilted her head. "Failed? To kill yourself, perhaps, which is a mortal sin no amount of devotion can absolve. Otherwise, I would say you've succeeded admirably." When I didn't speak, she went on, "You've proven that when you set your mind to something, nothing can dissuade you. *Quand même* should be your motto: 'Despite the odds.' It's the sign of a remarkable character, though you may not believe it now."

"But not the sign of a nun," I said, close to tears.

She shook her head. "But a sign of something, nevertheless." She leaned down to kiss my brow. "You must regain your strength. You are excused for the rest of the term." She drew back. "Your mother was here."

I stared at her.

"I sent word," she said. "Your condition was so grave, we feared last rites might be required. She was abroad, but your aunt Rosine sent her a telegram, at considerable expense, and she came at once. It was two weeks ago. You were in no state to remember her visit. She sat by your bedside for hours; I saw how concerned she was for you. She told me she would return again to see you."

As I remained dumbfounded, she went on, "When she does return, I suggest you find compassion in your heart and mend this rift between you. She's your mother. We only have one in this life."

I lowered my eyes. Julie had been here. She had interrupted her travels to visit me.

I didn't know whether to rejoice or to dread her next appearance.

I was able to walk and spend time outside by the time Julie arrived again. When she suddenly walked into the garden, dressed in a pink satin gown and matching capelet, a feathered bonnet atop her head, I braced myself for her avalanche of recriminations, aware I must look like a specter. Although the nuns had plied me with pottages— and I'd downed every one like a starving lioness—I was still severely underweight, my veins visible under my colorless skin.

I sat on a chair, wrapped in a shawl despite the balmy day. César, devoted as ever, slumbered at my feet. The summer term was almost over and the girls were impatient for the upcoming August reprieve, when they'd go home to spend a month with their families. I'd always welcomed the silence that settled over the convent during the summer holiday, for I never went home. Neither did Marie and a few others, so we enjoyed a much less demanding routine, allowed to tarry in art class and romp about the convent grounds.

Nervously watching my mother's approach, I was struck by the change in her. She appeared different somehow, though it took me a few moments to decipher it. When I did, I felt even more uneasy. Julie was still beautiful and overdressed as ever, but for the first time in as long as I could recall, she appeared entirely content.

"Sarah." She sat near me, on the very bench where Marie had first told me what our mothers did for a living. As Julie removed her gloves, I wondered how many smelly old men those well-tended fingers of hers had caressed.

Quand même, I found myself thinking. It could be my mother's motto, as well.

"Mère Sophie tells me you're feeling much better," she finally said, breaking the silence. "You do know everyone thought you were ready for your winding sheet? You terrified everyone. Mère Sophie, in particular, was beside herself."

"But not you." I wanted to shatter her impervious façade, though I wasn't sure what I hoped to hear. She had come to see me twice now. Surely that must mean she too was worried?

Her lips parted into the faintest hint of a smile. "You forget that

I know you—more than you know yourself. You did it all for attention."

"Attention!" I cried out, rousing old César, who whined. "I nearly died!"

"Indeed." She did not raise her voice. "You thought to defy me, first by that distasteful scene with the archbishop, then by flinging yourself about like Saint Thérèse of Lisieux until I couldn't bear to read another missive from Mère Sophie extolling your piety. And when you realized you were no longer my only child, you mounted a tragedy worthy of the actress Rachel herself. It was obvious to me. But then, as I said, I know you well."

I couldn't believe it. I couldn't comprehend how she could sit there in her fashionable dress and silly bonnet and utter such cruel, such *vicious*, things to me.

"It isn't my fault." My voice trembled. "You lied to me about everything: about what you are, and most of all," I gasped, breathless now with the need to wound, to inflict the same pain on her that she'd caused me, "you lied about my father."

She sat very still. "Is that what you think?" she said, after a long moment.

"Rosine told me everything. She said my papa sent you money for my care and insisted I be educated here, but not once did you ever mention him to me."

"Your *papa* now, is it?" Her smile turned cruel. "Shall I tell you about him? I did not spare you the truth to keep him from you. I hid it to spare you—"

"Rosine said it was complicated. Is that why you let me think I had no father at all?"

She let out an impatient sigh. "You are as unreasonable as ever." She came to her feet, tugging on her gloves. "As you apparently know everything, I see no reason to dissuade you. You are out of harm's way, so now is as appropriate a time as any for me to depart."

As she turned to walk away, I realized that if I let her go, I might never learn the truth, or at least what she deemed the truth. I might never know who my father was. Yanking my voice out of my throat, I said, "Maman."

She paused, glancing in annoyance over her shoulder. Then, seeing my expression, she returned to the bench, though this time closer to me. I might have reached out and touched her. "I . . . I want you to tell me about him," I said.

Without any further attempt to prepare me, she said, "His name was Édouard Therard. He was a law student at the Université de Paris; he kept a room in the Latin Quarter, not far from where I lodged at the time. I was nineteen, newly arrived in the city, and he was very handsome. He had thick dark hair and a wild temperament—" She paused, with a startling laugh. "Much like yours. You resemble my family in your appearance, but otherwise you are entirely his. He was so thin, he disappeared in the night when he wore black. He drank too much and lived under the burden of his family's obligations, which included a betrothal to a local merchant's daughter. Then he met me."

Hearing her describe my father made me want to plunge inside her, probe the depths of her untouchable heart and experience him as she had, when she still nursed illusions like any other girl.

"Did you love him?" I asked, for it was vital to me to hear that she had, that no matter what she felt about me, I'd been conceived in love, not by callous negotiation.

She understood. Immobilizing me with a glance, she said, "I wasn't yet a demimondaine, if that's what you imply. I rented a pit of a room. I was Youle van Hard, a Dutch Jew without a sou to my name. I worked as an assistant to a seamstress, like thousands of other girls. He met me in the shop when he brought in a pair of trousers that required mending."

"But did you love him?" I repeated, evading this revelation of her penurious past because it might weaken my resentment toward her.

She shrugged. "What did I know of love or young men who declare it? Nothing. Oh, I'd had one or two before him, but none I cared for. He was different. So alive. So full of anger and yearning to change the world. He wanted to see the Republic restored; he talked incessantly of politics, as if I had any concept of such things. He believed all men must be free to seek their destiny, regardless of rank or birth. You might say he was a revolutionary."

I had to hold back my torrent of questions, passion coursing through me until I longed to throw aside my shawl and dance about the garden. My father was exceptional, a man of ideals! Julie had confirmed I was like him, that I'd inherited his temperament.

Her next words brought me tumbling back to reality. "A revolutionary in speech, perhaps, but not in deed. When I discovered I was with child, I told him at once. What else could I do? I needed his support," she said, and I found myself holding my breath. "His behavior was commendable, that much I will say in his defense. He did not shirk his responsibility as far as your upkeep was concerned."

"Rosine said he wanted me raised as a Catholic." I clung to this paltry certainty, even as I sensed the world starting to shift, about to crumble in shards.

"What he insisted was that you not be raised Jewish. He acknowledged his paternity on your birth certificate, but he refused to allow me to publicly claim his name for you, which is why you were given my father's surname, Bernhardt, instead. I was never to mention his identity to anyone: that was our agreement, in exchange for his support. Then he went back to Le Havre and his respectable merchant's daughter. And there he remained." She glanced down at her folded hands in her lap. "He never asked to see you. He sent me a sum every month, but I never set eyes on him again."

It couldn't be. I refused to believe it. Only, I felt her words worm inside me and I knew that for once, she wasn't lying.

"As Rosine told you, it was indeed complicated, because I was a Jewess who'd borne a bastard. For all his grand speeches about men being free, women, it seems, were a different matter. He wasn't prepared to risk his future. It's a tiresome tale, all too familiar. I consider myself fortunate; he was honorable enough to admit his mistake and pay for it. Others cast such mistakes aside and pretend they never occurred. And his money helped me to depart that horrible seamstress's establishment and start my own life."

She went silent for a moment. "He is dead," she said flatly. "He died last year of a fever."

I sat there, sundered, longing to wail, to rend my breast like the agonized saints in the convent books. But in that devastating moment, I couldn't mourn what I'd never known. For the first time in my life, I felt entirely, horribly, grown up.

"He left you a sum in his will," Julie went on, "but like everything with him, it, too, is complicated. I managed to secure your board and tuition from his estate, seeing as he himself had insisted you be sent here. As for the rest . . ."

She gestured impatiently, as if to dismiss my pain at the news that the man who'd sired me, whom I had never met yet imagined so many times, was no more. Standing up and smoothing out her skirts, she said, "I shall return for you in August. We will go with Rosine and your sisters on holiday. The physician recommends a respite in the mountains to help heal your lungs. I know a lovely spa in the Pyrenees, at Cauterets."

I gazed up at her, dumbfounded. "And afterwards . . . ?"

"You'll finish your education here. After all, he did pay for it. Then we shall see."

Without another word, she left me, slumped on my chair.

Only then did I realize that much like my mother had, becoming someone else might be my only choice in life.

VIII

While I didn't look forward to spending time in the mountains with my family, given my relationship with my mother, I was eager to know my sisters. And once we arrived in Cauterets, I found that Jeanne was clearly my mother's favorite, arrayed in miniature versions of Julie's attire and giving herself too many airs for her age, making me suspect she was indeed Morny's child. But she could forget her hauteur when out of Julie's sight, reverting to being just a little girl as she joined Rosine and me on day trips to the local farms, where I found myself besotted by lambs and baby goats.

Régine, on the other hand, became *my* favorite. Nearly a year old, she was boisterous, wailing up a storm and grasping at my hair, my sleeves, anything she could take hold of to stake her claim. Perhaps because she didn't resemble any of us, with her olive skin and huge dark eyes, I saw her as someone apart, whom it was safe for me to love.

Julie remained aloof, our conversation in the garden having done nothing to bring us closer, as I'd hoped it might. Rosine made up for it with her ceaseless fussing over me, ladling soup and cheese and thick brown bread down my throat until I regained most of the weight I'd lost during my illness.

I returned to the convent fattened, and with just a nagging trace of my cough. Resuming my education, I also reclaimed Marie's friendship with much coaxing and gifts of chocolate, and we both made a new friend in lively, blond Sophie Crossier, whose family lived nearby and welcomed the three of us into their home on Sundays. With the onset of my menses, the nuns moved me into the older girls' dormitory, and my deportment and diction lessons took precedence. By the time I turned fourteen, I spoke like a Parisian, all trace of my Breton accent erased, and I could perform all the meaningless accomplishments expected of a bourgeois girl, such as straining tea into the pot, reciting poetry, playing the pianoforte, and conducting silly conversation about trivialities.

Yet I lived every day under the shadow of dread. On my fifteenth birthday, I'd be considered an adult per the convent rule, and my stay at Grandchamp must come to an end. Though I'd not given up hope of becoming a nun, I knew it would never come to pass. Mère Sophie had made it clear I wasn't suited to a religious life—another burden to bear, as all too quickly my fifteenth year loomed before me, in all its uncertainty.

A few days before my scheduled departure in August, Mère Sophie summoned me.

"You must remember everything we have taught you. You must accept God's will and obey His commandments. Your will is formidable, Sarah, but you mustn't allow it to lead you astray. I fear temptation will be your constant adversary." She didn't elaborate, but her intent was unmistakable: she knew what my mother and aunt did to support themselves, and while the nuns had prepared me to the best of their abilities, my choices were limited. Indeed, I could count those choices on one hand.

"I'm so afraid." My voice broke as I regarded her, this woman I'd come to love so much that I thought of her as more of a mother than the one who gave birth to me. "What will I *do*?"

"Let God show you the way," she said. "God and your heart. You will know. *Quand même*, Sarah. No one can force you into a life you do not desire."

The trouble was, I didn't know what I desired. Packing my suitcase with my linens and clothes, my worn Bible and well-thumbed rosary, I found myself in near despair. Julie had sent a landau to take me to Paris, but neither she nor Rosine came to accompany me.

As I hugged Marie goodbye, she burst into tears. "We must write to each other every day," she bawled, until I reminded her that she had to write to me first with her address, as she would be in Flanders. At this, she scowled; much like me, she had no choice. Her mother had accepted a proposal of marriage from one of her suitors, a "fat Flemish merchant who stinks of cheese," as Marie described him, and she'd only been granted an extra six months at the convent while her mother arranged their move. But she, too, would soon depart Grandchamp, while our friend Sophie, being younger than us, had just a year left. Sophie made me promise to visit her, which I knew I wouldn't do, though I assured her I would, trying to smile as my tears rose up to choke me when I proceeded into the courtyard to find the nuns assembled to bid me farewell.

They couldn't say anything to ease my desolation. I felt as if I were being evicted from the only home I'd ever known. Mère Sophie took me by the hand. "Remember to choose the life you want," she whispered as she walked me to the landau.

From the landau window, I watched her standing back as the contraption jolted forward, as I felt myself carried down the lane, out the gates, past the old oak trees shading the walls, taking me away from this holy world I'd become such a part of toward a world I feared would devour me whole.

Old César let out a mournful howl.

Seated alone on the red-cushioned carriage bench, I clutched a handkerchief that smelled of the lavender in the garden to my face and I wept.

Paris was still loud and crowded. It still stank, especially in mid-August, when everyone with the means to do so fled the city for the countryside. Regardless, as the scythed harvest fields of Versailles faded away and the bulwarks of the city loomed into view, my sorrow over leaving Grandchamp began to lift. An exciting city, bursting with opportunities; surely I could discover a path ahead here.

The coachman brought me down brand-new boulevards unfamiliar to me after six years of absence. I shouted at him—I had to, to be heard over the din—that he was taking me to the wrong district, but he ignored me, his cap pulled low over his brow as he steered past a riot of carriages and hordes of pedestrians.

We came to a halt before a white building on the rue Saint-Honoré in the 1st arrondissement, a fashionable area that I remembered from my excursions with Rosine. After I descended from the carriage and he handed me my suitcase, the landau took off, leaving me gazing up at the plaster façade and wrought-iron balconies painted in gleaming black, not peeling or rusted. He had made a mistake and left me stranded.

A woman bustled out from the building in a simple black dress, her mousy brown hair drawn into a net at her nape, accentuating her homely face. She reminded me with a start of Mère Sophie, though she was much shorter, with lively small brown eyes and the energetic air of an industrious sparrow.

A tiny bird of a lady, I thought, *une petite dame,* as she smiled, revealing tea-stained teeth. "You must be Sarah! I've been expecting you. I am Madame Guérard. I live above your mother's flat. Come, child. You must be exhausted from your journey. I've some lemonade and fresh croissants. Are you hungry? You must be. Did the good sisters of Grandchamp not give you anything to eat for your trip? How odd. Nuns should be more sensible. What were they thinking, to send a girl off to Paris without so much as a slice of cheese?"

She didn't await my response, babbling away as she hustled me into the building with its fancy gas lamps mounted on the lobby walls and up the winding staircase to the fourth floor, where she pointed to a door—"Your mother's flat"—then upward to the sixth, where she threw open a less impressive door and declared, *"Voilà!"*

I stepped into a cozy, if overfurnished, garret apartment, full of potted plants and—

"A cat!" I exclaimed.

"Ah, yes. My dear Froufrou," said Madame Guérard fondly, as the gray and white creature hissed at me and darted under one of the sofas. "She's old and cantankerous, I'm afraid. Like me. But she'll get used to you in time."

She—Madame Guérard, that is—didn't seem so old to me. As I unfastened my cape and searched for an empty spot to place it— every surface was cluttered with books or newspapers or random bric-a-brac—she went into the kitchen, returning moments later with a tray.

"Please, sit. Your mother told me you'd been ill. You must tell me all about it."

Easing onto the sofa with the least number of tattered cushions, I heard Froufrou hiss again. Madame Guérard set the tray on the table and proceeded to pour the lemonade. Once she'd seen me sip—it was deliciously bitter—and nibble on one of the croissants, she sat on a sagging chair that was evidently her preferred spot. To my delight, Froufrou vacated her hiding place to spring onto Madame's lap.

"You were saying," she began, as the cat purred under her caress, "you'd been ill?"

"It was several years ago," I replied between mouthfuls. I was famished. I could have eaten another four croissants. Would it be too forward if I—

"Go on," she said. "Take all you like. I bought them for you. I cannot possibly eat so many. Why, I'd burst out of my weeds!" She gave a jovial laugh, easing my timidity. Who *was* this woman? "Not like you," she added. "Why, you're no bigger than a sliver of soap. Ah, youth. Such a fleeting gift. Look at me. I'm a widow now. I lost my husband six years past. I was once as slim as you, though not nearly as pretty."

I studied her discreetly as I ate her croissants. She didn't look very old to me. She had no visible lines on her face except for the creases by her eyes when she smiled, and she smiled often. Her hair wasn't white. Her hands were chafed, but not spotted. No, not old at all, yet she was already a widow. It must be why she wore black.

"I'll put some flesh on those cheeks," she said, as I wiped crumbs from my chin. "You'll be plump and rosy in no time, with me to watch over you."

Clearly, my mother must have hired her.

"Are you to be my governess?" I asked, imagining that all the books strewn about indicated this was how she earned her living: educating courtesans' daughters.

"Me? A governess?" She let out another laugh. "Oh, no, *ma chérie*. Your mother has hired quite the impressive governess already. One Mademoiselle Branbender." She inclined to me, nearly toppling Froufrou from her lap. "She claims she once tutored a Romanov grand duchess. She is very learned. But not very happy, I'm afraid. She's come down in the world, through no fault of her own. Or so I've gathered. She'll take charge of your sisters' education, and I presume yours, as well. I'm merely the upstairs neighbor, whom Mademoiselle Bernhardt relies upon. I don't mind. I like to stay busy, and my poor Henri and I never had any children of our own. I like children very much." She paused, with childish eagerness herself. "I do hope you'll agree. I want us to be friends."

I did, too. I liked her. I enjoyed her garrulous conversation, spiced with bits of gossip and exuberance. My anxiety over my return started to ease. Nothing could go *too* badly if Madame Guérard was upstairs.

"You can visit me anytime. Consider my home yours." She paused. I heard unwitting trepidation in her voice when she said, "Your mother is very engaging, but also . . . very engaged. You need never feel alone whilst I am here."

I lowered my eyes. Apparently, nothing had changed as far as Julie was concerned. She wasn't even here to receive me, off with Rosine and their suitors of the moment.

And yet something *had* changed.

I was in Paris again, and I had made a new friend.

⸬

It was several weeks later, during which I slept in Madame G.'s flat in a spare room and tried to win over recalcitrant Froufrou, before Julie and Rosine arrived, laden with luggage, along with Régine and Jeanne, the former wailing and the latter pale with fatigue. I didn't fail to notice that my mother had taken them with her to wherever she'd gone, resentment curdling inside me even as Régine threw herself at me with an ebullient *"Ma sœur!"* When Rosine tried to pry her away, my sister spat at her, *"Putain.* Leave me alone."

"Quelle horreur," murmured Madame G. "Such language and not yet four years old."

Unpinning her bonnet, Julie sighed. "She repeats everything like a parrot. She doesn't understand a thing of what she says."

Madame Guérard's sidelong look at me conveyed that she believed my little sister knew exactly what she said. "Come see me later," she whispered, and she retreated upstairs, leaving me in the elegant salon of my mother's new apartment. Régine's sweet-sticky fingers adhered to mine as Rosine gave an apologetic smile. "We were supposed to be home last week," she said, "but there was a tedious delay with the trains. A strike of some sort. Have you been spending time with Madame Guérard?"

No, I almost retorted. *I've been drifting about your locked flat like a ghost.*

Julie was motioning her maid to the luggage heaped in the foyer; she hadn't yet spared me a glance. "See that you draw a hot bath," she ordered. "The girls must wash before they're put to bed. Régine." She turned to my sister, who glared at her. "Go with your sister Jeanne this instant. You can pester Sarah later."

Their maid looked about to drop dead on her feet. Taking my sisters in tow, along with armfuls of discarded detritus, she trudged down the length of the apartment hallway, Régine baying protest at the top of her lungs.

My mother finally lifted her eyes to me. "So. You are here."

I didn't dignify her remark with an answer.

"I have a bedchamber prepared for you," Julie went on, as Rosine took the opportunity to slip away. "I trust you'll find it adequate. But of course, you will. After years of sleeping in a dormitory, I imagine your own *chambre* will be welcome."

"I can share a room," I said. "It doesn't bother me."

"Doesn't it?" She floated to her settee, newly upholstered in expensive-looking green silk, discarding her fichu and gloves. I recognized other items from our old flat, those morose oil paintings of mountains and valleys, the assortment of urns, statues, and lamps with tasseled shades. But the rest was new, ornate, and overtly feminine—little gilded chairs that could barely accommodate a bustle, and tiny inlaid tables that looked as if they would collapse under the weight of anything heavier than a vase.

"No," I said. "I'd prefer to share a room with Régine."

"I can assure you that you do not. Jeanne will share with your sister." She gave me a terse look. "You are fifteen. A woman must have her own bed."

My hands clenched into fists at my sides as she went on. "I've employed a governess. Mademoiselle Branbender will instruct Jeanne and Régine, as I'll not see another daughter of mine put in a convent. You can take part in their lessons. You'll need something to occupy yourself while I decide what's to be done."

"*Done?*" My heart sank to my feet.

"Yes. I have certain arrangements in mind. You needn't ask for details, as nothing is settled. You will be informed when the time comes."

My entire body went taut.

"Yes?" said Julie. "Is there something you wish to say?"

"No." I kept my voice as cold as hers. "May I be excused?"

She nodded, with a moue of surprise. "It seems you've reaped

some benefit from that costly stay at Grandchamp. Your unfortunate illness and baptism aside, you appear to have learned manners.
Your bedroom is down the hall, the second door to the left."

I did not say another word. I hated her so much in that instant, I
could feel it thrumming like poison in my veins. I wished she were
dead.

But as I marched away, I wished I were dead even more.

IX

"She wants me to marry!" I burst into the flat upstairs like a windstorm, bringing Madame G. racing from the kitchen, where she was forever cooking or baking something to satisfy my appetite.

At the sight of her, I went still, panting. "She told me today. She wants me to meet with her and a notary to discuss the terms. This afternoon!"

With a dismayed cluck of her tongue, Madame G., whom I'd dubbed *ma petite dame* to my mother's irritation, steered me into her chaotic living room. Pushing Froufrou off her chair, she pushed me into it. "Some hot chocolate, I think," she said, her solution to all of life's vicissitudes. "Yes, that would be perfect. Wait a moment and—"

I shot out my hand to seize her wrist. "She told me he's a Dutch merchant, a Jewish man with a thriving cloth business in Lyons. He has agreed, though I'm Catholic and he's never so much as set eyes on me."

"Oh dear." She'd heard so many of my fears in the past months, when I'd repeatedly barreled up the stairs with some perceived affront—everything from the way I thought Mademoiselle Branbender regarded me through her pince-nez with regret when I took up watercolor painting, to Julie's increasingly terse remarks about my eccentricities—that her tone indicated she thought I exaggerated this latest upset, as well.

"Are you quite sure, Sarah? Julie told you this herself?"

I nodded, desperate. "Today over breakfast. She got up from her chair, in front of Rosine and my sisters, looked at me, and said, 'I believe it is time you wed. Clearly, you are ill-suited to gainful employment, so I see no other alternative.'" I shuddered as I recalled the impassive way in which my mother had delivered her indictment. "She said all I do is paint and mope about the house, and as Mademoiselle Branbender can't teach me anything else and I show no inclination to be of any use, marriage is my only option."

I expected Madame G. to utter her ubiquitous *"Quelle horreur,"* followed by a determined plot to thwart this terrifying proposition. Instead, she sat on the footstool before me and said, "Did you tell her you have no wish to marry?"

"Of course! I've never met the man. I surely don't care for him."

"But you might care for him in time. He could be a good man, and clearly he's an enterprising one, if he has a cloth business in Lyons. Perhaps you should consider it."

I sprang to my feet. *"Ma petite dame,* I thought you loved me!"

"Oh, I do, my child. As if you were my own." She wrung the kitchen towel in her hands. "I love you so very much, but you are so unhappy. Miserable. Your mother and aunt go out and leave you behind for hours on end; you have your sisters to see to, but you're not made to be a nursemaid, and they, too, will grow up in time, and . . ."

"And?" I was breathless with panic.

"You're nearly sixteen, Sarah. Girls like you must indeed do something."

I knew what she meant. She didn't say it out of spite or to hurt me; she did love me, like a mother, like Mère Sophie, but she only gave voice to what we'd both avoided until now. Girls like me, like my mother and her sisters—either we wed, as my aunt Henri-

ette had done, took a job in the sewing trade, or we became courtesans.

"I don't want to do *their* something," I said, as I felt an invisible
noose tightening around my throat. "I don't want strange men paw-
ing at me."

Madame G. said, "I think no girl wants that. Yet for many, it is
their only choice. That, or go begging in the street. Even an arranged marriage isn't so easy to find these days. That is why I think
you must consider it, if the alternative isn't to your liking."

"I can't. I won't." But the undeniable reality of her words deflated my rage. The truth was cruel. And unavoidable. "I could run
away," I suddenly said. "To Spain or Italy. I'll make a new life for
myself. Become an artist."

"With what, my child? You haven't a coin of your own to buy a
train ticket."

"I could sell my painting supplies—"

"Didn't you unearth those supplies from a coffer in your aunt's
closet? They were already used. Only a tinker would buy them and
it won't be nearly enough to make a new life for yourself."

I sank to my knees before her. "Can't you help me?"

She gave me a sad smile. "I would go with you, *ma petite*. But I
don't have that kind of money. I receive a small pension as a widow,
plus whatever Julie pays me on occasion—just enough to maintain
this roof over my head. We wouldn't reach Vichy with what I have
saved, much less Spain or Italy."

I struck my fist against my knee in frustration. "There must be a
way. I—I'll pawn some of Julie's jewels. That hideous Morny—
he's always bringing her baubles she never wears unless she's going
to the Opéra. She has plenty of jewels, and he has plenty of money.
Didn't you tell me he's the illegitimate brother of Louis-Napoléon?
He's practically royalty. He can replace whatever I sell."

"He *is* royalty. And if you show up at a pawnshop with your
mother's jewels, which are gifts from Monsieur de Morny, they'll
brand you for a thief and throw you into prison." She patted my

clenched hands and murmured, "Now would be the time for a nice cup of hot chocolate, yes?"

As she returned to the kitchen, I looked over my shoulder at Froufrou, who watched me with baleful eyes. "Shoo!" I hissed, and the cat lunged from the sofa to scurry under Madame G.'s bed.

If only it were so easy to do the same with my future.

With my belly full of hot chocolate and my ears full of Madame G.'s reassurances, I returned to the flat at the hour my mother had cited.

I entered the salon to find her guests sipping cognac and conversing as if they weren't about to destroy my life. I stood in the doorway, until Morny noticed me and inclined his head to Julie. She turned about with a smile as false as her greeting.

"Ah, there you are. Upstairs with your *petite dame* again?"

Thinking that flinging myself out the window, as I'd tried to do once before, might prove a satisfactory resolution, I saw the *duc* give me an unctuous smile. "All grown up, I see. But I vow, the claws are still just as sharp."

My mother's fingers snaked around my arm. "What do we say to monsieur le duc?"

"Pleased to meet you, my lord," I muttered.

"Pleased to meet me, she says!" He let out a guffaw. He'd grown stout and florid, and his mustachios were now entirely gray. "Clearly she doesn't remember we have met before."

It was on the tip of my tongue to assure him I most certainly did remember, but Julie had me in her grip, turning me to the other man in the room—a scrawny scowl of a man with wire-rim spectacles and the strict bearing of someone who thought himself very important. "This is Maître Clement from Le Havre. He was your father's solicitor and represents his estate."

Monsieur Clement cut short my sudden interest in someone who'd personally known my father: "So, we are all here on your account, are we?" he said, with a distinct lisp. "All these people with better things to do than find themselves beset by a rebellious daughter who ought to know what is best for her. You must be very pleased with yourself, mademoiselle."

I loathed him on the spot. I expected Julie to at least say something in my defense, as I was, after all, *her* rebellious daughter, but she only laughed in that glazed manner of hers and motioned me to a chair.

I sat, feeling as though I awaited the drumroll to my execution.

In an irritated tone, as if he'd been interrupted in mid-declamation, Monsieur Clement said, "The hundred thousand francs left to her in her father's will are intended as a temporal dowry. Therefore, it is incumbent to finalize these negotiations—"

"A hundred thousand francs!" I leapt up from my chair. I had money, left to me by my father. An inconceivable sum—a treasure, the very godsend I required to save myself.

Monsieur Clement stared at me as if in dismay to discover I had a voice. "To be paid upon the signatures of both parties," he continued, "upon the signing of the marriage contract and posting of the banns. Only these two items, notarized and witnessed by me, are considered binding terms for the release of the dowry from Monsieur Therard's trust."

"But it's my money," I declared, bringing everyone to a standstill. I turned to Julie, whose jaw was set. "I can return to the convent. I can pay to be accepted as a novitiate."

It was the only thing I could think of, my sole escape. With an exasperated wave of her hand, Julie said to the men, "Again with the convent. Do you now see what I must contend with? She is utterly without reason."

"Rosine told me a dowry was required to enter the convent," I said. "If so, we can offer the hundred thousand francs to Grandchamp and—"

"Offer?" interrupted Monsieur Clement. "Did you not hear it is a *temporal* dowry?"

"What does that mean?" I was doing my utmost to not lunge at him with my sharp claws, as Morny had called them. "It is still my father's bequest to me, is it not?"

"Not to do with as you please. A temporal dowry must be paid to your husband upon your marriage." Monsieur Clement eyed my mother. "Yes, I do see. Entirely without reason. I propose we move the matter to its conclusion. Monsieur Berenz is willing to take her sight unseen. Therefore, I've had his notary draw up the papers, which I'll witness today—"

"No." My voice, to my surprise, was calm. "I refuse to marry him."

He regarded me in astonishment as Morny chuckled. "Careful, lawyer. She has a temper. I've experienced it for myself."

"This—this is preposterous." Monsieur Clement directed his indignation at Julie. "You must tell your daughter to mind her tongue. When has such a thing been seen, a mere chit dictating what we should do with—"

"My money," I cut in. "I'm telling you what to do with *my* money, monsieur." I didn't know where my will sprang from, how I found the strength, much less the courage, to scold my father's solicitor. "He left that money to me. I can indeed do with it as I please."

"Enough!" snapped Julie. She never showed anger in public, let alone before a suitor as constant as Morny, but she'd gone beyond reason herself, enraged by my defiance. "You will marry him, even if I must drag you by your hair to the altar. You will *never* enter a convent. Never, do you hear me?"

Rosine bleated, "Sarah, please. You must marry, if you will not work."

"Who says I won't work?" I rounded on my aunt, causing her to flatten herself against her chair. "I never said it. I simply will not work as you do, on your backs."

My mother crossed the room in seconds, the swift blow of her hand against my cheek rocking me back on my heels. "Ungrateful," she hissed. "Ungrateful. Selfish and willful. Just like him. Only thinking of yourself, never considering the consequences of your actions."

In the stunned silence, as I felt the burn of her palm on my face, Monsieur Clement sneered.

With a yawn, Morny stood. "*Mon Dieu*. Such drama. I'm quite exhausted by it. *Chère* Julie, have your maid fetch my cloak and cane; I do not wish to stay for the second act."

Still quivering in rage, my mother started to reach for the porcelain bell on the side table when, to my disbelief, Morny shifted his watery gaze to me. I saw amused benevolence in his regard. "I fear we've reached an impasse. If the girl refuses to marry and a convent is out of the question, perhaps, given her evident talents, we should see her enrolled in the Conservatoire. Sarah Bernhardt, *tragedienne*. It has a certain appeal, don't you think?"

"The Conservatoire?" Julie's hand froze on the bell. "Does Monsieur imply she should become an *actress*?" She uttered the word in horror, as if he'd suggested I become a charwoman.

"Why not?" Morny approached the table beside her to tinkle the bell himself. "I understand she performed rather well in that little Nativity production at the convent, yes? The director of the Beaux-Arts is a good friend of mine; he's on the board of the Conservatoire. It can be arranged. She'll have to audition and complete the two years of training, but once she earns a place in the company, she'll earn a modest salary and have the means to support herself. Preferably," he said, sliding his mordent gaze back to me, "on her feet."

I whispered, "I never said I wanted to be an actress, my lord."

"Indeed. However, what you should now ask yourself is whether you want to be an actress *less* than a wife. It is a dilemma that only you, mademoiselle, can resolve."

The maid brought Morny his belongings. As he slipped on his cape and gloves, and my mother collected her shattered composure, he said, "It so happens that tomorrow night, I'll be attending Racine's *Britannicus*, staged by the Comédie. I'll send my footman with tickets and my carriage. I do hope you will join me."

Julie accompanied him out. I looked at Rosine, who appeared relieved, as if the matter were decided, even as Monsieur Clement gave a contemptuous snort. "An actress? This scarecrow in a dress? Not unless she can play the Grim Reaper every night."

I ignored him. What else was there to say? Morny was right.

An actress or a wife. My choices had just been laid out before me.

X

I had never attended the theater.

I knew of it, of course. The Comédie-Française, also known as the House of Molière for the esteemed seventeenth-century playwright who founded it, was one of only two state-sponsored acting companies in France, and it was where the actress Rachel, our Jewish icon, had made her debut and attained legendary fame as a leading interpreter of classical and contemporary roles. During the past listless months, with so little to occupy my time, I'd wandered our neighborhood and passed by the local theater, where the Comédie performed matinées. I'd seen the actors loitering outside smoking (a vice I found enticing) and painted scenery lugged through the back entrance. But I'd never seen an actual play, as only the privileged and fashionable could afford to indulge in such entertainment.

Julie must have had her own opinion, being a woman about town. She surely had an idea of what working in a theater entailed. I might have asked her, but she'd gone silent as a statue around me, as if I'd ceased to exist, and I avoided her the next day as much as possible, sitting in on my sisters' lessons and then creeping upstairs after lunch while my mother took her nap, to tell Madame G. what had occurred.

"Oh, that's a wonderful idea!" she exclaimed, to my surprise. "Acting would be the ideal profession for you. You can be independent and do as you like. And you needn't marry someone you do not love if you're performing onstage."

I observed her carefully, trying to detect whether the note of relief I heard in her voice was sincere. It was much like the expression I'd seen on Rosine's face—as if anything that eased the tension and set me on my path must be embraced, regardless of its actual benefits.

"Is it a profession?" I said suspiciously. "Surely, donning a costume to parade about for the public's amusement is but a step above doing the same in a salon."

Ma petite dame sighed. "Perhaps. But you needn't actually parade about a salon if you don't want to. And you'll have no need for a husband to please, either."

At this, I went downstairs to lie awake in bed until the time came to prepare for the evening. Rosine brought me a dress—one of hers, a castaway of gawdy blue taffeta, hastily adjusted with enough bows and ruffles to hide the tucked-in seams, as she was a good deal larger about the waist and bust. As soon as she laced me into it, I groaned. "I look like a bone in a lampshade. Must I wear this?"

My aunt nodded. "I'm afraid Julie insists. We are attending a performance with Morny. You must look as if you belong in his company."

On the ride in Morny's fiacre, I sat wedged between Julie and Rosine, both of whom were dressed to the teeth, jewels flashing about their throats and wrists, their cleavage amply revealed by the wide lace-trimmed scoop of their bodices. At the theater entrance, where distinguished members of society descended from lacquered black carriages gilded with family insignias, Julie seized my white-gloved hand. In a sibilant voice, she said, "Should you cause me any embarrassment tonight, I'll dispatch you to Lyons on the next train."

Her warning was unnecessary. My mouth hung open as we entered the Palais Royal, where the Comédie was holding that night's performance. I'd never seen such opulence and was dazzled by the lavish red carpeting, so soft under my uncomfortable shoes, and by the bluish hue of the gas jets mounted in swirled-gold lamps on the white silk-papered walls. Scarlet silk flared on the undersides of the gentlemen's ankle-length capes, their damask-patterned vests peeking from under their tailcoats, while the women swanned about in gowns so wide their skirts filled entire doorways, all in soft hues of cream, peach, and white.

The *duc* had his own box, naturally. Sitting beside him was a bear of a man, with shocking (at least, to me) caramel skin and piercing blue-gray eyes below a thicket of wiry red-brown hair. It astonished me. I'd never have thought to see someone like Morny, a titled aristocrat, with a man of obvious mixed racial blood.

"Mesdemoiselles Bernhardt!" the bearlike man boomed, rising to offer my mother and Rosine the front seats in the box. "Such a pleasure to see you." He spoke as if it were commonplace to encounter them here, rather than in Julie's salon. Then he lowered his gaze to me. "Can this be the scintillating Sarah Bernhardt I've heard so much about?"

Morny gave a lazy smile. "Mademoiselle, allow me to introduce my friend Monsieur Alexandre Dumas."

Even though I knew Morny had been the one telling stories about me, I couldn't curb my awestruck intake of breath. "The writer?" I said. For I knew who he was, and now understood his association with Morny: Alexandre Dumas was a celebrated novelist, his books serialized in the newspapers and taking Paris by storm. After Victor Hugo, he was considered to be France's greatest living writer.

"The same." He smiled. "Have you read my work, mademoiselle?"

"Yes," I whispered, and then I strengthened my voice, not wanting to sound like the gauche girl that I was. "*The Count of Monte Cristo* is one of my favorites—"

He clasped a big paw-like hand to his chest. "Why, she has the voice of an angel!"

Morny's smile widened. "Trust me, *mon ami*, you haven't begun to hear it. Wait till she raises it. A bassoon has less power."

Julie shot me a glacial look. "She always has her nose in a book," she said, sweeping to the seat vacated for her. "I keep telling her, it's very bad for a woman's intellect to read so much."

"Her intellect looks well enough to me," replied Dumas. He gave me a covert wink.

I took my seat beside my mother while the *duc* and Dumas settled behind us. The enormous crystal chandelier suspended like an icy sunrise above the house dimmed its gaslight. Three resounding thumps rang out, making me jump.

Leaning forward, Dumas said in my ear, "Pay attention, *mon ange*. The show is about to begin."

As the rustling of handbills and fans whispered throughout the theater, the orchestra began to play. The heavy gold-fringed velvet curtain rose with a *whoosh* to reveal a new world—pilasters and pastel clouds suspended over the seven hills of ancient Rome, populated by striding figures in togas and ivy wreaths. The emperor Nero was played by an actor of impressive stature, whose powerful voice reverberated thunderously. But it was the woman playing his mother, Agrippina, who most impressed me. Heavyset and swathed in a purple mantle, her fleshy arms encircled by serpentine bracelets, she was past her youth. Yet in her role as the vengeful empress-mother, her commanding presence eclipsed everyone around her, her encompassing gestures imbued with a majestic malice as she stalked the stage.

I was overcome in that moment by the realization that these were ordinary people, transformed by the alchemy of costume and lighting into epic figures, with the ability to transport those of us who beheld them to another realm, where passions erupted with volcanic force—grander and more tempestuous than anything I'd experienced in life. Here was a world where the commonplace ceased to exist, where mundanity had no place.

The theater was a world of magical escape.

Gripping the edge of the box with an audible moan, I leaned so far forward in my seat that I might have tumbled into the rows far below had my mother not pulled me back.

"Be still," she hissed. "Are you an idiot, to stare and moo like a cow?"

Dumas chuckled. "How can she not be enthralled? No one plays Agrippina like our Madame Nathalie."

Julie didn't even bother to watch the play. With her lorgnette fixed at her eyes the entire time, at intermission she turned to whisper to Morny: "Did you see Princess Mathilde? I hear she left her lover to take up with a degenerate. And Madame de Castiglione certainly has a nerve to show herself in public after the scandal. And was that the insufferable writer George Sand in the second tier? It was? Well, at least she had the decency to wear a dress tonight and not those intolerable trousers. Whatever is the world coming to, when a woman sees fit to go about in society in men's attire?"

I barely paid mind to her condescending comments. Neither did Rosine, who rose to partake of aperitifs before returning to the box for the final act, during which she nodded off. Clashing cymbals preceded a dénouement that had me straining to stand, to cry out at the magnificence of a spectacle that had swept me into the ancient past, so that I'd forgotten everything around me, the tumult of my existence, and the choice I still had to make.

But by the time the curtain fell, there was no longer a choice. I knew it from the moment the applause ricocheted around the house that I must become a part of this world.

As the lights came up and the audience rose to its feet, Julie turned her stare to me. "Is there no place where you can refrain from making a spectacle of yourself?"

Dumas intervened again. "You can hardly blame her. It was indeed a tremendous performance of what's always been an overwrought play." He smiled at me with a kindness that nearly made me weep. "Did you enjoy it, *petite étoile*? Was it everything you hoped it would be?"

"I have no words," I whispered. To my dismay, a tear slipped down my cheek.

"Well." He leaned close to me. "You'd best find the words. With that heightened sense of emotion and exquisite voice, I daresay you could be a sensation yourself one day."

XI

It was decided. The following month, I would audition for the Conservatory of Dramatic Arts and Music, known popularly as the Conservatoire. Julie harrumphed, even as Morny declared, "A splendid decision!" and proceeded to grease the wheels of mutual interest.

I plunged into preparation. Julie rolled her eyes when she found me scavenging through books brought from Madame G.'s flat, works by Voltaire, Molière, and Racine. I memorized every line I could, walking up and down my bedroom declaiming and adding the flinging gestures I'd seen Madame Nathalie make, until my mother drawled, "You needn't go to such trouble. You'll be accepted. Morny has seen to it."

"I still want to be perfect," I retorted.

She laughed. "You believe it so simple? You recite a few lines and—*voilà*—here comes the applause. You have no idea. This life you think you want is no better than the one you disdain. How do you think all those actresses pay for their costumes and paint? How do you think they keep a roof over their heads? They, too, require protectors. The salary you may eventually earn as an ingénue will scarcely pay for your daily sustenance."

"I don't eat much," I said, and her eyes narrowed. "And I already have a protector. Two, in fact. Monsieur de Morny and Monsieur Dumas."

She might have slapped me again; I could see she wanted to. Dumas had indeed taken a special interest in me. He came panting up the stairs to our flat every Thursday afternoon, but not to be entertained by her. Instead, he called for me, and in front of my mother's amused guests, he gave me instructions on my performance, calling out in his bass voice, "Not so fast. Slow down. Enunciate!" He wrote down exercises to perfect my rolling "r," and I drove everyone insane with my incessant pacing and recitals of *"Un très gros rat rongeait trois gros grains d'orge"*—"A very large rat gnawing three large grains of barley."

Dumas applauded me the next time he visited. "Yes, that's it. *Superbe*. But be careful to not drop your voice at the end of the line. Maintain the tempo. Heighten the emotion and breathe. You have a voice like silver. Use it. Let your voice convey the pathos and the audience will follow you. Never imitate. Find the character in yourself, *ma petite étoile*."

I loved that he called me his little star. To me, he was the father I'd always envisioned but never had. After he left, without partaking of her after-hours enticement, he always left a sum of cash— "for the girl's apparel," he said—and Julie would storm into her bedchamber with Rosine, where she shouted as my aunt begged her to calm herself.

"The ingrate!" Julie cried, so that my wide-eyed sisters and I heard her right through the door. "She says she'll not work on her back, so she does it instead with her eyes. She has that reprobate Dumas doting on her like a lovesick bull. 'For the girl,' he says. 'For my little star.' I can't abide it. Still a virgin and already she wreaks havoc on my affairs."

The tension between us grew so strained, with her suspicion that I seduced her suitors with my "outrageous ambition," that by the morning of my audition, I was a bundle of nerves, having surrendered every effort, and most of my meals, to my quest to succeed.

Being an actress meant far more to me than excelling onstage. Indeed, excelling wasn't my priority, though I believed it was. The urgency to escape my mother's grip, to get out from under her disapproval and caustic advice that I'd end up in the gutter like a thousand ingénues before me, coupled with her occasional plaintive appeals to heed reason, as Monsieur Berenz the merchant was still willing to marry me, had turned my life into a purgatory. Even the gutter seemed preferable to spending another hour in her presence.

She did, however, expend some of the money Dumas had left on a new audition dress for me. When Rosine unpacked it from its box, I moaned in despair.

"Black. I'll look like a widow."

"It's pure Lyons silk. Monsieur Berenz sent the cloth. Look." She held it to my chin as I stood before the tarnished mirror above my bureau. "It brings out the amber in your eyes."

My eyes, I thought—and my lack of figure. After I tried it on, I took one look at myself and realized it was worse than widow's weeds. I resembled an invalid. I'd developed a hint of bosom in my sixteenth year, but the dressmaker failed to take that into account, just as she'd apparently failed to confirm my other measurements, which I assumed my mother had provided—and no doubt, she'd sent outdated ones deliberately in order to embarrass me. The hem hung above my painfully thin ankles, exposing my white pantalettes. And the bodice constricted me like a corset (a contraption I never used, given my slenderness); its ruffled neckline smothered my throat and scratched like fingernails under my chin. Then I peered closer and noticed a burn mark on the bodice, made by the overzealous maid with the iron.

Rushing into the salon, where Madame G. waited to escort me, I cried, "It's scorched. Look here, right through the silk!"

Reclined in her *robe de chambre* on the settee, her hair loose upon her shoulders, Julie sighed. "It's barely noticeable. Fetch one of my fichus and a cameo to cover it."

"A fichu?" I regarded her, aghast. "That will only make it less appealing."

Rosine hastened to gather the items as Julie sipped her coffee. I passed my furious gaze over her. "Aren't you going to get dressed? I'll be late."

"Yes," she replied, "I will get dressed. Later. I have appointments this afternoon."

"You're not coming with me?" I didn't know why I was surprised. She hadn't once behaved as if my audition were anything more than a nonsensical act I would regret.

"I already told you, your acceptance is a given. I have it on the best authority. All this fuss over your dress and the rest of it is unnecessary."

"That's not true," I retorted. "Dumas told me no one can purchase a place in the Conservatoire if they lack the talent." I turned about as Rosine returned with the fichu. "Tell her. You were here the other night when he said as much."

Rosine avoided looking at Julie, draping the fichu over my shoulders and pinning it, lopsided, over the scorch with the cameo. "There," she murmured. "Much better."

"Never mind that," snapped Julie. "Did Dumas actually tell her such nonsense?"

Rosine kneaded her hands. "Yes. You were out with Morny, but Dumas came to help Sarah perfect her lines, and he did tell us that."

"And he should know." I returned my enraged stare to Julie. "He's a playwright, too. If I don't prove my talent, no matter what Morny says, the Conservatoire will not accept me."

"Well, then." Julie's voice turned glacial. "It should come as an immense relief that you're going there to be evaluated on your talent and not your attire, yes?"

Flinging another scowl at her, I grabbed my straw hat and hurried with Rosine and *ma petite dame* to the fiacre outside.

...

The Conservatoire's greenroom on Faubourg Poissonière was crammed with aspirants—youths and girls, even children, all clad in their Sunday best, fussed over by mothers and guardians as they frantically rehearsed their chosen selections, trying to refine their delivery even as the head usher called out their names from the roster in hand.

One by one, they exited through double doors into the hall beyond. From the bench nearby, where I sat with Madame G. and Rosine, I strained to hear what was occurring behind those doors, ignoring the usher's disapproving stare. In time, the doors opened again and the aspirants emerged, white-faced and trembling, some in tears.

I began to think this was a big mistake.

"Mademoiselle Sarah Bernhardt," said the usher.

Madame G. squeezed my arm. "That's you, child. *Merde*," she whispered, using the good luck charm for the theater. Standing on numb legs, I went to the usher.

"What shall you recite for us?" he asked in a bored tone.

"Second scene," I quavered. "Act Two. *Phèdra*. The role of Aricia."

"Ambitious. And who has been assigned to provide your cues?"

"Cues?" I echoed. Dumas hadn't mentioned any need for such, or if he had, I'd neglected to recall it.

The usher made an impatient gesture. "Mademoiselle, we have a very busy schedule, as you can see. The lines of the character with whom Aricia converses: *Who* will recite them?"

I shot a desperate look over my shoulder. Neither Rosine nor Madame G. knew the lines. "I . . . I didn't know," I stammered, returning my bewildered gaze to the usher.

"Then fetch the book and find someone. I assume you have the book with you?"

God help me, I did not. Even if I had known to bring it, I would have forgotten it after the fiasco with my dress. Glancing again over my shoulder at all the waiting hopefuls, no doubt ready with their books *and* someone to deliver their cues, I made an impulsive decision. I knew the entire parts of several plays by now, but all required cues; I had to change course.

"I will recite La Fontaine's 'Les Deux Pigeons' instead."

It wasn't the expected choice, judging by his bemused expression. La Fontaine's poem in rhyme was about two pigeons who bond in friendship until one of them, yearning for adventure, flies away. Caught up in a storm, stalked by predators and injured, he returns to his companion to roam no more. First written as a children's story, it had proven controversial because both the pigeons were male.

"This should be fascinating," he said sourly, and he escorted me into a cavernous hall, where the stage loomed before a long table, presided over by four men and a woman.

I could barely focus on them. In addition to his warning that no one could bribe their way into the Conservatoire, Dumas had told me the most senior actors of the Comédie were appointed to oversee student auditions. It was part of their responsibilities as fully pensioned members with a share in the company profits, but while they should be dedicated to discovering new talent that would ensure the future of the house, they resented the obligation because they were, in fact, auditioning their potential future replacements.

As I stepped onto the stage and curtsied, the usher announced in unabashed glee, "Mademoiselle Sarah Bernhardt will recite 'Les Deux Pigeons' by La Fontaine."

The woman snickered. "Does the girl think us still in the schoolroom, perhaps, to regale us with that tired fable?"

I looked up sharply, recognizing her voice. It was the actress Madame Nathalie, who'd enthralled me in her role as Agrippina. The woman was laughing with the man beside her. Without her lavish costume and makeup, she was just a fleshy matron. And her companion-in-jest with the broad shoulders was none other than the actor who'd played her son, Nero, though he, too, looked nothing like his stage persona—a heavyset, older man with a florid countenance. My sudden recognition that these actors who made their living pretending to be others were not benevolent magicians made me want to run out, fling myself at my aunt's feet, and beg her to persuade my mother to let me use my dowry to take the veil. I'd imagined this moment innumerable times since I'd seen *Britannicus,* envisioning myself commanding the stage with the same effortless presence. What I'd failed to imagine was how an actual audition would go.

You believe it so simple. You recite a few lines and—voilà—here comes the applause. You have no idea what you seek.

With my mother's reprimand in my ears, I opened my mouth.

"'Two pigeons were deeply in love. But one of them left their home. The days of pining are long, and long are the nights without you—'"

I heard a yawn. Another of the committee members, a silver-haired man with piercing dark eyes, called out, "Louder, please. We can barely hear you, mademoiselle."

"We hardly need to," said Madame Nathalie from behind her lorgnette. "We already know the story. If you keep asking her to repeat it, I daresay we'll be here all day waiting for that beleaguered pigeon to return to its mate."

Nero guffawed.

Something molten flared inside me. Their mockery reminded me of Julie's cruelty, her refusal to believe I could amount to anything but a woman like her. These people were professionals, supposedly here to evaluate my talent. How *could* they be so inconsiderate?

Stepping to the edge of the stage, I lifted my chin. "'A pigeon longed for his mate as I long for my sweet love,'" I sang out loudly, undulating my hands to evoke the shape of flight. "'I too await the flutter of wings, the sweet passage of love's return. He is gone, and I cannot find the happiness that was ours on the paths of lost time. Lovers, joyous lovers, say it again and again: Any absence is too long. It does no good to wander. Love passes, and the leaves fall with the turning compass of the wind.' "

As my voice faded away, I discerned a faint sound. I thought one of the members had taken to reciting alongside me in mockery, until I realized the sound was my own stifled breath. All five members, including Madame Nathalie, were regarding me in absolute silence. I curtsied again. "Thank you," I said, and saw them lean toward one another to murmur.

I started toward the exit, frantic to return to *ma petite dame* and Rosine, to bury my head in their skirts and lament my failure.

A voice detained me. "Mademoiselle Bernhardt, a moment if you please."

Turning around warily, I found the silver-haired man at the foot of the stage. "I am Monsieur Provost, a tragedian with the company. You were impressive." He looked over his shoulder to the others, asked, "Wasn't she impressive?" and they nodded their agreement.

"We think you have promise," Provost went on. "We will accept you as a student."

"Accept?" I thought I must have heard wrong. Looking past him to the table, I saw Nero with his arms crossed at his chest and Madame Nathalie wiping her lorgnette on her sleeve, while the others consulted papers. They did not seem all that impressed.

"You wish to be an actress, I presume?" asked Provost, and when I nodded, he sighed. "We believe you have the makings of a singer. Would a musical career interest you?"

"No," I managed to say. "I don't think I sing very well."

I had no idea if I did, even as he assented. "Then seeing as you'll not be singing, you may choose your principal instructor: myself or Monsieur Beauvallet"—he gestured to the actor who'd played Nero. "In addition to our performances onstage, we both teach at the Conservatoire. I can assure you, either one of us would be pleased to have you under our charge."

"You," I said at once. I also had no idea if he was any better than Beauvallet, as I knew nothing of either man, but he'd addressed me with respectful consideration and Beauvallet appeared to be in league with Madame Nathalie, to whom I'd taken a firm dislike.

"She chooses me," Provost announced to the committee.

Beauvallet scowled. "Naturally. You always did hold an attraction for *les jeunes filles*. Evidently, they share the same affinity for you."

Madame Nathalie snorted, tapping Beauvallet's arm with her lorgnette—"For shame!"—and Provost turned his gaze back to me. "We shall advise you of your acceptance by courier. Congratulations, Mademoiselle Bernhardt. Welcome to the Conservatoire."

When I burst out into the greenroom, the joy on my face was enough to bring Madame G. and Rosine to their feet. I had to restrain my triumphant cry.

I had done this on my own, and was now on my way to becoming an actress.

ACT II

1860–1862

Ingénue

It is not enough to conquer; one must learn to seduce.

—VOLTAIRE

I

"Mademoiselle Bernhardt, have you forgotten your lines again? Perhaps you can elucidate for us how this interminable delay makes you a better performer."

Provost motioned curtly as I stood before him. I hadn't forgotten my lines; I was searching for the right tone to convey them, yet as I struggled to satisfy his demand, he tapped his foot. "This century, if you please. By now, the audience has thrown their playbills at you and departed the theater in disgust. They come to see you *act*, not pantomime."

Haltingly, I launched into the soliloquy assigned by him. The role was the same one I'd been unable to recite for my audition: Aricia in *Phèdra*, and I struggled to find the emotion in the difficult phrasing, not that he cared a centime for my efforts.

"'Stunned at all I hear, my lord, I almost fear a dream deceives me. Am I indeed awake? Can I believe such generosity? What god has put it into your heart? Well is the fame deserved that you enjoy! That fame falls short of truth. Would you for me prove—'"

"No." Provost banged his pole on the floor. "What is this?" He strode to the stage. "Where is the *vérité*, the sorrow and fear that exalts Aricia?"

"But I—I thought you said you wanted me to recite the passage *à la mélopée*."

"*À la mélopée!*" He swerved to the other students. "Did I instruct Mademoiselle Bernhardt to recite the lines thus?" When no one answered—no one dared, searching their laps rather than risk falling prey to his monstrous condescension—he turned back to the stage. I had to fight the urge to recoil from his savage glare.

"Which are the accepted systems at this institution? Which are the acceptable styles developed in 1786 by one of our founders, Mole, who in turn imparted his impeccable expertise to the great Talma, Napoleon's favorite actor, and which have formed the principal foundation for our subsequent pupils, including your own idol, Rachel?"

Resisting my exasperation—did he never tire of extolling the Conservatoire's hallowed history?—and the urge to inform him that if Rachel had had to contend with his constant abuse, she'd never have excelled at anything, I replied, "*Chant,* emphasizing cadence and rhyme; *vérité,* concentrating on content and verse. *Mélopée,* by action, is allied to *chant* or recitation."

"And the differences between these systems are . . . ?"

"Declamation is the art of speaking verse with precision, tenderness, or fury. Fury and tenderness are opposed to precision, for precision is an attribute of technique, and represents *chant,* while tenderness and fury, being emotional attributes, belong to *vérité.*"

Not even he could accuse me of being remiss in my studies. During the last year, I'd done nothing else but devote myself to my art, every hour of every day, and often long into the night. I'd become a slave to it, learning every role assigned to me, no matter how secondary, scalding my fingertips on stubs of candles as I pored over plays in my room. It wasn't my fault that I was often tardy, living as I did a distance away, with Julie providing only enough for my transport on the horse-drawn omnibus either to or from the Conservatoire, but never both ways. It wasn't my fault that I chose to walk here in the morning rather than the evening, unwilling to risk my safety to drunkards and riffraff.

But Monsieur Provost, acclaimed tragedian and villain extraordinaire of the Comédie, as well as my personal tormenter, had no patience for such trivialities. With a malevolent smile, he said, "Mademoiselle, you have just proven that much like a babe at the teat, you can regurgitate whatever you suckle. Perhaps henceforth you can consider applying this prodigious talent for memorization to *applying* these systems in your performance."

Yanking my voice out of my constricted throat, I ventured, "Surely my goal should be to inhabit the character, regardless of whether I do it *à la vérité* or *mélopée*?"

"Your goal at this time," he retorted, "is to satisfy me." He banged his pole. "Again."

As I started to clench my hands, I stopped myself, extending my fingers instead. "'Stunned at all I hear, my lord, I almost fear a dream deceives me. Am I indeed awake? Can I believe such generosity? What god has put it into your—'"

Bang!

"Are you picking a pear from the tree?" snarled Provost. "What is that hand doing? Ismene, your confidante, has just revealed her suspicion about Phaedra's lust for Hippolyte, whom you adore. This is a moment of horror-struck revelation, not an invitation to pluck ripe fruit."

One of the students giggled.

Tears scalded my eyes. "I did this gesture before and you said—"

"I said, gesture *precedes* speech. You failed to do either. Again."

I made the attempt, but after four more thwacks of his pole and accompanying tongue-lashings, I couldn't bear it for another instant. Throwing my hands into the air, I shrieked, *"I cannot!"*

"You cannot?" he echoed. Behind him, the entire student body froze. "You just did. This is what I want to see: fury. Those arms, like laundry lines, stretched out as if to beseech the gods. You *can* do it, Mademoiselle Bernhardt. You will stay here until you do." Without turning his head, he barked at the others, "Dismissed. I shall see this lesson to its conclusion with Mademoiselle-I-cannot."

He stared at me as the students filed out, whispering among

themselves. As soon as the door closed, he sat down, leaned against his odious pole, and intoned, "Again."

It was dark, far past any hour to board the omnibus home, when I emerged from the Conservatoire. I was so fatigued I couldn't feel my body, my soliloquy running over and over in my head, for I'd not been allowed a break to so much as take a sip of water.

A shadow in the arcade sidled toward me. I mustered a smile. "You waited."

His name was Paul Porel; a chubby boy, not particularly handsome, but with a friendly smile and a thatch of curly brown hair. Almost eighteen, the same age as me, he was one of the only friends I'd made in the Conservatoire. Like me, he was in Provost's class.

"Of course I did." As he hitched his satchel onto his shoulder, I suddenly remembered that in my rush to depart upon Provost's exasperated leave, I'd left mine in the hall. "And your hat, too," he said, grinning as he took in my dejected expression. "I hope Monsieur Hateful didn't give you extra lines to learn."

I yanked my shawl about me. Winter was upon us, a bite of frost in the night air. "That man is a devil. How many hours did he keep me there? And just as I was about to faint from exhaustion, do you know what he said to me?"

Paul's grin widened. "What?"

"He looked me up and down, and said, 'Now, mademoiselle, you will remember that Aricia is a role you should never play.'"

Paul burst out laughing. "He adores you!"

I gave him a scowl. "He detests me. He thinks I have no talent; he's always telling me I'm thin as a skeleton and I move like one, too. You've seen how he constantly challenges me, and then, when I do precisely as he asks—"

"He says you've done it wrong," said Paul. "Remember when we performed that scene from *Zaïre* for him?"

I shuddered at the memory of the disaster that had been our misguided attempt to bring to life the scene from Voltaire's celebrated tragedy of the Christian slave captured by Muslims. Paul had played the Sultan and I played the slave Zaïre. We rehearsed it for weeks. When we performed it for Provost, he bellowed us off the stage.

"See?" I now said. We began walking toward his boardinghouse, our arms linked together to ward off the chill. "He detested me in that role, as well."

"He told you that you must have thought the audience had fallen asleep, because you kept turning your back to them. 'Mademoiselle, do you hear snoring, perhaps?'" Paul quoted.

"'Because if you don't,'" I continued, "'you should listen more closely.'" I cuffed his arm. "As I said, he must think I'm the worst student in the Conservatoire."

Paul's expression went solemn. "You are wrong, Sarah."

I paused, glancing at him. "Wrong? How so?"

"He thinks you might be the best. That is why he works you so much harder than the rest of us. He sees something in you that sets you apart."

"I doubt that," I said at once, though his compliment warmed me a little. "Even if it were true, Provost would be the last person to think it."

We continued for a block or so before I asked hesitantly, "Do you think I'm . . . ?"

He nodded. "So does everyone else in our class."

"Then why don't I have any other friends? All the girls and most of the boys shun me. I know they think I was only accepted because Monsieur de Morny arranged it."

"Did he arrange it?"

"He arranged my audition, yes. But I still had to audition, like everyone else. Provost himself told me at the time that I was impressive. He and that ogre Beauvallet—they both wanted me as their pupil. I should have chosen Beauvallet." I kicked a stray pebble from the cobblestones. "Maybe he wouldn't berate me every hour of every day. Come to think of it, he said Provost was fond of *les jeunes filles*. That's probably what sets me apart."

"Again, you are wrong. I happen to know Provost's taste runs to *les jeunes garçons*."

I gripped his arm tighter. "You never told me that. You never told me you were . . ."

He threw back his head, laughing. "Not me, you goose. I'm not his type, nor am I one of them. But that pretty blond boy in our class, Jacques Villette . . . haven't you noticed how Provost always casts him as the swain and croons that his limp wrists convey gravitas?"

"I hadn't," I admitted.

"And there's your problem. You don't notice. You rarely listen. You walk around with your mind somewhere else. That is why Provost hounds you. He thinks you have the makings of a great actress, but talent alone does not make a career. Training and focus do."

"Now you sound like him," I grumbled.

We reached his boardinghouse, a ramshackle building in a cheap district populated by students and drunkards. As I mulled upon his declarations and he searched his satchel for his latchkey, he said, "I suppose you also have no idea that you do have other friends at the Conservatoire? One, in fact, says she knows you very well."

I started. "Who?"

"Marie Colombier." He jiggled the key in the lock. "She's in Samson's class; she was accepted this year. She heard someone mention your name and started telling everyone you used to be best friends at the Convent of Grandchamp and she knew, from the moment you took the stage in a Nativity play, that you'd become an actress. She claims you played the role of Tobias so convincingly, when you opened your eyes and said you could see, everyone in the audience wept."

"I didn't play Tobias. I played the archangel." I paused. "Are you sure?" We stood in his boardinghouse's dingy foyer, with peeling plaster from the ceiling floating down around us.

"Yes, I'm sure. Do you know her?"

"I did. We were friends at the convent, but I thought she moved to Flanders." I followed him up the rickety stairs, ignoring the mice scampering between the warped floorboards. "And I didn't play Tobias," I said again. He hushed me, for though I'd spent the night here before when it was too late to go home, sharing his narrow cot and curled against him to keep warm, student renters weren't allowed to invite overnight guests. If we were caught, he'd be charged double and someone might send word to Julie, who believed I stayed with the other girls in their lodgings, if she even deigned to notice my absence.

As soon as we entered his tiny room with its hard cot, stool, and broken desk, I explained, as if it were of utmost importance, "Marie took my role as the shepherd. Another girl played Tobias. The girl assigned to play the archangel took ill, so I was given her place."

He chuckled. "Your friend Marie is a liar, then. And, I daresay, a bit of a slut, as well."

"A slut?" Unraveling my shawl, I snuggled into his bed, pulling the moth-eaten covers to my chin. "Why ever would you say that? And, Paul, do you have any cheese or bread? I'm famished."

He pulled out his plate from under the cot and lit the tallow light on the desk. With the rancid burning oil smoking up the room, we huddled on the cot and ate his stale bread and hard cheese, the only food I'd had since breakfast.

"You were saying Marie is a slut?" I prompted.

"That's what I hear." He chewed thoughtfully, mashing the hard bread into a digestible mush. "Some of the boys in Samson's class fancy themselves rakes. Samson recruits the sons of members of the imperial court, by-blows of minor officials and such. They think they're better than the rest of us. Not bourgeois. Marie goes out with them after class to that brasserie around the corner."

"Going to a brasserie hardly makes her a slut," I said, wondering how I'd failed to notice Marie in my goings and comings from the Conservatoire, and why, if she was talking about me, she hadn't yet approached me to renew our friendship.

"Does going with the boys afterwards down to the riverbank qualify?" said Paul.

I nearly choked on my bread. "She does that?"

"According to the boys. I haven't gone with her, so I can't vouch for their honesty."

I didn't know how to respond. The Marie I recalled had certainly been worldly; after all, she'd educated me about our mothers, so perhaps this was true. It brought the uncomfortable reminder that girls who surrendered their virtue were disparaged, while boys were expected to sow their oats as proof of manhood. As I thought this, I said aloud, "How ungallant of them to boast of it. If a boy said such things about me, I'd box his ears."

Paul chuckled. "I have no doubt. That is why they shun you. They like you very much, Sarah. They also see something different in you, but you scare them. Still, I suspect most, if not all of them, wish you'd go to the riverbank with them instead of Marie."

"Don't be ridiculous." I reached over to cuff his arm again, but before I made contact, he pulled away. In the slippery shadows, I couldn't read his expression.

"No," he said.

I peered at him. "What?"

"Don't do that. Don't treat me as if I'm your brother."

"But we're friends. I often think of you as . . ." My voice faded. When he started to collect the remains of our meal, evading my stare, I said, "Do you think of me like that?"

He shook his head. "I know you're not like Marie Colombier. And I'm not the son of an imperial official."

"But you think about it?" I wasn't sure why I wanted to know. My body, much as I neglected its basic needs, had begun to stir; I had felt inexplicable longings that had led me to furtive explorations in my own bed. But that quick probe with my fingers hadn't held my interest for long. It seemed such a waste of time, when I had so many lines to learn.

He looked up, into my eyes. "Of course I think about it. You are the most amazing, maddening girl I've ever known—and the most beautiful. I think about it all the time."

He thought I was *beautiful*? It wasn't an adjective anyone had ever used before to describe me.

"Don't you think about it?" he went on. "Not with me, but with others? There are many handsome boys at the Conservatoire, I suppose."

"Like Jacques Villette?"

He snorted. "You're impossible."

I couldn't say what made me do it. It was an impulse, like so much else in my life. I saw him with that bent pewter plate, his plump face downcast, crumbs about his chin and looking anywhere but at me, and I drew the covers aside. "Come here."

He froze. "I'll sleep on the floor tonight."

I patted the straw-stuffed mattress, scooting back until my spine was pressed against the damp wall. "You will not. You will put that plate away and get into bed. It's freezing. I insist. And blow out the tallow before we suffocate on the smoke."

He moved jerkily, as if he'd lost control of his limbs. As he squeezed onto the cot, tense as a spring about to snap, fumbling at the blanket to yank it over himself, I rested one of my hands on his chest and I felt it—the rapid thumping of his heart.

"It's like a horse racing," I whispered, and I trailed my fingers farther down, not sure of what I was doing yet hearing in the catch of his breath that I had the right idea.

His hand took mine before I reached his groin. "No. You . . . you will regret it. I'm nobody, the son of a shop-keeper. My family has no title. No riches."

"Neither does mine." I leaned over him to set my mouth on his lips.

He tasted of cheese. It was nice. Cheese and bread, and his quickening ardor, which, much as he tried to resist it, was gaining hold. When he thrust his tongue into my mouth, I drew back.

"Slowly," I whispered. "Remember, I'm not like Marie."

He said breathlessly. "Sarah, you are a goddess to me."

I almost laughed, but I held back because it wouldn't be appropriate. We groped and kissed, did all the awkward things first-time lovers do; we didn't remove all our clothes, just enough to feel the chill on our skin as we found those hidden places he'd thought so much about.

When he entered me tentatively, as if I might break, resting his weight on his arms and with his eyes closed, a look of such bliss washed over his face that it seemed as if he were entering paradise itself. I felt sharp pain. It hurt more than I'd expected. I clenched my teeth, urging him on because—well, it seemed like the only thing to do.

It was over soon enough. I was astonished, in fact, by how soon. He bucked and groaned, let out a cry, and spurted warmth onto my thigh. Lifting himself off me, he fell face-up, panting, as though he'd just scaled a mountain.

We lay in silence before I heard him whisper, "Sarah. I . . . I think I love you."

II

So, this was what all the fuss was about—what kings had sundered realms for, emperors forsook wives to claim, and countless playwrights spilled oceans of ink to exalt.

How absurd. Not that I'd disliked it. I could think of more unpleasant ways to spend an evening, but it wasn't at all what I imagined. Certainly, it did not amount to anything near the feverish passion I had for the roles I studied and hoped one day to perform.

Paul, however, was besotted. He offered to marry me, even as I said I was perfectly content to remain as we were. He did not like it. He believed because I'd surrendered my virginity to him—I had to scrub the stained sheets in the communal water closet down the corridor—we must proceed to the banns and the altar. He was concerned about my reputation, yet also apparently eager to continue sleeping with me whenever I was willing, which was less often than he preferred, as I couldn't absent myself from home *every* night.

I did not think it changed me. I was too absorbed by the revelation that after all my indignant condemnations, my strident refusal to ever be like my mother, in the end, the very act I'd disdained came down to a fleeting encounter of the flesh, not nearly the violation or indignity I had believed it to be. The only difference, I decided, was that afterwards, in her case, the man left suitable payment for the effort—which, if one discounted the social standing of being married, was probably more than most wives received.

Yet it did change me. Although I was slow to notice, my awakened carnality seeped into my person, coloring my voice, my gestures, the very manner in which others perceived me, so that one day after delivering a recital from *Zaïre,* the very play that had earned me his prior disdain, Provost grunted. "That wasn't bad. Not good, mind you, and not stage-worthy by any measure, but better. For you."

Coming from him, it was high praise. I could have hugged the brute.

Only then did I notice the other boys in the Conservatoire—to me, they were still boys, though to everyone else they were young men—eyeing me as I flew down the halls with my overstuffed satchel, my lips stained brown from the cheap bonbons I ate to stave off my hunger and save my coin, my hair escaping the pin stabbed through my chignon.

"What on earth are they looking at?" I asked Marie.

I'd gone searching for her as soon as I could, coming upon her one afternoon after deportment class, which was taught by an effeminate remnant of the Second Empire, replete with the lace-trimmed sleeve cuffs and rouged lips. Marie had been delighted to see me, kissing my cheeks as though we'd left Grandchamp yesterday. When I bullied her about keeping her distance, she shrugged. "I didn't want to be a nuisance. Everyone here seems so taken with you, while I'm . . . well, no one thinks I'll ever be a great actress."

"No one thinks that about me, either. We're friends. You never wrote to me, so the least you could have done was tell me you'd come to Paris, let alone were studying here."

"Flanders was a bore," she replied. "My mother was so occupied proving herself the perfect wife, she seemed very willing to let me come here to try my luck."

She was succeeding, at least to my eyes. She had a winning air that everyone flocked to, even the competitive girls, and through her I'd made more friends—or so I'd thought until now.

"They ogle me like wolves," I grumbled. "Must I fling rocks to keep them at bay?"

"Fling Paul Porel at them instead," said Marie, sticking her tongue out as we passed. A few of the boys made bold kissing sounds at her; she arched her rump, made even more curvaceous by her bustle. "They're mad with jealousy that you're with him and not them."

"They *know*?" I came to a horrified halt.

She glanced at me in amusement. "Sarah, surely you're not that naïve. Honestly, who would think it, considering what our mothers—or yours, now that mine is a respectable matron—do? Men always know. They can smell it on us."

"They can? Dear God, what if . . . ?"

She laughed. "I said men. Not mothers. Don't fret. I'm certain your *chère maman* has no inkling of your rendezvous with Porel. If she did, you'd have heard about it by now. Nothing enrages a courtesan more than a daughter who gives it away for free."

I wasn't reassured. Nor was I pleased. I sent Paul a note canceling our engagement that evening and went home in trepidation. Julie hadn't said anything to me; she barely acknowledged my presence these days. She was enlarging the flat, knocking down walls to make more space, as Rosine had engaged a new suitor—one evidently generous with his wealth. Half the flat was in chaos, scaffolds and tarps everywhere, Régine stomping around insulting the workers, while Jeanne complained that the wallpaper glue stuck to her shoes. Under the circumstances, my spending a few nights a week with "my fellow female pupils" had gone unquestioned.

As soon as I entered my room and unpinned my hat, my back aching from the weight of my satchel, Julie appeared unexpectedly at the door.

"May I ask where you have been?" she said, distinct frost in her tone.

I started to unpack my satchel. "At deportment class—"

"Liar." She came at me so quickly I didn't have time to duck before she delivered the blow. Reeling back from her, my temple throbbing, I heard her say, "I know exactly where you've been. After everything you put me through: the humiliation, the disparagement of me and Rosine before our suitors, our friends— Then Morny helps you into the most prestigious training academy for the dramatic arts, and what do you do? Play the whore."

I lifted my eyes to her. "He doesn't pay me."

"Then you're a fool. You'll wish for payment soon enough when he gets you with child. Those who do not pay leave. They always do."

I elected not to inform her that we'd seen to that potential complication; by mutual agreement, Paul never spent himself inside me. As she spun away, I said instead, "Maybe they leave you. Not me."

Her shoulders went rigid. "You'd best pray you earn such high marks that your instructors declare you the second incarnation of Rachel herself. Because I'll not give you another sou once you complete your training, regardless of whether the company hires you. Once you're done with your studies, you are on your own. Then we shall see who pays whom."

She stormed out, slamming the door so hard that a ladder toppled somewhere in the flat.

With a snarl of fury, I flung my satchel across the room, scattering my books. As they upended on the floor, underlined pages fluttering, I dropped onto my cot and sank my face in my hands. High marks, indeed. I must achieve more than that.

Only a contract at the Comédie-Française would save me now.

III

I told Paul we had to end our liaison. He was devastated, blubbering that he loved me, he would do anything for me.

I refused. "I only earned second prize in comedy and an honorable mention in tragedy last year. This is our final year. I must earn first prize in both to gain a contract at the Comédie. I've much studying to do and little time to accomplish it."

"Won't Morny see to your contract?" he said tearfully. "Why must you forsake me?"

I bit back a surge of anger. "Paul, please. We are not Romeo and Juliet. I don't want Morny to 'see to it.' I want to earn a contract by my own merits."

He was very unhappy and avoided me for weeks, while the other boys turned aggressive. I had so many invitations for coffee and pastries at the brasserie, I might have lived off their largesse. I turned down every one. If I wasn't studying, I was sleeping. I was punctual for every class; I even tolerated the deportment fop with his crop, which he flicked across my shoulders—"Upright, mademoiselle. Glide. You're a queen at court, not a nag dragging the milk cart."

The month before my final exams, I prepared without cease. Provost had assigned me two challenging scenes selected to display my versatility, but all of a sudden, he fell gravely ill. Samson was appointed to assume his place, and he informed me that my monologues from *Zaïre* and Molière's *Les Femmes savantes* were ill-suited, replacing them with Delavigne's *La Fille du Cid* and *L'École des vieillards*. Neither suited me better, with their long-winded verse, but Samson insisted, despite my objections. As he was one of the appointed judges for my exams, I couldn't disobey him.

Then Rosine declared that I must have a new hairstyle for "Prize Day," the euphemism for that grueling week of exams, on the very morning of my appearance. The coiffeur proceeded to fuss over my unruly mop—"She looks like a harem slave"—and employed an arsenal of hot irons and combs to wrangle my hair into fat coiled ringlets. The oily pomade used to set the froth in place stained my new dress; when I arrived at the exam hall, sweating and disheveled, I resembled a harem slave nearly drowned by a flood.

Standing before the judges—Samson, Beauvallet, the lorgnette-wielding Madame Nathalie, and two others from the Comédie—I recited my scene from *La Fille du Cid* with a sob breaking in the back of my throat. It didn't enhance the drama. My comedy scene was indeed comedic, but not because of my delivery. The pomade had dried and cracked, my hair springing up from its imprisonment as if I'd been electrified.

Only pride kept me upright. Madame Nathalie compressed her lips, while Beauvallet looked outraged. Samson gave a malign grin of contentment.

As luck would have it, Julie had decided to accompany me to my exams, and her knowing smile undid me on the carriage ride home. "That certainly did not go as planned. I must tell Rosine we can never employ that hairdresser again."

Madame G. waited for me with her ubiquitous pot of hot chocolate. For once, I couldn't bear her sympathy. I went into my room and shut the door, crawling into bed to plunge my head under my pillow. If I'd had a vial of poison, I would have swallowed it.

Hours later, after my sisters went to bed and Julie and Rosine departed for their evening engagement, a knock at my door preceded Madame G.'s voice: "Sarah, are you awake?"

I moaned. "I wish I wasn't. I wish I was dead."

She stepped inside. "Surely it's not as terrible as all that."

"It's worse." I sat up. Her mouth drooped as she took in the greasy mess of my hair. "No one will ever hire me. I was dreadful. I—" I choked back another onslaught of tears. "I have no choice but to marry that horrid merchant from Lyons. Julie will see to it."

"Then she'll be very disappointed to hear you received this." From her skirt pocket, she removed an envelope. "It came for you this afternoon; I retrieved it from the courier before your mother saw it. Knowing how she feels, she might have burned it and claimed it never arrived." She smiled as I sat still, afraid to take the envelope from her.

"What . . . what does it say?" I whispered.

She set it in my hands. "Read it for yourself. It's from the Comédie."

Trembling, I unfolded the envelope:

We request the presence of Mademoiselle Sarah Bernhardt, graduate of the Conservatoire and second-year prize honoree in comedy, to sign her six-month contract as a pensionnaire at the Française tomorrow morning at ten o'clock.

"Signed by Édouard Thierry, administrator-in-chief of the Comédie-Française." I looked up in disbelief. "They're offering me a contract. I won first prize today in comedy." The irony did not escape me. Given my performance, it was precisely what I deserved.

She nodded. "You see? Not as terrible as that."

I lunged across the bed to hug her, laughing and crying at the same time. I didn't know how it had happened, how I'd managed to survive what surely must have been the most disastrous exam in the Conservatoire's history, yet somehow I had.

Tenuous as it might be, I had a future to look forward to.

ACT III

1862–1864

::

The Slap

I embrace my rival, but only to strangle him.

—JEAN RACINE

I

My dress was puce satin, like boiled cabbage. Rosine had it adjusted for me, another of her castaways, the suitor who financed the remodeling of our flat having also provided her with a plethora of new frocks. To add distinction, she loaned me a matching bonnet and parasol, as well as her new luxury eight-spring barouche with its coachman.

Julie made no comment upon hearing of my good fortune, but as I prepared to depart, she did something unexpected. Slipping a turquoise ring from her finger, she handed it to me with the cryptic words "Miracles can happen." Too overjoyed to spoil the moment, I accepted the ring and rode in my aunt's barouche to the Comédie-Française like an empress.

Upon my arrival at the entrance, I pranced up the steps twirling my parasol and nearly collided with a man leaving the building.

Samson gave me a sour smile. "Mademoiselle Bernhardt. What an unexpected surprise." He lifted his eyes to the barouche. "And such splendid equipage. I'm pleased to see you've not suffered too much from your unfortunate exams. Indeed, you appear to have recovered with remarkable resiliency. To what do we owe this pleasure?"

"I'm here to sign as a *pensionnaire*," I replied.

His supercilious regard faltered. "You are to . . . perform here?"

I waved the note. "By invitation of Monsieur Thierry."

His voice darkened. "My, my. His lordship de Morny certainly has a long reach. Shall we expect one of your sisters to be studying at the Conservatoire next year?" Before I could respond to this, he added, "I wish you *bonne chance*. You'll certainly need it," and he stalked down the stairs.

My joy crumbled into cinders.

Morny. He was responsible. Again. He had arranged this contract for me, and I couldn't claim I'd had to audition to earn it, unless I counted my horrid performance at my exams as an audition— which I did not. First prize or not, I'd been catastrophic.

As I hurried into the theater, my mother's turquoise ring loose on my finger, I had the unsettling thought that my acceptance couldn't have been a spontaneous act of generosity on Morny's part. As impossible as it seemed, Julie must have informed him of my debacle at my exams and had him put in a word for me. If so, her rare kindness held a hidden barb. Was her ring her way of reminding me that whatever I achieved, I owed to her?

I wouldn't dwell on it. I was here now, an ingénue in France's most prestigious acting company. I must prove myself worthy of it. Entering the famed greenroom of the Comédie's main theater, its *foyer des acteurs*, with its curved upholstered velvet sofas and cushioned armchairs under the lavish crystal chandelier, a gift from King Louis-Philippe himself, I took a moment to linger before the portraits of all the acclaimed actors who had graced the Comédie's stage. Rachel hung there in her pride of place, her slim, dark-eyed splendor immortalized in her regal costume as Mademoiselle de Belle-Isle, a role written for her by my own patron, Dumas.

"I'm going to be like you," I whispered. "Dumas told me I could be a sensation, as you were." I crossed myself and said a quick prayer, for Rachel had died of consumption three years past, her tragic loss convulsing Paris.

"Mademoiselle Bernhardt, may I ask why are you dallying?"

Whirling around, I saw Provost limping toward me, leaning on a cane as he'd once relied on his pole in class. He looked emaciated. "After the considerable effort expended on your behalf, it's most ill-advised to keep our administrator waiting."

"Oh, monsieur." I couldn't hide my relief. "I'm so happy to see you. I'd feared . . ."

"Not dead yet," he said dryly. "Come. Marvelous as she was, Rachel isn't going to sign your contract for you." He glanced past me into the empty room. "Are you alone?"

I nodded, seeing his bloodless lips purse.

"You're not yet nineteen. We require your mother's signature. No matter." He motioned to me. "You can sign now and Madame Bernhardt can witness it later." As he led me into Thierry's office, he said, "I regret that my illness came upon me so precipitously. The scenes Samson selected for your exams were very unsuitable."

"I did tell him. I begged him to let me perform your selections, but he didn't listen."

"Why would he? He saw an advantage and he seized on it." He paused, taking in my bewilderment. "He hoped to ruin your chances. He knew that had you performed my selections, you would have won first prize in both categories, despite the incident with your coiffure. He had his own student to promote. She performed your scenes instead."

I was aghast. "But that's a terrible betrayal. You are colleagues."

He chuckled. "And you still have much to learn. There is no such thing as collegiality in the theater. You will find actors are capable of anything in order to succeed."

His words dampened my elation.

Monsieur Thierry was an efficient, obviously very busy man who made short shrift of having me sign my contract, at a salary of fifty francs a month, which was indeed, as my mother had warned, barely enough to cover my meals.

Provost escorted me back to the barouche. "As I must take a leave from my teaching obligations due to my illness, Thierry has agreed to let me prepare you for your debut. I will select your roles and supply your expenses for costumes and such. You will need a makeup box, as well, which I shall provide."

I almost embraced him, my eyes swelling with grateful tears.

He shook a finger at me. "Don't thank me yet. I expect you to work harder than you ever did at the Conservatoire. The theater is not the classroom. You cannot forget your lines or cues onstage. The entire cast depends on you; they'll expect professionalism at every performance. The Comédie has an illustrious history," he said, reverting to his familiar harangue. "If you fail here, there are no second chances. Music halls or back-alley cabarets are all you can look forward to—if that."

"Yes," I said. "I promise to work as hard as I can."

"Harder. There must be nothing else in your life henceforth. No friends or family, no outside distractions. Performing must be your entire life." To ease the impact of his words, he gave me one of his infrequent smiles. "You can be great. You have it in you. But—"

"Talent alone doesn't make a career," I said quietly. "Training and focus do."

He harrumphed. "See that you do not forget it." He stood in the doorway as I mounted the carriage. I restrained the urge to wave goodbye as he watched me depart.

Not since Mère Sophie had I been so willing to sacrifice myself to please someone.

II

As was customary, the announcement appeared in the newspapers and on playbills in the arcade of the Française: *The Debut of Sarah Bernhardt as Iphigénie by Racine*. Seeing my name in print thrilled me, even if the role itself was daunting, laden with all the challenges Provost had highlighted. Though I wasn't expected to give a defining performance in my debut, as he assured me to my relief, and would perform several other roles besides Iphigénie in succession, all chosen by him, I must still prove my worthiness to be on the Comédie's stage if I hoped to have my contract renewed.

In the weeks leading to opening night, I indeed had no other life. Every waking hour was devoted to learning my lines and rehearsals. Even Marie, who still had a year left to complete at the Conservatoire, complained I never had any time for her. I couldn't help it; I was now a member of the Comédie, working with far more experienced actors, all of whom treated me with the same regard as they would any untried ingénue, which was scarcely any at all.

And Provost was merciless. He shouted and banged his cane, pushing me past endurance, so that I returned home late at night in such exhaustion, I could barely undress before collapsing into bed. At dawn, I was up again, shoving a croissant down my throat as I readied myself to depart for the theater, while Régine sulked and Madame G. sighed, saying I was gone so much these days, my sister feared I might never return. To assuage Régine, I started bringing her with me to rehearsal, armed with sweets and strict orders to sit still and be quiet. Julie and Rosine neglected her terribly, flitting about Paris and beyond on their engagements, often taking Jeanne with them, but leaving Régine with Madame G., who, kindly as she was, couldn't curb my youngest sister's tantrums. Yet in the theater, Régine turned surprisingly docile, her little form upright in the front row as she raptly followed the fantasies on stage.

Long before I felt ready, the evening of my debut was upon me. As I prepared to leave for the theater, Régine wailed that she wanted to go with me. Madame G. had to hold her back, for I couldn't bring her tonight. Debuts were sold-out events, attended by critics eager to assess the crop of new talent, or lack thereof. Much as I adored her, Régine would be a distraction, and who knew how she'd behave in the chaos backstage.

Provost was waiting impatiently, for I was late. He spared me a lecture, thrusting me into my tiny dressing room to oversee my makeup. My costume no longer fit; I'd lost too much weight and the toga-like robe exposed my bony arms. When I suggested adding sleeves, he snarled, "If you can sew them on in five minutes, by all means do so."

Hearing the audience taking their seats beyond the curtain churned my stomach. As I waited for my entrance, all of a sudden, I felt faint. I knew this feeling, though I hadn't experienced it since the play at Grandchamp. I looked in panic at Provost.

"*Le trac,*" he said. "Most players suffer it. You'll forget it once you take your mark."

"Has anyone died from it?" I whispered, for I felt as if I might.

"Never," he said, and on my cue, he pushed me forward. "*Merde.*"

No amount of rehearsal could have prepared me for the vertiginous sensation of standing on that immense platform, the gas flames in the footlights seeming to shine directly into my eyes, the mass of people waving fans and playbills or peering through their lorgnettes. I imagined myself under a gigantic paw, paralyzed for an endless moment before the actor playing Agamemnon strode to me, and I clutched at his arm.

I croaked out my lines.

"What did she say?" someone shouted from the upper loge.

In the scene when I implored Achilles to save me from Eriphile's envy, I remembered to throw out my arms, but failed to turn to the audience to declaim my lines, as Provost had drummed into me countless times. Something inside me compelled me to reach out instead toward my fellow actor with my gesture of imploration; as I did, a man in the audience issued a ribald "Have a care, Achilles, lest she impales you on her toothpicks!"

Laughter roared through the house. I wanted to die.

Staggering backstage at intermission, I found Provost wringing his hands. "Why?" he implored. "Just tell me why, after everything I taught you. Why turn aside from the audience at such a crucial moment?"

"I . . . I don't know," I quavered. "I didn't think. Forgive me."

"Oh, I forgive you," he retorted, "even if Racine in his grave never will."

He strode away. Stifling my desperation, I hurried to my dressing room. It was only then that my anger spilled forth; I would have swiped the little table clean of my cheap makeup tubes had I not two more acts left. As I grabbed the stick of greasepaint to dab at the rivulets carved by sweat on my cheeks, my reflection stared back at me: huge eyes in a pinched face that, despite the heavy paint, had gone as colorless as my costume.

I heard Mère Sophie as if she stood beside me. *Despite the odds . . . it's a sign of greatness, though you may not believe it now.*

Savagely, I scrawled *Quand même* in greasepaint across my mirror, squashing the stick. "You can do this," I told myself. "You *must.*"

I felt more in control during the next acts, mindful to do everything as Provost had instructed, not deviating once from the established choreography even though I thought I must resemble a marionette, my strings manipulated by an invisible conductor. I wasn't certain if I actually was any better, however, until the curtain fell and Provost gave me a terse nod.

His lack of advice made me realize better wasn't good enough, as I discovered the very next morning when the fearsome critic Sarcey published his notice of the play: "Mademoiselle Sarah Bernhardt, the latest *pensionnaire*, carries herself well and has near-perfect pronunciation. Unfortunately, that is all that can be said of her at the moment."

It wasn't devastating—he reserved his most acerbic remarks for the production values, which he deemed "an embarrassment"—but Provost assured me that Sarcey had put me on notice. "Your next performances must be flawless. While a *pensionnaire*'s debut rarely garners high praise, it is our testing ground for future status. Thierry thinks granting you a contract was a mistake. Not even Morny can save you if you prove him right."

I plunged into rehearsals for my subsequent roles as Henriette in Molière's *Les Femmes savantes*, which had won me second prize at my exams, and the lead in Eugène Scribe's comedy *Valérie*. Provost had me stay late at the theater to go over my lines and movements until he felt I'd mastered both to perfection.

Because of his diligence, I experienced no further mishaps, though *le trac* overcame me every time before the curtain rose. I even vomited once, moments before my entrance. But my plays were well received, judging by the audience's response, and helped to restore my frayed confidence—until Provost delivered Sarcey's latest critique. We sat in the theater, where I'd arrived early to refine my final role of the season as Hippolyte in *L'Étourdi*, written by Molière, patron saint of the Comédie.

As I recited from the column that *L'Opinion* devoted to the venerable critic, my voice broke. " 'Mademoiselle Bernhardt has excellent carriage and a lovely face; one might even say that one day she may become a beauty, but as an actress, she's rather unremarkable.

Which is not to anyone's surprise. It is inevitable that most *pension-naires* will never excel—'"

I lifted my horrified gaze to Provost. "How can he judge me on my very first year?"

Provost gave a sigh. "Sarcey is our most feared and respected theater critic. He can judge you because it is his job to do so."

"But you told me, debuts rarely garner praise. Not even Rachel had any acclaim at first. The critics barely noticed her first role as Camille in *Horace*. It took months, and several more roles, before she—"

"Your knowledge of Rachel's career and desire to emulate her are noteworthy," he interrupted. "But she's dead now, and we urgently require another of her stature."

"How can I gain her stature if no one will give me the chance?" I stabbed my finger at the newspaper. "Rachel didn't become renowned overnight."

He lapsed into pained silence before he said, "Alas, becoming renowned overnight is the order of the times. The few who seek to fill Rachel's shoes are aging. We have no time, let alone patience, to wait for an ingénue to grow into her talent."

"Then I must do something different," I replied.

Provost gave me a contemplative look. "Am I to understand you have objections to my method of instruction?"

I forced myself to return his stare.

"Yes?" His voice was impassive. "This would be the time to state your concerns."

He'd never requested my opinion before, and though now he did, I still had to gather up my courage before I said, "You know how much I respect you, how honored I am by your trust in me—"

He held up his hand. "Mademoiselle, I didn't ask for flattery."

I swallowed, trying to find the words to express aloud what to me was barely coherent, an innate instinct that felt almost primal and became clear only when I was onstage. "It doesn't feel natural," I said at length. "How can I become my character unless I'm allowed to discover her for myself? When my performance is so ordained in advance, I can't *feel* it."

"I see." To my relief, there was no overt censure in his tone. "I've undergone great pains, and considerable risk to my own reputation, to take you under my charge. I have guided you in the traditions of this house: to declaim toward the audience, so your emoting can be seen; to precede every line with a precise gesture that conveys the pathos in the verse; to support the ensemble and not your individual self. This is our established precedence. It is how things have always been done at the Comédie."

I lowered my eyes. How could I explain to this man, who'd earned his senior status from a distinguished career playing hundreds of roles, that his established precedence was impeding me? That while I had no experience to draw upon, something within me told me that what I must do to earn acclaim was not adhere to tradition, but rather inhabit my character in such a way that her humanity transcended her particular circumstances to stir the hearts of everyone in the audience.

He leaned toward me. "I must insist that you say what you think, mademoiselle."

"I've no wish to imitate what others have done before," I finally whispered, terrified by my admission. "I want to be different. Isn't that how Rachel achieved success?"

He went quiet for such a long moment, I thought I'd transgressed beyond redemption. Then he said in a voice that sounded almost apologetic, "You are correct. To be different from everyone else is indeed the path to success. Those who achieve greatness in our profession do so by setting their unique stamp on every character they play. They must have not only the talent, but also the daring and ambition to prove themselves on the stage." He paused, lacing his hands as he picked his next words. "I've seen many come and go through this house in my years as an instructor, but no one quite like you. It is why I've risked as much as I have. But," he added, before

I could react to his unexpected praise, "even our Rachel had to start somewhere. Even she had to follow the rules at first. Defiance at this time will not serve you. Moreover, my influence can only extend so far."

I swallowed. "Meaning?"

"Meaning every company needs competent actresses for secondary roles, but I fear that is all you can expect for now. If you wish to deviate from my instruction for your final performance of this season, I will permit it, within reason. It is in both our interests that you deliver your best, even if Hippolyte isn't the role to elevate your profile."

"Nevertheless," I replied, "I will play her as if she can."

He allowed me to make limited changes, mainly in how I declaimed. Rather than turning to the audience to deliver my lines, I engaged with my fellow actors and imbued Hippolyte with my own vulnerability. I was perfect, Provost assured me when the play closed. But Sarcey hadn't bothered to attend. He had issued his verdict on my debut and I'd therefore performed to a near-empty house.

My debut season ended in late July, as did my contract. I had no idea if I'd be called back, returning in dejection to the flat, where Régine was overjoyed to have me home. To fill my spare time, I resumed my painting, filling canvas after canvas, trying to forget my theatrical venture, which I feared wouldn't amount to anything more. I saw no reason why the Comédie would care to renew my contract, given my inauspicious notices, and the vast unknown of the future stretched like an abyss before me. Painting at least relieved my desperate uncertainty, even if it, too, could amount to nothing more than a pastime.

"You should try to exhibit your work," remarked Madame G., looking over the stack of paintings cluttering my bedroom. "These are so lovely. You are a talented artist."

"Do artists have an easier time of it than actors?" was my morose reply.

"You will hear soon enough from the Comédie," she assured me, unfailing as ever in her optimism. "I know you will. Just give it time, my child."

I wanted to believe it, wondering if Provost was right that the Comédie always needed girls like me. The Conservatoire churned us out like loaves of bread, hundreds of aspirants. Competent mediocrity, it seemed, was not in short supply.

And as Sarcey had pointed out, most never succeeded.

Was I destined to be one of them?

III

My contract for the following year was renewed, albeit begrudgingly, with Provost warning me that Thierry had informed him that if I were not "his favored pupil," he'd have shown me the door. This time, Julie bestirred herself to accompany me to the signing. Thierry turned obsequious, declaring himself "overjoyed" to include me in the company ranks for another year, and to please give his regards to Monsieur de Morny.

I gritted my teeth until we were back in the carriage. "Morny again. Does he own the Comédie, per chance, that he can snap his fingers and they'll do whatever he says?"

Julie eyed me from under her parasol. "Perhaps you should show gratitude that he still has an interest in this so-called profession of yours. It's not as though you've done anything to deserve it."

"I most certainly have! I studied for two years at the Conservatoire and have done nothing but dedicate myself heart and soul to—"

"Yes, yes." She tilted her parasol to shade her face as the carriage took us down the avenue. "We're all well aware of how devoted you are to your craft. Unfortunately, it would appear your craft is not so devoted to you." She sighed. "You're simply not suited for the stage. You are too thin and pale; your voice might be distinctive, but you have no presence." She delivered this condemnation in serene indifference. "But you might end all this unnecessary suffering if you only do as I suggest."

"Marry that merchant, I suppose," I snarled, "who can hardly be the prize you claim if after all this time he's still available."

"We get what we pay for. If marriage isn't to your liking, let me instruct you in a less burdensome way to earn your keep." She didn't look at me as she spoke, her eyes fixing on some remote point beyond the carriage. "You might find the success you crave elsewhere, should you apply yourself. Look at Rosine; she has a permanent suitor now. Not once has she had to endure being ravaged by critics before the entire city."

"Never. I'd rather bed with curs than sell myself."

She chuckled. "As you wish. But fifty francs a month won't detain the fleas."

I was enraged by her reminder of my helplessness. Though I had a new contract, I couldn't see it as an achievement if Morny had been behind it, and gnawing fear beset me that I'd end up playing insignificant roles to barely full houses for the rest of my life.

On January 15, 1863, the new season officially began with *La Cérémonie*, the company's annual tribute to Molière—a sacrosanct event held with due pomp. All the company actors were required to attend, dressed in costume from the playwright's most famous works, lining up to place a palm frond at the foot of his bust—brought center stage for the event from the greenroom—and recite a selection of his noteworthy lines. As the member of least status in the Comédie, I was given the task of bearing the laurel wreath, which I had to hand over to Beauvallet for placement on the bust's marble curls.

I practiced carrying the wreath at home, solemnly parading down the corridor carrying a veiled hat, Régine scampering at my heels as Julie watched from the salon. When Jeanne asked, "Is she attending a funeral?" Julie broke into peals of laughter.

I didn't care. It was my first participation in this time-honored ritual; minor as my role might be, I must fulfill it without mishap. I must show the entire company that I, too, held our founding father in the utmost respect.

Régine begged me to take her with me. "Please let me come. Please, Sarah. I'll be good, just like at your rehearsals. I'll sit there and watch."

"I don't think it would be appropriate," I said gently, but as she burst into tears, Julie remarked, "What possible harm can she do? It's not as if you're resurrecting Molière."

I glared at her. Who was she to tell me what harm Régine might do, when she never paid my younger sister the slightest mind? But the tears rolling down my little sister's face persuaded me; she was only eight years old, so young and innocent despite her unpredictable temper, and she loved me so much. She would sit for hours, joyfully ripping apart her dolls while I painted. She was never happy when I was gone, Madame G. told me; she wept for hours, refusing consolation, thinking I'd abandoned her.

"Very well," I told Régine. "But you must promise to be on your best behavior."

"I promise." Régine wrapped her arms around me. "I love you, *ma sœur*. I love you more than anything. I love you more than these nasty *putaines*."

The frozen look on Julie's face was worth it. I dressed Régine in a white frock, tied up her dark curls with a satin bow, and brought her with me to the theater.

Thierry frowned; a child at the ceremony was unheard of. There were invited patrons of the house, as well as the journalists obliged to pen saccharine praise of the occasion. I told Régine to stand aside by the entry pillars at the edge of the stage, out of view of the audience, and wait there as I took up the wreath.

"You are not to move," I told her. "Do you understand? Not one inch."

She nodded, her eyes gone wide as she took in the company in their extravagant historical costumes, all portraying roles from Molière's most famous plays.

The company advanced in pairs to the stage, where Beauvallet oversaw their palm frond offerings like sacrifices. Suddenly an outraged cry rang out—"This brat is on my train!"—followed by Régine shouting, *"Vache! Leave me alone."*

Reeling about, I saw the redoubtable Madame Nathalie, garbed in a pompadour wig and colossal gown, gesturing angrily at Régine. Determined to obey me, my sister refused to step aside, though she had somehow ended up on Madame's immense train. With a cry of indignation, Madame Nathalie yanked at her train and upset my sister's balance, causing her to stumble backward into the entry pillar.

Régine let out a shriek as she toppled the plaster pillar, falling to the stage and cutting her forehead. I flung aside my wreath to rush to her.

Madame Nathalie swerved to me, gripping my arm. "This lowborn urchin you've brought here—it's an outrage. Who *are* you to insult the House of Molière thus?"

"You told me not to move," cried Régine. "The fat cow shoved me."

I saw red. My long-simmering anger at my mother, my failed debut, the humiliation of my exams and my audition, where this woman had treated me with such contempt—it all came boiling to the surface. Before I could stop myself, I threw out my hand and delivered a stinging blow across Madame's overly rouged cheek.

It reverberated like a thunderclap. As she stood stunned, the imprint of my fingers on her jowl, the entire company let out a horrified gasp. It was Madame's cue; flinging an arm to her forehead as if she were a doomed heroine, she dropped in an epic swoon—right upon hapless Coquelin, a fellow actor.

I went immobile, my hand still lifted. Pandemonium erupted. The callboys and stagehands rushed to assist Coquelin, flattened under Madame's bulk. Beauvallet barked, "Water! Someone fetch a glass of water!" Someone obliged, only they misinterpreted his intent and tossed the contents of the glass on Madame, smearing her makeup and eliciting a yelp from Coquelin: "*Mon Dieu*, must you drown me? Get her off me before I'm crushed."

Régine let out a cackle. I looked over at her, splayed on the floor, her skirts crested over her pantalettes, and I couldn't resist my own giggle. It was a farce worthy of Molière himself. Even the invited public, who'd abandoned their seats to crowd to the front of the stage, began to laugh, the journalists scribbling in their notepads as fast as they could, while the stagehands hauled Madame to her feet. She was moaning as if she'd been struck by a mortal blow.

Helping Régine up, I wiped the blood from her forehead with my sleeve, not hearing Provost's approach until he said, "God help you, this time you've gone too far."

I met his stare as he motioned. "Apologize to Madame Nathalie this instant."

"I certainly will not." I turned from him to smooth Régine's disheveled skirts. "She should be the one to apologize, for being so beastly to a child."

From behind us, Madame Nathalie blared: "We are dishonored. *La maison de Molière* is defiled. Remove that filthy Hebrew and her devil sister from my sight this instant."

Provost's shoulders slumped. "Sarah, if you don't make amends, your career will be over. You'll have no one to blame but yourself."

I took my sister by the hand. "So be it," I said, and I led Régine out of the theater—for all I knew, forever.

IV

"She refuses to heed reason," exclaimed Julie. She'd forced me out of my room, where I'd sat brooding for days, informing me that Morny had arrived to see me. Dragging myself into the salon, I avoided his sardonic gaze as I sank into a chair, braced for his outrage. Although I'd never solicited his help, he had given it. He'd put in a word for me at the Conservatoire and at the Comédie; he'd petitioned his friends to help me, and I'd repaid him with scandal.

To my surprise, he let out a chuckle. "Let's not pretend we are on the verge of ruin. I've read about it in the newspapers. As has all of Paris by now."

"It's in the newspapers?" My entire being went cold at the thought. But of course there had been journalists present, who'd witnessed everything.

"Did your mother not tell you?" said Morny. "Your name is on everyone's lips—the brazen ingénue who dared to strike a senior *sociétaire*. *Le Gifle*, they're calling it: 'the Slap.' No one," he added, with a smile, "claims you were unprovoked."

I couldn't believe he actually appeared amused. I'd never liked him, not since he'd tried to finagle a kiss from me years before, but at this moment, I was very grateful for his wit.

"Thierry sent us a letter." Julie shot a glare at me. "If she makes an apology, he'll reinstate her. It's the least she can do. No one can get away with such intolerable behavior."

"The apology is a formality," said Morny. "The Comédie hasn't enjoyed this kind of publicity in years, and Thierry knows it. Everyone now wants to see the young actress who—"

"Struck a *sociétaire*," I interrupted. "Not the publicity I'd hoped for."

"Ah, but you have it. I'm suggesting we do something with it."

"Such as what?" said Julie, and I steeled myself for his repetition of the litany my mother had already heaped on me: that I must abase myself before Madame Nathalie and do penance. Julie didn't care if the renewal of my contract would seal my relegation to minor roles till the end of my days. All she cared about were the ramifications, for she had a horror of any attention that might cast her in an adverse light. A courtesan like her relied on discretion, the illusion of respectability, not on the wives of her suitors or her suitors themselves gossiping about her daughter's defiance.

Instead, he said, "May we assume an apology is out of the question?"

"She put her hands on Régine first—" I started to say, and Julie cried, "Impossible! She thinks she can do as she pleases, whenever she pleases, and there'll be no—"

Morny cleared his throat, bringing my mother to a standstill. "Sarah is wise to not risk further humiliation. Even if she makes her apology and returns to the Comédie, Madame Nathalie will not tolerate her reinstatement. Madame is a pensioned member, with a reputation to uphold; she will make it her mission to ruin Sarah's career."

"What career?" snapped Julie. "She never had one to begin with."

"True," he replied. "Yet she might have one now."

I felt a jolt of interest. After Julie's tirades and her threats to throw me into the gutter, where it seemed I was determined to end up, any hope, however thin, was welcome.

Morny said, "Her name holds some recognition. Others will wish to hire her."

"Others?" echoed Julie doubtfully.

"The Gymnase, to be precise. I'm acquainted with its proprietor, Monsieur Montigny. He's staging clever farces for a less discerning clientele and making quite the profit. He has inquired about Sarah's availability."

Julie let out a gasp. "But it's on the Right Bank, a common music hall for the rabble."

"Indeed. Montigny is an astute businessman. His establishment has become very popular with the rabble, as you call them, and they can make a reputation."

"No." Julie was trembling. "She can never perform in such a place. I forbid it."

"Then what, my dear, would you have her do?" Morny's unspoken intimation hung between us. "My offer stands. If you wish to pursue it, you must let me know. Montigny is always looking for fresh talent. Only," he said, retrieving his cane, "don't wait too long. The Slap will not stay fresh indefinitely."

After he departed, Julie paced the salon. I watched her warily until she whirled to me. "Before I will consent to another kindness from Morny, you must prove your willingness to deserve it. Otherwise, I shall write to Berenz in Lyons and see you wed within the month. You're not twenty. You require my signature on any contract you sign."

"You can't force me to marry," I said, although I feared she might.

"Perhaps. I can, however, put you out of this house. And you'll not last a month on the street, I assure you." She paused. "If you do as I ask, I shall see your dowry paid to you in full, to use however you like."

"I thought my dowry was dependent on my marriage," I said, immediately suspicious of her unexpected offer. "Didn't that notary say the terms of my father's testament were irrevocable?"

"What does he know?" she replied. "A notary is not a solicitor. A skillful Parisian lawyer can challenge the terms of any testament. But in order to hire one, you'll need money—and not the kind of money you'll make in clever farces at the Gymnase."

I clenched my teeth. She regarded me, unblinking as a snake.

"What," I finally said, "would you have me do?"

"Engage a suitor at the Opéra, but not someone we already know: he must be a new acquaintance, and one wealthy enough to demonstrate your value."

I swallowed my revulsion, wondering when she'd grown so cold, so ruthless as to pander her own daughter. But as I also recognized I had no other option, to my surprise, it didn't seem so terrible. I remembered how it had been with Paul, how easy. Surely one way was much like the other; it was only a matter of perspective. I couldn't crawl back to the Comédie—Morny was right, Madame Nathalie wouldn't tolerate it—and the Gymnase was the last place an actress wanted to be. If I could secure the money that my father had left me, it would give me the freedom to seek a respectable acting position elsewhere.

"Very well." I stood. "One time. After that, I decide my own future."

V

Julie and Rosine spent weeks grooming me. Between the subtle gestures, the complicated use of my lorgnette and fan, and Rosine's repeated exhortation that "when he's present, your suitor must be your lord and master," I began to regret my submission. I should have accepted Morny's offer on the spot. But he didn't return to the flat for the entire month, no doubt advised by Julie to make himself scarce while she prepared me. And he must have been satisfied enough by the prospect, for when he next appeared, it was in full evening attire, with his carriage and footmen at the ready.

When I emerged in the sumptuous white satin gown that Julie had had altered for me, along with her prized suite of pearls, my hair styled in a loose coiffure to highlight my slim neck, Morny crooned, "Mademoiselle, you are ravishing. Like a virginal swan."

Were it up to him, he would have been my first suitor, but it wasn't up to him; this was to be my test, my punishment for humiliating myself at the Comédie. I must attract someone worthy, whom we didn't know. Those were the rules, imposed by Julie.

We proceeded to the Opéra, that bastion of tradition, where between arias and aperitifs, the demimondaines plied their illicit trade. Morny put his box at our disposal. As the curtain lifted and the opera began, Julie elbowed me. Removing my lorgnette from my beaded bag, I raised it to my eyes with a practiced curve of my glove-sheathed arm.

"Now," she whispered, "search the crowd as if you are looking for no one in particular, and see if someone in particular is looking at you."

Since this was to be in essence a performance, I decided to exploit it, inhabiting my new persona in all her freedom and bondage, thinking if I ever managed to step onstage again, I could use what I'd learned. But my hand quivered as I wielded the lorgnette; I didn't see anything at first, only a haze of shadowy figures. I was about to shift the glasses to the stage and enjoy the opera when I caught sight of someone staring back at me.

I started, training my lorgnette with a casual air toward the person in question. Dumas's expansive smile filled my eyes. He was sitting across the house from us in the opposite box. But he wasn't the one I focused on; beside him sat a dark-haired man with a proud forehead and raptor-like stare, who returned my appraisal in blatant candor.

"*Who* are you looking at?" hissed Julie. She shifted her lorgnette; I heard her mutter, "God save us. Dumas." Then she went still. "Rosine, who is the gentleman with the writer?"

As Morny chortled under his breath, my aunt peered through her glasses. She gave a stifled exhale. "Comte Émile de Kératry. A lieutenant colonel in the Imperial Guard."

"Is he rich?" said Julie, making me wince.

"Very," drawled Morny. "And extremely adept at employing it."

Julie lowered her glasses with a sigh. At intermission, she and Morny vanished, leaving me with Rosine. The opera resumed. I didn't want to search the house again like a flower vendor. Instead, I reclined in my seat and shut my eyes, letting the music wash over me. I'd had so little comfort these past weeks, so little peace. . . .

A voice murmured near my ear: "Monsieur Dumas tells me you are an actress."

Turning my head, I found myself gazing into deep-set green eyes with impossibly long lashes.

The man smiled. "Are you?"

My mouth went dry. "I . . . I was."

His smile widened, displaying perfect teeth. "I understand you recently had an altercation with a certain *sociétaire*, as well. Congratulations."

"Congratulations?" I thought he must be mocking me. It was only then that I noticed Rosine had disappeared, leaving me at the mercy of this Comte de Kératry.

"Why, yes." He was obviously well bred, with high aristocratic cheekbones and thin lips that managed to appear supple. His hair, which had looked dark from a distance, was actually light auburn, slicked to his scalp with brilliantine. "It was high time someone gave her a proper dressing-down."

I suddenly let out a laugh. "You tease me, monsieur," I said, almost not recognizing the seductive vibrato in my voice, though I'd been perfecting it for weeks in anticipation of just such a moment.

"I would do more," he said. I froze as I felt him reach across my seat to touch my hand. Then he withdrew. I looked down to see a calling card on my lap.

"I will send a carriage for you tomorrow at noon," he said, as I stared at the expensive cream card embossed with his address. "I trust we are in agreement, Mademoiselle Bernhardt?"

He knew my name. He knew about the Slap. It sent a chill through me; I felt as if he'd singled me out in the way a wolf sets its sights on the most vulnerable prey, the one most likely to be brought down by a quick clamp of its jaws.

I forced myself to lift my eyes to him. "I believe we are."

"*Demain*, then." He bowed, departing the box.

Moments later, Rosine returned to me in a fluster. "Well?" she asked, tugging anxiously at her necklace, as if I'd just received a long-dreaded diagnosis.

I handed her the card. "He says he'll send a carriage for me to-morrow."

Tears surfaced in her eyes. "Oh, my child. Just wait until Julie hears of it. You've outdone yourself on your very first night. Not even she in her prime could have snared such a prize." Rosine leaned to me with a confidential whisper. "She put you to the test and now she'll be beside herself with envy. She was quite certain you would fail tonight."

"Then I'm delighted to disappoint her," I replied.

The *comte* sent his carriage to take me to his palatial townhouse by the Tuileries, where he had a luncheon served for just the two of us by a host of liveried servants who never looked at me.

His seduction was practiced, but not routine. He did not behave as if anything proposed was his due, but rather made me feel as if I were the only woman in the world he'd ever desired. I wasn't deceived. Julie had spared me nothing, assuring me he was one of the most sought-after gentlemen in Paris, with a wealthy family and title, in addition to a position at court—all of which made him the consummate rake.

When he led me upstairs to his bedchamber, where the linen sheets were already turned down on the bed and the window shutters half-closed, lending the sumptuous gilded room a watery shadow that I assumed was intended to enhance the mood, my heart was pounding so hard, I could feel it against my ribs. His lips felt cool on my nape as he leaned in to me from behind to kiss my skin.

"No perfume," I heard him murmur.

I froze. I hadn't even thought of scenting myself in the painstaking hours before his carriage came to fetch me, closeted with Rosine as the two of us agonized over which dress and hat I should wear, while Julie made herself absent, declaring she had an engagement—a deliberate ploy, for now that I'd accomplished what she had thought impossible, she wasn't pleased that, in turn, she must honor her end of our pact.

With a knot in my throat, I said, "I didn't know which perfume you'd prefer, my lord."

"Ah, no." He took me by my shoulders, turning me about to face him. His cravat was undone about his lean neck. Up close, his eyes were so green, they reminded me of cat eyes. Or wolf eyes, I reminded myself. I must never forget that I was now his prey in every way. He was going to get his money's worth. "Don't pretend to be a woman you aren't," he said, his fingertips tracing the line of my jaw. "Perfume isn't your style. Nor is any of this. Is it?"

"No," I whispered. And I raised my hands to his chest, setting my palms against it, hard to the touch, sculpted from horseback riding and fencing practice, or whatever it was men like him did to pass the time. As I felt my fear uncoiling, I was determined to contain it.

"What do you want of me?" As soon as I spoke, I realized I'd made a mistake. I had revealed the one weakness that bared my inexperience, but his smile only widened.

"I want you to be yourself, Sarah," he said, his voice pausing on my name. "I can have women like your mother any time I like. But someone like you is rare."

"I'm not a virgin," I told him impulsively. Rosine had equipped me with a tiny skin-bag of pig's blood, which she'd explained I must keep hidden on my person and somehow prick open at the appropriate time to stain the sheets. I'd left the little falsehood in my cloak, thinking there was no way to accomplish it. How on earth was I supposed to hide the bag if he undressed me completely?

He laughed low in his chest; I felt it under my hands before he turned me back around to deftly undo my stays. "Virgins don't interest me," he said, as my dress slipped off to pool at my feet. "Rarity, on the other hand . . . When one can have anything one desires, rarity becomes very special. It is the only thing that is most difficult to acquire."

I heard him divest himself of his clothes, standing still as he pressed his naked length against me, his mouth at my ear: "Now, tell me what *you* want. Tell me how I can please you."

I almost blurted out another inappropriate truth—I wanted his money, of course—except that as he guided me to his bed, I found I didn't care about that anymore. I'd never been treated like this by a man. None save for Dumas and Provost had ever regarded me as someone who mattered; even Paul, for all his fumbling ardor, had only wanted to possess me, to marry me and call me his wife, without ever asking what I might desire in return. The very fact that this stranger with his exquisite manners and intrepid tongue, who'd purchased me like a piece of furniture for the afternoon, would ask what I wanted sent a bolt of triumphant flame through me.

This was true power. The power Marie had cited when she told me at Grandchamp about our mothers, only she'd misunderstood it as much as me. This was a power that most women, especially those like Julie, squandered, cheapened in transactions cloaked by salon propriety, because they couldn't comprehend that power like this was priceless. No matter what it might cost to obtain, to exert such power was to command respect—and respect was worth more than gold to a woman.

"I wish to be seen," I heard myself say, as he lowered his head between my thighs.

He went still, his eyes lifting to me. "Seen?" he repeated.

"Yes." I met his gaze. "If I'm so rare to you, show me. Make me feel it."

He chuckled. "You do realize we already have an agreement?"

I nodded, putting my hands on his head. "But rarity can't truly be bought, can it?"

"It depends," he replied. "In your case . . . we shall see."

After that, there was no more conversation. For several hours, I basked in the ardor of a man who knew exactly how to arouse me. Nothing I'd experienced with Paul could compare; for the first time in my life, I felt the hot rush of blood in my veins, my thighs clasped around his waist as he drove into me, filling me with pleasure. After it was done and I lay splayed on his now-rumpled sheets, feeling as though I drifted in a warm sea, he rose and went to a cabinet, still naked, so confident in his allure as he lit a match to a cigarette and stood at the window, the ebbing daylight rimming his musculature in gilt.

I had to ask him. "Why do you do this?"

"This?" He didn't look at me as he blew out a plume of smoke.

"Yes." I righted myself on my elbows. "A man like you—you could have any woman you want for free."

He ran his hand over his chin. "That is precisely why I do this."

I felt myself frown. "I don't understand."

"You do." He glanced over his shoulder at me. "You just showed me how much you understand. You wish to be seen for who you are. Is it so strange for me to want the same?" He gave me a quiet smile when I didn't reply. "Women always think that men like me hold every advantage. And in most respects, we do. But we aren't immune to the same needs that women have, only we're never allowed to admit it."

I considered for a moment. "You want to be loved?" I said, thinking it highly unlikely; he didn't seem like a yearning romantic to me.

He let out a throaty chuckle, extinguishing his cigarette in a crystal bowl on the cabinet. " 'Love' is a term we use to claim exclusive ownership. My horse probably knows more about love than most people. It's not love I seek, but freedom, to be whoever I am. Women see my title, my family name and net worth—to them, I'm but a means to an end. You can never be loved by those who think you'll be their salvation. If I choose to pay for my pleasure, then the line is clear: there can be no confusion or expectations."

"Well, I don't know about love or horses," I replied carelessly, "but your means can certainly be *my* salvation."

As he threw back his head and laughed again, making me cringe at my crassness, at my breaking of some intimate spell, I saw gratitude in his eyes and heard it in his voice.

"This is your rarity, Sarah: honesty. And you are right, it cannot be bought. You must never try to sell it." He gestured past the bed to a set of double doors in the wall paneling. "My bathing quarters are in there. Please, take your time. I'll wait for you in the library downstairs."

I availed myself of his facilities, which were luxurious, with hot running water, a bidet (both Rosine and Julie had stressed the importance of this to avoid "complications"), and enough lotions and oils to stock an emporium. After I dressed, he escorted me to his carriage. With an insouciant smile, he said, "Your mother has invited me to her salon next week for a musical soirée. Should I attend?"

"She sent you an invitation?" I suppressed a snort of derision. "When?"

"This morning. Before I sent my carriage for you."

"In that case," I said, "you mustn't deprive her of your company."

"I look forward to it." He reached into his robe pocket. Without fanfare or explanation, he extracted an envelope. On the ride home, I opened it.

He had paid me thirty thousand francs.

◼

He attended the soirée. Morny was there too, along with Rosine and her suitor. Though Kératry's rank was comparable to Morny's, he did not flaunt it. He laughed and told lewd jokes that made Rosine blush. He played with Régine, who found him fascinating, and complimented simpering Jeanne. Julie sat at the pianoforte that she'd had installed in the renovated salon and had me sing chansons from the Conservatoire, music lessons having formed part of my curriculum to strengthen my voice, while he watched from the settee with Régine, his indolent eyes never wavering from me.

I did not depart my mother's house with him; that would have been indiscreet. But I went to see him the next afternoon and many afternoons thereafter. Within three months, I'd earned several hundred thousand francs, more than in my entire time at the Comédie.

Then one afternoon as I took my leave from his townhouse, Kératry handed me the envelope and said, "The Prince of Ligne is a friend of mine from Flanders. He's coming here to visit Paris on his annual trip. Would you be amenable?"

I was fastening my cloak. "Of course. You must spend time with your friends."

"Sarah." The mirth in his voice made me pause. "That isn't what I mean."

It took me a moment to comprehend; when I did, I felt sick. "You want me to . . . ?"

He said, "Not if you're averse. You said my means can be your salvation. He has more means than I do." His voice softened. "Remember what we spoke of: no confusion or expectations. I have no desire to claim exclusive ownership of you."

"Yes," I said, struggling to recover my composure. "If he's so inclined."

"I believe he will be. Allow me to make the arrangements."

I should have been elated. I knew from what Marie had told me years ago, and from what I'd witnessed with my own mother, who held fast to Morny as if she otherwise might drown, that obtaining a suitor of wealth and constancy was a coveted feat; to be recommended to others of his ilk heralded a courtesan's certain rise to fame. And when I told Julie of what Kératry had suggested, despite her sour look, she had the grace to say, "I never thought I'd hear these words coming out of my mouth, but you've shown yourself to be more resourceful than I supposed. Perhaps I can now rest assured that once I find myself obliged to retire, I'll be seen through my old age in the comfort to which I am accustomed."

She vanquished any elation I felt. It wasn't only the thought that she believed I'd carry on the family profession indefinitely, but my shame at the savage pride her admission brought me. Quite unwillingly, I had surpassed her and begun to enjoy myself; it was too easy, this business of pleasure and money. I now understood why so many women braved the perilous arena, as the deed itself was nearly as enticing as its rewards.

The realization brought me to my senses.

I brought my tin stuffed with francs to the table where Julie and Rosine sat over breakfast. "I have enough to hire a solicitor," I declared, as Julie frowned. "I want my dowry released. And have Morny speak with the Gymnase. It is time for me to return to the stage."

VI

The Gymnase was indeed a frivolous establishment, one of Paris's ubiquitous so-called boulevard theaters, where nightly brawls competed with whatever nonsense played onstage. There was no Racine or Voltaire on the playbill; no one would have understood them or cared. Comedic farces of mistaken identity and lurid tales of crime, infidelity, and fatal affairs, penned by unknown playwrights, were performed instead for an uncouth and inebriated crowd.

The pay was pitiful, the roles equally so. And I did not like the managing director, Montigny. A circus entrepreneur, he believed theater should be entertainment, not art. Despite my scandalous departure from the Comédie, I had been trained by its instructors at the Conservatoire, where actors were deemed professionals with a tradition to uphold. Montigny only hired me at Morny's recommendation because my name had been in the newspapers, and he believed it had marquee value. Yet, as such matters went, my name disappeared from the papers soon enough, and he didn't capitalize on whatever value remained, relegating me to secondary roles, which, he said, "make the best of your odd looks." He was astute in this regard. His other actresses were all buxom and pert. I stood out among them like a waif.

Nevertheless, I took the undeniable step down in my fortunes as an opportunity to escape the courtesan trade, if not to hone my craft.

The rigid expectations of the Comédie had felled me; here, with lamplighters bustling about and vats of water readied overhead lest the footlights ignite a conflagration, with ringing bells to capture the audience's fickle attention, often in vain, I wasn't expected to do much of anything.

The terror of *le trac* deserted me. No one cared if my gestures lacked precision or if I missed a line. No one noticed if I turned my back. Indeed, as the other actresses advised me, the audience preferred to see our backsides whenever possible.

What mattered was that I was performing again.

In between appearances in such forgettable productions as *Madame Steals a Kiss,* I met with Kératry and his friend, the Prince of Ligne—not together of course. Soon, a few others approached me, based on Kératry's recommendation. None were boors or brutes; they made generous offers, which I accepted, but I refused to sacrifice whatever principles I had left. I must make ends meet, but that, I vowed, was as far as it could go.

Julie didn't contain her disappointment. "Why must you debase yourself at that dreadful place? I fail to understand it, when you're having such success elsewhere." But that was all she said. No doubt she thought my time at the Gymnase would come to a premature end, as it had at the Comédie—not because I'd find myself in any trouble (performing there was demeaning enough, as she never ceased to point out) but because my other activities would prove more lucrative. In a rare display of magnanimity that betrayed her motivation, she offered me the newly renovated apartment next door, intended for Rosine. My aunt located another flat nearby, courtesy of her suitor, allowing me privacy to conduct my affairs—or as much privacy as I could find with my sister Régine underfoot, scowling at the various gentlemen who arrived to escort me about town.

Occupied from dawn to midnight, rushing from my afternoon liaisons to the Gymnase at night to throw on whatever horrid costume had been assigned so I could prance onstage to recite inane lines like *"Un baiser? O non! Non!"* I was too distracted to notice anything was amiss.

Until Marie Colombier did.

▪▪

We met at the brasserie by the Conservatoire; she was about to take her final exams, she told me, and Samson had assured her of a contract at the Théâtre du Châtelet.

"It's not the Comédie," she said airily. "But then, I never intended to be an actress."

"No?" I eyed her over my cup of coffee.

She toyed with the ruffles of lace at her throat. "Girls like us have two choices. Or three, if you include marrying the first rogue who comes our way. I'm not suited to the first choice—not like you, *chère* Sarah. My mother left that pursuit years ago, as you know, and unlike yours, she offered me no encouragement. So, the theater it must be."

"There are other choices," I said.

Marie laughed. "I suppose so, but shop-keeping is so tedious. No, acting suits me for the moment. As I said, I've no wish to be another Rachel. And I'm prepared for what comes next. Even if I'm not engaging suitors at the Opéra, I've found a protector who can ensure I live as comfortably as possible. Given the meager salary at the Châtelet, I've no intention of subsiding on gruel. I'll perform onstage and save whatever I can on the side, until a suitable husband comes my way, like my mother before me."

"Is Samson your protector?" I asked, knowing full well what he was capable of doing to promote his ingénues and her equal lack of compunction in bedding him for a contract.

"What of it?" Her voice sharpened as she directed her gaze over my new green wool walking dress and smart hat. "You're hardly one to judge. You seem to be doing quite well for yourself these days, despite that unpleasant incident with Madame Nathalie. I sincerely hope your protector cares as much for you in return. Otherwise, your dismissal from the Comédie will feel like a blessing by comparison."

I laughed. "He's a suitor, nothing more."

"So, you're indulging others than the dashing *comte*?"

"Naturally. Émile is generous, but neither of us seeks a permanent arrangement."

"Oh?" She curled her hand at her chin. "You might tell yourself that. You might even believe it. But it's plain to me that while there may be others, you desire only him."

I went silent, biting my lip before I reached for my cup. "It is true that I prefer him," I admitted. "In fact, I'm considering forgoing my other engagements. With my obligations at the Gymnase, I have no time, and Émile offers more than enough."

"And are you taking precautions?" she said. When I failed to reply to this unexpected question, she exclaimed, "Sarah, are you mad? Do you *want* to get with child?"

Incredulous laughter burst from me. "Don't be so dramatic, Marie. It's impossible." Yet even as I spoke, I knew it wasn't. Both Julie and Rosine had inculcated in me the importance of thoroughly rinsing my private parts after my encounters—and for the most part, I'd done so. But there had been occasions when I'd wondered if those hasty splashes of water were sufficient. Julie had advised keeping a close eye on my menses and adding vinegar to my bidet douches whenever possible, which made me scoff. I could hardly ask Émile to go down to the kitchens to fetch me a bottle of vinegar from his pantry after an afternoon of passion. And while I could bring a small bottle of the stuff in my bag, the thought of emerging from his bathroom smelling like a salad was equally unappealing.

"It is not," Marie said, reading my thoughts. "It's not only possible, but probable if you let him spill inside you. Men like Émile de Kératry do not fulfill obligations to girls like us. You'd best be prepared." She regarded me with discomfiting intensity. "And regard-less of whether you've realized it yet, I believe you are already with child."

I recoiled from her so fast that I knocked over my cup. As I heard coffee dripping off the table onto the tile floor, I said angrily, "I most certainly am not!"

"I wish it were so. But you have all the signs: Your skin is glow-ing. You have color in your cheeks that I've never seen before. You've put on weight. Have you been tired of late? Do you feel nauseous or bloated? Have you missed your menses?"

I paused, thinking it was a mistake to have met with her. "Of course I'm tired," I said after the waiter came over with a scowl, obliged to mop up the mess I'd made. "I run from my apartment to the theater every day. My sister Régine practically lives with me, so I must attend to her in addition to everything else. It's only to be expected I should . . ."

As my voice faded into sudden silence, I recalled that I'd recently vomited before two of my performances at the Gymnase. I'd thought it an inopportune return of *le trac,* although I did not feel the accompanying panic that rendered me immobile, just an odd queasiness that persisted for several hours. As for my menses, surely it had been last month or the month before. . . .

"Dear God," I whispered in dawning horror.

Marie nodded. "Indeed. Sarah, whatever are you going to do now?"

I came to my feet, clutching at my parasol, moving outside as if a rough wind buffeted me. She followed me. I stood gazing at noth-ing, lost in an inner storm.

"There are ways to rid yourself of it," said Marie. "Herbs and such. Your mother or aunt must know. If it's early enough, it will require only minor discomfort."

She spoke as if she knew from experience. I thrust out my hand. "Please. Say nothing more." I walked away from her toward the boulevard, thinking I should hire a hansom to take me home. I was due at the Gymnase in a few hours. I should lie down and rest.

Instead, I wandered aimlessly until I found myself poised on a bridge over the Seine, staring down into the murky waters and thinking of Marie and the Conservatoire boys, stealing down to the riverbank to fondle and grope.

I wasn't one of those girls. I would never be so careless as to—

Except I was. And now that the possibility had been broached, there was no escaping it.

That night, I performed the role of a jilted Russian princess. It required me to skip about like an idiot, blithely unaware until the dénouement that a temptress had connived to steal away my husband. It was a terrible play and I was terrible in it. My mind was elsewhere; I moved like a sleepwalker, uttering my lines without conviction.

Montigny scolded me. "You've been appalling before, mademoiselle, but tonight you exceeded your own low standard. I don't pay you to perform as if you were dead."

"You barely pay me at all," I retorted. "And your own standard is execrable."

"If your fine Conservatoire sensibilities are so offended by our common stench, I suggest you take them back to the *maison de Molière*. I can find ten other girls in a minute to perform as badly as you."

I stormed out, only to find that Julie and Morny had come to see me in the play on a whim, lauding it over the masses and amused by the spectacle.

"My poor Sarah," Julie clucked when we arrived home. "You were so ridiculous as that foolish princess. And before Morny, too. Don't you think it's time you admitted you'll never amount to anything as an actress?"

Ignoring her, I went to my apartment. Régine had fallen asleep on my settee in the little parlor. As I drew a shawl over her, I gazed at her face, so innocent in repose. When I sat beside her, she instinctually reached for me, nestling her cheek against my hip.

I finally allowed my dismay to overwhelm me. I'd never wanted this. Régine was more than enough to make me think I must never bear a child of my own. Children were so fragile, so easily wounded and deeply scarred. My own childhood played before my eyes; how I'd longed for a mother's love even when I didn't know it, to feel that someone strived for my happiness before their own. I had no example to emulate; I knew nothing of rearing a babe. I was nineteen. If I gave birth now, how would I cope? How would I protect my child from the very sorrows I had endured?

By the night's end, I'd reached my decision. As Madame G. came in with our breakfast tray—"Sarah, you look as if you haven't slept"—I went to the desk where I kept paper and ink, and wrote a missive to Kératry.

Then I saw Régine to her lessons, tidied up my apartment, and asked Madame G. to sit down. Quietly, I confessed my predicament.

"Oh, my poor girl," she said. We sat for a long moment in silence before she asked, "Can you inform the father, if you know who he is?"

Her voice was so devoid of condemnation, I almost started to cry. I showed her the letter.

"What if he refuses to have any part of it?" she said.

"I don't know." I knotted my hands in my lap. "Julie will disown me. She'll refuse to release my dowry. I'll forsake any chance I might have at a theatrical career. Everything tells me I should not keep this child, but God help me"—my voice fractured—"I cannot bring myself to be rid of it. I want it, even if everything tells me I shouldn't."

"Then you shall have it." She embraced me. "You are not alone. I am here."

After dispatching my letter to Kératry, I waited. I thought he must be the father—I'd spent more time with him than anyone else—but I couldn't be certain, as I'd entertained others, such as his friend the Prince of Ligne, who'd spent a week with me during his trip to Paris. I didn't even know how far along I was. Madame G. had me recline so she could probe my abdomen like a midwife, but she had no experience to determine it, either.

I performed at the Gymnase every night. The situation with Montigny grew unbearable as he threatened to sack me because I didn't appear to even be trying anymore, reciting my lines as if I were "dusting the props." I told him I wasn't trying because his productions didn't deserve the effort, but I knew I was sabotaging myself, that my humiliation and fear of what lay ahead were clouding my judgment. If I was going to bear a child, I would need the means to support it. Kératry's willingness to help remained uncertain, and this job was the only means I had.

The other actresses were sympathetic. Sensing my plight, they fussed over me and brought me endless cups of chamomile tea, warning Montigny to make himself scarce whenever he appeared at the dressing room door, as if he had a mind to throw me out.

After an entire month passed without word from Kératry, I made my way to his townhouse under a torrential July downpour. It was early evening, the time when he was most likely to be at home, but as I neared, the house appeared shut up. Many aristocrats left the city in the summer for their country estates, and my heart sank at the thought that he'd not only ignored my letter but absconded to avoid an encounter with me. Yet as I moved into the front courtyard, my mantle drenched about my shoulders, I discerned the sound of faint laughter coming from an upstairs window and glimpsed telltale gaslight flickering between the closed white shutters.

I went still. He had warned me that he wasn't a man from whom I should expect anything but payment in full. Despite our few confidences and mutual physical ardor, we barely knew each other. And he hadn't sent a reply to my letter, though he must have received it if he was here, as it seemed he was. Still, I had to allow him the opportunity, I thought, recalling Julie's words to me about my father: *At least he was honorable enough to admit his mistake.*

Perhaps Kératry would prove honorable, too. It couldn't be uncommon for men like him to find themselves in this situation, just as it wasn't uncommon for girls like me. I would never know unless I directly addressed it with him. He had to be told. He might not want anything more to do with me or the child, but he'd been generous thus far, and I needed money, as much as I could get. Julie had appropriated what I'd given her to hire a solicitor, as requested, but nothing had resulted thus far from our suit to claim my dowry. Whatever I earned, I spent on living expenses and my so-called career, as I had to pay for my costumes and makeup at the Gymnase. If Kératry elected to end our association, he might at least compensate me with a large bank draft.

Bracing myself, I rang the doorbell.

I waited a long while, ringing again several times before the door finally opened. The bland-faced butler intoned, "Does Mademoiselle have an appointment?"

I was shivering, soaked to my skin. "Please tell my lord the *comte* that I wish to—"

"The *comte* is not presently at home. If Mademoiselle cares to leave her card, I will see it delivered once he returns."

A burst of distant feminine laughter from upstairs made me push past him into the black and white marble foyer. "Émile!" I called out.

"Mademoiselle Bernhardt, you do not have an appointment," protested the butler. "My lord is—"

"You *do* know my name." I turned to him. "After all this time of serving me luncheons, I'd begun to think you were deaf, as well as blind."

The butler gaped at me. Behind me, footsteps came down the staircase. Kératry said quietly, "Sarah. What are you doing here?"

He wore his silk *robe de chambre,* fastened hastily at the waist so that his muscled chest was exposed. His hair was tousled, his lips bruised. I knew that look; I had seen it many times. He was entertaining a lover.

"Can we speak in private?" I said, grappling with my sodden mantle.

He gestured to his library. As I stood with my teeth chattering, more from nerves than cold, he poured me a brandy. "Well?" he said, in faint impatience. "Unless I'm mistaken, we do not have an appointment today."

"I sent you a letter." I gulped the brandy. "Didn't you receive it?"

He assented, taking the glass to refill it. Without looking at me, he said, "I regret that I cannot be of assistance. I can't imagine what you expect."

"But the child is yours," I exclaimed.

His smile, when it surfaced, was icy. Snatching the glass from him, I drank it down again. "Sarah," he chided, as if I'd tracked mud in on my boots, "it seems you have forgotten our arrangement. Must I be the one to remind you this is an unfortunate result of your profession? I suggest you discuss it with your mother and do whatever needs to be done."

"Whatever needs to done? I'm going to bear a child. *Our* child!"

"How can you be so certain?" His smile widened, cruel now, like the wind outside. "Because when one sits on a rosebush, one can hardly tell which thorn gave the prick."

I had known this might be his response. It didn't surprise me, but I was still incensed. Throwing the glass aside and hearing it shatter, I said, "You are no gentleman."

"And you were never a lady. I've said all I intend to say on this matter. Now, if you will excuse me, I have other matters to attend to." He started to move past me. "Will you require my fiacre?"

"I will *not* require your fiacre," I replied, my voice rising despite my efforts to control it. "But perhaps you should introduce me to your other matter upstairs. She might be interested in discovering your true character."

He paused. When he returned his gaze to me, I recoiled.

"I suggest you be careful henceforth," he said, in a voice that by its very lack of emotion exuded menace. "Do not test my patience, for I will deny whatever claims you care to make. Not only will I deny it, but I will ensure all my friends hear of how you sought financial gain at my expense. It will end your engagements, not to mention those of your mother and aunt. If you cannot exercise restraint for their sake, consider your sisters. They, too, will no doubt be launched in due time. If you persist in this untenable stance, they shall have to be launched elsewhere than in Paris."

I regarded him in horrified disgust. I had known from the start that this was my ultimate peril: to be discarded as a toy that no longer served. But the sordid reality of it, the callous indifference, felt as if he had tossed acid in my face.

"You—you bastard," I whispered.

He stepped aside. "The only bastard here is the one you say you carry. Now, please leave my house. Needless to say, our association is over."

I pulled up my mantle. "I never want to see you again." I tried to sound haughty, as uncaring as him. But my voice caught and he heard it, for he replied, "I'm relieved that at least in this regard, we are in perfect agreement."

He did not follow me as I marched through the foyer, out the door into the twilight.

The thunderstorm crouched over the city. Trudging back to rue Saint-Honoré, my feet sopping in my ankle boots, my hands numb as I clutched the wet mantle at my throat, I did not feel my tears, mingling with the rain like droplets of ice.

VII

"I must leave," I told Madame G.

We sat in my parlor, hovering over the charcoal brazier. Outside, rain blanketed the world, flooding the Seine's embankments and turning the streets into rivers. The worst storms in twenty-odd years; Paris had become a swamp, the sky a thundering mass of black cloud hurling fury down upon us. It fit my mood to perfection.

She let out a worried sigh. "An unwed woman with child. Where can you go?"

"I don't know. I cannot stay here. My reputation will be ruined. Besides," I said wearily, for as my pregnancy advanced, it seemed perpetual exhaustion was to be my bane, "no one wants to see a girl *enceinte* onstage, much less in their bed."

"But your contract . . . didn't you sign for a year at the Gymnase?"

"I'll resign. I missed my matinée yesterday, so Montigny will sack me anyway. He's been threatening to do so for weeks and now I've given him the perfect excuse."

She gnawed at her lip. "Sarah, can't you speak to your mother? She herself has borne children under similar circumstances. I should think she, of all women, would understand."

My smile felt bitter on my lips. "She'll make me pay in blood.

She'll lock me in this apartment until the child is born and give it away to the ragman." I met Madame G.'s perturbed eyes. "You've seen how she treats Régine. To her, Jeanne is her only child."

"Then your aunt. Rosine has always been tenderhearted. Surely she will help you."

I had considered telling my aunt, but shied away from her uncertain mercy. She'd left me that night in the box so Kératry could make his advance; she was beholden to the rules that governed a demimondaine's existence. If Kératry learned I'd kept the child, he might see it as a threat. Rosine wouldn't risk her livelihood by incurring the *comte*'s wrath.

"Rosine is preoccupied with her suitor," I said. "And she always defers to Julie."

Madame G. went quiet before she ventured, "I do have some savings. Not much, but whatever I have is yours."

I reached for her hand. "You've been a true mother to me. I shall never forget it. If ever a time comes when I can repay you, I will. Every last sou."

"It's not necessary. I love you as if you were my own. And this babe you carry—I want to help you raise it. I always wanted a child. I lost two in the womb. Then my Henri fell ill, and the chance to be a mother passed me by."

I felt close to tears again. "For now, you must promise to look after Régine. She'll need you more than ever. She won't understand why I've left her."

"You needn't ask. Régine can live with me." She rose, kissing my forehead. "It's late. Do try to get some rest. You must keep up your strength."

I went to my damp bed, but I lay awake for hours, listening to the rain pebbling on the rooftop, running my options over in my head. I tallied the few francs I had; together with whatever Madame G. gave me, it might be enough to purchase a one-way coach ticket to Brittany or Normandy, and a room in a cheap boardinghouse. I could work in a tavern until I started to show. By then, I'd have saved enough to—

I had no idea what came next. The future yawned before me like a chasm, a jagged pit where I might fall endlessly, tumbling into darkness without reaching bottom.

You'll not last a month in the street, I assure you.

Hearing Julie's words like a prophecy, I rose to gaze out the garret's narrow window. The rain was falling in blinding sheets.

With any luck, it would drown us all.

I sent my letter of resignation to the Gymnase and feigned a cold. Julie expressed no concern. She knew Madame G. would tend to me, and she was occupied preparing for her annual autumn soirée, when all her suitors, having returned to town from their summer holiday, came to be entertained.

"I trust you'll have recovered by then," she remarked to me. "I want you to perform chansons. Morny likes it so much when you sing."

I nodded, thinking she and Morny were in for an unpleasant surprise. But I couldn't leave immediately; the storms had created chaos for travelers, and I hadn't yet decided where to go. In my mirror, I examined myself. My stomach was still flat, though the nausea had worsened along with my fatigue, especially in the morning. I shouldn't have resigned so impulsively from the Gymnase. I might have made amends to Montigny, toiled a few more weeks for the extra pay. I considered contacting one or two of my suitors, but quailed at the thought. I had no desire to play the courtesan now, even if I doubted Kératry had said anything hostile about me. I was certain he'd put the entire incident from his mind, an unsavory episode not to be discussed—unless I went about declaring my discontent or was seen with a babe on my hip that I claimed was his.

One evening after I saw Régine to bed—she sensed my distress and clung to me, wanting me to read stories to her and play with her shattered dolls—a knock came at my door. When I opened it, Dumas stood on the threshold in his great wet overcoat, an astrakhan hat crammed about his head. I smelled the rain and the faint odor of spirits about him, but he otherwise appeared sober, and the penetrating look he gave me made me step back and say faintly, "Isn't Julie at home?"

I hadn't seen him in months, though I knew he still attended my mother's salon whenever he felt the urge. In fact, I realized with a surge of guilt, I hadn't seen him since the Opéra and my first encounter with Kératry. He must have heard through my mother's salon that the *comte* and I had become lovers and no doubt, knowing Julie, of my subsequent success elsewhere; seeing me now, like this, he would quickly discern that my much-vaunted achievements had amounted to nothing. I didn't want him to see it. I couldn't bear for him, of all people, to be disappointed in me—his little star, of whom he'd had such hope.

"I didn't come to see her." He trudged into my room, too big for its narrow confines, removing his hat and gloves but not his coat. "God's teeth, it's like Siberia in here."

"I'm sorry." I tried to rouse a smile, tugging my shawl about me. These days, I went about in layers because I couldn't afford to waste money on coal for heat. "It's going to be a harsh winter," I added, thinking I should offer him coffee, which I also didn't have. "If it's started to rain this early."

"Not as harsh as what Montigny just told me," he retorted. I went still. "I saw him at the Gymnase tonight," Dumas went on. "He was very unhappy. He says you are irresponsible and reckless." He stared at me as he spoke, forcing me to avert my gaze. When I failed to reply, he said, "Sarah, it so happens I went to see him because I've written a new play that I wish to debut in his theater, to see how his audience responds. It's not finished yet, but it's a cut above his usual fare, and I want you for the lead role. Imagine my disappointment when I found you had resigned." He took an envelope from his waistcoat and set it on the table. "Without your final pay."

Sinking into a chair, I told myself not to cry. No matter what, I must not cry in front of him.

"Sarah, whatever is the matter?" He stood over me, looming and inescapable. I knew I couldn't avoid his questions, just as I hadn't been able to avoid his trust in me when he helped prepare me for my audition to the Conservatoire. "I know you can be temperamental, but to leave the Gymnase thus, after the Comédie—do you deliberately wish to never work in the theater again? Morny refuses to intercede on your behalf anymore."

"I don't expect him to," I whispered. I couldn't look at him.

He cupped my chin, forcibly lifting my face. When he saw my expression, he sighed. "As I suspected." He lowered himself onto the footstool before me, overwhelming it; I expected to hear it crack and collapse under his weight. "Have you told him?"

"I tried. Kératry claims I cannot possibly know he is the father and disavowed all complicity in the matter."

Dumas growled. "The scoundrel. I tried to warn them that night at the Opéra; I spoke to Morny at intermission. He knows very well that Émile de Kératry has too much money and too few scruples. But Morny told me it had been decided; you'd chosen him and your mother approved. I did not intervene further. I wish I had."

"Nothing would have deterred me," I said, grateful for his kindness even as I struggled with mortification that this effusive man, who'd been the first to believe in my talent, could find me in such a desolate state. "I made a pact with Julie."

"For the dowry, I presume." He chuckled at my startled look. "Don't be surprised. Morny is not discreet. Your mother thinks he cares, but those like him can only care so much. He takes interest in your family because he believes your sister Jeanne is his and has decided to leave her a bequest in his will. He's not honorable by any measure, but more honorable than most of his ilk, as you have learned."

The confirmation of my long-held suspicion about Jeanne's paternity brought me no consolation. It only reaffirmed the likelihood that my mother would throw me out, now more than ever before. She would never risk Morny's censure, and the *duc* would not approve of my bearing Kératry's bastard if the *comte* had come down against it. Men like them shared a common ethos: to protect one another, above all else.

"Yes," I said quietly. "I've learned that much, at least."

He considered me, his large hands twitching on his wet trouser legs as if he might touch me. I thought if he did, I would fall apart.

"Do you have a plan?" he finally asked, and I found myself telling him everything, unable to stanch my outpour of anguish. "I should never have allowed him such liberties. I was warned, time and time again, of what might occur if I failed to take precautions."

"Yet you still want to bear his child?" he said, and when I nodded, swallowing, he sat in silence, one of his hands at his chin. "You know I have a wife and children I adore?" he said at length. "Yes? Well, let me also tell you, I have other children by other women. Too many, in fact." He gave a startling laugh. "I never could say no to a pretty face. Why else do you think I must write constantly? To support my brood, of course. Precautions aren't always effective; trust me when I say if they were, I'd be more solvent. But I love all of my children, and would never leave them on their own. What Kératry has done is not only ungallant, it's inexcusable. You are not to blame for his lack of morals or sense of honor."

His affection as he spoke of his family pierced me like a knife. He seemed to sense it, for he leaned to me to say quietly, "You must forget Kératry. Those like him can indeed disavow themselves and do everything they threaten. They have a vengeful streak when crossed."

"I have no wish to ask more of him." For the first time since my confrontation with Émile, fury ignited my voice. "I grew up without a father. My child will have me."

"You needn't martyr yourself. I will help you, if you'll let me." He finally did what I had dreaded: he took my hands in his. "I know you are afraid. I know because I, too, have experienced hardship and rejection. Look at me: I'm descended from slaves. But I forced open doors that would never have opened otherwise, because of my persistence. I am proof that any one of us can rise above our obstacles. No one ever believed I would become a celebrated writer. I proved them wrong. One day, so will you."

His encouragement only made me feel worse; what I'd faced was nothing like what he had, and what had I done with my advantages, save careen from misadventure to catastrophe? Looking into his keen gray-blue eyes, so distinctive against the caramel hue of his skin, I whispered, "You also have tremendous talent. Persistence is nothing without it."

"Are you saying you do not? Bah!" He waved his hand in the air as if to dispel a noxious odor. "Didn't you hear me say I wrote my new play with you in mind for the lead?"

"Unless your lead is a disgraced pregnant courtesan, I fear you'll have to find someone else," I said, with a weak smile. "I don't think I'll ever perform again. I've discovered I'm not suited for a life in the theater."

He came to his feet, once more filling the room with his expansive presence. "I hear your mother, and I like it not. Why would you say such a thing when you've not yet found your place? Everyone has setbacks. Every player who finds success must first fight for it."

"But I . . ." I had to lower my gaze from him again. "I'm not like every player. I question too much. I can't seem to bring myself to perform like everyone else. There is no place for someone like me on the stage."

He paused. His voice softened. "That is precisely why I know you can succeed. I've plenty of experience in the theater, and the best players always question. You *will* perform again, Sarah Bernhardt. I'm as certain of it as I am that I must die with a pen in my hand. Those of us who invite the muse cannot escape her."

"I thought Montigny informed you how well my muse did for him."

He glowered. "What does that charlatan know? He runs a gutter theater, where he expects pewter to shine like silver." He leaned to me. "The play can wait. As I said, it's not finished yet. I can wait. The world can wait. You cannot. This child must be born and cared for, but never let me hear you say again that you'll not return to the stage. I refuse to accept it." Cupping my chin, he looked intently into my eyes. "Never forget that I saw you experience your first play. The passion in your soul can't be denied. You were born to be on the stage, and unless you do as fate ordains, you will lead a very miserable existence."

I could no longer contain my sorrow, my sense of utter loss and defeat. In a voice choked by tears, I said, "What shall I do?"

He sank to his knees on the floor, once more clasping my hands in his.

"What shall *we* do," he said. "Leave it to me. I have the perfect solution."

VIII

The perfect solution, it turned out, was Brussels. Dumas had good friends there, a married couple named Bruce. He wrote to them, explaining my situation, and they agreed to receive me. They were childless. Should I decide to relinquish the babe, they promised to raise it as their own.

Still, my departure obliged me to submit to the inevitable family conference. By now, Julie had discovered that I'd left the Gymnase. Morny must have told her, but she'd kept it to herself, no doubt because she believed I'd finally decided to abandon my ill-chosen stage career to pursue my engagements. Dumas's announcement that I was instead suffering from nervous exhaustion and needed time away didn't please her in the slightest.

"She has resigned from that dreadful establishment. Why should she go all the way to Brussels when she can rest here?" Selfish to her last breath, Julie stared at me in annoyance, not wanting the plans for her autumn soirée to go awry. She needed me at her pianoforte, singing my lungs out for her suitors.

"She must get away from Paris," Dumas said. "Your daughter is unwell. You need only look at her. She must recover her health without distractions."

"How much time?" Julie kept eyeing me. I had to resist draping my hands over my stomach, thinking my mother saw far more than she let on. But she'd never admit as much before Dumas; he might not be a regular suitor, but he was still someone she couldn't offend. Many of his friends were regulars. One ill word from him, and they could stop calling. "She wasn't working that much."

"You call three matinées a week and six nightly performances, in addition to her other activities, not much?" exclaimed Dumas. "At such a pace, she'll perish before her twenty-first year. I should think you'd rather she seek respite now, before she ends up in her grave."

Julie assumed an appropriately chastened expression. "Well." She gave a strained smile. "If you think it best, *mon ami*."

"I do. My friends will look after her. Brussels is perfect. No one knows her there, and her absence for a time will help repair this imbroglio with the Gymnase."

Julie gave a sigh. "She should never have worked in such a place. She's not suited for the stage. But as you say, we cannot risk another scandal. I concur entirely on that account."

Scandal being her worst nightmare; she'd send me all the way to America to avoid it.

Dumas booked me on the train, with Julie saying nothing more as I packed my trunks. I had the suspicion she knew exactly why I was leaving and believed I'd turned to Dumas to arrange for me to deliver and give away my child. If so, she saw no reason to interfere, providing I didn't bring my shame to her threshold. She might have borne three daughters under similar circumstances, but she'd never condone it from me, not when the child I carried might threaten her arrangement with Morny and Jeanne's inheritance.

I didn't care to contemplate what would happen when she discovered the truth.

॥

I found Brussels quaint. Compared to Paris, with its ceaseless noise and endless variety of entertainments, the Belgian city felt provincial, and too well suited for my much-touted respite. With the exception of daily promenades about the square for shopping and afternoon tea, there wasn't much to do, and by October and my twentieth birthday, my pregnancy could no longer be disguised, relegating me to the house.

At Dumas's suggestion, Madame Bruce and I devised an explanation for my extended visit. I was a recent widow, my husband the victim of an unspecified illness, leaving me *enceinte* and alone. Not that the neighbors questioned. The mere sight of me, looking so forlorn, was enough to assuage any doubt about my misfortune.

My seclusion and Madame Bruce's plentiful board did wonders. My face in the mirror was still angular, but the hollows in my cheeks filled out, and the dark circles under my eyes from my sleepless nights faded. I hadn't realized how terrible I must have looked until I saw how much better I now appeared. Still, my body more or less resembled a taut string with a knot in the middle; the enlarging bump startled me at first, as it seemed to materialize overnight, though the persistent nausea subsided, a blessed relief.

With little else to do, I spent my days on the settee, nibbling chocolates and reading every play I could find. Bookshops in the square sold imported publications from Paris as well as abroad. I immersed myself in the works of Shakespeare, thrilling to the macabre Lady Macbeth and maligned Desdemona. But it was Hamlet who most enthralled me. Although the French translation of the play was poor, I'd never read a more perfect character or more exquisite lines. Drifting to sleep as I recited, "Doubt thou the stars are fire; doubt that the sun doth move. Doubt truth to be a liar; but never doubt my love," I dreamed of playing the tormented Danish prince, a skull in my palm as audiences swooned at my feet.

And for the first time in my adult life, the seclusion allowed me to reflect. I came to recognize that in many respects, I'd been my own worst enemy. Every opportunity handed to me I'd set out to thwart. I did not regret striking Madame Nathalie or leaving the Gymnase— neither was worth regretting—but I did regret disappointing Provost. Like Dumas, he had believed I had something that set me apart, and what had I given him in return? Tepid performances and disdain, never taking myself as seriously as he did, performing the *role* of an actress rather than believing it in my heart. Provost's methods may have curtailed my ability to personify my characters, but he'd given me the stepping stones to launch my career. He'd told me that with time and patience, I might deviate from the standard rules.

I also regretted having succumbed to Julie, trusting so little in myself that at my first falter, I fell into her snare. Émile de Kératry had dishonored his responsibility, but I'd allowed him to do so by letting myself be blinded to who he was, by the power I thought my conquest of him gave me. Although I'd failed to realize it at the time, like so much else in my life, I'd done it out of spite, to bait Julie's envy. Having the *comte* in my bed had been my ill-chosen weapon to counter her domination over me.

I now understood how much my relationship with my mother had poisoned me. It had to end. I could no longer let myself be ruled by her or the past. Henceforth, I must make my own way, even if I perished in the attempt. *Quand même* would be my sole guiding star. I would return to the stage, accept any roles offered. I'd work as hard as I could until I proved to myself, and to the world, that acting was my destiny. Nothing would ever make me doubt myself again.

But I forced open doors that would never have opened otherwise, because of my persistence. I am proof that any one of us can rise above our obstacles.

Dumas's words were emblazoned in my heart. If he could still believe in me, I must believe in myself. Everything I had done up till now might warrant my regret, except for this: I did not regret the new life growing inside me.

To me, my child was the unexpected gift that would restore my freedom.

I was nearing my seventh month when Dumas sent urgent word from Paris. While entertaining in her salon, my mother had suffered an apoplexy.

Bidding hasty farewell to Monsieur and Madame Bruce, I boarded the next train, arriving at the flat disheveled and with my belly jutting under my cloak. Rosine was on the stairs; when she caught sight of me, she gasped. I shoved past her, not caring to hear her bleated query as to why I'd kept it a secret; why had I left my family, who would have seen to my comfort? Ignoring her protest that Julie was abed, I barged into my mother's room. The curtains were drawn, the odor of burnt herbs and medicine souring the air. Perching on the edge of the bed, I took my mother's hand.

Her papery eyelids fluttered at my touch. Her appearance shocked me. I'd left a plump, tidy woman not yet forty-five, only to return to a gaunt invalid I barely recognized. She did not seem to know me at first. Then her parched lips moved and I heard her whisper, "Sarah."

"I'm here, Maman." My voice choked. She looked so frail, so unlike herself. All the hatred I'd nursed toward her drained from me. I should never have left. I should have stayed and done battle with her. Maybe if I had, she wouldn't have taken ill.

Her gaze lowered to my belly. Her hand slipped from mine.

"You should not have come," she said. "You bring disgrace to my house."

With Régine clawing at my skirts, barraging me with questions interspersed with ferocious accusations that I'd gone and left her with the *putaines*, I installed myself in my apartment. Madame G. was overjoyed to have me home; as she helped me remove the dust sheets and replenish the larder, she fretted that I was doing too much, I would tire myself and harm the baby.

"Nonsense." I placed her hand on my stomach. "Feel her. She's kicking up a storm. She's a Bernhardt. She keeps me up half the night."

I was certain I would bear a girl. It ran in our family. We were all daughters.

"Still, you mustn't overexert yourself," insisted Madame G. "Let Rosine care for your mother, while I see to you."

I submitted to her care. Rosine had assured me that my mother was improving. Morny had hired the best physician in Paris, and while frightening and debilitating, her apoplexy had been mild. With time and rest, she would recover.

"But," said my aunt sadly, "I fear she may never be the woman she was."

What she meant was that Julie might never be the courtesan she'd been. As for the woman herself, any transformation remained to be seen.

I did not hold out hope, not as far as I was concerned. Instead, I dedicated myself to preparing for my child's arrival.

IX

"Sarah, you must push," said Madame G. "Push, for the love of this child."

Outside, December had cloistered Paris in a heavy snowfall, like a shroud. To me, the world beyond these four walls had become unreachable, as I lay trapped on my bed like a beast in the field, writhing to expel the mutinous burden inside me.

The ordeal had taken me by surprise. My pregnancy had proceeded without mishap; indeed, I'd felt so fit that I swathed myself in a cloak every day to embark on brisk walks about the city despite the chill, the weight of my belly scarcely an inconvenience, though I took pains to disguise it. My appetite had been hardy, and my color good. I'd refused the services of a midwife, over Madame G.'s objections, stating I had no need for one. I had enough with her and Rosine, who'd moved back into Julie's flat and went between my mother's bedside and my apartment. I could deliver my babe without trouble, I declared; there was no reason to fear the birth would be any more arduous than my pregnancy.

But once the pangs overcame me, I found myself caught in its maw, the pain building until it was all I knew, my cries and howls of protest sundering my ears.

I thought I would die. I heard Rosine whisper to Madame G, "Her hips are too narrow. We must fetch a midwife," and I screamed,

"No! No one else!" bringing them rushing to my side as I grasped at their hands. "No one else can know. Please." In my delirium, I was terrified word would spread throughout Paris of my condition. Everyone would learn that Sarah Bernhardt, disgraced former *pensionnaire* of the Comédie and tawdry disappointment of the Gymnase, had left her employment to give birth to an illegitimate child, dooming my career before I had the chance to revive it. I had to support my child once it was born, and the only resource I had was the stage. I would never entertain suitors again, not after this.

I focused on my waning strength as Rosine peered between my legs. "I can see it. Sarah, it's here. Push!" and I bore down on the obstacle lodged in my womb.

"Again," cried Rosine.

"I *can't*," I wailed. "I cannot do it, God save me."

Then, through my pain and despair, a weakened yet still-firm voice declared, "Let me see," and I gazed through the haze of sweat on my face to Julie, leaning on a walking stick, her robe seeming to float upon her diminished frame. She motioned to Rosine. "Get up off your knees and spread her legs more. I'm not about to lean over."

To my mortification, she stared between my splayed thighs. A dreadful silence fell. Then she said, "The child is turned around. It will kill her. You must pull it out."

Rosine lifted a hand to her throat in dismay. My mother looked directly into my eyes. Her emotionless expression chilled me. If I died, then the problem I presented died with me. She would no longer have to contend with my character, my insistence on living outside the established norm; she wouldn't have to explain my child or cajole me into submission. She would mourn, see us to our grave, and have two fewer worries. Jeanne would follow her example, while I'd proven an incorrigible disappointment.

I shrieked in mindless rage, sundering the pain-thickened air.

As Rosine recoiled, Madame G. abandoned her post by my bed to plunge between my legs. I felt her hands stab at my bruised opening. The pain was so immense, my senses darkened. Just as I thought death had come to claim me, relief surged through me in a shuddering rush and Madame G. cried, "The child is born!"

I couldn't lift my head as she and Rosine severed the cord, turning to the basin of rose water and stack of clean cloths. I waited, breathless, for the cry that would tell me my daughter was safe; when it did not come, I heard Julie snap, "Wipe that mess from its mouth," followed by taut anticipation before the wail sounded— piercing, distraught as a mewling cat, and music to my ears.

Grappling against my exhaustion, I righted myself on my elbows. Julie stood immobile, Jeanne and Régine staring wide-eyed from the doorway behind her. My aunt slumped against a chair as Madame G. turned with the swaddled bundle in her arms.

"Perfect," she breathed. "A perfect—"

"Boy," intoned Julie. I tore my gaze from Madame G. "A son," my mother said to me. "Now you will know true suffering. One can hardly train a son to be of any use." With these words, she limped out, shooing my sisters before her.

Ma petite dame set my babe in my arms. "He's so beautiful, Sarah." Tears moistened her eyes. "A beautiful baby boy."

I looked down at his wizened face, his mouth puckering as he prepared to release another yowl. He was the ugliest thing I'd ever seen, yet nothing had given me greater fulfillment. Love unlike any I'd felt overcame me, filling me to overflowing.

He had grown inside me. He was mine. All mine.

"What shall you name him?" asked Madame G.

"Maurice," I said without hesitation, for no reason I could think of. The name, like my son, had just come to me. "Maurice Bernhardt."

ACT IV

1865–1871

The Odéon

Curiosity is one of the forms of feminine bravery.

—VICTOR HUGO

I

"I need money." I took a sip of my coffee, hoping my confession didn't sound as peremptory as it felt. "Caring for a babe on a pittance . . . it's impossible."

Paul gave a dejected assent. I'd asked him to meet with me, sending a note to the Odéon, where he toiled in minor roles, seeking to establish himself. Of the few friends I had left, he seemed the one most likely to be sympathetic, though I hadn't counted on his immediate offer of marriage or his sullen pout when I refused.

"I don't want charity," I hastened to add. "I'm prepared to work at whatever I can. Only"—I sighed, finally letting my fatigue reveal itself—"no one will hire me. It seems the scene with Madame Nathalie and my departure from the Gymnase are not so easily forgotten."

He stuck out his lower lip. He'd grown a beard for his latest role and I found its rough thickness disconcerting on his still-boyish face. It seemed inconceivable that only a few years ago, I'd lain with him and discovered the dubious pleasures of the flesh.

"I could ask Provost," he said at length. "I do still see him, on occasion."

I shook my head. "I don't think that would be wise," I replied, though in truth, if he'd said he would ask Madame Nathalie herself, I should have been hard-pressed to refuse. The past six months since

Maurice's birth had been so fraught with turmoil, I was now desperate. No sooner had I risen from bed to nurse my child than an explosion ensued with Julie, who, although not yet recovered from her apoplexy, proceeded to barge into my apartment because "that bastard's infernal crying" was keeping everyone awake at night. "Muzzle him," she demanded, banging her cane on the floor like Provost. "Or find yourself another abode. I'll not abide my suitors being deafened by his caterwauling."

We embarked on an epic battle that brought half the building to my door. I called her every name I could think of, threatening to bear a hundred bastards to drown out her "ungodly fornication"— never mind that she wasn't doing much of it these days. While Madame G. implored us to reason and Régine cried in despair to hear us shouting at each other, Julie threatened to evict me if I did not leave her premises within the week.

"Clearly," she said, "this roof is too small for both of us!" She limped into her apartment with me raging behind her. From her desk, she extracted an envelope and flung it at my feet. "There. I have done my part as promised. That is the settlement the solicitor negotiated on your behalf. Take it and go."

I opened the envelope to count the billet of francs. "This is only half of my dowry," I said, raising my eyes to her. "Where is the rest of it?"

"Retained by the estate in the unlikely event you should marry." Julie sniffed. "Very unlikely now, after what you've done. No man wants to raise another's mistake."

"Tell the solicitor I want the rest released immediately. I have no plans to marry, now or ever." I pocketed the envelope. "I'll be out by next week."

Packing up my belongings, I used my newfound money to rent an apartment on rue Duphot and hire a neighborhood girl, Caroline, to help me with Maurice. Régine plunged into despair at my departure, wailing in fury, but I couldn't take her with me. I could barely afford to support my son, but I promised I would bring her to live with me as soon as I was able, and Madame G. assured me she would look after her.

My new apartment consisted of a cramped living room and two bedrooms the size of closets. I installed myself and Maurice in one, leaving the other as a spare for when Madame G. came with my sister to visit and assist Caroline while I went out in search of employment. To no avail, as I soon discovered. My reputation preceded me and no theater manager was inclined to test it for himself. I scoured the newspapers for casting calls and haunted every audition, only to earn one offer to perform in a cabaret chorus. Although sorely tempted, I knew my limited dancing skills guaranteed another failure.

Paul now lifted his mournful gaze to me. I tried to smile. "Please, do not ask again. You are very dear to me, but neither of us would be happy with me as your wife."

He looked discomfited. "I do know of . . ."

"Yes?" I said eagerly.

"A daguerreotypist." He paused. I tapped my foot. "He's always looking for people to sit for him. He was a caricaturist before he became fascinated by the camera. He's successful; he's taken portraits of many important people in Paris, including Dumas. His name is Félix Nadar. He pays a sitting fee. I could mention you to him, if you like."

"Do so," I said at once. "How difficult can it be? One just stands there and—"

"He might want you to pose . . ." Paul's voice faded into another awkward silence.

"Oh." I went quiet for a moment. Then I said, with somewhat less enthusiasm, "I suppose it can't be helped. Very well. Give me his address and I'll apply."

"It's not so formal, Sarah. Let me arrange a meeting."

I didn't know what to expect, but I had vague imaginings of a dark attic in a disreputable district, reeking of varnish and chemicals. Instead, at the appointed hour, I arrived at a lofty attic on the brand-new boulevard des Capuchines, flooded by dust-mote sunlight streaming through overhead louvers and cluttered with *objets d'art*—busts, statues, paintings, coils of fabric—as well as the pervasive odor of albumen and the unmistakable stink of rotten egg.

Monsieur Nadar was an unkempt giant who reminded me of Dumas, his red-gold hair springing in disarray about his balding pate and his fingers stained silver from his craft. But he was charming from the start, complimenting me on my ensemble—my much-worn green walking suit—as he showed me his gallery of daguerreotypes, which presented startling realism, capturing as no other medium I'd seen the mercurial faces of his subjects.

"Here is Monsieur Dumas," he said, motioning to the portrait of my benefactor, seated in all his majesty upon a massive chair, "and here's Madame Sand," featuring the infamous cross-dressing writer in a demure caplet and ruffled gown, looking nothing like her reputation. "As you can see, mademoiselle, I'm very dedicated to my endeavor."

He was, indeed. I stared in awe at a series of photographs of Paris, taken from an astonishing height and offering a bird's-eye view of the city in breathtaking detail.

"I was the first to employ a camera on a hot-air balloon," he said. "They all thought me mad, claiming a spark would set the contraption aflame and send me crashing to my death, but they weren't so critical afterwards once they saw the results. The emperor himself has commissioned me to do a series for him of the palace at Versailles."

"You've been up in the sky?" I turned to him in a daze. "What was it like? It must have felt as if you were flying. So free and unencumbered . . . how marvelous it must be to step into a basket and find oneself lifted far from earthly cares!"

He smiled. "You sound like a dreamer, and one with the spirit of an adventurer."

"Hardly." I returned to his photographs. "But I would very much like to see the world like this one day, so vast and neat, and—"

"Laid out like a carpet at your feet?" His smile widened. "I wonder if my camera can capture the sheen on your skin?"

I made a conscious effort to not avert my eyes. "Is it necessary?"

"I'm not asking you to disrobe if you're unwilling. My subjects pose on an entirely voluntary basis." He paused. "Perhaps just your shoulders . . ."

I would have sat for him without pay; I found his art magnificent. But the fee he cited was significant, sending me scurrying behind a Chinese screen in the corner to undress, about to step out in my petticoat when he said, "I've set up a pillar and length of velvet by the wall. Use the velvet to drape yourself. You must remove your chemise so the straps do not show. You can tell me when you are ready."

Moving to these objects, I grappled with the red velvet, which was heavier than it appeared. I nearly toppled the pillar, too, which was hollow plaster. As I yanked the velvet about me and slipped my chemise to my waist, I wondered if the other things scattered about the attic were also fake, illusions that only became real through his lenses.

"Ready," I said, with a catch in my voice.

He turned from the camera mounted on a brass-tipped tripod to survey me where I leaned with an elbow on the pillar, clutching the velvet to my throat. "Might you loosen your hair? And perhaps employ the mantle with less modesty?" He gave me a nod as I complied. "Much better. Now, please be still, mademoiselle. Monsieur Porel tells me you're a gifted performer. Emulate for me. Only do so with your expression, not your body."

He wanted me to *act*? I hesitated. I felt ludicrous, the velvet scratching my bare skin (it was cheap, its underside a rough grosgrain), my position stiff and unnatural. Easing my elbow on the pillar, I closed my eyes and took a deep breath, thinking of Maurice, the way he woke every morning, chortling, kicking his little legs and making fists in the air as he grabbed for my teat. My small breasts couldn't produce enough milk for him, the greedy mite; I had to hire a nursemaid, whom I could ill afford, but Maurice liked to suckle me nevertheless, despite barely squeezing out a few mouthfuls and leaving my nipples chafed.

Nadar raced behind his camera, throwing the short black curtain over himself. "Now stand very still. Don't move. Yes, like that. Perfect, mademoiselle."

I was surprised it took so long. After he emerged from the camera, replacing the glass plate at the back and taking the used one to a table, I realized I wasn't going to see the results immediately when he explained, "Processing takes time. I'd like to shoot a few more, if you don't mind?"

"I don't." He was paying me, after all. "Do you want me to try another pose?"

"Yes, please. In profile this time." He watched me adjust myself. "Oh, that's marvelous. You have such arresting features. Perfect for the camera."

"And quite the nose," I quipped. "A critic once said I might one day be deemed a beauty." I stifled my laughter as he adjusted his apparatus.

"Don't move," he said.

I spent the better part of that afternoon with him. He took several portraits, which I was eager to see. He asked me to return in a week, handing me an envelope with my fee. "You're a pleasure to work with. Any theater company would be fortunate to hire you. Do come back. And if you have friends who might be interested, please refer them to me."

I floated from his studio as if I were in his hot-air balloon, the money tucked inside my bag and my heart warmed by his praise.

It wasn't the stage. But it was a start.

II

I returned to Nadar's studio several more times, first to see my pictures, which were so arresting and unlike how I saw myself that I felt as if I were looking at a stranger, my face seductive and pensive, my hair a thicket of curls, darker in photographic hue than reality. I thought I looked much older, sophisticated and mysterious.

"A Parisian sphinx," declared Nadar.

One afternoon, as I toyed with a fan and allowed him to photograph a tantalizing glimpse of my breasts, two young men and a woman arrived—sending me plunging behind the screen to cover my indecency. When I emerged, flustered, I found they, too, were there to sit. While Nadar prepared, I conversed with them and discovered they were actors from the Odéon, friends of Paul's, who, like me, sought to supplement their limited income.

I'd not been in the company of actors in so long that I found myself tongue-tied, wondering if they'd heard of my aborted spell at the Comédie. They had. The woman exclaimed, "You're the Slap!" laughingly telling me that many actors in Paris deemed me a heroine for it.

"Such an insufferable battle-ax," said the pretty blond woman, her blue eyes shining mischievously. "She no doubt deserved it." She paused, regarding me. "And I cannot help but wonder how you, Sarah Bernhardt, can fail to recognize me."

"Have we met?" I searched my memory, not recalling her at all until her smile widened, exalting her dimples. "We were friends at Grandchamp. I'm Sophie Crossier, though I now go by Croizette. You came to my house on Sundays with Marie Colombier."

"Sophie!" I couldn't believe it. I embraced her in joy and soon we were nestled together on the sagging couch, sharing reminiscences of our time at the convent and of our mutual friend Marie, while Nadar posed the men.

"Don't you find it unusual that the three of us became actresses?" said Sophie, eying the men, who were engaged in a seductive embrace for the camera. "Not like Grandchamp at all, is it? Imagine the good sisters' horror if they knew what goes on in Paris these days."

Having already seen Nadar's collection of illicit erotica, which was sold under the counter in kiosks around the city and earned him a tidy profit, I wasn't shocked, though I had to agree the nuns would certainly be. Instead, I asked, "Is Marie still performing? She didn't seem so enthused by it the last time I saw her." I made sure not to mention that the last time I'd seen her was when I'd discovered my pregnancy.

"If you can call it performing." Sophie gave a sigh. "I think she only went into the theater because she thought it would be easy. As a result, she's not made a name for herself at the Châtelet. The notices for her debut in *La Jeunesse du roi Henri* were not kind."

"Critics can be savages," I said, recalling my own unremarkable debut and feeling a pang of guilt that I had not sought out Marie since delivering Maurice. "Look at me."

"But I thought . . ." She frowned. "Marie told me you had left the stage to pursue other engagements. She mentioned a certain *comte*."

A burst of incredulous laughter escaped me. "She actually told you that?"

"She did. As reluctant as she is to learn our craft, Marie is an expert when it comes to gossip. I did find it strange at the time; everyone seemed to think you had such promise at the Conservatoire, according to Marie. She sounded rather jealous, if I can be candid."

I almost laughed again, thinking no one should ever envy me. "Well, she was wrong," I said, averting my eyes in sudden embarrassment at my predicament. "I was obliged to take some time away from the stage and I'm not having any luck returning to it. I may be heralded for the Slap, but not so much that a theater cares to hire me."

Sophie made a commiserative sound. We sat in silence for a long moment before she said, "I could put in a word for you at the Odéon, if you like. It's sponsored by the government, like the Comédie, as you know, but we're not so beholden to tradition. Our associate director, Duquesnel, might be very interested to hear you're available."

I was startled by her offer. "You would do that for me?"

She laughed. "I realize it's not something any actress should do for another, but we are friends, are we not? More importantly, I'm under contract at the Odéon, and our ticket sales are . . . Suffice to say we could use a promising new talent." She paused. "Providing you can deliver a suitable reference."

I thought of Paul's offer to contact Provost. "I could ask," I said.

"Then allow me to talk to Duquesnel." She pressed her calling card into my hand, leaning close to me to whisper, "We must prove this fable of your retirement is entirely unfounded." As I started to thank her, touched by her generosity, she added, "And allow me a word of caution, Sarah: be careful of Marie."

Paul agreed to approach Provost. As months went by without word from him and my money started to dwindle, I forced myself to pay a visit to Julie to demand the remainder of my dowry. She cited vague legal entanglements, and I did not have the strength to argue. She was entertaining again on a limited basis, but I could see how fatigued she was. She was no longer the courtesan she had been, relying on a few steadfast regulars and old Morny, whose devotion remained constant even as his health declined. I thought the inescapable eventuality of his demise must torment her, and I would have pitied her had I not resented her lack of any inquiry about Maurice. She remained impervious, as if the birth of my son had never occurred. Rosine, on the other hand, slipped me extra money as I left. "For the baby's clothes," she whispered.

Nadar's studio offered my sole artistic outlet, both in the novelty of his company and that of his revolving coterie. He often had gatherings of threadbare sculptors, writers, composers, and painters, drinking absinthe and debating the merits of art while waiting to be photographed. I rediscovered my passion for painting, setting up an easel in my living quarters, and began experimenting with sculpture, as well—all of which laid further waste to my income. Bills piled up for my paint tubes, clay, gesso, and other necessities of my *moi*, as I dubbed my quest for artistic fulfillment.

I ignored the debts, until the proprietor of my apartment came banging at my door. Hiding in my room with Régine and Maurice while Caroline haltingly explained that Mademoiselle Bernhardt was not at home, I heard the proprietor retort that he would ensure Mademoiselle Bernhardt would never be at home again, at least not in *this* particular home, unless she paid her overdue rent by the end of the week.

I no longer had a choice. If I was going to survive, something had to be done.

Nadar informed me that an aristocrat had seen my pictures and inquired. Although I had sworn to never again risk the vagaries of the trade, I accepted the aristocrat's invitation to tea and soon found myself accepting a great deal more.

It paid the rent.

Then Madame G. suggested a move. "There's a cottage in the borough of Auteuil. Monsieur Dumas was at Julie's salon the other evening and he asked about you. When he heard you were living here, he was outraged. He says it's no place for a new mother. He's offered to pay your entire rent for the first year. There's more room," she went on hastily, as I began to shake my head. "He was most insistent. He says you cannot possibly raise a babe here. The rats alone—" She shuddered. "They swarm the gutters at night."

"I'm more concerned about the rat badgering me for rent every week," I said, but she had a point. My apartment was run-down, infested with vermin. I had spread lye in the corners to smother the fleas and raised Maurice's bassinet on bricks, maintaining watch over him at night, armed with a broom to keep the rodents at bay. I was sacrificing my own sleep to protect him. He hadn't suffered so much as a sniffle, but the thought that he might fall ill terrified me. I would never forgive myself if my son suffered because of my pride.

I gave a nod. "Tell Dumas I will accept his offer, but only on the condition that he lets me repay him as soon as I can."

The cottage was charming, with a rose trellis over the doorway, squeezed between new apartment buildings and a boulevard carved out of the rubble of a demolished hamlet, renovations instituted by our emperor that were converting this western district into one of Paris's latest residential areas. I suspected the rent was far higher than I could ever afford, but Dumas was present to welcome me, looking diminished, thinner than I recalled, yet waving aside my concern as his hired men moved in my furnishings.

"If you're going to hold court," he said, when I stepped into the living area and gasped, finding it wallpapered in pristine white silk, with vases of fresh lilies and lilacs on every new marcasite-topped table, "you must hold it in style."

I hadn't planned on it, but I understood his intent. I could no longer evade my penury. I had Maurice to maintain, as well as Caroline and Madame G., for she had expended all her savings on me, along with most of her monthly pension.

Turning to Dumas, I embraced him. As he caressed my nape, I heard him murmur, "Ah, my little star. What I wouldn't give to be twenty years younger and ten kilos lighter."

I would have gladly taken him to bed as he was, out of gratitude and affection, for he was my one constant in a world that seemed to shift daily under my feet, but he laughed and told me he had others to satisfy his needs.

"I want more from you," he said, kissing my cheek. "You must become my Rachel."

Thus did I inaugurate my salon. Through Dumas and Nadar, I gathered a select roster—young aristocrats with a bohemian flair; foreign banking managers; artists without much money to spare but more than enough ambition to compensate; and the occasional theater critic, who wasted no time in promulgating the delights of my company to others in his circle. I accepted donations, of course, but my main focus was to cultivate a unique style, as Dumas had suggested. Because I couldn't afford a dressmaker, I began wearing eccentric ensembles cobbled from secondhand bazaars, combining male waistcoats with walking skirts and inventive hats I decorated with knickknacks, along with flamboyant scarfs. I adopted several street dogs I'd found scavenging in the neighborhood; I washed and brushed out their coats, then let them loose among my guests. Coming upon an old coffin at a rummage sale, I bought it on impulse— a narrow sarcophagus lined in tarnished satin, which I propped on a bunted dais and reclined in to greet my visitors, reciting the *Fleurs du mal* by Baudelaire. Nadar photographed me in it, and reproductions of the picture made their way into various shops, where women gasped in horror and purchased them by the dozens like an occult souvenir. Nadar gave me half the profits.

Encouraged by the attention and influx of money, I decided to hold private exhibitions of my paintings and sculpture, inviting other artists to exhibit with me, and also began organizing readings from unpublished plays. A few minor critics attended these readings and wrote about them, which put my name, albeit in tiny print, in the newspapers.

It was during one of these impromptu readings that I finally allowed myself to indulge that instinct, which had hampered me during my time at the Comédie. As I had no need to impress anyone save my callers, all of whom were delighted to grant me license, I invested my readings with my spontaneous interpretation of the character, avoiding unnatural declamation at the attendees and emoting instead to those reciting opposite me—all impoverished actors like me, in dire need of a contract—gazing upon the object of my despair or desire, and allowing the character to reveal herself.

Reveling in a confidence I'd never experienced onstage, I began to think that regardless of my reputation, perhaps the very asset which Provost believed set me apart also posed an insurmountable obstacle to my future employment. For me, acting wasn't a task steeped in mind-numbing denial of one's self; it was a willingness to plunge into my depths and allow myself to be vulnerable, to excavate my heart for my character's truth—even if it wasn't how things were done and most certainly not what Provost had taught me. It went against everything the House of Molière stood for, in fact, where the systemic application of tradition provided the sole path to recognition.

Dumas attended my readings, lending the occasions gravitas, and beamed in paternal satisfaction as the playwrights whose works I performed wept once I finished, telling me they were overcome to see their words brought to life in a manner they'd never expected.

"Did I not tell you as much?" he said to me. "You were born for the stage. It's in your blood."

"Unfortunately, no stage at the moment wants my blood," I replied. "Or rather, my blood is apparently all that will suffice to atone for my sins."

"It will happen." He kissed my cheek. "I've never doubted that one day you would become a great actress. Perhaps now, for the first time, you can believe it, too."

I wasn't certain of any greatness on the stage, but I was secure in devising an ambiance of sophistication unlike that of other courtesans. I refused to call myself one, in fact. I wasn't a woman for hire. I was an arbiter of art and its stimulating effect on our primal nature.

In my salon, the sole rule was *modernité*—to delight in the way of life of our modern age and fulfill our artistic responsibility to it.

Word soon spread, with invitations to my salon sought after by those seeking to forgo the habits of their fathers. Younger aristo-cratic men, as well as the sons of bankers and industrial magnates, flocked to my evenings of poetry, play readings, and art, to my in-formal seating on Turkish cushions spread on the floor, to my spir-ited debates on politics or the latest novel—everything that eschewed the pedestrian rigidity of the established demimondaine, who never offered an opinion worth heeding.

By 1866, word reached as far as the Comédie.

Paul sent a message. Provost had agreed to see me.

III

"You understand it's quite impossible," Provost informed me from across his desk. I had arrived punctually, knowing how he detested tardiness, but perversely also dressed in an iridescent crêpe-de-chine tunic with appliqué sleeves and an oversized coolie hat rimmed with tiny bells—a creation of mine, causing him to eye my ensemble with the same contempt he'd displayed during my instruction at the Conservatoire. "Leaving aside that disaster at the Comédie, you disregarded the terms of your employment at the Gymnase to flitter off to who knows where. And," he added, with a sniff, "these tales I hear of a salon, of poetry recitals from a coffin, and all sorts of déclassé people doing garish things. Do you think these gyrations can gain you a respectable position in the theater?"

I almost reminded him that my gyrations had certainly gained his attention, but lowered my head instead and set my hat to tinkling as I murmured, "I needed time to find myself, but I am here now. I intend to do whatever is required to prove my talent."

He harrumphed. "Can you turn back time?" But his sarcasm belied the faint hope I saw in his eyes. It sent a thrill through me. He had not forsaken me. Otherwise, he would never have bothered to reprimand me with such fervor. "You are irresponsible, careless, and too temperamental. You lead an impolitic life yet think no one notices—"

"Oh, no," I said. "I do not think it goes unnoticed, judging by the full-capacity attendance at my salon every evening." I spoke deliberately. As much as I needed his recommendation, I would no longer be bullied into marching to the Comédie's baton. I wasn't here to be reinstated by the Comédie; I was here to gain a reference to a more modern, if less acclaimed, playhouse.

His gaze narrowed. "*This* is what I mean, this utter disregard for the way things are done. You are not above the rules. Yet you behave as if you are, and thus I'm at a loss as to how I can recommend you to the Odéon, despite Monsieur Duquesnel's inquiry of you."

"He has inquired?" I bolted upright in my chair, making my hat chime like Notre Dame.

"Mademoiselle." He sighed. "Must everything be punctuated by those ghastly bells?"

Removing my hat, I ran my hands over my hair, which in the summer humidity sprang around my face in what I was certain was yet another display of my rebelliousness.

"He has," said Provost. "I would never have agreed to see you otherwise. Apparently, he is willing to offer you a contract." Again he sniffed. "It doesn't come as a surprise. Duquesnel is a known libertine who revels in the unconventional. He has turned the playbill of the Odéon into a rather unorthodox affair. However, his senior partner, Monsieur de Chilly, is not of the same caliber. And I understand you've encountered de Chilly before."

"I have?" The name eluded me.

"How quickly we forget. According to Duquesnel, you auditioned last year at the Ambigu for the role of a shepherdess in *La Bergère d'Ivry*. De Chilly was present."

"Oh." I slumped. One of the innumerable auditions I'd endeavored to forget, for I had arrived late, as usual, with breast milk stains on my bodice. De Chilly had cut me short, declaring me unsuitable for the part with the remark "Whoever heard of a shepherdess who never eats?" alluding to my slenderness, rather than my unmentionable past.

"I wasn't at my best. I was so tired from—" I cut myself short, not wanting to admit the truth. "There were kerosene lamps on-stage. It was so smoky I could barely see."

"One need not see in order to perform. Sight is the least of the senses one should employ—which you would know were your dedication as noteworthy as you claim."

I gave a deflated nod. Perhaps he had given up on me. Perhaps he'd only agreed to see me to unleash his vitriol for my past behavior, which had no doubt cost him his own share of grief at the Comédie, considering he'd championed me.

Then he said, "I must be assured that this time you truly intend to do as you say. I'll not be made a laughingstock again. If you wish to return to the stage, you must devote your entire being to it. Nothing less will suffice."

"I will. I want this more than anything."

"Wanting is not enough. In order for me to recommend you, I require more than the mere desire to succeed; every ingénue in Paris has that. What I require—no, I *demand*—is a dedication that precludes everything else: your salon and admirers; your painting or sculpture or whatever else happens to catch your fancy. Acting—and acting alone—must be your sole pursuit."

"Yes. I promise." Even as I spoke, my gut twisted at the thought of Maurice. I could relinquish my salon and its amusements, the lovers and money that came with them, or at least set them aside for as long as required. But my son—I couldn't just abandon being a mother to him. Yet if I accepted an offer from the Odéon, acting must come first, even before motherhood. Otherwise, I should leave now. I could not humiliate Provost with another failure.

Yet I did not rise. I did not thank him and make my exit. Although it sliced off a jagged piece of my heart, if this was the sacrifice I must make, I was prepared to do so.

He sat quiet for what seemed like an eternity before he said, "Before I will consider offering a reference, I must know why you left the Gymnase in the manner that you did."

I went still. If I lied and he later discovered the truth, he would repeal his support of me. Although he was no longer my instructor in practice, part of me felt he always would be, even if I'd learned that most of what he'd imparted wasn't how I wished to proceed.

"I was with child," I finally said.

He went quiet again. "I see," he said at length. "And this child is now . . . ?"

"With me. I am raising him on my own."

His expression underwent a curious softening. "You are very brave to admit this."

"Am I? It can't be so unusual. I should think other actresses you've known have found themselves in a similar predicament."

"Indeed. Yet not many would willingly reveal it to someone who can provide a reference for gainful employment." He pushed a sealed envelope across the desk to me. "My letter of recommendation. See that I do not regret it."

As I put the envelope in my fringed bag, he said, "A word of advice, mademoiselle. You mustn't allow the reason for your departure from the Gymnase to become common knowledge. Paris may be a large city, with others who share your predicament, but the world of the theater is very small."

Nodding at his advice, I replied, "I promise to make you proud. One day, you will tell everyone that you launched the career of Sarah Bernhardt."

His mouth twitched. "I sincerely hope so. Otherwise, Sarah Bernhardt shall be the one who regrets ever having crossed my path."

I proceeded directly to the Odéon on the Left Bank, near the Luxembourg Gardens, arriving with sweat dripping down my temples beneath my hat from the simmering July heat. Monsieur Duquesnel greeted me as if he'd been expecting my imminent arrival—an elegant man in a beige linen suit, with tousled fair hair and indolent hazel eyes, appearing to be only in his early thirties—younger than

I'd supposed—and evidently versed in wielding his considerable charm. Taking my hand, he lifted it to his lips. "*Enchanté,* mademoiselle. I've heard much about you, but your beauty is gravely underreported."

A practiced voluptuary, but I could tell by his smile that I was hired, reference or not. I was about to ask when I might sign the contract when he inclined toward me, his breath tinged with tobacco and mint. "My partner Monsieur de Chilly insists on meeting you. A mere formality, you understand, but required to conclude our arrangement."

He guided me to an upstairs office heaped with scripts and playbills, colorful posters of past attractions framed on the walls. From behind the desk, a small, bespectacled ferret of a man in a frock coat, with a bald pate and the demeanor of a banking official, snarled, "And who is this, if I may ask? Another of your strays?"

"My dear de Chilly," lilted Duquesnel, his hand still cupping my elbow, "this is the lovely young actress I mentioned to you earlier: Mademoiselle Sarah Bernhardt."

"Ah." De Chilly's scowl deepened. "The infamous girl of the Slap. I'll have you know, Mademoiselle Bernhardt, I don't believe you possess any talent. Scandalous ladies who wish to perform abound in this city, and we cannot hire every one. Were it up to me alone," he went on, with an accusatory look at Duquesnel, "you would not be offered a position here."

His supercilious tone brought back unwelcome reminders of every theater manager I'd encountered thus far, prompting me to say, "And were it up to you alone, I would not accept it."

Duquesnel chuckled, as if such acrimony between his players and his business partner was routine. "Now, now. Let us save the drama for the stage, shall we?" He motioned to de Chilly. "The contract." Then he paused, with some drama of his own, turning to me with an air of bewilderment. "I trust you are of age?"

I nearly laughed in his face. "Monsieur, I'm in my twenty-second year."

"You do not look it," he said, and de Chilly snapped, "The reference first. That is my condition. Either she provides a suitable reference or there's no contract."

Removing the envelope from the bag, I handed it to Duquesnel. He did not open it. "You see?" he said to de Chilly. "I have no doubt it's in perfect order."

"It's from Monsieur Provost," I said. "You will indeed find it in perfect order."

"Order or not, Provost owes me for this," retorted de Chilly. He yanked a paper from the stack by his side. Duquesnel inked a pen. Leaning over the desk, I signed, my belly fluttering as if I had swallowed a thousand butterflies.

I was an actress once more, employed at the Odéon.

"Now." Taking me by my arm, Duquesnel led me from the office, away from de Chilly's malevolent stare. "We must discuss the roles I'm considering for you. I believe we should start with . . ." With his murmur in my ear, I allowed myself to be seduced.

I understood. My roles were secondary. Sophie Croizette had recommended me as promised, and imparted extra incentive to pique his interest. He had heard of my salon and apparent willingness to perform, both onstage and off.

I did not care. If this, too, was the price required of me, I would pay it. He wasn't unattractive, and I sensed that, much like my suitors, he had no interest in permanent arrangements. No doubt, bedding new hires was a ritual he indulged by rote.

All that mattered was that I now build a career to eclipse all others.

IV

"I don't understand why you're so concerned," said Sophie. We walked in the Luxembourg Gardens, swathed in our cloaks as we took a brief respite from rehearsal. The chill of late autumn frosted the air, the chestnut trees shedding their foliage to lay a brittle carpet of russet and gold at our feet. "Yes, your performances haven't caused much of a stir thus far, but Duquesnel is steadfast in his support. He allowed you to interpret your roles as you see fit and even offered to pay your salary out of his own purse to keep you on, over de Chilly's objection."

I glanced at her. Sophie was vivacious and ambitious, but with none of the undercurrent of rivalry that characterized Marie, with whom we'd renewed our friendship and whose first comment upon seeing me again was an astonished "Why, Sarah, you're looking so well! I thought you'd given up acting."

She herself had not looked well. I noticed her bonnet was frayed at the edges, and she was diminished in appearance, betraying that she wasn't living as well as she'd planned, despite Samson's patronage—which she ought to have anticipated, given that actors, even those with senior status, were hardly paid well. As I recalled Sophie's warning about her, I also did not fail to mark her disappointment that I had resurfaced; nevertheless, she admitted her time at the Châtelet had been as inauspicious as mine at the Comédie, and she wasted no time in entreating us for a referral, saying she urgently required a change of venue.

I told her I was in no position yet to suggest new hires but once we returned to the theater, I asked Sophie to do so, instead.

"Sarah, why on earth would you want me to refer her?" said Sophie in surprise. "Marie only wants to come here to seek opportunity in whatever you may achieve."

I sighed. "Perhaps. But I can't forget we were once friends in our childhood. I refuse to be petty. Her silly jealousy hasn't served her at all, as you saw. She's barely making ends meet, and none of us should willingly cast a fellow player out into the streets."

"Your generosity is admirable," Sophie said. "I fear she'll not appreciate it."

De Chilly proved amenable enough, encouraged by a personal recommendation from Marie's patron, Samson, at the Comédie, though he might have questioned why Samson couldn't secure Marie a position there. And Sophie was right, for no sooner did Marie sign on at the Odéon than she set herself to making eyes at Duquesnel. As he and I were lovers, he ignored her advances, driving a deeper wedge between Marie and me. I might not have cared had there been mutual attraction between them; I hardly expected Duquesnel's fidelity, but I knew Marie had only attempted to seduce him to usurp my place in his bed and secure her tenuous new rank at the theater.

"I regret my generosity now," I told Sophie as we paused by a bench near the palace. "Marie seems determined to upstage me at every turn."

Sophie laughed. "I did warn you. Fortunately, Duquesnel oversees casting and Marie was hired only to play secondary roles. She can never challenge your position."

"What position? Duquesnel's affection thus far hasn't extended to my roles: Marivaux's *Jeu de l'amour*, with lines as ancien régime as the costumes. Then Armande in Molière's *Femmes savantes*—another ignominy." I blew out my breath in frustration. "I thought we were supposed to be an innovative playhouse."

"Sarah, you've been here less than a season." By the fountains, a gaggle of schoolchildren was being herded by nuns, making me think of Grandchamp. "Your role as Zachariah promises to be very innovative indeed," she went on. "No one has staged *Athalie* like this in ages, with the Greek chorus. Tickets have sold out weeks in advance."

I gave her a weak smile. I had campaigned mercilessly for the role of the high priest's young son. While it wasn't the lead, which Sophie had secured, it still required considerable skill, as I would be playing an adolescent boy murdered at Athalie's command. Many, including Voltaire, considered *Athalie* to be Racine's finest work, his final play about the King of Judah's widow, who abandons her Jewish faith—something I was familiar with—in order to rule. I'd been rehearsing obsessively, hoping my incarnation of Zachariah would finally earn me the notice I craved, if only to silence de Chilly's frequent demands that Duquesnel void my contract and put Marie in my place, for she had wasted no time ingratiating herself into de Chilly's good graces.

"You're going to be sublime." Sophie linked her arm in mine again. "You've been shining at every rehearsal. The entire company thinks so."

I didn't want advance praise from my fellow players. Praise was treacherous when I felt as though I might never amount to more than second-rate. I missed Maurice, whom I'd left in Madame G.'s care in Auteuil, rarely setting eyes on him, as my obligations required me to spend most of my time at the theater or in Duquesnel's townhouse. I missed Régine, now eleven years old and miserable with Julie. I missed my salon and my artistic pursuits, for which I no longer had the spare time. Looking back over the past four months, I doubted my willingness to return to this cloistered world where I so rarely felt at ease, where my every flaw was laid bare for others to scrutinize and tear apart.

"We'll see," I muttered, as we started to return to the theater. A swirl of snowflakes suddenly powdered the air. As I saw the nuns flapping their arms at their errant charges, the children ignoring them as they jumped about in delight at this magical manifestation of winter, I felt a pang, thinking that I was missing the chance to be together with Maurice during his first snowfall.

Sophie nudged my ribs. "You'd best do more than see. Marie is playing your sister Salomith. You must outshine her. Otherwise, she may take it into her head again to upstage you both in the play *and* in Duquesnel's bed. Now, that would be disastrous."

I had to laugh, despite the sense of peril her words sent through me.

Survival required that I make myself indispensable.

On opening night, I stood in the wings, dressed in Zachariah's tunic, oblivious to the chaos around me as I swallowed an acidic taste and fought off an inopportune resurgence of *le trac*. I hadn't experienced it since my return to the stage; I now understood it only beset me when I was about to embark on a role upon which I'd pinned too much hope.

De Chilly burst upon us moments before the curtain was due to rise. "Half the students for the chorus have failed to appear," he gasped, always in a fluster on opening night. "Some illness felled them, tonight of all nights. And with Sarcey in the front row!"

I froze. "Sarcey is here?" For a second, I feared I might actually vomit.

"Of course he's here," said de Chilly impatiently. "After all the attention lavished on this production, all the publicity Duquesnel insisted on, what else did you expect?"

Hearing his name, Duquesnel strolled over to us, as serene as de

Chilly was not. "We'll have to adjust the chorus. Can we make do with whoever has shown up?"

"No," de Chilly snarled. "Two boys with a cough do not a chorus make. We'll look ridiculous; the audience will jeer us out of the house." He started to swerve away when Duquesnel said, "Sarah can sing the refrain. She has exquisite tonality, and the training."

De Chilly gaped at him. "The *entire* chorus? She has her role to perform."

"There is no chorus when the players are onstage," Duquesnel reminded him.

Glancing at Duquesnel, I realized his intent. He sought advantage in the turmoil to exalt me, but surely he must also know Sarcey had savaged me when I was at the Comédie. To put me in such an untenable position might bring about the premature end to my career, as de Chilly himself declared:

"Have you lost your mind? A woman singing the chorus? Impossible." He scowled at Duquesnel. "I'll not abide doling out refunds for tonight's performance. It would be a disaster, after everything invested in the production. We'd have to close our very doors. Gather up the male players who are not in the first act and have them sing it. It won't be perfect, so we can only hope the play makes up for the defect. And do it fast."

He stalked off, leaving me with Duquesnel, who looked after him with a lazy smile.

"You can't be serious," I said, as he turned his smile to me. "The future of the house depends on this play. I'll make a fool of myself—"

"You will not make a fool of yourself," he said calmly. "None of the male players has your voice. I'm not sure they even know the entire refrain. You do. Best take your mark."

"But I'm not wearing a chorus robe," I protested, my dismay spiraling into panic. "I'm already in my costume!"

"Never mind that. There's no time. Sarah," he said, "I trust you."

I turned to the cast. Sophie gave me an encouraging nod, having overheard, while Marie, her face lathered in white pigment as my older sister, seemed about to break into a gloating smile. I hadn't seen it until now, not fully, her envy and secret hope that I'd fall flat on my face, clearing her way of a rival. The girl who'd once declared she never aspired to become a great actress had evidently lied.

Gathering my resolve as the orchestra tuned their instruments, I hastened to the other side of the curtain, where the chorus was meant to stand. I drew a deep breath, closing my eyes as the rush of velvet and creaking ropes announced the curtain's rise.

The cavernous vastness beyond, the sudden loss of sensation that always left me feeling as though I were submerged in dark water, overwhelmed me. Sarcey was here, the very man who'd helped ruin my fledgling career. He would recognize me, the disgraced *pensionnaire* whose sole accomplishment to date had been to strike a senior actress.

I missed my cue. As the music faltered, laughter drifted from the audience. Then the orchestra began the refrain anew and I stepped forward, envisioning my salon, my dogs running about, nipping at legs; the laconic men on my white settee, smiling, sipping brandy, as I regaled them with a music recital or declamation of poetry.

I began to sing.

The sound of my voice was disconcerting, seeming too light for the enormity of the house, lost in the muted maelstrom that made up an audience. Yet when no jeers ensued, no catcalls or insults, I grew bolder, lifting my voice higher, chanting of the sultry heat of Judea, the soughing of palm trees, and the buttresses of Athalie's fortress. I'd never believed I had a talent for singing, but the chorus music swept me up in its beauty, so that I forgot I stood alone on the stage, singing verses composed for more than a single voice—and not a woman's. Duquesnel had revived the play's original staging from the time of Louis XV, adhering to the purity of form Racine had intended, but to use only one person to sing the entire chorus—it was unheard of. In doing so, he had turned what was supposed to be an homage to the playwright into a controversy.

When I finished, I braced for the uproar. Sudden applause rocked me back on my heels. I stood, incredulous, as voices bellowed, "Brava!" and then a hiss came from behind me—"Off! The play is about to start"—and I scrambled backstage for the first act.

I didn't have any lines until the second act, when Zachariah made his entrance. But as I stood shivering, sweat dripping down my nape, Duquesnel looked at me from where he stood in the wings and his sardonic smile conveyed everything I needed to know.

"'Sarah Bernhardt is a revelation,'" I read aloud from Sarcey's latest newspaper column as Duquesnel reclined naked in bed. "'She charmed the audience like Orpheus.'" I pirouetted to his desk, retrieving the personal note I'd received from Sarcey after my numerous curtain calls. "And he wrote me this private message. He thinks I have a bright future ahead, should I continue in my present vein."

"Extraordinary," drawled Duquesnel, his eyes at half-mast. Reaching to the side table for one of his noxious cigarillos, he struck a match to it. "He has forgiven you. But, my darling, de Chilly will not soon forgive me for defaming *Athalie*."

"Why ever not? You saved the production. No refunds were required."

"Nevertheless." Duquesnel blew out smoke. "He gave me quite the scolding for setting you to singing the chorus alone. He believes it was too great a risk and now insists we must stage something entirely orthodox for our spring season."

Flushed by my success, I would not let de Chilly's sourness spoil the moment. "But he's already consented to Hugo's *Ruy Blas*, hasn't he? You've had the advance announcements distributed."

When he'd first told me about his ambition to bring Hugo's venerable drama to our stage, it plunged me into excitement. Perform-

ing one of the playwright's works was the crowning ambition of
every player, and *Ruy Blas,* set in seventeenth-century Spain, where
an indentured poet dares to love the queen, was considered his finest. Though ill-received by critics at its debut in 1838, it had gained
immense popularity among companies and audiences alike for the
beauty of its verse, and I'd begun to memorize my lines, determined
to win the role of the queen.

Duquesnel sighed. "Sarah, not even we can ignore that play's
message of political reform. Hugo took himself into exile to protest
Louis-Napoléon and is publishing critiques of the empire from
abroad; his very name has made him a rallying cry for malcontents.
De Chilly is adamant. As our emperor has come down against Hugo,
so must we. No *Ruy Blas.*"

"But you're our artistic director! Tell de Chilly it's your decision."

He chuckled. "De Chilly has majority stake in the company: that
means he controls our purse. I can't override him. It would be the
end of the company if I made a habit of flouting him at every turn.
Instead," he went on, before I could express my outrage, "he's
agreed to Dumas's *Kean.* I trust you will be satisfied if I cast you as
Anna Damby?"

I let out a gasp. "She's the female lead. De Chilly won't abide it.
What about Sophie?"

He gave an indulgent smile, as he might with a recalcitrant child.
"Sarcey had nothing laudatory to say about Sophie in his notice, did
he? She's competent, but not up to the task of Anna Damby. And de
Chilly is aware of Dumas's high regard for you. Leave it to me.
You've proved what you can do in *Athalie.* The time has come for
your leading role."

Tears filled my eyes. "Dumas will be beside himself with joy," I
whispered.

Duquesnel inched down the bedsheet, exposing his hardness.
"As I am. As you can see, Sarcey's praise has exerted a rather salu-
brious effect on me."

Throwing myself upon him, I surrendered to his lovemaking. But as he thrust himself into me and moaned, I was not thinking of his pleasure.

My only thought was of how I would soon astonish them even more.

V

Dumas's *Kean* was a tragedy about the famous English actor Edmund Kean, who had died only ten years before. My role as the young woman who earns his tempestuous affection was different from any I'd played—elegant and nuanced, perfect for displaying my versatility. But on opening night, anger erupted from the Left Bank students in the audience, who'd expected, as promised by our prior announcements (an oversight that de Chilly regretted with chest-pounding laments), a performance of Victor Hugo's *Ruy Blas*.

Standing in the wings in Anna Damby's dark blue gown, I heard the rioters clashing outside, the shouts of "Hugo! Hugo!" and thumping of their fists on seatbacks as our more civilized patrons hissed at them for silence. The hammer blows that preceded the curtain failed to stifle the uproar; as the students directed their harangues toward Dumas himself, seated in pride of place in the upper box, I thought he must be mortified to be accused of usurping the revered Hugo.

I spun to de Chilly. His bald head was dappled with sweat, his eyes wide with horror under his spectacles as he delayed the curtain's rise. "You must *do* something. Before they tear this entire house apart!"

He moaned. "What can I do?" Between his ubiquitous opening night nerves and the clamoring mob, he was about to collapse.

"You're the senior company manager. Go out there and threaten to call in the gendarmes. It was your decision, after all," I said, not without spite. "You canceled *Ruy Blas* to avoid controversy, and now we have your much-feared revolutionaries about to storm our stage."

"No. We must cancel the performance. It's the only solution. I'll not—"

"Cancel? After all our work? Certainly not!" Pushing past him, I strode through the curtains onto the stage, into a blast of roaring voices.

I stood perfectly still, glaring out at faces I couldn't see. Rabble. Muckraking louts. This was the theater, not a cheap tavern by the Sorbonne.

"We want Hugo! Down with imperial tyranny!" someone shouted. *"Hugo! Hugo!"* chanted the crowd, in voices so thunderous, the very chandelier rattled overhead.

Lifting my chin, I stepped to the footlights. Thinking this unruly crowd was fully capable of uprooting the seats to build barricades, I felt my hand quiver as I lifted it in a plea for silence—only when I looked, I saw my hand wasn't quivering at all.

They were just boys, insolent louts like those who'd ogled me in the Conservatoire, licking their lips and hoping I might tarry with them at the riverbank.

"Mes amis!" I called out. Another roar made me sharpen my voice to a whiplash. "Friends, silence please." As reluctant quiet fell, I forced out a smile. "You defend your cause for justice. Must you do so by blaming Monsieur Dumas for the absence of our esteemed Hugo? Surely we have room in our hearts in France for two master playwrights."

Someone laughed. I set a hand on my hip. "Now, shall I perform for you tonight or would you rather we brought in a guillotine to cut off some heads?" The laughter increased, along with a round of hearty applause. Looking into the front row, I caught sight of the dapper Sarcey, smiling cryptically up at me.

"Sarah. *Ma belle* Sarah, marry me!" bellowed a swain from the crowd.

"Propose to me later," I cried. "After the play."

Reeling around, I pranced back through the curtains, where de Chilly stood openmouthed. For the first time in our association, I had left him flabbergasted.

"Wait five minutes," I said. "Then lift the curtain."

Under Duquesnel's direction, and with advice from Dumas, who'd been so elated to hear I was playing one of his roles that he'd attended our rehearsals, I'd devised a unique portrayal of Anna Damby. Instead of the traditional victim, I transformed her into a stout-hearted muse. Having poured my very being into the role, I refused to be dissuaded by the lingering tension in the air as the curtain rose on the first act. But I felt it, even if there were no further outbursts. Dumas's clever tale of the caprices of success managed to capture even this intemperate audience, and when I took my curtain call, the applause was effusive, with bouquets of ragged rose stems flung at my feet, their blossoms missing because, during the earlier rampage, the louts had trampled over the flowers brought by my admirers.

The next day, Sarcey exulted in his column: "Sarah Bernhardt is a marvel—so natural in her style, innovative and unaffected. She may have tamed Kean onstage last night, but in reality, she tamed our Parisian lions."

De Chilly snorted when I showed him the notice. "Perhaps I owe Provost a debt."

To my delight, the writer George Sand, who'd been in the audience, approached the company to stage her work. She asked to meet with me in person. Now in her sixties, wreathed in a constant fog of cigarette smoke, she wore a dowdy dress, having forsaken her penchant for male attire. I found her intoxicating nevertheless, her declaration that "female ambition strikes a blow against society's obstacles" sending shivers down my spine. Madame Sand's ambitions had defied convention, her parade of lovers, including the composer Chopin, causing an uproar even as she forged a career in her own right. To me, she personified our *modernité*, where gender should pose no impediment to fulfillment.

"I fear I might die if I don't achieve my dream," I told her, passionately grasping her tiny hands in mine when she came to my dressing room.

She smiled, lighting another thin cigarette, her long-featured face showing a hint of jowls, but her dark eyes still piercingly youthful. "And what might that dream be?"

"To become the most celebrated actress in France," I declared. "More acclaimed than Rachel herself."

Until that moment, in my dressing room with my dented greasepaint tubes scattered across my scarred table and my costumes hanging like skins on hooks on the cracked wall, I'd never voiced aloud this deepest yearning that had driven me past every shoal. As soon as I did, I realized how absurd and vain it must sound.

Madame Sand contemplated me. "You're surely aware that in the theater, most especially in the house of your former employers of the Comédie, to seek recognition is the height of vulgarity—a degradation of one's dedication to the craft, and of the craft itself."

My voice quavered as I asked her, "What would you say, madame?"

She chuckled. "I would say that until one achieves the recognition, one will never obtain the dignity one deserves, especially if one is a woman."

I sagged in relief, having feared I might have offended her. She was perhaps the only woman I'd met since Mother Superior at Grandchamp whose respect I craved.

"Moreover," she said, "I believe you could be very celebrated. No other player on the stage has dared defy the ordained order as you do. You refuse to conform to expectation; this is why I want you to play the leads in my *François le Champi* and *Marquis de Villemer*. They are perfect for you, as I informed that toad de Chilly myself," she added, with a gravelly laugh.

With this coup, my future at the Odéon was assured. De Chilly agreed to renew my contract at two hundred francs a month. It was enough to pay my overdue bills, if not my outstanding debts, and see to my household.

Taking a respite for the Christmas season, I rushed home to be with my son. It was there, while I basked with Maurice and Régine, that fortune finally found me.

It arrived with my mother—of all people. She'd bestirred herself at word of my success, brought to her salon by Dumas himself, who'd wept openly over my portrayal of his Anna Damby. Escorting sullen Régine, almost twelve now and contrary as ever, Julie entered my home and gave my crowded living room a long, appraising look. Her gaze narrowed at my dogs, chasing each other and nearly upsetting the table on which sat the cage confining my new African gray parrot, Bizibouzon—a gift from Dumas. Bizibouzon cawed, shedding feathers and dots of excrement upon half-open boxes heaped under his cage, spilling chinchilla stoles, metallic-threaded wraps, and other items—all congratulatory gifts from my admirers—which I hadn't yet found time to acknowledge.

"Well," she remarked, in a tone she might have employed had she found me squatting over a firepot in a back alley. "You appear to be doing quite well for yourself."

"Not as well as you presume," I replied. "These are all gifts from my public, not from suitors."

Her eyebrow lifted a fraction. "Is there a difference, I wonder?"

Her apoplexy may have left her with a pronounced limp and reduced her salon to a few loyal intimates—Morny had recently died, leaving a bequest in his will for Jeanne—but Julie remained as impervious as ever. Dumas had extolled my talent to her, and she must have seen the notices of my performances by Sarcey in the newspapers, but as far as she was concerned, I was still her wayward daughter, her eternal disappointment.

Fortunately, I was now better equipped to deflect her sting.

While Régine played with Maurice, already on his feet and staggering about with stoic determination, obsessed by three pet turtles I'd adopted and let roam the house, Caroline served us tea. Julie eyed the silver pot with my initials as she tested the quality of the cups. "Limoges." She lifted her gaze to me. "Expensive. Yet you persist in keeping this quaint abode, so far from the center of town."

"I prefer it. I've no need for another residence."

"I should think not." She gave a tight laugh. "With this menagerie to attend."

I glared at her. "Must we?"

She sipped from her cup. "As you wish. You've always done as you pleased."

I sighed. "How is Jeanne?" I said, hoping a change in subject would ease the blade of resentment between us. "I thought you would bring her with you."

"Whatever for? She's with Rosine, of course, preparing for her debut."

My cup clattered onto its saucer. Dismay sharpened my voice as I took in her bloodless expression. "You wouldn't dare. She's— what? Fourteen?"

"Nearly sixteen. And unlike some, Jeanne has a care for her mother."

"If you require money," I retorted, "you need only ask."

She stiffened. "A mother should never have to *ask*."

Gritting my teeth at her insufferable tone, I went into my bedroom, banging my shin on my old coffin as I pulled open the bureau drawer. I deposited the envelope containing the first installment of my new salary onto her lap.

I met her cold regard. "I don't want Jeanne or Régine subjected to your salon. There's no reason. I'm making more than enough to see to their upkeep."

She pocketed the envelope. "Perhaps you shouldn't be so hasty. You've had some success of late, I'll admit, but this kind of life . . . it's hardly reliable, is it? The theater is not the real world, much as you may wish it so. How many older actresses do you know?"

"Plenty. No salon. Send Jeanne and Régine to Grandchamp, instead."

From behind us, betraying she had sharp ears despite her apparent obliviousness, Régine snarled, "I'm not going to some smelly convent." Then she let out a hacking cough—an ugly sputter I didn't like, as if whatever she had in her chest was too thick to expel.

"Is Régine ill?" I said, alarmed not only for my sister's sake but also because she was so close to Maurice, who'd abandoned the turtles to tug insistently at her skirts to join him on the floor. Although my son was a paragon of health, I was ever vigilant.

Julie shrugged. "She insists on running about without shoes. She catches cold."

"Then she must stay here with me," I said impulsively. "Madame G. tends to Maurice every day, and I now have Caroline. I'll enroll Régine in the local school for the new year." I refrained from adding that my sister desperately needed the oversight. Julie and Rosine had left her to her own devices too long; she had the demeanor of a street urchin.

"Whatever you say." Julie flicked her wrist, but she'd never do as I said. She might leave Régine with me because it suited her, but Jeanne was another matter. My mother had inculcated her sense of duty in my other sister, her perennial favorite, so much so that she had no compunction in offering her up to that pack of well-heeled wolves at the Opéra.

Before I could respond, Julie reached into her discarded cloak to remove a sheaf of papers. "I almost forgot. This parcel came for you at my flat a few days ago. I have no idea why. Perhaps whoever sent it thinks you visit me more often than you do."

I snatched it from her. "I suppose you've opened it, too, though it's addressed to me."

"Me? I hardly care," she said.

I lowered my eyes to the handwritten message scrawled across the top page:

Chère Sarah, My Coppée wrote this and I immediately thought of you. Shall we entreat D. to let us stage it together? It is a trifle, really, but so charming!

   Your friend, Marie

One of the Odéon's senior *sociétaires*, Marie Agar was an older actress of the sort my mother claimed didn't exist—and a kindly soul, who'd never shown me a moment of arrogance. François Coppée was her much younger lover, a civil servant, very thin and doleful, who sometimes came backstage to visit Marie, but had never said a word to me that I could recall. I would never have thought he was a writer, much less a playwright.

Turning the page doubtfully, I found the title: *Le Passant*, "The Passerby."

Julie looked up from her tea. "Another love letter from your adoring public?"

"A play sent by a colleague." Though I was intrigued, I made myself set the sheaf aside as if it were of no importance.

She waved her hand. "Far be it from me to interrupt your brilliant career." As I hesitated, taken aback by her unusual, if sarcastic, willingness to indulge me, she said, "It's not as if we have much more to say to each other. Don't mind me."

I almost smiled. Money. She had come here only for money, and now that she had it, she was merely passing the requisite time until she could take her leave.

Settling opposite her on my shawl-draped sofa, I read. It was indeed a trifle, as far as the plot: a troubadour in Renaissance Florence romances an aging courtesan on a moonlit terrace. The role of the courtesan was obviously intended for Marie; the seductive troubadour, Zanetto, I assumed, given my embodiment of Zachariah, was for me. While the story was hardly unique, the verse was marvelous, imbued with longing and bitter regret. The role of Zanetto, in particular, so enraptured me that I forgot my mother was still sitting there, drinking tea, until she said, "It's getting late. I have an engagement this evening."

I suspected she did not, but I accompanied her to the door, where she fastened on her cape and ignored Régine and Maurice as they rolled about on the carpet with my dogs.

"I'll send Régine's belongings over tomorrow. Including her shoes." She pecked my cheeks and limped out to her carriage without a backward glance.

I had Caroline take Maurice up for his bath, and turned my attention to Régine. My sister sat sprawled amidst the debris of her games with my son, plucking up her rumpled dress to reveal tattered stockings under her pantalettes. Her lace-up boots were flung aside somewhere; as she lifted her eyes to me, those strange eyes in which so little of what she felt could be read, I said, "*Ma sœur,* if you wish to live with me, you must go to school."

Régine scowled. "Why? Jeanne never goes to school."

"She may not, but I did." I crouched beside her, tucking her skirts down over her knees. "I enjoyed it very much. The nuns at the convent were so kind to me; they taught me many things. How to read and write. How to draw. Even how to act. You like seeing me perform on the stage, don't you? I first performed in a play at my school. Had I not attended, I might never have discovered that I wanted to be an actress."

She contemplated me, a furrow creasing her brow. "Julie says you only became an actress to defy her. She says you never cared for anyone but yourself."

I gave a start, not having expected these words to come out of her mouth. I realized in that moment that I'd never attempted to have an actual conversation with Régine, that in many respects, I'd treated her much as my mother did—like a feral creature who must be tolerated and subdued, lest she caused more upset than she was worth.

"Julie doesn't know me," I replied quietly.

"She doesn't love you," said Régine, again startling me. "Just as she doesn't love me."

Abrupt tears welled up in my eyes. I blinked them back. "Does it hurt you?"

She shrugged, looking down at her dress, her hands bunching up as if she wanted to ruck her skirts past her knees again. "Why should it? I've never loved her." She returned her gaze to me. What I saw there caught my breath. For the first time, I beheld the wounded child who'd always known she was unwanted, who'd never felt a mother's affection or care, just like me before her. I saw myself reflected in her strange haunted eyes, only the reflection was distorted, clouded by the helpless fear that Régine had converted into rage.

It was her sole defense against a life she couldn't understand. Unlike me, my sister had not found any outlet for the pain and grief inside her.

"You'll never abandon me, will you?" she whispered. "You won't send me away, as she did to you?"

"Never." I embraced her, pulling her taut body against mine, feeling every bone under her skin as if I held a captive bird. "I promise," I said, my voice thick with tears.

She clung to me. Against my chest, I heard her say, "I'm never afraid when I am with you, Sarah. I'm always afraid when I am not."

I understood then that she was as much my child as Maurice was. She had only me to safeguard her, to guide her past the chasm of Julie's indifference, toward a future she might make her own, if she discovered the will to do so.

I wasn't certain if she would. But while she had me, my sister must never fear again.

VI

"What do you think?" I said as Duquesnel finished reading and set down the play. Christmas had ended, and I'd eagerly come to the Odéon to find him bleary-eyed from the festivities, facing a stack of overdue invoices left on his desk by de Chilly to review.

"You say Marie's lover, that mousy clerk, wrote this?" he asked. When I nodded, he gave a wry chuckle. "Who would have thought? The man stamps papers at the Ministry of War for a living." He had read it very quickly, and judging by his slight grimace as he'd done so, I suspected he didn't share my opinion of it.

I leaned to him, stroking a lock of his fair hair back from his brow. We hadn't been together during the holidays, and I hoped my gesture conveyed enough seduction to soften the doubtful look on his face. "I think it can be a success. Love duets have such popular appeal, and it's only two acts, so it's perfect to inaugurate the charity benefit. A simple production. Two characters, one set. Marie Agar and I can provide our own costumes, and use whatever props we have here. It won't cost any money."

"Sarah, it's the theater. Everything costs money." He tapped his finger on the sheaf, his expression perplexed. "While our benefit is for charity, it precedes the opening of our season, so we must present a notable repertoire. No one knows who this Coppée is."

"Not according to Marie. She tells me he has numerous literary contacts and has already published a well-received volume of poetry. The staging of his first play will bring his friends to the house, which won't be bad for business. And you need something fresh to open the benefit. Don't you always inaugurate it with a new work?"

He leaned back in his chair to evade my caress, for he was no fool. "Unfortunately, I do need something. De Chilly has left it up to me, as usual. He doesn't countenance these benefits, claiming we should only hold ones that actually benefit *us*—though we can't ignore our civic duty. We receive government sponsorship and must contribute our share in return." He grimaced. "I optioned another work, but the writer is a drunk and claims he needs extra time to revise it. With our benefit less than three weeks away."

"Then the timing is perfect. This play is finished and has such unique charm—"

"Not to mention a unique character for you to stake your claim to before anyone else."

"Why, yes. It's not been staged."

Duquesnel eyed me. "All our wealthiest patrons will attend. I should think you'd be eager to perform something"—his fingers tapped the play again—"less inconsequential."

"I have a good feeling about it," I replied. "I can't explain why."

"Neither can I. It's not Hugo or Dumas, but under the circumstances, we have no other choice. I'm not about to issue another advertisement for new playwrights." Before I could declare my excitement, he added, "Nevertheless, I must consult with de Chilly first; I'm in no temper for another scolding. He might not wish to be bothered by the details, but if he dislikes what I select, I'm the one who must hear about it."

Seeing as I'd been the one to bring the play to Duquesnel's attention, de Chilly had to make an acerbic comment about allowing me more liberty than any player should be allowed. But with the other play unfinished and the upcoming season to oversee, he gave terse consent to opening the benefit with *Le Passant*, providing we saw to our own costumes and set décor.

With so little time to prepare, Marie Agar and I went to work. I paid out more than I should have for a custom-made doublet; I wasn't broad in the hips, so I could wear hose, but the doublet must be authentic. After poring over research books, I found an illustration of one in the fifteenth-century Florentine style, with white-satin slashing and dagged sleeves in crimson velvet, and a tailor willing to create it in the allotted time.

On January 14, 1869, our charity benefit opened to a full house. The annual benefit brought out the best in society, so that along with a beaming Coppée, Dumas and George Sand were also in attendance. None of us were prepared, however, for when de Chilly burst into our dressing room in a panic, exclaiming, "Her Highness Princess Matilde is here tonight, with several ladies of her court!"

"His Imperial Majesty's sister, no less," remarked Marie Agar to me, as de Chilly blustered out again, barking orders at the stage-hands. "Oh, Sarah—the princess herself is about to see our little play. My darling Coppée must be a bundle of nerves."

I could see she herself wasn't the least bit nervous. Dressed in a Renaissance gown from another production, she was delighted to be the center of attention. Her skill as a tragedienne had made her a staple in the company, but with the passing of years she'd been relegated to secondary roles. Tonight she was again the lead, in a part written to exalt her talents.

Except now, I must overshadow her with my own talent. With the emperor's sister in the audience, I had to steal the show.

We went to assume our places. In the wings, I adjusted my shorn hair under my cap. I'd experimented with various ill-fitting wigs until, in a fit of pique, I took a pair of scissors to my mane, shearing it to a shoulder-length page-boy cut. Duquesnel was horrified, but Marie Agar proclaimed it "enchanting," mollifying my dismay at my impulsiveness. I greased it enough to subdue its frizz, and in my new doublet and tights, I felt boyishly lithe.

The curtain lifted to tepid applause and the distinct murmur of ongoing conversation. Because the benefit opening always featured a new work, not a venerated classic, no one present expected much. Thinking I might have erred in my enthusiasm, I felt anxiety surge in my veins as Marie began her soliloquy in her rich, vintage voice and I awaited my entrance.

"'Commend me to summer nights,'" I sang out, striding onto the stage with a lute in my hand. "'For travel far and wide. A modest supper, such as hazard may provide, beneath an arbor set aglow by sinking sun . . .'"

I heard the sudden silence as the lure of the verse and Italian setting captured the audience's jaded attention. Too much plum pudding and seasonal cheer had made our Parisians maudlin; they were, as I'd hoped, ripe for this ditty that didn't require any effort on their part.

I had decided to put my instinct to the test. This was unlike my previous performances, as none, save for an unexpectedly absent chorus, had provided me the opportunity. My other roles had been weighted by significance, penned by celebrated playwrights and performed countless times before, but this part was new, and one I might make entirely mine. Avoiding the overt deep tonality and broad gesticulations that characterized a woman in a male part, I imbued my troubadour with a silken voice, feline gait, and deliberate sensuality. I knew my naturalistic approach might come across as inept, even ludicrous. An actress playing a man wasn't novel, but an actress obscuring her femininity in the part was. No actress wanted to *look* like a man while in a male role; they always exaggerated masculine traits to render them unrealistic, so their innate womanhood would shine through. I wanted to play Zanetto as a conniving youth fully aware of his beauty, who knows exactly how to captivate his hapless, older conquest.

And it worked. Before the curtain fell and the silence was shattered by a roar of applause, I knew whom it was I had truly seduced.

We took four curtain calls before we had to remove ourselves for the next performance. De Chilly exulted backstage that he'd known all along it would be a success; I refrained from reminding him that, as usual, he took credit where none was due. I was too elated to care. I'd not missed a single line. Zanetto had flowed out of me as if I'd been born to play the part. A troubadour created by a minor poet had proven what I could do.

Le Passant became an overnight sensation. The critics heralded its unassuming appeal, and my tremendous appeal in it, with de Chilly establishing it as a paid venue for the house. Tickets sold out weeks in advance as word spread. I didn't miss a single one of the 140 performances, not even after an impromptu conflagration from an errant candle ravaged my cottage, obliging me to seek a flat in the same suburb. I mourned the loss of my turtles—my son, sister, dogs, and parrot escaped, saved by Caroline—but I still went to work every night.

And Princess Matilde was so taken by the play that she eventually sent us an invitation to perform it for the emperor himself at the Tuileries Palace.

We waited for hours in the appointed hall while a reception for visiting dignitaries was held elsewhere. Marie was now beside herself with apprehension. I directed my nervous energy into my obeisance, practicing it over and over until Marie gasped under her breath, "Sarah," and I looked up to find Emperor Napoleon III striding toward us.

"I believe I liked the third curtsy best, mademoiselle," he said—a short, rather fat man with ginger-hued mustachios, a forked beard, and a receded hairline, clad in a formal blue uniform with a medal-bedecked sash. Behind him trailed a line of courtiers and his Spanish-born empress, Eugénie, all done up in ringlets and flounces. Rumor was that Louis-Napoléon had once romanced my idol Rachel; his watery blue eyes now gleamed lasciviously as Marie and I curtsied and went to the cloth-draped dais prepared as our stage.

After our performance, he congratulated us with unabashed enthusiasm. I didn't know the truth about his alleged liaison with Rachel, but I saw his empress turn away as he breathed in my ear, "My sister was right, Mademoiselle Bernhardt. You are indeed a rare talent." He lowered his voice, and his gaze, to my hose-sheathed thighs. "Were I not otherwise occupied, I might ask to see more of your exquisite charms."

On our carriage ride back, Marie Agar laughed. "You enchanted him! Did you see how he looked at you? *Mon Dieu*, the empress herself didn't fail to notice. You could be his lover, Sarah. Imagine the scandal. You'd certainly become Rachel's successor then."

I smiled. Dear Marie. Unlike her namesake, Marie Colombier, she'd not begrudged me a moment of adulation. I adored her for her selfless, and decidedly unthespian, ability to set aside her waning ambitions to see mine fulfilled. Of course, she'd reaped benefits, too, about to retire on a high note, yet she seemed genuinely pleased by my disproportionate success, which had indeed overshadowed hers.

"No doubt he says the same to every actress," I replied. "He's a Bonaparte, after all."

"Perhaps. But he did not try to seduce *me*."

The next day, our gallant emperor sent gifts—a bejeweled brooch for me, embedded with so many diamonds spelling out his initials that had I ever need to pawn it, the proceeds would keep me debt-free for years. Marie received an exquisite rope of black pearls. Within days, the newspapers were peppered with salacious innuendo that Louis-Napoléon had commanded me to court for a reprisal of my performance—in his bedchamber, no less.

Nonsense, of course, but nonsense that Duquesnel wasted no time in turning to our advantage. He had no compunction dropping hints to critics and journalists that I now shared my favors at court, not if it would fill our seats. As for me, I reveled in the attention. I'd worked hard for it, and now I wanted to savor every moment of it. What was the harm in being touted as the latest imperial paramour, of whom Louis-Napoléon had dozens? Gossip sold tickets, and with de Chilly's approval, Duquesnel prepared a roster of leading roles for me, under an extended four-year contract.

I was now earning enough to hire a cook to assist Caroline. I also reestablished my artistic salon. As the Odéon's newly minted lead actress, I must live up to the role. Rehearsals and performances took up most of my time, but after-work hours were devoted to my soirées, where I could make personal contacts and coyly respond to whispered inquiries as to whether Louis-Napoléon's prowess in bed was as tireless as rumor had it.

I threw myself into my work and my life, unaware that both were about to be eclipsed by tragedy.

VII

It started with Otto von Bismarck, the portly statesman appointed minister president of Prussia by King Wilhelm I. Upon uniting the fractious German states, Bismarck had rattled his saber over Austria and stirred up persistent talk of conflict with France.

I paid the disquiet no mind. I was about to perform in a new comedic play written exclusively for me by George Sand, titled *L'Autre*. The role promised another success, if I could get it right. Extra rehearsals were mandated by Duquesnel, who invested significant advance publicity in Madame Sand's play. Although she declined to impart advice or oversee rehearsals, she would of course attend the premiere. Everything must be perfect.

When Rosine unexpectedly arrived at the Odéon, racing into the theater as I rehearsed one of my most challenging scenes, her appearance startled me. She'd never so much as come to see me perform, so I ignored her as she stood panting below the stage, staring up at me, bunching her gloves in her hands until Duquesnel remarked, "Perhaps your house is on fire again," and motioned me to see why she was here.

I drew her aside. "Whatever is the matter? Can't you see I'm rehearsing?"

She whispered frantically, "You must come with me at once. Jeanne has taken ill."

I glanced over my shoulder. Duquesnel was frowning. "Is it so serious that it cannot wait until I've finished?" I said, turning back to Rosine. I had steered clear of Julie's ploy with my sister. I knew Jeanne had attracted her first suitor at the Opéra—and it was all I wanted to know. I vowed not to interfere, showing my displeasure by not visiting my mother if I could avoid it. Until now, I had avoided it—entirely.

"You must come." Rosine seized my hand. "Sarah, please. Jeanne needs your help."

Excusing myself with the promise to return as soon as I could, I accompanied Rosine to the flat to find my mother pacing outside the bedchamber, her mauve skirts making an angry rustle, her face pinched. She turned sharply at my entrance. "Why is *she* here?" Julie said to Rosine. "I can't imagine how you think Sarah can improve matters."

The insinuation that I'd only make matters worse alarmed me. I peeped into the bedroom to find Jeanne white as her nightgown, her hair matted with sweat as she moaned on her pillows and the maid applied compresses to her forehead.

"What's happened to her?" I turned back to my mother.

Julie lifted her chin. "What else? She failed to take the necessary precautions. We all fall in love so easily, it seems, until we must deal with the consequences."

I went still, meeting her impervious stare. "Are you saying she's with child?"

"Was. She took it upon herself to be rid of it."

"Dear God." My hand gripped the bedroom doorknob. "How?"

"With herbs, I suppose. Followed by a visit to a back-alley crone." Anger tinted Julie's cheeks, belying her careless tone. "Had she only come to me." She shot me a venomous look, laden with everything she'd never voiced about my own pregnancy. "It's really so simple to avoid these complications, if one seeks the proper advice."

I was trembling with rage. "When did you ever give us proper advice?" I hissed at her. "We must fetch a physician this instant." I started to the front door, needing to escape the flat before I completely lost control of myself and assaulted her.

Julie cut me short. "No physician. If there's any scandal, she'll be ruined before she's begun. She's young. Healthy. She will survive this, and learn her lesson while she's at it."

I drew to a halt, incredulous. "You cannot mean to let her suffer."

"The worst of it is done. Go back to your play," said Julie.

Rosine implored, "Julie, please. Sarah can pay for a discreet physician—"

"No." Julie stared at me, rendering me frozen with her spite. "I've had enough of her *charity*." She spat out the word as if it left a nasty aftertaste in her mouth.

Clenching my hands lest I actually strike her across the face, I said, "Then I will move in and care for her myself."

Julie flinched. "There's no need. Rosine has overreacted, as usual. Jeanne has a fever at the moment, yes, but she's expelled the—"

I took a step to her, taking savage pleasure in her recoil. "I'll have Caroline bring my pets, Maurice, and Régine. Madame Guérard is upstairs. We will stay here as long as required." I looked past her rigid stance to Rosine, who appeared about to weep in gratitude. "I'll need your help," I told my aunt. "I have a play to open. And while we are here," I added, returning my stare to my mother, "you will conduct your salon elsewhere."

I marched out before Julie could say another word, flinging open the front door with such force that it swung against the wall, cracking the plaster.

I must do this for my sister, I told myself as I hailed a hansom to the theater. For Jeanne's sake. Yet deep within, the residue of poison inside me started to drain, the last venom of my flight to Brussels leaving me at last.

This time, my mother would indeed pay for my charity.

Living with Julie, my aunt, my five-year-old son, my rambunctious dogs and squawking parrot, in addition to my rebellious younger sister, who detested the flat almost as much as she did Julie and made no bones about it, proved a test of my forbearance. Rosine rallied to my order that Jeanne must be attended at all times, washing her with a tincture of chamomile and feverfew to ease her malaise, and ensuring her sheets were changed and laundered daily. Jeanne slowly began to show improvement, sipping broth and gritting her teeth from the spasms in her private parts. The bloody discharge had ebbed, though whatever she'd done to herself had caused damage. It would be at least another month before she was back on her feet.

Julie went about her days as if I didn't exist, but it was her utter lack of outward concern for Jeanne, whom she'd treated so preferentially, that most infuriated me. If I could have thrown her out into the street, as she'd so often threatened to do to me, I would have. Only her agreement to not entertain at home and Rosine's constant presence upheld our uneasy stalemate, my aunt murmuring that Julie wasn't uncaring, but Jeanne had gone and done the unforgivable, giving herself so recklessly after she'd seen what could happen—

"Did she have a choice?" I said, glaring at my aunt. "Did Julie ever ask *her* what she might want? No, Julie did not. Nor did she give Jeanne any advice on what might happen other than what she gave me, which is scarcely enough to prevent a chill, let alone a child." My voice caught. "Julie should never have put her in this position."

Upon my inquiry, Jeanne refused to disclose her suitor's name. I didn't press her; it made no difference, but my anger was so fierce, resurrecting memories of my humiliation by Kératry, that I poured my turmoil into my play, creating a performance that critics hailed as my most accomplished yet. Madame Sand was delighted, as were Duquesnel and de Chilly, who raked in record receipts. Ironically, my fame increased, even as I raced from the theater to my mother's flat every night, losing too much weight and fueled by nerves.

Finally, Jeanne was well enough to leave her sickbed. Before Julie could reassert her authority—I knew she'd dress Jeanne in white and send her back to the Opéra, regardless that my sister had scarcely recovered—I announced that upon the closing of my play in mid-August after sixty-five shows, I would take a respite. I was exhausted from work and the situation at home, but still worried enough about my sister that I invited the family to join me. We would spend a week enjoying the healing waters of Vichy; as I offered to pay the expenses, I thought no one would protest.

Naturally, Julie did. "Absolutely not. Jeanne is in no state to be seen yet in society."

"Vichy is not society," I said through my teeth. "It's a spa. Where sick people like Jeanne go to take the cure."

"No." Julie turned from me. "I forbid it."

"You must go instead," urged Rosine, as my mother walked away and I contemplated hurling a nearby vase at her departing figure. "You're so thin. You barely eat or sleep. You go to Vichy and we'll care for Maurice and Régine."

"Never," I said.

I returned with Caroline, Régine, my son, and my dogs to my flat. Caroline offered to come with me and look after Maurice and Régine in Vichy, but it was a spa, after all, with no activities for children, so Madame G. dissuaded me. "They'll be bored to tears and will distract you. Leave them with us. You never have any time to yourself."

I hesitated, not wishing to part from my son or sister, even though it was just for seven days, which was all my contract allowed. The Odéon had closed for midsummer repairs; once I returned, I would embark upon the extended season Duquesnel had prepared for me.

Upon my shoulders now rested the house profit. They had anointed me their lead actress and neither he nor de Chilly was going to let me forget it.

Packing my bags after a tearful farewell and strict instructions to Caroline to see that Régine attended to her studies and Maurice didn't spend every minute romping with our dogs, I boarded the train to Vichy for what I hoped would be a restorative holiday.

VIII

"Ridiculous!" I flung the newspaper with the blaring headline onto the glass-topped table in the resort's atrium. Finches chirped in cages over stone urns spilling ferns, as immaculate waiters circulated with pitchers of the sulfurous waters, but Vichy itself had emptied overnight, the news that Napoleon III had declared war on Prussia sending vacationers rushing to the train station to return home. I wasn't pleased. Here I was, looking forward to a respite, and the moment I left Paris, the entire world imploded.

Across from me sat a well-upholstered matron of Madame Nathalie's ilk, all bustle and ringlets despite the heat. She peered at me over her pince-nez as if I'd stepped on her hem, then at the paper I'd tossed aside. She let out a sigh. "His Imperial Majesty must defend our honor. France has been sorely impugned by those dreadful Huns."

"Must he do it while I'm on holiday?" I said, and she gave an indignant huff.

Yet he had, nevertheless, and I began to fret. Caroline was devoted to Maurice and Régine, but she couldn't be expected to oversee them in a city thrown into upheaval by fear of war. I should return, even if it couldn't possibly be as terrible as the newspapers claimed. How could our emperor endanger us by fighting Prussia? It was inconceivable. No doubt this was just more of that insufferable saber-rattling by that menace Bismarck and boastful posturing in return by Louis-Napoléon. Still, I couldn't dismiss it entirely out of hand, lest I risk being stranded in Vichy should the inconceivable turn out to be true.

Packing up my valises, I braved the infernally crowded station, bartering, demanding, then begging and overpaying for a spare ticket on the last overbooked train to Paris. I had to stand the entire way, my valises at my feet. There were women clutching handkerchiefs to their tearful faces; ashen husbands, brothers, and lovers sat rigid at their sides, no doubt already envisioning themselves charging across the battlefield in full dress uniform to defend our alleged impugned honor.

It made me sick. I thought it a lunacy of the highest order and was relieved I didn't have to sit across from one of those stalwart gentlemen as he comforted his distraught wife, muttering of intolerable Prussian aggression. I wasn't one to hold my opinions to myself, so it was just as well that I was left to sway like a maidservant in the corridor.

Once we arrived in Paris, my disdain crumbled. A pall of smoke obscured the sky, but no one seemed to know exactly what was happening. Rumors ran amok that the Germans were about to assault the city, and Parisians had responded as one might expect at such a terrifying possibility. With utter disregard for any facts or reason, those who could closed up their houses, flung themselves and their families into hansoms or private carriages, loaded up carts with their valuables, and fled to the countryside.

Locating a spare hansom at the *gare* proved futile. The clamoring multitude brandished fistfuls of francs, depositing entire bank accounts into coachmen's laps for the short ride across the Seine. I might have walked, but I had no place to store my luggage, without risking it being stolen, as pandemonium reigned in the station. I counted myself fortunate when a passing milk vendor saw my frantic waving and stopped. Thrusting my fare at him, I clambered into the back of his cart amidst rusted tins and the sticky residue of milk spills, perching as best I could and holding on for dear life as he drove me toward my mother's district. I reasoned it was the logical place to start; I could commandeer Julie's private equipage to go to my apartment, reunite with Maurice and Régine, and decide what to do next.

"Is it true the Prussians are upon us?" I asked the grizzled milk vendor. His beret was jammed about his ears and a cigarette dangled between his lips.

He snorted. "Do I look like Louis-Napoléon's general to you, mademoiselle?"

"But all this smoke in the air . . . it's not from their cannon fire?"

"Our new government has seen fit to torch the Bois de Boulogne and every other tree within fifty miles of the city," he replied. "No forage must be left for the enemy." He gave me an acerbic look. "Not that anyone has set eyes on the enemy yet."

Once we arrived in Julie's arrondissement, the smoke dissipated. In its place, an eerie calm prevailed. The chestnut-lined streets were deserted; a discarded newspaper bearing the dreadful headline fluttered down the pavement in an unfelt wind, that stir of empty space that could be so unsettling, when everything went quiet, still, like an audience in a darkened theater, waiting for the play to start.

"Where now?" he asked.

"Up ahead." I pointed to the building. There was no one outside. Where had everyone gone? Were they all indoors, huddled under the tables, waiting for Prussian cannonballs to shatter their windows?

I leapt from the cart as soon as he reined his nag to a halt. Grappling with my valises, I found the building's entry door ajar. The foyer was empty. As I heard the clip-clop of hooves on the cobblestone road grow fainter behind me, the hairs on my neck stood on end. Times past, this district had been so full of pedestrians and the clattering of carriages, I would never have discerned the sound of a single cart.

Standing in the foyer with my bags heaped about me, I called out.

My voice echoed into the vacancy, increasing my alarm. Where *were* they? Surely my own family had not been so reckless as to depart the city without sending me a telegram—

Footsteps came clattering down the staircase. When I saw Madame G. peering over the wrought-iron balustrade above, I breathed again. "Finally. Come, *ma petite dame,* help me with these bags."

She inched down the stairs, glancing at the door at my back as if she anticipated an eruption. Scowling at her, I handed her two of my smaller bags while I shouldered the valise, climbing the staircase to Julie's door. When I paused, she said, "They're not here."

I stared at her. "Where have they gone?"

"I don't know. Your mother . . . she took them. She said . . ." Madame G. faltered.

"What? What did she say?"

I expected a hasty explanation that, given the situation, Julie had decided to escape to some mountain haven before she and Rosine found themselves entertaining Prussians in their salon, until Madame G. muttered, "She said, why should you be the only one to take a holiday? You'd barely walked out the door for Vichy when she decided to leave, as well."

I wanted to kick my mother's closed door with my pointed ankle boot. "Let's go upstairs. I must sit for a minute."

In her flat, I dropped onto the sofa as Madame G. brought me a tepid cup of tea and a plate of stale macaroons. I noticed boxes on the floor, haphazardly filled with a mishmash of items, as if I'd caught her in mid-packing.

"What is all this?" I asked sarcastically, though I already knew.

She made a helpless gesture. "They say we're in danger. I thought it best to prepare."

"By packing up your books and . . . is that Froufrou's pillow?" Her beloved cat had died years ago. "Honestly. The Prussians are not invading. Everyone has gone insane."

"But there is a war." A tremor crept into her voice. "We are at war with Prussia."

"The emperor might be at war. We are not." I drank my tea, trying to steady my nerves. Julie had left with my aunt and Jeanne, taking her equipage, of course, and I needed reliable transport to my apartment. I supposed I could walk, but as soon as I mentioned it, Madame G. exclaimed, "Oh, you mustn't! It's too dangerous to be out in the streets."

"Do I look like a Prussian soldier to you? Who will trouble me? I must fetch Maurice and Régine. They're with Caroline. . . ." I paused as she averted her eyes. "What is it?"

She shook her head in mute distress.

I almost lunged at her before she said, "Your mother took them with her. She had Caroline bring them here. I'm so sorry, Sarah. We did tell her you must be informed, but you know how adamant Julie can be. She said as you went away, forsaking your obligations, why shouldn't the boy and Régine go with them? Régine was most unhappy about it."

I clenched my hands so tightly, my nails cut into my palms. "How dare she? *Where* are they? Where did she take them?"

"She didn't say." Madame G. looked ready to abase herself. "But I'm certain wherever they are, it must be safer than here."

"With a war about to explode around us?" I cried, and as my voice resounded in her garret, I realized all the worry I'd kept at bay had finally overwhelmed me. I felt light-headed, on the verge of frenzy. My son, my child—he was with Julie, while I was here, in a city about to be invaded.

"What shall I do?" I said, loathing my own helplessness.

"Stay here with me," quavered Madame G. "What else *can* you do?"

After three days of seclusion, I couldn't abide another moment. The Prussians weren't marching in yet, I informed Madame G., and I decided to make my way to the Odéon. I needed information. Afterwards, I'd proceed to my flat on the rue de Rome. I was worried about my pets and could only hope Caroline had had the foresight to tend to them, as she hadn't with Maurice and Régine. Madame G. kept telling me that my maid had no idea what Julie was planning when she was summoned to bring Maurice and Régine, and she burst into tears when Julie snatched my son and sister from her, then sent her away.

Perhaps, but I was still irate. I thought my mother must have mentioned where they were headed, but in the fluster of the moment, Madame G. failed to hear it. If Caroline knew where my son and sister were, I was going to fetch them myself despite the entire Prussian army or even King Wilhelm himself. Even if I had to walk the entire way.

I soon discovered it wouldn't be so simple.

Hailing a carriage was impossible, for there were none to be found. I had to trudge on foot to the 4th arrondissement, my feet blistering as I tried to wave down overladen carts and anything else on wheels, to no avail. As I neared the Odéon, I saw the marquee empty, the glass-enclosed placards by the ticket office displaying shreds of last season's playbills.

Then I began to notice the men in tattered blue and white uniforms, so covered in grime and rusty splotches that at first I thought they were vagrants who'd stolen military attire. Some held each other upright, staggering down the boulevard, the few passersby going out of their way to avoid the pathetic sight. Others huddled in exhaustion in the Place du Châtelet before the Odéon, gaunt and bleary-eyed, too tired to even reach out their palms to beg for a sou.

As I passed them, I couldn't stop staring. Like inert mounds, they lay there; like refuse, discarded and left to rot. The sight of their haggard, haunted expressions drove through me like a blade. These were not vagrants. These were our soldiers, sent by our emperor to fight for our cause. I had no idea why they were here and not off killing Prussians, but in that moment, it didn't matter. How could they be left unattended like this? Had we lost all sense of duty or pride?

At the theater, I banged on the front doors until a rheumy stagehand with cataract-filmed eyes cracked open the portal. "I'm Sarah Bernhardt," I barked at him. "Let me in this instant." Inside, I found the Odéon in dismal shape, already a ghost, the chandeliers draped in dust cloths, the detritus of the interrupted repairs—stepladders, hammers, and pails with hardened plaster—strewn about like the relics of an apocalypse.

The stagehand responded to my pointed inquiries by telling me that the directors had closed the theater and were preparing to depart Paris. He didn't appear to recognize me.

"But they haven't left yet?" My voice caught as I began to understand the situation must be dire indeed for de Chilly to abandon his place of business. Duquesnel, yes; I could see him leaving. He wouldn't want to be caught up in any trouble, but de Chilly always kept an eye to profit. If he'd forsaken this theater, where he spent more time than with his own family, the situation must be more severe than I thought.

"Monsieur Duquesnel is still here—" the stagehand started to say.

I bolted past him to charge up the main staircase, past the second-tier boxes to the third floor, where the offices were located.

When I burst in, my heart in my throat, Duquesnel looked up wearily from a stack of papers on de Chilly's desk. "Sarah. I thought you were in Vichy."

I looked around him. The office was in disarray, drawers yanked open, the safe where receipts were stored open and empty, papers strewn everywhere, as if a windstorm had gusted through the room and overturned anything not bolted to the floor.

"We're at war," I said, breathless.

"You heard." He looked as tired as the soldiers outside, his shirt collar askew over his rumpled waistcoat, days of stubble on his cheeks, and his eyes sunken in shadow. The sight of him only added to my alarm; ever the dandy, Duquesnel would never before have let himself appear so disheveled. "Not the most opportune time to return, I'm afraid. I was just finishing up here. We are, of course, closed until further notice."

I drew in a shallow breath. "Is it truly so bad?"

He gave an arid chuckle. "Sarah, we've lost the war. The emperor was defeated and captured at Sedan. A new government has declared itself as our Third Republic and removed itself to Tours, leaving us under the defense of the National Guard, which vows we must never surrender, for whatever that's worth. A catastrophe. The end of France as we know it. Did you not see the soldiers outside or read any newspapers? The Prussians are a day or so away. Within the week, Paris will fall under siege."

I had to reach for a chair, though I couldn't sink onto it. Duquesnel came forth and toppled the pile of playbills on it to the floor. "Sit. You look like a catastrophe yourself. Why did you come back? You should have stayed in Vichy."

"My son . . ." Tears sprang to my eyes. I couldn't stop them as I choked out the news that my mother had taken Maurice away with her to who knew where.

Duquesnel lit a cigarette and handed me his case; I rarely smoked, finding the vice, as so many vices, more enticing to behold than indulge, but I now took one, striking the match with a trembling hand and coughing on the acrid inhale.

He regarded me. "If Maurice and your family have left, it's for the best. You should leave, too. Our new government may vow to resist, but we have no emperor. No order. A provisional government is only that. Whoever stays in the city is doomed."

I returned his gaze. The resignation in his expression enraged me, bringing back the haunting sight of all the men outside in their soiled uniforms. "Like those soldiers in the Place? Are we going to let them just die there? Let Paris die? Let France die because of Louis-Napoléon and his absurd nonsense?"

"Really, Sarah, I don't see what we can do about it." Duquesnel turned back to sorting through the papers on the desk. "We'd barely started the repairs before this absurd nonsense, as you call it, erupted. We can't stage plays to an empty house and—"

"Who said anything about staging plays?" I cut in, with more censure than he deserved. He'd been a complacent lover and champion, so I should have shown some empathy. After all, he only stated the obvious. Instead, I had to swallow my disgust at his cowardice, his unwillingness to look beyond his own interests. "If the theater is closed because of this silly war, we might as well put it to good use."

"Good use?" he echoed, as if I'd uttered an obscenity.

"Yes. Those soldiers out there fought for Louis-Napoléon. For us. They need our care. Why aren't they in a hospital where they belong, rather than left to wander like beggars?"

He sighed. "Every hospital is full. We have more wounded soldiers than beds to accommodate them. What part of our defeat and the Prussians coming to lay siege do you fail to understand? Most of Paris is fleeing as we speak."

I stood, stubbing my unsmoked cigarette in his ashtray. "Then we must care for the soldiers here. We'll turn the theater into an infirmary."

"An infirmary? Here? Go home, Sarah. Fetch whoever is left of your family and get as far away as you can. This is not the time to play the lead actress."

I stepped toward him, my heels crushing the playbills underfoot. "This is our city. Our country. We *must* do something. I have nowhere to go. Those soldiers have nowhere to go. And *you* have nowhere to go. We can do this much. I'll oversee everything," I said, focusing on the despair beyond our doors and this shred of hope, of purpose, to move forward amidst the incomprehensible. "Do you want us to be called cowards who abandoned our nation in her hour of need?"

"I hardly think our cowardice is of any concern," he replied, but his voice thawed. "An infirmary . . . De Chilly will have an apoplexy. But," he added, "the House of Molière will have an even greater one, once they hear we opened our doors to wounded soldiers. The Conservatoire has already been requisitioned as a military ward, so your suggestion is, as always, inconvenient, but the height of current fashion."

I had to stifle sudden laughter. Publicity. He never failed to glean an opportunity. I didn't care, reprehensible as it might be. Whatever moved him, providing he allowed it.

"True. And once this war is done, we'll be called heroic. Imagine our box office then."

"Or fools who let themselves be trapped in a city under siege." He paused. "How do you propose to go about it? We'll need supplies. Food. Cots. Dressings and medicine. Nurses and doctors, if you can find them. You'll have to offer something in return."

"I can sell the jewel Louis-Napoléon gave me," I said, thinking quickly "We can also request donations from those of our patrons still in Paris. They know my name; they came here to see me perform. Surely not everyone has fled yet. And our new government cannot want our legions dying in the streets; it's terrible for morale. I'll petition whomever I must. If the Conservatoire has been requisitioned, they must be in need of more infirmaries."

He let out another sigh. "I suppose you can try. The National Guard has set up its headquarters in the Tuileries. As for de Chilly, he's in no position to complain, as he left the city three days ago. But," he said, as I turned to the door, "you must oversee everything yourself. And if the situation becomes as dire as I believe it will, we cannot stay. We may not have anywhere to go, but once the Germans march into Paris, we'd best find some place to hide, because they'll grant us no quarter."

I glanced over my shoulder at him. "Can I use your fiacre?"

"Yes." He lowered his eyes to his papers. "Be careful. A horse and carriage are more valuable right now than your imperial jewel."

The driver wasn't amused, but Duquesnel had given his permission, so the ill-tempered man had no choice other than to convey me to the rue de Rome, whipping his horse into a lathered froth and shouting dire threats at anyone who sought to impede our passage. Not that anyone did. Paris looked deserted, our once-lively streets devoid of activity, the cafés and restaurants shuttered, with only a few stragglers crossing our path, pushing wheelbarrows piled with belongings, though where they intended to go with their candelabras, fine china, and paintings was a mystery to me.

While I gripped the fiacre's upholstered leather seat as we rattled over the cobblestones, the reality of what we faced clutched me like a talon. Paris was bracing for the unthinkable: a foreign army, glutted on carnage, marching toward us to sack us into submission. I could only imagine the hysteria at the *gare* as people clamored to get onto any remaining trains, perching upon the very carriage rooftops, providing they could get that far. But not everyone would escape; not everyone had the means or a place to escape *to*. A siege might be horrible, but being trapped in the countryside by an encroaching Prussian army would be worse. At least in Paris, we had some form of resistance. This provisional government must have troops at the ready. Here, we could shelter in place as our forces battled the incoming assault.

Or so I kept telling myself as the fiacre came to a halt outside the building of my new apartment, barely occupied by me since my cottage had burned down. After instructing the scowling driver to wait, I climbed the stairs to the second floor, rummaging in my bag for my keys when the door creaked ajar.

Caroline's wan face peered out from behind the chain latch. "Mademoiselle Bernhardt?" she said, as if she, too, failed to recognize me.

"Who else? Undo the latch this instant."

As soon as I entered my apartment, which was submerged in gloom from the curtains drawn over every window, my four dogs rushed at me, barking and yelping, leaping up to be petted, lavishing me with desperate affection. As I caressed them, their ribs were palpable under their lusterless fur.

"Are you starving them?" I whirled toward Caroline.

"Not at first, but . . ." She kneaded her dress. She looked no better, thin and very pale, as if she'd been secluded indoors for weeks. "There's no more meat in the shops."

"How can there be no meat?" I declared, but my indignation was muted. I'd left her plenty of money, but if food was growing scarce, francs couldn't be eaten.

She let out a moan. "I tried to stop her, but she insisted, even though I begged her to let me notify you first. I would have gone with them, but the dogs, your parrot . . . How could I abandon them here?"

"You might have asked Madame Guérard to care for them," I said, as the dogs sat at my feet, gazing imploringly at me as if I had steaks stashed in my pockets.

She nodded in abject misery. "I didn't think of it."

"You certainly did not." I forced myself to soften my voice. "But I know my mother too well to believe you might have prevailed against her." I paused. I feared the very question, but it had to be asked. "Do you know where they went?"

"To Holland. To visit your grandparents, she said."

"Impossible. I don't recall her once mentioning my grandparents, even in passing."

"She claims she's been sending them money all these years. She said it was time they met their granddaughters and her grandson in person."

I clenched my jaw. "The nerve. *Her* grandson. Whom she called a bastard to my face before throwing both of us out of her house."

"But he's safe," said Caroline. "There's no war in Holland, is there?"

"Not until I get there." I heaved out a sigh. "There's nothing to be done about it now. Pack your things and leash the dogs. And my parrot. Cover his cage. We're leaving."

"To Holland?" she said, in astonishment.

I snorted. "To my mother's flat. She left Madame Guérard an extra set of keys. I want dog hair and bird droppings on every one of her settees and rugs. Once we settle in and I attend to what needs to be done, then we shall go to Holland to fetch my son."

Ignoring the driver's protests, I instructed him to strap the valises to the back of the carriage as Caroline, my dogs, and I squeezed onto the seat, my cawing parrot in his cage on my lap. We were driven at jolting speed to my mother's district, the driver so furious by the time we arrived that he was spewing threats of getting caught by the Prussians while ferrying me back and forth. I gave him a handful of francs to mollify him and coax him to help us lug the valises to my mother's door.

Madame G. went white at my demand, but she unlocked the flat. Unfastening the leashes, I watched my dogs bound into my mother's salon, catching Maurice and Régine's scent and tracking them all over the apartment, mournfully howling when they failed to locate my son or younger sister.

"Food," I said to Madame G. "They've not eaten in days."

"We won't, either, if we give them what we have. Sarah, all the market stalls are empty. Whatever is available is extremely overpriced—" At my glare, she went silent.

We fed the dogs. The poor creatures devoured the boiled chicken we served on my mother's china, and Caroline filled my mottled parrot's dish with apple slices.

"Now what shall we do to sustain ourselves?" said Madame G. "That was all we had. Besides the vegetable soup on my stove, the larder is empty."

"We'll make do." I sat on the settee, cradling my lapdog Lulu as she gratefully licked my face with her poultry-tinged tongue. "You and Caroline will go out tomorrow to buy up whatever you can find, while I go to the Tuileries to petition this new government of ours."

"Petition?" Madame G. regarded me, aghast, as much at my statement as my command that she must venture into the city with Caroline. "What for? They won't give you a thing. We're at war; whatever they have must be reserved for the soldiers."

"We'll see about that." Exhausted, I closed my eyes, snuggling my dog close.

I didn't know if they would grant me anything or shout me out of the headquarters, but I wasn't going to take refusal for an answer.

IX

Sandbags barricaded the Tuileries. Volunteer soldiers patrolled the grounds, clad in an assortment of ill-fitting garments and armed with assorted weaponry. At least not every able-bodied man had deserted us in our hour of need, but my courage quailed as I presented myself at the front gate and was led into an inner courtyard and before an imposing desk, there to impede unauthorized entry. The able-bodied men stared at me in my bonnet and bustled skirts, for I'd dressed for the occasion and the weather. It was unusually cold for September, with the bitter frost of winter already chilling the air.

The officer seated at the desk ran an ink-stained finger down a list scrawled in a ledger. "No," he said. "We have no Sarah Bernhardt here."

Despite my ire—was he deaf?—I repeated in as sweet a tone as I could muster, "I'm not on your list because I'm not expected. I'm here on official inquiry, however. I am the lead actress at the Odéon and we wish to open a—"

"Actress?" He chortled. "You're early. The siege hasn't started yet. Wait awhile. You may be of use later." His intimation was crude, causing the soldiers nearby to guffaw.

I lifted my chin. "Who is in charge here, my good man?"

"You're looking at him, mademoiselle. At your service." As he leered, I said again, in a far less dulcet tone, "*Who* is the prefect of this establishment? You've no idea whom you are addressing. I once performed before His Imperial Majesty. I'm not accustomed to insults."

In my coat pocket, I had Louis-Napoléon's jewel wrapped in a handkerchief. I was prepared to pawn it, but not to this lout.

His face closed into a snarl. "And our prefect, Comte de Kératry, is not accustomed to receiving actress whores in his headquarters."

His disparagement was lost in the faintness that overcame me. I must have swayed, lost my color, for as his expression faltered—having the actress whore collapse at his feet would not do—I heard myself say as if from across an abyss, "Comte de Kératry?"

He recovered his superiority. "Were we not aware who the prefect is, mademoiselle-actress-who-performed-before-His-Imperial-Majesty-himself?"

I forced myself to not turn about and flee. "Please inform the *comte* that Sarah Bernhardt is here. We . . . we are previously acquainted."

"Are you, now? Shall we set you up in the empress's bedchamber or would you prefer—"

"Enough." Kératry's voice slashed him to silence. "How dare you."

I lifted my eyes. I didn't want to, but I did. And there he stood, handsome as ever, in a blue wool greatcoat with its lynx-fur collar upright about his angular jaw, his mustachios trimmed to waxed points, his green eyes locked on me as he said to his officer, "We do not disparage civilians here." To my amazement, he extended his hand. "Sarah, come with me."

I followed him into the palace, through gilded passageways to one of the imperial secretariat chambers. He motioned to a plush red velvet chair opposite his desk. "Please accept my apologies. As you've just seen, we may be all that stands between France and ruin, but our National Guard sorely lacks proper manners."

I couldn't speak, unable to fathom that of all the men in Paris, the prefect of our defense was none other than the very man who'd sired my son and thrown me out of his house, whom I'd vowed to never ask anything of again. In my skirt pocket, the jewel felt like a rock. I couldn't offer it to him. It was unthinkable of me to attempt to bribe him.

"Sarah," he went on quietly, sensing my dismay. "I can see this is as much of a surprise to you as it is to me. Why are you here?"

I swallowed. I found no judgment in his expression, only a profound weariness that mirrored Duquesnel's, who even now was laboring alongside hired carpenters to remove the rows of seating in our theater to make room for cots.

"I'm the lead actress at the Odéon," I finally said.

"I know. And, as I understand, applauded by Louis-Napoléon himself."

"Not everything they said about us is true," I replied, bristling.

"I do not doubt it. What can I do for the lead actress of the Odéon?"

"We . . ." I strengthened my voice. "We request a permit to open an infirmary in the theater." I paused once more, expecting his incredulous laughter. But he regarded me in sober consideration, as a gentleman should. If he saw no reason to cite our last encounter, neither would I. Yet I also thought I saw relief surface in his gaze. He might not mention it, but he hadn't forgotten. It would have pleased me under any other circumstance.

"Are you certain?" he asked at length, and when I nodded, he said, "Permit granted. I assume you understand the responsibilities. The Prussians have been sighted on the outskirts of the city. We've dispatched regiments to keep them at bay and sent word for a parlay with their generals, but they'll insist on unconditional surrender. Which, of course, we cannot concede. There'll be many wounded before this siege is done, and we'll need every infirmary we authorize to remain open for the duration."

"Of course. We require—" I searched my tasseled bag for the list of supplies I'd drawn up with Duquesnel.

"Everything, I presume." He took the list from me but didn't peruse it. "I have supplies here. Medicine. Dressings. Food. I can give you milk, cheese, vegetables, sugar, potatoes, legumes, eggs, and coffee. And live hens and geese, if you have a place to pen and slaughter them. Did you bring a cart or shall I have the supplies delivered this afternoon?"

"This afternoon?" I echoed, taken aback by his efficiency.

"It is why you're here, isn't it? Not everyone wishes to serve our cause; that you do means something. I'll inform those of my friends who remain in the city, as well. The Rothschilds, for one, are supporters of the arts. I'm sure they'll be willing to assist, once they hear you're involved. Your name carries weight, and not only for a slap."

He hadn't forgotten a thing. "Would that we could resolve this silly war with a slap to Wilhelm and Louis-Napoléon," I remarked.

He smiled. "Alas, I fear they're too occupied slapping each other."

My gaze faltered, dropping from his face to his fur collar. "If we're going to last for the duration, we'll need coats to keep our patients warm." It was a perverse impulse on my part, and I wondered why I felt the need to humiliate him after all this time. In the end, he'd done me a favor. He'd given me my Maurice.

He emptied his pockets onto his desk and removed his coat. "My scarf, as well?" He reached to the white silk cravat at his throat.

"That won't be necessary." I grasped the coat, bundling it under my arm as I came to my feet. "But please tell your friends that all articles of clothing would be welcome."

"I will." He stepped from the desk as I made toward the door. "Sarah," he said, bringing me to a halt.

I went still.

"Did you . . . ?" His question hovered between us.

"Do you truly want to know?" I said.

He sighed. "No."

"Then we mustn't ever speak of it again."

Before the fiacre, his greatcoat clasped to my chest, he bowed and took my hand, kissing it. Then, without a word, he returned to his office.

I climbed into the carriage. Halfway to the theater, I lifted his coat to my face.

It smelled of him. It did not move me in the slightest.

⋮

I rallied Marie Agar, Sophie, and Marie Colombier, along with four other company actresses who remained in Paris. We donned the winged headdress and smock of the Red Cross, submitting to a hasty training course provided by a head nurse dispatched by Kératry, leaving me in no doubt that despite my enthusiasm and our bounty of supplies, we were as ill-equipped as possible to tend to actual patients.

However, our ward was equipped enough to compensate. We penned the hens and geese in the courtyard, and kept burlap sacks of supplies in the basement, along with our stored props and the up-ended theater seating. Rows of tidy cots now lined the auditorium, with an operating table set up on the stage. Then we enticed the soldiers loitering in the Place du Châtelet, by doling out hot soup from a charcoal stove in the lobby. We discovered most of the soldiers weren't gravely injured, merely stragglers who'd survived the rout at Sedan and made their way to Paris, like a herd of lost cattle. A few had minor wounds, which we cleansed and bound. Once they were attended, we sent them to the Tuileries to be conscripted. Kératry needed as many men as possible, and he'd fulfilled his promise to me in abundance.

His society friends, including the Rothschilds, donated wine, chocolate, clothing, and other necessities, which he dispatched on municipal carts, along with a letter assuring me that should I require anything, I need only send word. He didn't come in person to inspect our ward, but his message was plain, as was his intent. This was his apology for his prior abuse of me. When I had least expected it, he redeemed himself. That he didn't inquire again about Maurice was, to me, an act of mercy. He had said he'd never acknowledge my child as his, and much as I appreciated his redemption, I did not want to share my son.

Nevertheless, I was determined to prove my commitment. Yet as September ebbed into a frigid October, with Prussian cannons now heard firing on the outskirts, no patients arrived at our ward. It was disconcerting, as day after day we waited, expecting a deluge, only to find ourselves re-counting the stacks of donated linens and blankets, the rolls of pristine gauze, and the precious boxes of laudanum vials.

"Are you certain we'll be nursing soldiers at some point?" yawned Marie Colombier as I stood in the lobby, gazing out into the Place. "Because this is quite the production, without an audience to reap the benefits."

I refused to look at her, watching a few pedestrians walk past, bundled against the chill, but no longer scurrying as if the sky were about to fall on their heads. As the weeks dragged on without a single skirmish to remind us that we were under siege, Paris had reverted to a semblance of normality—if not entirely, as we now had Prussians barring safe passage outside the city, but enough so that cafés and restaurants had reopened and those who hadn't fled ridiculed those who had, remarking that our coastal resorts must be very crowded, indeed. For some, the situation even became one of illicit profit, with newspaper advertisements offering guided tours to view the Krupp cannon blasts from nearby rooftops, as if it were all a passing lark.

"The war isn't over, Marie," I said.

"I wonder if it's even begun," she replied.

"If it's such an inconvenience," I snapped at her, "you can leave whenever you like."

She stifled another yawn. "Whenever, perhaps, but not wherever. With all the roads closed, there's no place to go. I rather think

I'd enjoy an invasion about now, if only to put an end to this tedium."

I had to agree. It was a bore, but it wasn't going to stay that way. At some point, our defenses would be put to the test and Marie would receive the excitement she craved, though it might not be the excitement she envisioned. Once she was elbow-deep in gore, I doubted whether she would have the courage for caustic asides.

At night, I tossed and turned. We had plenty of food, thanks to Kératry, and Madame G. knew how to preserve so as not to waste. I rescued a few of the pluckier hens from the theater pen and let them loose in my mother's flat; they'd lay fresh eggs for us, I told Madame G., as Caroline giggled, for my dogs chased after them and the hens ended up high on Julie's bed to evade pursuit, nesting on her satin cushions. It suited me immensely. Let my mother return to find her precious boudoir a mess of feathers and chicken excrement.

But Maurice was never far from my thoughts. I wondered how he fared and if he missed me. I pictured him in Holland, tripping over quaint bridges spanning canals, then a vise clamped across my chest as I imagined Julie whispering venom in his ear. She was quite capable of it; she would turn my son against me to prove she held the upper hand.

I'd almost decided to abandon the infirmary and beseech Kératry to help me reach Holland when the shelling began.

X

The prized chandelier overhead, mummified in layers of felt as ordained by Duquesnel, who must have begun to regret indulging me, rattled ominously as another explosion nearby shook the Odéon.

From the bedside where I was binding the stump of what had once been a soldier's hand while he writhed in agony, I glanced at Marie. She was cringing, her smock splattered in blood. I'd had to relegate her to our lesser wounded, if any could be deemed such, for as the siege took an abrupt turn, so did our time of waiting. Even as the most brutal winter any of us could recall assailed Paris, cutting short those careless jaunts to view the cannon fire from rooftops, the Prussians had mounted an equally ruthless assault, cutting off our supply routes and bombarding us day and night. The soldiers of our battered defense began to flood in, conveyed in carts or upon the shoulders of their compatriots, presenting such horrific injuries that I had to bite back a surge of vomit. Many were delirious, with gangrene setting in, but I set myself to cleansing their putrid wounds, a lavender-drenched mask tied about my nose and mouth to douse some of the stench. Marie, however, swooned and had to be revived with smelling salts. She soon showed herself as inept at nursing as she was at acting.

"They're going to bring the very roof down about our ears," she now cried out, as I jabbed my finger at her, ordering her to see to the

invalids she'd been assigned. Around us, the din of moans and im-
plorations for a priest, for their mothers, or for a dose of laudanum
rose like a wretched score, punctuated by the howls of those unfor-
tunates undergoing impromptu amputations on the stage, where
Marie Agar, despite her age, had taken to collecting the severed
limbs to be burned outside on a pyre, though I thought it a waste.
We'd chopped down every prop and set, even the seats removed
from the theater, for kindling, and still we were blue with cold, our
breath wreathing us in icicled clouds. Frostbite was a constant concern, both for us and for our patients. Had it been up to me, we'd
have burned the severed limbs in the furnace for heat.

"Stop it," I hissed at Marie Colombier, my patience, of which I'd
never had an excess supply, strained past its limit. "You'll frighten
our patients. No one is going to bring—"

She glared. "Our patients are half-dead already. The Left Bank
has been shelled to cinders! The Prussians are at our gates. How
long must we pretend?"

"Enough!" I strode to her and seized her by the arm. "We have a
duty to perform. We've raised our flag to alert those barbarians that
we're an authorized medical facility. I'll not hear another word of
abandoning it, no matter how many shells they throw at us."

She was trembling, though she had enough self-possession to
wrench her arm from my grip. "It's over," she spat at me. "There's
famine everywhere. Not a cat or dog or pigeon left in the city that
hasn't been turned into soup. Every animal in the zoo of le Jardin
des Plantes has been butchered; people are paying out their life's
savings for a quarter kilo of elephant or perishing of starvation.
There's nothing left of your precious cause, and the Prussians don't
care a fig for your wretched white flag. I do *not* intend to die here, no
matter how much acclaim you may seek for your patriotism."

I almost struck her. I had to clench my fist to my side, meeting
her eyes, her defiance marred by the fear I saw there—a fear I'd
seen in the others, as well, though I'd tried to ignore it, just as I'd
tried to ignore the same fear scrabbling in the pit of my being.

"You're a coward," I whispered.

"So be it. Coward or not, I'm leaving." She tore at her smock, flinging it aside. "No one's going to have a bust commissioned for surviving the siege, Sarah. If you want to end up as a Prussian prisoner of war for headlines, you can do so without me."

I might have hit her then, out of rage and frustration, for she only spoke aloud what the others must be thinking. From a staff of twelve or so actresses who had flocked to my call for assistance, we were down to four—myself, Madame Agar, Sophie, and Marie—plus Madame G. and Caroline, both of whom I'd dragged from seclusion in our flat to oversee our supplies, of which, as Marie had declared, we had nearly nothing left.

But my anger was cut short by another earth-sundering blast. This time, the entire theater swayed. As I rocked back on my heels, I heard in impossible clarity the creaking of the overheard chains holding the chandelier in place, and then, in a horrifying suspension of time, so that everything seemed to pause, the chains rupturing.

"Our patients!" I staggered toward the row of cots with a cry, just as the chandelier came crashing down in a deafening explosion of crystal shards.

Chaos erupted as I dove onto the cots to protect the wounded, lacerating my hands to yank the inert men from under the glass-covered blankets, shouting at the others for help. Madame G. rushed to assist me, as did Sophie and Caroline, but once we'd managed to pair the men together in the few spare cots outside the site of the fallen chandelier, most of them too far gone with pain to even be aware they'd nearly been crushed, I looked to where Marie stood.

She'd gone immobile, her mouth agape in horror. I knew then, with a dreadful capsizing of my heart, that she was right.

"The basement," I said. "Move everyone into the basement. Now."

"The basement?" echoed Sophie, her coif askew and her pert blond charm subsumed by fatigue. "Why?" She lowered her voice as she marked the fury in my stance. "To feed whatever rats are still swimming down there?" When she reached for my shoulder, I flinched. "Sarah," she said. "The pipes have burst from the cold. The basement is flooded with sewage. The men will die down there just as well as they will up here. Or perhaps not as well, if the theater collapses and buries us alive in the basement."

"No." My voice shuddered. "These men will *not* die under my watch."

Marie let out a coarse laugh. "And here it is at last, our lead actress's soliloquy."

I whirled on her, this time fully intending to slap her, but Madame G. halted me with a hesitant "What about Julie's flat? We have spare beds there. . . ." Her reassuring smile was more like a grimace. "At least we'd be safer, yes?"

I met her hollowed eyes, marking the fatigue that weighed on her, on all of us. I had to assent. "We also have extra food there, and—"

"No." Duquesnel came into the theater, no doubt alerted by the fall of the chandelier. Though he'd allowed the requisition of the theater, he'd kept his distance once my ward was established, living in his office upstairs. "Sarah, we must see every patient transferred to the Hospital of Val-de-Grâce." He lifted his voice over my protest, thrusting a shred of paper into my hand. "Orders from Kératry. Every civilian-run ward must close."

"It . . . it cannot be." I didn't glance at the paper, crumpling it into my smock pocket. "The military hospitals are overflowing. There's no room."

"Nevertheless, these are his orders." Duquesnel kept his gaze on me. "We've done all we can. The Prussians are determined to destroy the city; Kératry says either we surrender or we'll perish in our own rubble."

"But . . ." I turned to the others, all of whom except Marie averted their eyes. She gave me a look of gloating satisfaction, as if this were a play where she'd finally succeeded in upstaging me. "Now?" I returned my gaze to Duquesnel.

He nodded. "As soon as we can. We can use my fiacre and the supply carts out back." He managed a tremulous laugh. "Be glad I refused when you wanted those carts dismantled for firewood or we'd be carrying your *invalides* to the Val-de-Grâce on our backs."

I swallowed a surge of tears. Duquesnel saw it, but he knew me better than I supposed. He did not offer any consolation. He took charge instead, ordering the women and the lone elderly stagehand with the cataracts to prepare our patients for transfer.

We may have done everything we could, but as another shell exploded in the Place, the impact reverberating through the Odéon's walls, I feared nothing would be enough to save us.

Once more, Madame G., Caroline, and I huddled in my mother's flat with my emaciated dogs—my poor parrot had succumbed, to my despair—as the shelling continued, lighting up the smoke-charred sky with an infernal glow and permeating Paris with the stink of charnel and sulfur. It was such a nightmare, such hell on earth, that it defied comprehension. I couldn't understand how we, the pride of Europe, revered for our exquisite civilization, had fallen so low, our crown jewel of a city in our now-extinct empire buried in debris, with starvation and cholera stalking those of us who remained.

"How could they have let it go this far?" I demanded, pacing the flat while Caroline eyed me wearily and Madame G. retreated to her garret upstairs, unable to bear my ranting. "When shall it end? Must we die in the ruins of our own country"—I rounded on Caroline—"while hiding behind bolted doors? Kératry shut down our ward because he said we had to surrender, but thus far, I've seen no sign of it."

My maid had become so drawn and pale, she resembled a ghost. We all did, every soul left in Paris. I couldn't look at myself in the mirror, appalled by my spectral gauntness. When I twisted my hair into a chignon in the morning, strands of my hair clung to my fingers. My gums were bleeding and I'd lost a back tooth; it came out as I gnawed on a rot-soft apple core. I didn't even feel it until I was staring at the broken molar in my palm.

"We can't endure much more of this," said Caroline, my dogs lying listless at her feet, too tired from hunger to move. I'd had a confrontation with Madame G. over my pets' survival; as the last of our food dwindled, she suggested we must do as everyone else: Butchers were paying for domestic animals, according to the amount of flesh that could be harvested. As the poor creatures were certain to die anyway without sustenance—

"Not my dogs," I shouted at her. "We'll eat you first!"

She burst into tears and fled. I apologized to her later, but as I now regarded my emaciated animals, I couldn't evade the dreadful reality. Unless we indeed resorted to cannibalism, we'd soon have no other choice.

Pausing at the window of my mother's salon, boarded up to keep the explosions from shattering the glass, I peered into the street through the haphazard nailed slats of wood hauled from the Odéon to replace the broken shutters. The streets were deserted. Although thousands were still trapped in Paris, the entire city felt devoid of life.

"I should go." I tugged my shawl across my shoulders. I had to envelop myself in layers against the cold when I headed out to search for food in the lull between the shellings. "There might be something edible today in our so-called black market." I snorted. "Overpriced and spoiled as it may be."

"You only found that cabbage and rancid meat yesterday," Caroline said. "Who knows what the meat even was? No matter how much we boiled it, it was still tough as a leather sole."

"Cat." I trudged to the door. "The butcher said it was cat. Or was it rat? I can't recall. Whatever it was, the women were about to slit each other's throats over it, until I offered up Julie's pearls and the butcher declared it mine."

Caroline crossed herself. She hadn't shown any particular de-
voutness before, but now she'd taken to fingering her rosary constantly as shells burst in the distance, making the sign of the cross as
if the Holy Virgin were about to descend from heaven to save us. It
obviously gave her consolation, even if I wanted to tell her that God
cared no more for our plight than the Prussians.

"Clean up the kitchen," I said instead, for I'd set down old playbills and newspapers for the dogs, not daring to take them out, lest a
starving citizen tried to steal them for slaughter. As if they'd sensed
the danger, my dogs had obliged. "And check on Madame Guérard," I added, wrapping another scarf about my head. "I'm worried about her. She barely ate a mouthful of our leather sole last
night."

"Please be careful," implored Caroline as I pulled away the chair
that we kept lodged under the doorknob, to deter looters prowling
the district, risking life and limb to break into dwellings. "Don't be
gone long. It's not safe."

"Yes," I said, but as I went out, I thought a German shell striking
me dead as I bartered my mother's earrings for inedible meat would
make a fitting epitaph.

I'd barely reached the end of the district, my mitten-swathed
hands shoved into my coat pockets to clutch the dull kitchen knife I
carried for self-defense, my lungs wheezing in the thick chill of the
morning, when I saw two soldiers shambling toward me.

I went still. I should return to the flat, but I didn't want to run and
bring attention to myself. I was scarcely a prize in my current state,
but I'd heard bloodcurdling tales of violations taking place as the
city succumbed to anarchy. A shell strike would be quick, maybe
painless. Rape at the hands of a pair of desperate soldiers would not.

Then I saw the soldiers were as weak as me, staggering under a
mishmash of clothing to ward off the cold, without visible weapons.
Their pained gait and the palpable despair in their faces transfixed
me. I stayed immobile as they neared, for they appeared aimless, as

though they had no idea where they were heading, like those soldiers I'd seen in the Place, which now seemed a lifetime ago.

In a voice gone hoarse from the cold, I heard myself say, "Is it
over?"

I didn't know why I asked. There was nothing to indicate it, but
something about their slumped shoulders, their pathetic clinging to
each other, compelled me to it. One of them glanced at me with red-
rimmed eyes, as if he'd been weeping. "Yes," he said. "An armistice
was signed at Versailles. We were ordered to disarm, mademoiselle."

"Armistice? Not unconditional surrender?" It hardly mattered,
providing this ordeal came to an end, but it mattered very much to
me in that moment. If we'd negotiated terms for our surrender, at
least we could retain some shred of our dignity.

The soldier gave a joyless nod; as they continued onward, perhaps toward homes they'd not seen in months, I burst into tears.
Right there on the street, with a blade in my pocket. I wept for myself, for France, and for everything we had lost.

"It's over!" Bursting into the flat, I startled Caroline, her hands
laden with bags of urine-sodden paper from the kitchen. Madame
G. must have heard me depart, for she was at the table, setting out
cutlery for our nonexistent breakfast. My dogs, roused by my fervor, bestirred themselves to yelp piteously from their perch on my
mother's settee.

"The siege," I explained, seeing *ma petite dame*'s confusion. "I
just came across two Republican soldiers who told me an armistice
was signed at Versailles."

"Blessed be." Madame G. dropped onto a chair. "We can eat
again."

"And not elephant or cat." I swooped to my pets to hug their
skinny heads. "I must find Kératry and ask him to help me send

word to Holland." Unraveling my layers, my relief that the siege had finally ended stoking welcome heat in my shallow flesh, I scavenged in Julie's little desk. "Is there any paper or ink left? The telegraph lines are shut down. I hardly think I can hire one of those balloons they used for reconnaissance to send a message—"

I paused, as much at the sudden silence when there should have been rejoicing as at the disquieting sensation of something being withheld. Turning to the table, where Caroline stood as if petrified with the dripping bag, I looked at Madame G.

"What now?" I asked.

"They're not in Holland." She was too fatigued to mince her words. "Didn't you read the note Kératry sent you when he closed the ward?"

I stared at her. "No. Should I have?"

She sighed. "Sarah, he also sent word of your family."

I plunged into my bedchamber, digging through my heaped clothes for my Red Cross smock. I found it stiff with caked blood under my tattered stockings and undergarments, as laundering was impossible. From the front pocket, I extracted that deceptive slip of paper Duquesnel had handed me. I could barely read the minuscule writing, though it was precise: like everything else about him, Kératry's penmanship was excellent.

I collapsed to my knees. When my howl erupted, Madame G. rushed in to stand over me in helpless despair.

"Bad Homburg," I cried. "They're in *Germany*."

XI

"Sarah, it's out of the question. Have you failed to consider the consequences of such an endeavor, just as you apparently fail to understand the situation our entire country finds itself in?" Kératry regarded me over his paper-strewn desk in the Tuileries; within the palace itself, little had changed except for the pervasive cinder dust coating everything. Outside, however, Paris was in wreckage, every tree cut down for fuel, with corpses festering under the rubble on the streets, and shell-ravaged buildings prone to collapsing without warning, so that voluntary crews were already tearing down every structure that couldn't be salvaged.

"We have peace now, don't we?" I insisted, having traversed the ruined city in a hired equipage, in my least soiled dress and bonnet, determined to make an impression. "The Prussians are retreating and—"

"Retreating?" He gave a terse laugh. Though he wore an elegant tailored suit—no imperial uniform now, for we had no empire—he looked underweight and haggard. "They're still roaming the countryside, plundering as they please. The armistice is a farce. Our Third Republic gave in to every one of Wilhelm's demands, allowing him to proclaim himself the Kaiser at our palace of Versailles. He's the new German emperor, and that devil Bismarck is his lackey, demanding Alsace-Lorraine in exchange for releasing Louis-

Napoléon into exile. What we lost Prussia reaps. We've surrendered our standing and our honor."

I'd never thought I'd see him, a scion of aristocratic privilege, moved to such despairing patriotism. Lowering my gaze to my hands in my lap, I shifted them to hide the missing buttons on one of my gloves and the threadbare fingertips.

"You did send me the message," I reminded him.

"I sent it so you could know your family is safe, not to incite you to this madness."

"Safe?" I lifted my eyes, my voice sharpening. "In enemy territory?"

"In a spa at Bad Homburg. They are free to return here whenever they like. Bismarck isn't refusing our citizens abroad safe passage, but considering the situation, it would be best for them to remain wherever they are until safe passage is assured."

"He's my son." I couldn't maintain my calm or stay true to my avowal that we must never speak of Maurice. "She—she took him there without my permission. I would never have allowed it. A spa in Germany, while we were under siege . . . it's beyond belief."

"Be that as it may, it's also beyond belief that a woman alone should undertake such a journey. You would be risking your own safety, perhaps your very life."

"Then I will risk it." I came to my feet. "With or without safe passage. I survived the siege. I can survive a trip to Bad Homburg. And I won't be alone; my maid will accompany me."

He met my stare for a moment, laden with everything unspoken between us. Then he sighed. "I have this entire city to oversee. I won't fight one woman. Do as you will." He took up a pen and wrote on a paper, stamping it with his insignia. "A pass. If you can book a seat on one of the provision trains, this might allow you to cross the border. The Prussians are controlling every entry and departure, so a pass signed by a former officer of a disgraced former empire is only that. If they refuse, do not say you weren't warned."

"I consider myself warned." I pocketed the paper. As I turned toward the door, he said, "Wait," and I heard him open a drawer. When I looked around, he was extending a pistol to me. "If you don't know how to shoot it, just point and hope for the best."

I retrieved the pistol. "I know how to shoot," I said. Even if I did not.

I couldn't decide what was worse. The supply train crammed with refugees who stank of fear and unwashed skin, the sated Prussian soldiers, drunk on victory and our vintage wines, halting the train at intervals to board and loot—though they leeringly referred to their wholesale ransacking as "inspections"—the lack of food or potable water, or Caroline's insufferable litany of prayer.

"Will you please stop invoking God?" I hissed, once we finally arrived in the town of Homburg after a harrowing twelve days, which had involved every kind of transport from the supply train to a goatherd's trap to walking for hours over unpaved roads. My feet throbbed in my tissue-thin boots; my clothing was stained and my hair an unsightly mess. I glared at her, trudging like a penitent beside me, as we neared the immaculate vision of marble pantheons looming before us like a mirage, surrounding by healing waters.

"Who else can save us but Him," she moaned, "now that we're in the enemy's maw?"

"Maw indeed." I flung out my arm. "Do you see any wolves here? Look about you. Parasols on the terrace. Waiters with tea service. Why, it's like Vichy. Only," I snarled, recalling my aborted attempt at a holiday before I'd been plunged into this nightmare, "they speak German here. They're also Protestants, so unless you want to be burned alive as a papist, I suggest you put away that rosary and refrain from invoking the saints."

Caroline recoiled and said nothing more, though I could tell she was terrified of what lay ahead—and it wasn't the Prussians that she most feared.

It took me a half hour of haggling with the reception staff, most of whom pretended to not understand me although they must have acquired some French as a matter of course, considering this spa was, or had been, as frequented by French society as by Prussian. Finally, the manager on duty took it upon himself to answer my irate demands by requesting another possible name, as he had no Bernhardt listed in the register.

"Youle van Hard," I spat out at him. "My son is Bernhardt. Maurice Bernhardt."

"I see." He sniffed. It hadn't occurred to me in my impatience that of course Julie traveled under her own name. And Bernhardt, as the manager's sniff implied, reeked of Hebraic origin. Evidently, they didn't serve Jews in the spa of Bad Homburg.

"We do have a Mademoiselle Julie Youle van Hard registered—" the manager started to say.

"Where?" I cut him off.

He gave me a pointed look. "Given the hour, I assume she and her family are about to partake of luncheon in our dining room. Would Mademoiselle care to register for a room? Only our registered guests are allowed into the dining area."

I clenched my jaw, feeling the pistol in my bag poking my ribs as I filled out the form. I had brought whatever money I'd managed to scavenge from my apartment, hiding it in the lining of my bag, but I didn't know if it would be enough or if French currency would even be accepted. I didn't care. Let them arrest me for my unpaid bill, if they chose.

"I'll have you know I'm a celebrated actress in France," I informed the manager, who accepted my deposit of francs readily enough.

"Then your visit is an honor for us," he said dryly, handing me the key to my room. "Will Mademoiselle Bernhardt require any assistance with her luggage?"

"Mademoiselle's maid will." I thrust my tapestry bag at Caroline. "Go to the room," I told her. "And draw me a hot bath. This won't take long."

I marched into the gallery, past guests idling on wicker chaises and sipping tea as if just across the border our country weren't struggling to evade the Prussian heel. I heard plenty of French spoken as I stormed past; apparently, Julie wasn't the only one who lacked any conscience or pride. But when I entered the gilded salon, with its linen-draped tables and cultivated air of refinement, a violin quartet playing Bach, and observed the guests feasting on cooked ham, shellfish, and fresh fruit, my stomach lurched and my mouth, bone-dry from the road, flooded with saliva.

Food. Actual edible sustenance. As a waiter drifted by, bearing a platter of langoustines and oysters on ice, I nearly pounced on him. Instead, I scoured the room in mounting rage until I caught sight of them by the bay windows overlooking a rose garden.

When I saw Maurice, my knees started to buckle underneath me.

Weaving my way through the tables to them, I went unseen, until Régine looked up with her habitual scowl, a preposterous bow atop her head, and cried, *"Ma soeur!"*

Julie turned in her chair, a napkin at her lips. She froze as I reared before her.

"How *could* you?" I passed my furious gaze over her, in her white day gown and straw bonnet adorned with satin cherries, her coiffure a confection of ringlets, then I stabbed my gaze at Rosine, who went white. Régine threw herself from her chair at me. Clutching my sister to my side, I beckoned Maurice, who rose uncertainly from his seat beside ashen-faced Jeanne.

"Mon fils," I said. "Come give your poor *maman* a kiss."

How could he have grown so much in so little time? He'd just turned six—I had missed his December birthday because of his absence—but this solemn, handsome child with his long legs and thick auburn hair brilliantined to his scalp, enhancing his deep-set, amber-hued eyes, appeared much older to me. My heart cracked in my chest when I saw him hesitate, as if he didn't know who I was.

"Go." Rosine gave him a nudge. "She's Sarah. Your mother."

Tears choked me as his eyes lit up in recognition. I enveloped him with my other arm, falling to my knees as everyone stared and Régine bayed her joy. I breathed in his scent, my precious boy, and through my overwhelming relief that he was well, unharmed, and with me once more, I lifted my eyes to Julie.

"Poor *maman*, indeed," she said. "All the way from Paris, no less—and looking as if she crawled here on her hands and knees."

Over lunch, Julie protested she saw no reason for haste, even as I took Maurice by his hand and marched him up to my room, Régine scampering beside us. I reveled in a hot bath, spent the afternoon with my son and sister in the garden, ate dinner at a separate table, with Julie avoiding a single glance at me from hers, then went back upstairs to squash myself between Maurice and Régine on the bed, with Caroline on a truckle beside us.

The next morning, I packed up my belongings. When Julie and Rosine came upon us in the lobby as I was returning my room key and settling my bill—I barely had enough to cover it—Julie exclaimed, "Are you leaving already? Honestly, Sarah, this is ridiculous. Paris is no place for any civilized person to be right now."

She was right. I knew I was being reckless and unreasonable. Given the situation, Paris was indeed the last place I should willingly take my son and sister, but the very thought of letting them remain here, in Prussian territory, hardened my resolve. France might be in chaos, yet it was still our country and it was where we must be. Moreover, I certainly would not stay here myself nor let my son be influenced any further by my mother's wiles.

"We will make do," I retorted. "You may stay as long as you like."

Rosine bleated, "Jeanne isn't fully recovered yet; we only came here so she could take the cure, as you suggested."

"In Vichy. I suggested she take the cure in Vichy." I kept my eyes on Julie, who said coldly, "We might have been recognized in Vichy; our suitors take their families there on occasion. Besides, with all the tiresome talk of war, I thought it wiser to go on holiday outside of France. We've come here often enough in the past. It's a perfectly respectable resort. There was no harm—"

"*No harm?* Does your respectable resort have no newspapers?" I snarled.

I hired a cab to take us to the center of town. After repeated inquiries, I discovered passenger trains were departing to Paris on a sporadic schedule. Of course, Julie refused to stay behind, arriving with Jeanne, Rosine, and their mass of luggage at the station where we waited to board the train, declaring she'd been so humiliated by my precipitous arrival and departure she couldn't possibly remain in Bad Homburg.

On the train, which would only take us to a *gare* outside Paris, requiring us to hire another conveyance to the city, Julie lamented the entire way. "Like peasants," she said, casting accusatory looks at me as if I'd planned the war to inconvenience her. "When we were perfectly comfortable at the resort."

I refused to say another word to her. By the time we reached Paris after an interminable train ride that took nearly three days, and hired a carriage at considerable expense that she had to pay, seeing as I had no more money, she was seething with fury in her dainty silk shoes and askew bonnet.

Once we entered her flat, she went cold. Madame G. had taken my dogs to my apartment and done her best to tidy up, but the evidence of our occupation was clear. I smiled to myself as I saw Julie pause in her boudoir and sniff at the lingering smell of chicken before she said flatly, "I'm quite sure penning animals in my house as if it were a barnyard gave you much pleasure."

She had seen the city as we'd been driven through it, the disaster
of it, piles of demolished buildings and rubble-strewn boulevards,
people searching for food and fuel; but to her, the most egregious
act of the calamity was my uninvited invasion of her home.

"For the moment," I said. I left her there, with her luggage about
her, Jeanne faint with exhaustion, and Rosine distraught at the upheaval. I returned to my apartment with Caroline, Régine, and
Maurice, where my dogs were overjoyed, leaping up to slather the
children with affection. As I heard my son laugh aloud for the first
time since we'd departed Bad Homburg, I realized that, like Paris
itself, we had to rebuild. I must get back to the business of living if
I was to support my family.

But my joy at being reunited with my boy and sister, and my satisfaction that I'd taught Julie a much-needed lesson in the process,
turned out to be short-lived.

XII

"Must they burn down Paris all over again?" I stood upon a wooded hill in Saint-Germain-en-Laye, clutching the reins of my mare as I stared toward the city, from which emanated plumes of smoke and the scattershot echo of cannon fire. "After we only just survived the Prussians by the skin of our teeth, how can they turn on each other like this? It's appalling."

Beside me was my latest *affaire de coeur,* a robust, green-eyed Irish lieutenant in the Republican Army. I'd met Arthur O'Connor in the spring of 1871, during the social rounds I'd undertaken to attempt to restore my theatrical career in the brief lull following the siege. In addition to our incineration of our seating and scenery for heat, the Odéon had been badly damaged by the shellings, and we had no means to repair it. To raise the necessary funds, I'd set myself to paying visits to our patrons—many of whom demurred, citing France's precarious state—and attending political galas, where I delivered passionate appeals about the urgent need to safeguard our irreplaceable artistic institutions. O'Connor was at one of these galas and introduced himself; like many foreign adventurers, he'd enlisted in our army in an international demonstration of solidarity.

Word of my efforts during the siege had preceded me, allowing me to be well received and obtain some donations, but I soon learned our Third Republic and the National Guard, which defended Paris from the Prussians, were at odds, the Guard vehemently opposed to the disarmament. When National Guard soldiers who'd joined a socialist groundswell in Paris calling itself the Commune murdered two Republican generals, the entire Guard declared itself autonomous from Republican authority, initiating our *semaine sanglante*, the Bloody Week—plunging us once more into chaos.

I had found O'Connor a charming and useful diversion, until I now heard him chuckle. "Sarah, my pet, the Communards are a radical nest of vermin, but they take their cause very seriously. They'll not see the emperor restored under the Third Republic."

"Who said anything about the emperor?" I replied, wondering if the raging fires would reach the Odéon and consume what little was left. "You know I've spoken to those now overseeing our government, and not one of them mentioned wanting Louis-Napoléon back on the throne. All agree it's best if he remains in exile. Surely there are more sensible ways to decide who is most suitable to guide us without torching the Tuileries?"

As I spoke, I thought of Kératry, whom I'd seen at a charity event where I'd performed for those left destitute by the siege. He'd looked much like himself again, impeccably groomed in evening wear. Kissing my hand after my curtain call, he said, "I'm relieved to see our heroine of Paris survived her voyage to Bad Homburg."

I'd gone still with dread that he'd ask about Maurice. He did not. He merely smiled, informing me he had resigned his post and was departing on an extended continental tour. "You might consider doing the same," he said. "I fear the siege was only the start of our downfall. Many in Paris are calling for the city to declare its independence from our new government. Even that traitor Hugo has declared his intent to return from abroad, no doubt to incite the rabble to revolutionary fervor."

Kératry's disparagement of our lionized writer didn't surprise me; he'd always been an ardent Bonapartist, like most aristocrats, and Louis-Napoléon had detested Victor Hugo. But the unexpected news that our greatest living playwright, whose plays had been banned under the empire and in which I longed to perform, was returning to France sent me racing to O'Connor, who arranged for me to attend a planned reception for Hugo. If I could meet the playwright in person and secure his agreement to stage one of his works at the Odéon, a slew of donations would surely follow.

Only days before the event, word came that my beloved Dumas had died of heart failure, having lived long enough to see his beloved France torn asunder. He left behind a legacy of over thirty novels, numerous plays, and other works, as well as four surviving children, his bereaved wife, and countless mistresses. My mourning for him, whose generosity had set me on my path, was cut short by a sudden swell of violence, with mobs of working-class Parisians storming down the boulevards waving red flags and chanting *"La république démocratique et sociale!"*—a slogan that must have frozen the aristocracy's collective blood. Civil war soon broke out between the National Guard and the Republican Army, which vehemently opposed the Commune's equalitarian ideology.

With fighting once again in the streets, thousands had to flee Paris. I'd had no choice but to accept a benefactor's offer to move my family, including irate Julie, Rosine, and Jeanne, to his *petit château* in Saint-Germain. My benefactor was a wealthy Jewish banker who'd donated a significant sum to the Odeon's restoration; he was also elderly and not overly inclined to bed-sport, which suited me. I had no intention of resuming the courtesan trade on a permanent basis, but for the moment, I had to protect my family and shore up my own decimated finances, without excessive demands on my time. O'Connor sniffed out my trail and installed himself in the vicinity during his leave, displeased by my other arrangement, though I'd never given him an intimation that our affair was to be exclusive.

From my saddle, I now turned to regard him. He sat aside his horse like a living statue, a splendid specimen of manhood, with his thick red-gold hair and muscular shoulders. He took me riding in the afternoons, seeing as my evenings were occupied, and I enjoyed his rugged ease on horseback. Indeed, I enjoyed much about his rugged ease, but I found his careless sarcasm infuriating.

"Seeing as you care so much," I said, "shouldn't you be down there with your fellow soldiers, defending Paris from this nest of vermin?"

"What? And miss my delightful argument with you?" he replied, smiling.

"It is not an argument. That city is my home. I'd barely started to perform again, and now this—another catastrophe. What if they burn down all the theaters?"

He gave a hearty laugh. "Sarah, you are truly heartless. Are you angry because Paris is again under siege or because they've had the effrontery to interrupt your career?"

"How dare you!" I kicked my mare's sides to canter away, but his hand shot out to seize the reins from my hands. "Let go this instant," I cried. "You are a cad!"

"I've never denied it. But you didn't answer my question."

"Your question doesn't deserve an answer." I glared at him. "Needless to say, our association is at an end."

He started to laugh again, then suddenly went quiet. He did not release my reins.

"Did you hear me?" I said. "Let me go. Contrary to what you think, I am *not* your pet."

"Sarah." He was staring past me toward the woods. "Be still."

I swiveled about in my saddle. A rustling in the bushes preceded what looked like a harmless vagrant staggering from the forest— but then I saw that he held a rusted pistol, and was croaking out a patriotic stream of vengeance made unintelligible by the sudden pounding of my heart. His wavering shot missed me by a handspan, causing my mare to rear and throw me to the ground. As I blinked in pain from the stony impact, I heard another shot and looked up to see O'Connor had dismounted, his rifle leveled at the vagrant.

"No!" I cried, as the cowering man fell by a tree, a bullet wound in his thigh. "You brute," I shouted at O'Connor. "He's French! Don't shoot him."

"He shot at us," said O'Connor. "Filthy Communard."

The man—who wore a near-unrecognizable uniform coated in filth—moaned, blood spurting from the wound in his thigh. I could see he was beyond exhaustion, that he'd made his way here from the savagery in the city, no doubt witnessing countless horrors along the way. I made a soft soothing sound, as I might to a wounded animal, while he regarded me with pain-clouded eyes. The pistol went limp in his fingers. "I won't harm you," I said, moving toward him, tugging up my habit to rip at my petticoat. "I'm a nurse. Let me bind—"

The shot tore into his forehead, slamming him against the tree. I stared in horrified disbelief as blood streamed down his dead face, then turned in rage to O'Connor.

"He wasn't going to shoot at us again. You . . . you *murdered* him."

"I did." O'Connor sheathed his rifle under his horse's saddle, wiping his gun-powdered fingers on his trousers. "He would have burned down all your theaters."

I swayed in sudden light-headedness. When O'Connor reached out to me, I slapped his hand away and then saw the blood spattering my hand. I could also feel it on my face—the blood of a countryman, shot by a foreigner.

"Sarah," I heard O'Connor say, "this is war. I am sworn to defend the Third Republic."

Mounting my quivering mare, I turned to the château. I did not say another word to him. He was right, but I had just seen the beast lurking under his skin. Men, I had learned, were capable of any excuse to do evil.

ACT V

1871–1879

Mademoiselle Révolte

To drift with every passion till my soul
is a stringed lute on which all winds can play.

—OSCAR WILDE

I

"Must I play that insipid shepherdess till the end of my days?" I made a disparaging motion from where I reclined in a high-necked tea gown in the salon of my flat, my dogs at my side, as my new friend, the painter Georges Clairin, sketched me for a portrait. "The prose is execrable. De Chilly and Duquesnel seem to have lost all concern for our reputation in their zeal to see us in business again."

My other attendees sat on my overstuffed couches, among tasseled pillows and animal pelts. I had returned to Paris to resume my shattered life. The Commune had ended in bloodshed, mayhem, the familiar barricades, and wanton destruction. With our Third Republic established, evidence of our insanity was all around us—our ample boulevards created by Napoleon III's favored minister, Haussmann, strewn with debris from fallen buildings; storefronts gaping like open wounds, shattered and looted; the Tuileries a charred ruin and the column in the Place Vendôme torn down, leaving a jagged pit in its place. With gas lines in dire need of repair, we had to rely on handheld lanterns, and transportation was so unreliable that hiring a public cab was a feat. Everywhere, the fetid stench of death lingered in the air like a noxious reminder of our folly.

It would take years for Paris to regain her luster, but patience was not a Parisian virtue. I'd certainly wasted no time in reestablishing my salon and my theatrical footing, just as those with the means set themselves to reviving their own particular versions of civilization. Restaurants and cafés reopened, featuring menus that, while not a horn of plenty, at least offered more than minced rat or pigeon à la carte. Charity galas were held, and the Odéon, cobbling our repairs as best we could, finally opened its doors, doused with a new patina of gilt and offering seating for our 1871 autumn season, our first in over a year.

"And what does Duquesnel have to say to your complaints?" drawled Arthur Meyer, another new friend and a rising critic, who was giving Sarcey a run for his rapier wit. Plump and short as Sarcey was slim and tall, Meyer enhanced his bohemian flair by donning knotted cravats, pearl-studded shirt cuffs, and voluminous frock coats, along with an incongruous peasant-style beret.

"He defers to de Chilly," I grumbled, waving my hand in annoyance. "Nothing controversial or exacting. According to them, we've had enough exacting controversy."

Georges cast a despairing look at me from his easel, imploring me to retain my serene countenance, required for his art. Duquesnel and I were no longer lovers; that had ended with the siege, just as my liaison with O'Connor ended with the Commune. I was in no mood for love or its approximation, though I still found myself obliged to entertain my banker on occasion, to afford the expense of setting my household to rights. I had my family to feed, and my contractual salary at the Odéon was well in arrears.

"Such a pity," Meyer said with a pout, though he didn't sound sympathetic; he was distracted by the languid dark-haired youth—an aspiring actor—posing for Clairin's apprentice by the windows. The young man, whose name escaped me, indulged the critic's infatuation. Meyer might be on the rotund, acerbic side, but he commanded esteem among his peers and was thoroughly detested by Sarcey. With Paris in shreds, Meyer's recommendation could be the difference between a living onstage and starvation.

As the young man shifted his sultry gaze toward him, Meyer said, "Execrable as it may be, your *Jean Marie* has been a success, with all your notices, including mine, praising your performance as that in-sipid shepherdess."

"It's a comedic trifle," I replied. "What we need to stage now is something important. Times have changed. Even the Comédie has had to adjust its playbill."

Meyer gave a malicious smile. "The House of Molière must cer-tainly have lowered its standards if they saw fit to hire Marie Co-lombier."

I felt a scowl crunch my face, prompting another look of despair from Georges. It had come as a shock to learn that Marie, who'd earned no praise for her acting, had absconded to the Comédie—at their invitation. At first, I couldn't believe it, until I'd seen her on their playbill, featured in a dramatic role she was entirely unsuited to perform.

Extracting a silver case from his waistcoat, Meyer lit a cigarette, though he knew I loathed the smell in my flat. "Perhaps de Chilly requires more time to get his house in order." He paused, to lend his words emphasis. "What might you suggest instead, Sarah?"

"Hugo's *Ruy Blas*," I said at once. "We were going to stage it before the siege. His Queen of Spain is ideal for me and I know the role by heart; I was memorizing it before we had to replace it with Dumas's *Kean* and those student louts rioted in the house."

"Well, the louts won't be rioting now. Their university is a cra-ter. Not to mention Louis-Napoléon despised that play, but with our emperor gone and Hugo back where he belongs, hailed as a heroic defender of our *liberté*, it would indeed be the perfect opportunity."

"Precisely what I told Duquesnel. Yet he keeps saying it's not the right time."

Meyer cast his gaze about the room, as if he might glean a solu-tion behind my potted ferns and painted screens. "Like you, I be-lieve Duquesnel is mistaken. I happen to know Hugo would be very much in favor of seeing his *Ruy Blas* revived in Paris."

"Oh?" I eyed him. Like every critic who relished lambasting us onstage, he had an equally avid ear for our backstage gossip.

"Hugo is residing with his friend Meurice," Meyer went on, though I already knew as much. "I've been invited to dine with them on occasion. After all, Meurice is his devoted ally, and he confided to me that Hugo is very eager to see his work on a French stage."

I forced out a smile, even if I wanted to wring his neck for not seeing to it that I, too, was invited to Hugo's house. "I'm well aware of their years-long friendship. Meurice is also a writer; I happen to know he collaborated with my dear Dumas."

"Do you also happen to know his current mistress is Jane Essler?"

I froze. "The actress?"

"The same."

I took a moment to compose myself. "Does Hugo want her to play the role?"

"Meurice hasn't said as much. But she's enjoyed tremendous acclaim in London and has performed at the Odéon in the past, as you must also well know. I think it likely that Meurice is pressing Hugo to allow her to make her mark here, once they secure the appropriate venue."

"Not at the Odéon," I snapped. "I am the lead actress there."

Meyer exhaled smoke, his commiserative air unable to disguise his glee that he'd caught me unawares. "I assume that's why Duquesnel and de Chilly have delayed answering Hugo's request to stage the play—"

"They delay answering *Victor Hugo*?" My voice rose in outrage, as much at the news as the revelation it had been kept from me. "Have they lost their reason, along with their spine? We'd be the first French company to stage one of Hugo's plays in nineteen years! It would make the Odéon more renowned than the Comédie."

"Not to mention make you our most renowned actress," added Meyer.

I unclenched my hands, just as Clairin threw up his in exasperation at my inability to stay still. "What else?"

"Only that Hugo wants the players to audition for their roles." Meyer grimaced. "At his home. Apparently, he won't allow the play to be read in the theater."

"But that's preposterous. We always audition in the house; it's where our roles will be performed."

Meyer tapped ash into my Limoges teacup. "And there we have it."

"Can't he be persuaded otherwise?" I said. "He wasn't in exile so long as to forget how we conduct business."

"I assume Duquesnel and de Chilly have tried. According to Meurice, either the Odéon agrees to the terms or Hugo will apply elsewhere."

"He'll go to the Comédie." I was overcome by panic.

Meyer drew on his cigarette. "That is a possibility. But what can you do? You cannot audition outside the theater. It would set an appalling precedent, both for the theater and for you, as Meurice would waste no time in comparing you unfavorably to Mademoiselle Essler."

I swallowed, looking at Clairin standing there in his smock, with his fingertips smeared with charcoal and a lock of chestnut hair tumbled across his forehead. I might have taken him for a lover were I in the mood; he'd certainly expressed his willingness. Now, he returned my gaze in mute sympathy. He wasn't an actor, so he had no insight to offer.

From the corner where the young man was posing, Clairin's apprentice said in a voice so low I almost failed to hear it, "Perhaps *you* might persuade Monsieur Hugo."

I peered at her. She was a mouse of a young woman, with overpoweringly melancholic dark eyes in a pinched face, and the long-fingered hands of a sculptress. What was her name? Louise something . . . Abbey? No. Abbéma. Louise Abbéma. I couldn't see her work from where I was sitting, so I stood and went to her easel, Clairin declaring that at this rate, he wouldn't complete my portrait until the next century.

She'd captured the youth's sinuous indifference in a few bold charcoal lines.

"This is remarkable," I said. "You're very talented, Louise."

She lowered her eyes. As the youth slipped away to whisper what no doubt amounted to an offer in Meyer's ear, I asked her, "How do you think I could persuade him?"

Her little face with its piquant features took on a concentrated expression. She didn't hasten to reassure me, as I expected, that she had no experience to draw upon, but that the lead actress of the Odéon mustn't be demeaned even by the great Victor Hugo. Instead, she appeared to grant my request every bit of consideration before she said, "A note informing him of how one ought to treat a queen might suffice."

"A note?" I let out a sudden laugh. "Only that?"

"It depends on what the note conveys, Mademoiselle Bernhardt."

She lifted her gaze. Such eyes. Like an ancient in a child's soul. She couldn't be more than fifteen; in the wake of the siege and collapse of our empire, many young women were now obliged to earn their keep, but she had an air of privilege about her, which she would have to possess to choose art as an occupation. Female artists were usually denigrated for their inferior work, with few admitted to the coveted annual exhibition at the Salon des Artistes—although judging by what I'd seen, I thought she might prove an exception.

"You must paint me one day, Louise," I said impulsively. "And please, call me Sarah."

"I would like nothing better, Sarah," she replied, and a frisson of something akin to pleasure trembled in my veins. It surprised and disconcerted me.

I returned to my settee, retaining my pose long enough for Clairin to capture his sketch. After he and Louise packed up their utensils and bade me farewell, the youth slinking at their heels, Meyer came up to me, his hat in hand. "*Ma chère*, you should be more careful on whom you bestow your affections, if you wish to impress Victor Hugo."

I tapped his shoulder. "She's but a child. Besides, I'm not in-clined that way."

He smiled with a hint of teeth. "Children grow up. And inclina-tions change."

I delayed until the evening. I had the night free, so I supped with Caroline, Régine, and Maurice, tucked my son into bed, read to him, then paced my empty salon, where Caroline had drawn the drapes before retiring for the night.

Tugging back the heavy curtains, I gazed into the dark streets, where handheld lanterns bobbed like spectral lights in the winter mist.

It depends on what the note conveys, Mademoiselle Bernhardt.

Turning to my desk, I inked my pen and, before I lost my nerve, wrote:

The Queen has caught a chill, and her lady-in-waiting forbids her to go out. You, better than anyone, should know the etiquette of our court. Pity your Queen, monsieur!

No signature. It was unnecessary. Sealing my small note in an envelope, I wrote the address of Meurice's home on it and left it for Caroline to deliver.

I couldn't sleep. I kept thinking I should submit to the demand, berate Duquesnel for keeping it from me, and agree to read wher-ever and however Hugo ordained.

But when I woke in the morning, Caroline had left with the note and Madame G. had arrived to tend to Maurice and Régine, though my younger sister approached her fifteenth year and required some occupation in life other than playing with my son or driving Julie mad with her tantrums.

Caroline returned hours later, with sacks of groceries. I couldn't believe it. "You went all the way to the market?" I said in dismay.

"Yes." She looked confused. "We have fresh vegetables and fruit now. And meat."

"Never mind that," I snapped. "What about my note?"

She removed a crumpled envelope from her pocket. "His reply," she said, and she hurried into the kitchen to avoid my fury at her disregard for the urgency of the matter.

Tearing open the envelope with trembling fingers, I unfolded his note.

I am Your Majesty's devoted servant.

II

In keeping with his reputation, Victor Hugo was a lion of a man, with cropped silver hair and a weathered countenance that belied the intensity of his stare. Despite his paunch and stiffened gait, Hugo behaved much younger than his sixty-nine years, drilling us for hours on end on the stage, growling out the specific intonations required for his verse.

Upon signing the contract at the Odéon, Hugo informed de Chilly and Duquesnel that I'd won my coveted role "with a mere note." De Chilly gave a sour smile. What else could he do? Hugo's novel *Les Misérables* was enjoying a massive revival, after having set off a storm of controversy upon its publication during his exile, with outraged cries among the aristocracy calling for his head, in much the same way the novel portrayed the gross injustice between rich and poor. It was selling thousands of copies in its latest edition, renewing Hugo's iconic status. To stage his *Ruy Blas* was a coup that de Chilly couldn't deny, as evidenced by his immediate printing of advance playbills and advertisements.

HUGO RETURNS, his newspaper headlines blared, and in smaller print than pleased me: WITH SARAH BERNHARDT AS THE QUEEN.

Every day, I arrived for rehearsal full of excitement. As soon as Hugo appeared in his rumpled waistcoat, his battered copy of the play under his arm as he took his seat in an armchair before the stage, I feigned indifference. But I was very much aware that while he was merciless with the cast, he appeared oblivious to me. Not once did he suggest an improvement to my delivery, though I over-played my lines just to see if I could capture his attention. Instead, he waved me aside and proceeded to harangue the others, stabbing his hands in the air—"This year, if you please. We open in less than four weeks"—while the players hastened to fulfill his exacting in-structions.

Perched on a nearby table one morning during our final week of rehearsal, I swung my legs and gnawed my fingernails, pretending boredom, letting out a loud sigh as he made adjustments to the scene in question, in which I didn't appear. I kept my gaze on anything but him, until one of the stagehands approached to slip a folded paper into my fingers.

When I read it, I burst into laughter, bringing the rehearsal to a halt.

A Queen of Spain, honest and respectable, shouldn't sit in that fash-ion on a table.

Lifting my eyes to him, I saw Hugo hadn't turned around, but when the time came for me to take my mark, he criticized me with vehement focus.

Two days later, he requested that I pay a visit to his home.

"Should I emote like this?" I stood center stage in his parlor. " 'To shun despair, I gave my soul to dreams, and sought for their indul-gence the solitude of lonely walks. In one of these I found, while resting for a moment, a bouquet of the flowers I most loved. I won-dered whence they came, but I knew someone cared to please me; and with their fragrances inhaled a sense of ecstasy—a thought that someone loved me.' " I paused. "She's both melancholic and hope-ful in this scene. Which emotion should I emphasize more?"

He regarded me with a curious smile. "Which do you think?"

"I'm asking you. You are the playwright. You must have a preference for how you wish to see the scene performed."

His smile widened. "Ah, but you don't truly want my advice. I don't believe I've met an actress who wanted advice less."

"I most certainly do," I said indignantly. "Why else would I have come here?"

He reached up a hand to stroke his impressive beard. "Mademoiselle Bernhardt, as you can imagine, given my age I've enjoyed quite my share of feminine attention."

I saw it then, the lustful spark in his eyes, which until that moment I hadn't recognized. I set my hand on my hip. "Monsieur Hugo, I can't imagine who you suppose I am."

"A magnificent actress," he said. "Judging by this performance. You needn't go to such trouble, however. I believe we are of the same mind."

I held his stare. "And as you can imagine, I, too, have enjoyed my share of attention. I'm not so easily satisfied."

His laughter rumbled in his chest. "I expect nothing less."

▪▪

February 19, 1872. Opening night. Dressed in a white-silver brocade gown and filigree coronet, I drew in slow breaths, battling a resurgence of *le trac*. Knowing why I was afflicted by the near-incapacitating fear didn't alleviate its upheaval; I felt as if I stood on a sinking ship as the first act began and I assumed my place for my entrance.

At his post nearby, de Chilly looked frantic, as always. The house was full to capacity. We'd sold out weeks in advance, abetted by his publicity and the fact that Hugo himself was attending this long-anticipated revival of a play that, at its premiere years before, hadn't garnered any notice. No one had paid it any mind, in fact, until Louis-Napoléon came down against it. Now, with all of Paris embarking on a new era, all of Paris had purchased tickets to attend.

"No one's applauding," de Chilly whispered to me. "Listen. The first act is nearly over and no one's made a sound. They hate it."

"They do not," I hissed back. "They're waiting." For me. Everyone was waiting for me. Although Ruy Blas was the titular character, the play depended on its queen—and on my rendition of her.

At my cue, I walked onto the stage under a red canopy borne by livery-clad pages, into the papier-mâché garden, with my chin held high.

Tonight, I must conquer every heart in Paris.

"You were *sublime,* Sarah. Tonight, you proved your talent to the world," exulted Sarcey, pressing my hands in his. "No one before has given Hugo's prose such vigor."

We stood in my overcrowded dressing room, every tabletop drowning in flowers as well-wishers crammed through the narrow door to congratulate me. I was still in my regal costume, having barely finished my curtain calls before de Chilly motioned me backstage. It seemed as if everyone who'd seen the play was now attempting to fit into my dressing room. I felt cornered but not unhappy as I smiled at Sarcey—this same man who'd ruined my fledging career with his indifference, now fawning over me—and sneaked glances over the milling crowd toward the door, anticipating Hugo's entrance.

De Chilly was trying to curtail the invasion, if not very well, while Duquesnel stood to one side, smoking with an air of immense satisfaction. Our premiere had been a rousing success; the applause at the end of the final act thunderous, the audience leaping up to shout my name. For a dazed moment, I hadn't known how to react; I'd felt the performance in my bones, the yearning and despair of my betrayed queen, but to hear such acclaim, the cry of "Sarah, our Sarah!" hoisted to the Odéon's newly gilded rafters—it kindled a sensation unlike any I'd felt before. This wasn't *Le Passant,* a ditty performed for charity, which had earned unexpected acclaim; I had just performed a role written by the most respected writer in France. I felt as if I were floating when I emerged to take my curtain calls, the very air bursting alive with petals, every bouquet in the house tossed at my feet.

At my side, Sophie, who had played my lady-in-waiting, said, "They'll devour you now, Sarah. I sincerely hope Marie Colombier hears of this night."

"Oh, she'll hear of it," I replied, as Sarcey turned away and Meyer came forth with a wry, knowing smile. "Let her be warned."

"Warned?" Sophie shot me a puzzled look, but before she could say anything else, I saw Hugo at last, his silvery hair and black-clad bulk pushing through the door as the crowd parted before him like the Red Sea.

He had to stop, accept homage from all those eager to bask in his triumph. For it was his triumph as much as mine—more so, in truth. I'd proven my talent, but Hugo had proven his resiliency. From disgraced exile to returning hero, he'd regained his status. Watching him smile at the effusive compliments, I recalled his rough hands on my bare skin. I'd enjoyed our liaison; despite his age, he had extraordinary stamina. Of course, it must end. He had other mistresses, and neither of us was inclined to exclusivity, but for its brief duration, it had been one of the most gratifying interludes of my life. Once, as he'd teased me toward *la petite mort*, he whispered in my ear, "I think you're not nearly as satisfied as often as you should be," and I'd laughed through my climax.

He was right. And he'd taken pains to remedy my lack.

Impatient, I watched him trace his trajectory as hands reached out to touch his sleeve and oblige him to pause. Just as I thought I'd have to make my way to him, I caught sight of a dark-eyed man by the dressing room door, leaning against the wall with his arms crossed at his chest. He wore a costume from the play, though I couldn't for the life of me recall which role he'd performed. Under his mane of curly black hair, his magnetic eyes were fixated on me. I wondered how I'd failed to notice him before, with that muscular build, sculpted jawline, and Roman nose, like a classical statue come to life. Nonetheless, I found his heavy-lidded stare unsettling. I couldn't tell whether he regarded me in admiration or disdain.

"Who is that?" I asked Sophie, through the side of my mouth.

"Have you gone blind? That's our own Hugo."

"Not him. Beside Duquesnel."

She followed my gaze. "Surely, you can't be serious. He's an actor with our company: Jean Mounet-Sully. He's performing the role of Ruy Blas's page."

"Is he?" I forced myself to look away. "Why is he looking at me like that?"

She laughed. "Perhaps because he's in the play and you don't know who he is. Duquesnel only hired him for the season, but I believe he's done well enough tonight to earn a contract. He'll make an impressive leading man one day, don't you think?"

"I suppose so." Sailing forth, I went to Hugo, accepting his whiskered kisses on my cheeks and feeling his furtive pinch on my backside.

"You'll always be my queen now," he chuckled in my ear. He turned to the crowd, lifting our clasped hands. "Wasn't she everything a Queen of Spain should be?"

The room broke into applause. A sudden rush, more pleasurable than anything he'd done to me in bed, overcame me. I saw myself at Hugo's side, the daughter of a courtesan, whom no one save my dear Dumas had believed would amount to anything, the defamed girl of the Slap, of the frivolities of the Gymnase, the frightened mother who nearly lost everything to bear her illicit child. Every humiliation had brought me to this hour; I could revel in my achievement. I was the toast of Paris. I'd made my theatrical mark.

Except that as Hugo beamed and I feigned humility, even as I couldn't repress my proud smile, I saw that brooding actor, to whom I'd never said a word, turn and disappear through the door into the passageway beyond, like a reproach.

III

I t was inevitable, Meyer said. After two hundred sold-out performances of *Ruy Blas* and countless columns dedicated to my emergence as "a passionate revelation"—as if I hadn't been toiling on
the stage for years—the command to return to the Comédie, thinly
veiled as an invitation, was only to be expected.

"You've become our most celebrated actress," he said, as I paced
my otherwise empty salon, for of course he'd ignored my abrupt
cancellation of my habitual gathering so I could have some time to
myself. "You were declared a heroine of our Republic for your val-
iant efforts during the war, and souvenir shops are selling thousands
of those portrait postcards of you as the Queen of Spain. The Française can't afford to ignore you any longer. I should think you'd be
pleased. This is what you wanted all along, is it not?"

"Surely not." I turned to him. "The Comédie threw me out into
the street."

"As I recall, you left them after you slapped a *sociétaire*."

"They still never believed I had any talent. The only reason they
want me back now is because I've proved them wrong."

"With a considerable increase in salary to atone for their error."

"How would *you* know that?" I demanded, immediately suspicious. Was he responsible? I wouldn't put it past him to have extolled my merits to the managing director of the House of Molière.

If I left the Odéon to return to the Comédie, he could take credit for it and score another victory in his ongoing battle against his rival Sarcey.

"My dear, if they hadn't, you wouldn't be in such a state. One doesn't cancel one's entire day for a minor sum. And regardless of the Odéon's success with *Ruy Blas*, I doubt they can match whatever the Comédie has to offer."

"Twelve thousand a year," I breathed. "Twice my current salary." I couldn't hide the unwitting satisfaction in my voice, that the very company that nearly ruined my career now wanted me so desperately they had offered a fortune.

"You're worth every franc," said Meyer. "Unlike de Chilly, the Comédie knows it."

I turned from his remorseless expression, looking upward as Régine and Maurice chased each other upstairs, their footsteps pounding on the floorboards and threatening to crack my salon's ceiling plaster. Both of them should have been in school, but they'd begged me to let them have the day off, and I'd been too beset by my turmoil to argue. Downstairs, Caroline was instructing my maids—I'd hired two neighborhood girls to assist with the endless cooking and cleaning, as well as a butler—while Madame G. oversaw the enterprise, for she'd taken permanent residence with us, her aged bones faring better in my well-warmed flat than in her decrepit garret across town.

I had to pay the bills, see to everyone's welfare. And while my mother and I staked our mutual distance, I must pay for her upkeep, too. Rosine had settled in with her suitor, but from what my aunt told me whenever she came to visit, my sister Jeanne suffered more than scars from her near brush with death. The trauma lingered and she'd resorted to opium, which clouded her judgment and ability to conduct herself as required. Julie had thrust her back into her salon, but Jeanne was attracting few suitors, with none constant or wealthy enough to grant our mother any peace of mind.

The increase in my salary would satisfy all of it, but I still couldn't bring myself to consider it, even if I knew Meyer was right in asserting that the Odéon couldn't possibly hope to match the offer. As if he sensed my hesitation, he said, "Surely you don't intend to decline their invitation? The Comédie will only abase itself once."

"Is it an abasement?" I turned my gaze to him. "Or merely an opportune way to increase their receipts? I hardly think Marie Colombier is attracting record audiences."

"Does it matter? You know very well the Comédie is still considered our most prestigious theatrical venue. We've all fallen on hard times since the end of the empire, but their status remains inviolate. How can you refuse them?"

"How can I not, after everything the Odéon has done for me?"

"You've done far more for them. You forget you were the one who lured Hugo to their stage." He stood, gathering his coat. "I cannot tell you what to do, but I will suggest that you think very carefully on it. To become a *sociétaire* at the Comédie will gain you a prestige you can never achieve at the Odéon. It may be harsh, but it's true nonetheless."

I saw him to the door. Once he departed, I started back to my salon when Maurice, his hair disheveled and face flushed, my pack of dogs at his heels, came running to the top of the staircase. He called down breathlessly, "Mama, can we have a pony?"

"A pony!" I looked up at him in amazement. "Whatever for?"

"So I can ride it," he said, with a puzzled look.

Régine appeared beside him, equally disheveled. "He keeps wanting to ride me," she sneered. "I told him boys should only ride *putaines* or ponies, and I am neither."

Seeing the mounds of her small breasts indenting her bodice, her black tresses tumbled about her sharp-boned face, I was struck in that instant by my failure to mark her transition into womanhood. Her enrollment in school hadn't brought about the change I'd hoped for. She was not an adept student and had failed to discover an interest to sustain her; indeed, her instructors had informed me that my sister suffered from a distortion of the mind that would, in time, require institutionalization. I refused to countenance the possibility, insisting she merely needed to grow out of her childhood. Now, the abrupt realization that she might never grow out of it made my decision. If Régine couldn't support herself or live unsupervised, she would require a full-time companion, which only I could provide. In order to do so, I must negotiate with the Odéon. I couldn't take on the extra expense on my current salary.

"Get to your books at once," I said. "I don't want to hear another sound out of either of you until supper. Am I understood?"

Maurice scowled at me. Régine let loose a cackle, but the laughter strangled her and incited one of her increasingly frequent coughing fits. She bent over, hacking, pressing a hand to her chest as if she lacked for air.

"Ma petite dame!" I cried, and Madame G. rushed out from the kitchen. Climbing the staircase behind me, she went to my sister as I instinctively pulled Maurice aside, blocking his view. Madame G. assisted Régine into the small parlor off my bedroom, where I'd set up my neglected sculpting and painting, along with my battered coffin. Here, she sat Régine on the settee as my sister, gone so pale that I could see the veins in her temples, struggled to draw a full breath.

I felt Maurice wince under my hands on his shoulders when Madame G. lifted her face to me. "We must summon the doctor."

"No," croaked Régine, still defiant as she gasped for air. "I hate that old goat."

"He examined her last month." I resisted the urge to shove Maurice behind me. "He told us it's another of her summer agues, nothing to be concerned about."

"It's not an ague." Madame G. held out her hand; I froze at the sight of blood spotting her fingertips. I knew what it meant, but my mind shrank from it. It wasn't possible. Régine was just sixteen.

"Yes. Send for him at once." Swallowing a surge of tears in my throat, I steered Maurice to his room down the hall, which looked as if a storm had ripped through it, books and clothes and toys strewn everywhere. "Clean this mess up. Then finish your lessons. Tomor-

row, you'll return to the academy, and every day thereafter. No"—
I held up my hand—"enough, my son. It is time you stop running
about with Régine and attend to your studies. Don't you want to
grow up to be a proper gentleman?"

"I want to grow up to be a player like you," he said.

I smiled. "How can you know what you wish to do in life until
you finish your education and learn everything there is to know?" I
wanted to dissuade him, to cite the toil and travails of a player's life,
which often never amounted to anything but sacrifice and disillusionment. But I'd never heard him mention any ambition until now,
and when he said, "Don't you want me to be a player?" I replied,
"Only if it's your calling."

He considered. "Régine says I write wonderful stories. Maybe I
could be a writer instead? Do I need to go to the academy to be a
writer?"

"You write stories?" I was taken aback. How had this happened?
How had I failed to notice this about my own child?

Going to his upended bureau, he took out a small parcel of notebooks. Untying the ribbon binding them, he spread them on the
floor at my feet. I knelt down to open their pages, filled with his
handwriting and accomplished illustrations that brought a gasp to
my lips. "You did all of this?" I said in amazement.

He nodded. "My teachers say it's not a proper occupation, but I
like writing stories."

I thought suddenly of Dumas, of his rescue of me while I was
pregnant. Had the spirit of my late benefactor somehow imprinted
his essence on my unborn child?

"I must read these," I said, gathering up the notebooks.

He pouted. "If you like them, can I have a pony then?"

"If you complete this year with outstanding marks, I'll consider it."

He gave a dejected nod. As I turned to the door, he said quietly,
"Is Régine going to die?"

I went still, unable to speak for a moment. "She has weak lungs;

that's what the physician told us. You mustn't force her to exert herself."

"She's the one who forces me." He collected an armful of his clothes, trudging to the bureau. "She comes here and empties out the drawers, then makes me chase after her."

"Yes, she's untamed. Like—like a pony," I said haltingly, "before it learns to accept the saddle." My metaphor was clumsy and I didn't want to say more, but the unsettling way he contemplated me brought the unbidden question to my lips. "Has she ever . . . ?"

He frowned. "Ever what?"

"Touched you," I whispered, overcome by a deep sense of guilt and shame. But I had heard Régine's earlier remark about *putaines*. She'd been raised in my mother's household, where she'd been exposed to things no girl like her should see. She was now at an age when the sexual impulse was natural, and where else might she experiment?

"All the time," he said, without hesitation, as any seven-year-old boy would with a tempestuous older sister, which was how he regarded Régine. There was no abashment in his reply; what I'd feared had not come to pass, despite her callous comment.

I forced out another smile. "Very well. Mama must go to the theater now, but I'll be back later tonight. See that you complete your lessons. Or no pony."

"What about a new turtle?" he said hopefully.

I had to laugh, even if mirth was the last thing I felt.

That evening, I gave my final performance in *Ruy Blas*. I waited until after the curtain calls, bouquets of flowers, and endless backstage greetings; once everyone from the cast had departed for the late supper party at a popular restaurant arranged by Duquesnel to celebrate the end of our season, I went upstairs to his office, hoping to catch him alone before he left. Instead, I found de Chilly hunched at the desk with a pile of receipts and pen in hand, his shirtsleeves held up by armbands as he prepared for a long night of tallying the profit. Heaving a sigh at the sight of me, he said, "Sarah, why are you still here? Much as you abhor punctuality, Duquesnel expects you to be on time tonight. Need I remind you that you and Hugo are his guests of honor? A needless expense, which he insisted on."

I would have preferred to conduct this difficult transaction with Duquesnel first, but in the end, de Chilly had the final word. Only he had the authority to increase my pay. To counter my trepidation, I remembered what Meyer had said about my contributions.

He went still as I set the Comédie's offer before him. "What is that?"

"Read it for yourself."

His gaze narrowed. "I have no need." He brushed the letter aside. "I'm in no temper for whatever you and Sarcey have concocted for my entertainment."

"Sarcey?" I said, curbing my ire at his supercilious tone.

"Oh? Have we suddenly ceased to read our own notices? Your friend the critic has been lamenting to all and sundry that the Comédie has failed to live up to its standards by having no one to match your peerless splendor," he said with a sneer.

"I didn't know." And I hadn't, to my chagrin, believing Meyer to be behind it. But of course, it made sense. Meyer had only incited me to action because he knew that regardless of the vitriol in Sarcey's pen, the venerable critic valued his reputation too much to personally persuade me to abandon the Odéon. Meyer decided to do it instead, knowing that if he succeeded, he could still assume full credit.

"And here I thought you and the critic were the best of friends," de Chilly said. "In any event, lest you think I'm a fool, let me also inform you that the Comédie wants nothing to do with you. I know their managing director, Monsieur Perrin, personally and he cringes at the mere mention of your name."

I sensed at once that he sought to incite my doubt, yet still I had to take a moment to collect myself. De Chilly and I had never been

on good terms, but he'd allowed Duquesnel to rescue me from ignominy; begrudging as he may have been, he'd given me the means
to return to the stage when no one else would. I owed him that
much.

"For a company that wants nothing to do with me, they're offering a considerable sum," I said. "Six thousand more, in fact—"

"Impossible. They are in no position, not if Rachel herself came
back from the dead. And certainly not after their dismal run this
season."

"They've offered it, regardless. I have my future to consider."

His face flushed red; he half rose out of his chair, stabbing the
pen in his hand at me. "You only have a so-called future because of
us. You also have a contract here to consider. We made you whoever
you think you are, and have allowed you more latitude than any respectable company should."

His deprecatory manner squashed my hesitation.

"My latitude brought Victor Hugo himself to this house—"

"With a mere note. Yes, I'm very aware of your persuasive
charm. As is, no doubt, all of Paris by now." He eyed me with derision. "I have no idea how you manage it, but I suppose some men
prefer to pick their teeth after a meal. In my time, we preferred our
women with actual meat on their bones."

"How dare you." I took an enraged step toward him.

"I dare," he retorted, "because you trespass beyond decency. Did
you think playing the whore with Hugo would allow you to swing
this guillotine over our heads? If so, you are very much mistaken.
You've earned some acclaim, for the moment, but it is not cause for
anything more than we've given, regardless of how much you
choose to give others."

My efforts to remain composed faltered as I recognized the depth
of the resentment he nursed toward me. He refused to take pride in
my accomplishments because had it been up to him, I would never
have accomplished anything, so he must resort to degradation instead. I'd prepared to cite my mounting household costs—for as the

first actress of the Odéon I must be seen to live in style—as well as the upkeep of my family; even, if necessary, the tragic situation looming over Régine, though I still held out hope that the physician would prescribe a remedy. I'd rehearsed it all in my head as I'd removed my paint and costume; now my entire script went from my head as I heard him demeaning my importance—an importance I had earned with my sacrifices, regardless of who had provided the means. In his inflexible stance, I heard my mother, berating me for my foolishness. I heard Kératry, telling me he couldn't be held responsible for my mishap. I heard everyone who'd set obstacles in my path and forced me to surmount them.

"I know you never wished to hire me," I said. "Yet here we are. And you cannot expect me to stay for another season when I can earn twice what you pay elsewhere."

"Like you, what I want is of no account," he replied. "I do, however, expect your compliance. Moreover, our contract demands it."

"Then I shall break our contract."

His expression darkened. "Let me warn you now, do not test me further."

"You're the one testing me," I exclaimed. "If you will not increase my salary, what else can I do?"

"And you think you'll find success at the Comédie?" he snarled. "You have no idea of what awaits you, if you dare. Monsieur Perrin will never tolerate your caprices as we have. He cannot afford it. And you cannot afford to go against us."

"You give me no other choice," I said, my voice trembling with rage.

"Oh, but I do. Attend your celebratory party and report here in a week for our next season. That is your choice, as detailed in our contract."

Meeting his stare, I whirled to the door.

"Mademoiselle Bernhardt," he bellowed.

I paused, hearing his next words aimed like knives at my back.

"If you sign a contract anywhere else, I will pursue legal recourse. Have no doubt, your name will be in every newspaper, though in far less laudatory terms. And I can assure you, the Comédie will *not* be amused. You will regret this hour for the rest of your life."

I couldn't feel my legs as I took the staircase to the lobby and out the back door to my fiacre. Only once I was being driven toward my flat did I realize my hands were clenched so tight, every one of my fingers ached. My entire person felt taut, about to snap.

I had no doubt de Chilly would do exactly what he threatened.

Nor what I must do, regardless.

IV

The Comédie smelled of stagnant repertories and yellowed play-bills, overlaid by funereal solemnity as the company assembled in the greenroom, with its sacred bust of Molière, to receive their assignments for the upcoming season.

It was my first appearance as its new member, although my return had been heralded in the newspapers, with Meyer and Sarcey dueling in rapturous anticipation over what my return to France's most venerated stage would signal for its diminished fortunes. Neither spared the superlatives, declaring, "Sarah Bernhardt's engagement at the Française is a revolution. Poetry has entered the domain of dramatic art," and other similar statements of grandiosity that did nothing to endear me to the company director, Monsieur Perrin.

Upon signing my contract, Perrin—a slender man with angular features and a rigid demeanor—regarded the inkblot spilled in haste under my signature as if it were a criminal offense before he said, "Allow me to welcome you to the Française. I trust this unfortunate situation with the Odéon will not delay your commitment."

"Not at all," I replied, appalled that he'd already heard of de Chilly's suit against me for six thousand francs, the exact amount of my increase in salary, which he claimed was the loss the Odéon would incur due to my illegal voiding of our contract.

"I should hope not. Duquesnel sent me a chastising letter, as apparently you were deemed under contract. I must insist all my players in this company avoid extraneous publicity."

As I left his office, Marie Colombier appeared in the corridor as if on cue. She must have been lying in wait for me, but she pretended to be surprised, though it was obvious she was not.

"Sarah. Why, this is . . ."

I took some satisfaction in her effort. "My engagement here has been in the newspapers for weeks, as Monsieur Perrin just informed me."

Never one to hide her antipathy for a perceived rival or disguise her current position of favor, she abandoned the pretense. "Yes, but none of us actually thought you'd forsake the Odéon or incite such a scandal."

"De Chilly refused to let me depart amicably," I replied. "And there's no need for concern. I've worked here before. I am aware of how things are done."

"Are you?" She gave a tight smile. "Because your ensemble suggests otherwise."

I smiled back at her. "My ensemble is by Jacques Doucet. Isn't it charming? He designs the most current fashions. Look, no bustle."

I could tell by her prim light-blue dress with its oversized bustle and lace-trimmed neckline that she had no idea Doucet was Paris's most innovative couturier, nor that I'd had a personal hand in designing my tailored shirtwaist and narrow skirt, along with the belt studded with talismans that was slung on my narrow hips. But the pièce de résistance was my hat, featuring a desiccated bat nested in coiled black velvet ribbon. Given the popularity of my image from *Ruy Blas*, I'd sat for a portrait by Nadar in the hat and he'd had it reproduced for the shops, where it was earning us a tidy profit, with the extra bonus of steering public conversation away from my professional imbroglios to my unfathomable eccentricity.

"And do you think that hat is charming, too?" said Marie. "Because let me assure you, Madame Nathalie will not be impressed. She protested your contract here most vigorously."

By now, it was clear we weren't really discussing my choice in attire, and it pained me to hear us descend to this level, exchanging barbs like aged courtesans over a suitor.

"Marie," I told her, "I am not a threat to you. I never have been."

"A threat?" She let out a careless laugh that failed to disguise her discomfort. "Sarah, you always did think too much of yourself."

"Do I? Or is it you who always thinks too much of me?"

Despite her obvious dismay that I'd dared broach the subject of our rivalry, which she herself had instigated, she still couldn't repress a snide chuckle. "I'm quite well positioned here and do not see you as a threat. I simply wished to offer you friendly advice. The Comédie is not the Odéon."

"How kind of you." I made myself lean forward to kiss her cheeks; as she flinched at my unexpected gesture of affection, I whispered, "You haven't changed a bit, *chère* Marie."

Still, I feared she might be right as I beheld the august players of the House of Molière, all of whom regarded me as if I'd defiled their musty halls with my intolerable modernity. I couldn't believe that in the nine years since my departure, nothing had changed here. Our empire had disintegrated, our city had been besieged and plundered twice, yet within these walls where the portraits of the deceased testified to the faded glories of the past, time had ceased to move. The assembly looked as *ancien* as the horsehair-stuffed settees, with Madame Nathalie in particular, grown stout as a hippopotamus, glaring at me from her pride of place among the senior *sociétaires,* a penciled beauty spot quivering on her jowl as if she were a royal mistress in Versailles.

What had I done? How could I have voluntarily left a company where I reigned supreme for this antiquated den of famished lions?

I steeled my resolve. In making my name here, I'd conquer the highest bastion of the theatrical world. More immediately, the extra income was essential, and as I thought this, I bit back the sorrow that was never far from my heart these days.

My sister Régine was suffering from advanced consumption,

confirmed by the physician who'd managed to examine her despite her flailing and insults. When he informed us, I burst into tears, even if Régine would have none of our pity. Through wretched bouts of coughing, she begged me to let her stay, so Madame G. and I set her up in my bedroom, while I took to sleeping in my coffin in the parlor. The physician recommended a drier climate, citing it could extend Régine's health, but for now she was too weak to travel, so while Madame G. installed herself at her bedside, I'd swallowed my pride and gone to Julie.

"Paris is too damp in the winter," I explained, as Rosine began to weep. "She needs the dry air of the Pyrenees. Perhaps among the three of us, we can—"

Julie gave a regretful sigh. "I always knew that child would bring nothing but grief."

I suddenly had no outrage left to vent on her. She made clear by her pronouncement and evident circumstances—her salon devoid of callers, her prized pianoforte draped in silence as Jeanne languished in opiate-induced obliviousness—that Régine's fate depended on me, as always. Once my sister recovered her strength, I must send her to the spa on my own. Much like the Comédie, nothing had changed in my mother's house, even as the present devoured whatever remained of the past.

Hearing my name announced, I brought myself to attention. Perrin stood in the center of the room with the roster. "Sarah Bernhardt will play the lead in Dumas's *Mademoiselle de Belle-Isle*. Rehearsals to commence next week at—"

I started to my feet. Everyone turned to me in disbelief when I said, "I thought we'd agreed on Junie in *Britannicus*. It's far better suited to my premiere—"

"*Premiere?*" echoed Madame Nathalie, as Monsieur Perrin fixed his glacial stare on me. "How easily we forget. It is not a premiere when one must make amends for past mistakes."

I turned to her; she was ensconced on a gilded chair and surrounded by the privileged and outdated pillars of authority who'd lashed me through my training at the Conservatoire. I sorely missed my instructor Provost, now retired due to chronic ill health, as he would have surely taken me under his wing. Instead, I confronted a wall of stolid resistance that might as well have been a firing squad. In their pitiless stance, I saw that every one of them had protested my engagement and was resolved to campaign for my failure, hastening my second and final dismissal from their ranks.

Madame Nathalie met my gaze. "Yes? Have you anything else to say, mademoiselle?"

I did. Plenty, in fact. The torrent scalded my mouth, but the last thing I needed was a confrontation with her on my very first day.

She snapped open a fan to stir the dust about her. "I'm relieved that at least you appear to have learned some discretion during your time at that Left Bank playhouse, if not any discernible improvement in your taste in clothing. Is it a Hebraic custom, perhaps, to parade about with a dead creature on one's head?"

No one laughed. It wasn't done at the Comédie. Had the same remark been aimed at me at the Odéon, there would have been an eruption of hilarity, with me storming about in mock outrage while the company nudged my ribs. Here, her pronouncement was absorbed with the solemnity of a religious decree.

Perrin said flatly, "I believe you and Monsieur Dumas were acquainted before his untimely demise. He would be pleased to see you bring one of his most beloved works back to our stage, as you did with Monsieur Hugo. Lest you've forgotten, it was also Rachel's favorite role."

I hadn't forgotten. "Yes," I murmured. "Monsieur Dumas would be pleased." I expected Madame Nathalie to deliver another indictment on my unacceptable conduct with playwrights, but she merely allowed herself a satisfied snort. She was perfectly aware that despite Rachel's acclaim in the role, the play itself was one of Dumas's least accomplished—a romantic melodrama without the classical heft required to elevate my stature.

"This is not the Odéon," Perrin went on, echoing Marie's words

to me and confirming my assumption that he partook of her mediocre talent after hours. "Here, we perform as a company, devoted to
our unique specialties. I trust that is understood." Specialties, as if
actors must be consigned to one specific type of role until the end of
their career. I felt ill as I assented, because to say another word
would surely result in my dismissal, as I had a mind to inform him
precisely what I thought of his selection for my debut, as well as his
precious specialties, all of which were destined to undermine me.

Returning to my seat, I caught Marie's spiteful glance. As I felt
hot anger surge in my chest, I forced out a smile. They'd not get the
better of me this time. Much as I longed to give the entire House of
Molière another well-deserved slap into our present age, I'd bite my
tongue and dedicate myself to the work, until the opportunity presented itself.

For it would. It must. Much as it might try me, fate always favored me in the end.

And as I sat there, barely paying heed as Perrin recited the other
designations, from lead roles to secondary parts for the new *pension-
naires,* I saw him, among the new hires, his stare fixated on me from
across the room. That dark brooding actor from the Odéon, who
had watched me in much the same manner after my triumph in *Ruy
Blas.*

I averted my gaze.

Clearly, his contract hadn't been renewed at the Odéon, and I
still couldn't tell if he admired or disdained me, but his presence
gave me unexpected relief.

At least someone here knew what I was capable of.

V

"A disaster." Gulping down my third cup of coffee, I beckoned the waiter to serve me another. "After I implored Perrin. Why ask me to return, only to humiliate me? My dreadful notices can't be helping him or the house. And that serpent Marie—she's sleeping with Perrin, naturally, and everyone knows it. She's never been discreet and she couldn't contain her glee when Perrin assigned her the best roles for the season."

"Sarah." Sophie regarded me in exasperation from across the table in the café by the Tuileries, where we'd taken to meeting every month or so, ostensibly to keep up our friendship. "No one forced you to sign with them. You knew how they operate. I suppose Perrin expects you to prove yourself. Marie has been there for several seasons already."

I stared at her. "How can I prove myself if he won't assign me a decent part? Must I declaim my skills during intermission?"

Sophie sighed. "Do whatever you did to win favor at the Odéon. You're always so impatient. It was one play. Perrin won't dismiss you. He risked too much to steal you away, so you must now persuade him to assign you whatever roles you want for the next season. Remember how much he's paying you. And he has agreed to *Britannicus*, yes? You'll shine as Junie, and everyone will soon forget the unfortunate *Mademoiselle de Belle-Isle*."

"Not everyone. Sarcey practically crucified me in his column. After all his fanfare about my poetic entry into the dramatic domain."

"He also said by the third act, you were the Sarah Bernhardt who mesmerized us in *Ruy Blas*." Sophie shrugged. "You give him too much credence. Critics are like newspapers. One day, everyone is reading them, the next they're lining a finch cage." She sipped her coffee, unperturbed, as well she should, for in the wake of my departure from the Odéon, she'd filled the void with her rubicund glow and shapely figure, assuming my place on the stage and no doubt in Duquesnel's bed. Not that I could reproach her for it; as she said, I'd done this to myself.

"I can only shine as Junie if I have someone other than a relic with false teeth to play Britannicus. Perrin clings to his notion of player specialties as if Molière might rise from his tomb should we dare do anything different." I couldn't keep the tremor from my voice, recalling the first time I'd beheld Racine's epic drama and been swept into my ardor for the theater. "I will *not* play Junie with one of their moldering specialties. It would be a farce."

She smiled. "Then you must find yourself another Britannicus. Jean is now at the Comédie and I'm quite sure he's as eager as you to exalt himself."

"Jean?" I pretended ignorance.

She clicked her tongue. "Mounet-Sully. You know perfectly well who he is."

"A lowly *pensionnaire*," I said sourly.

"Who's been receiving excellent notices for his debut. Why must you mount such resistance? To play Junie, you require a suitable Britannicus. All you need to do is find him and convince Perrin. Surely if you could manage de Chilly, you can manage Perrin."

I winced, lowering my gaze. "The poor man. I feel terrible that I never had the chance to ask his forgiveness."

"You do not. You feel terrible that de Chilly dropped dead from a paralysis attack before you could counter-file for those six thousand francs he won against you in court. His passing is lamentable, but life must go on. And so must we. With de Chilly gone, we're staging more modern works now at the Odéon." She paused. "Had you only waited a bit . . ."

Despite my chagrin, I couldn't curb my laughter. "I never thought I'd say this, but you've become a creature of the theater: entirely without scruple."

"As are you, when it comes to your *moi*. Sarah, have you ever seen Jean perform? He's marvelous. He just needs the role to prove it. I also happen to know he left the Odéon because of you."

"He did not," I scoffed, though the notion intrigued me.

"Duquesnel himself told me that Jean applied to the Comédie the moment he heard you were going there. I suspect he must be in love, to follow you around like that."

"How can he possibly be in love? He doesn't know me. And what I require is a Britannicus, not another stray dog."

"You have a way with dogs," she said. "All you have to do is collar and train him."

With my inauspicious play at an end, the Comédie limped toward its season finale, Perrin mandating last-minute changes to the repertoire after the disappointing reception of *Mademoiselle de Belle-Isle*.

Still, the hallowed Salle Richelieu in the Comédie's theater, with its whipped-cream marble balconies and azure velvet curtains—all of which had the faded air of having seen better days—was half-empty when I slipped in to take my seat to see Mounet-Sully perform in the role Sophie claimed was earning him such excellent notice.

I didn't expect to be impressed. The play was a wartime drama penned by a new playwright whom Perrin had inexplicably patronized, perhaps as a concession to the current mood in Paris, where classical fare must be counterbalanced by more accessible works.

Still, it was hardly the vehicle for an actor to prove his mettle, even less so than my recent effort.

Yet when he appeared onstage as a wounded Prussian soldier taken in by a naïve country maiden, with whom he predictably falls in love and for whom he must sacrifice himself, I felt the intensity under my skin as the hush fell over the theater. His magnetic presence was undeniable; all eyes were drawn to him, with his robust body silhouetted by his soiled uniform, his mass of black curls disheveled about his forehead. Despite his saccharine lines of regret for what Germany had done to France—a ludicrous sentiment that should have made me and anyone else who'd survived the siege laugh—he delivered his soliloquy in a voice resonant as an incoming storm, enveloping us in his plea to not judge him by his nation's sins. He made a silly play unforgettable with his pathos, and I was especially moved to see him hold his own against Madame Nathalie as the maiden's treacherous mother, who betrays him to the Republic.

It wasn't until the final act, as the curtain dropped upon his bullet-riddled corpse and grieving maiden, that I realized I had actual tears on my cheeks.

Opportunity had not failed me. I had found my Britannicus.

I sent a note backstage, inviting him to tea at my home. It was proper enough; although we hadn't spoken a word, he struck me as a man who valued propriety. I had no qualms about what I planned, however. He was still an actor, and actors were ambitious; I was certain he'd rather not toil in mediocre crowd-pleasers for the rest of his career. Already in his thirty-second year—I had made inquiries—which made him only a little older than my twenty-seven, his window of opportunity was narrowing. If he didn't gain a leading classical role soon, he might never achieve one.

Still, I took extra care that my household was put to rights, or as right as it could be with a half-dozen dogs, which I kept rescuing because I couldn't bear to see them starve in the streets, the myriad birds I let loose because I despised cages, and my motley assortment of cats, few of whom I'd bothered to name after they managed to slink in through the kitchen door, lured by raw chicken left by Maurice and braving pursuit by my dogs to perch atop my overcrowded bookcases like sphinxes.

Oh, and my puma, Clotilde. She had come to me from the zoo, where I'd donated a large sum toward its restoration after the ravages of the siege and the Commune. Born in captivity from a mother who died in wretched conditions during the upheaval, the cub fell sick when her claws and fangs were cruelly removed. The zoo director told me he would have to sell her or put her down, as he was severely understaffed and unable to provide for her care. I offered to take her off his hands; armed with raw meat and plenty of goat's milk, I nursed her back to health. She was perfectly tame, like an oversized house cat, though my other cats took care to keep out of her way. My dogs, on the other hand, braved her lazy swipes to entice her to play. Her favorite spot was at Régine's feet. For hours, she reclined there, a sleek guardian, meticulously grooming herself as she oversaw my sister.

Despite the dire prognosis, Régine had begun to improve, if not enough for a trip to the Pyrenees. Madame G.'s attentions returned sparse color to her gaunt cheeks and abated her cough, especially when she gave her a medicinal syrup brewed by a nearby apothecary. I suspected this mysterious syrup must contain laudanum, for after she imbued it, Régine seemed to drift away, more serene than I'd ever seen her, murmuring nonsensical endearments to Clotilde.

Hardly a regular household, but I wasn't asking Mounet-Sully to move in. Still, on the day of his arrival, I set the maids and Caroline to shooing the cats from their fur-infested nests atop the bookcases and luring the screeching parakeets and canaries into the white-wicker cages that usually sat empty in the corners, surrounded by a jumble of potted ferns in *chinoise* urns and my sculptures-in-progress on clay-spattered pedestals.

"See Monsieur Mounet-Sully directly into the parlor and serve the tea," I ordered Caroline, who regarded me in amazement, for I often had callers, as well as many friends who came by whenever they pleased, and I never dictated their reception. Indeed, I often forgot anyone was due, going off to a luncheon or to sit for Nadar or visit with Clairin, only to return to find my parlor full of grumbling guests who'd waited for me for hours.

I couldn't understand my own anxiety as I selected a discreet mauve gown with lace at the cuffs and asked Madame G. to assist with my coiffure as I sat in my bedroom at the dressing table, while Régine dozed. I'd moved back into my room to sleep by my sister at night, having seen how *ma petite dame* limped about in the morning, her arthritis exacerbated from the truckle cot at Régine's side, which she had been using instead of her own mattress in her bedroom down the hall. Madame G. chided: "Only if you don't bring that dreadful casket back in here. Do you think it appropriate for your sister, in her condition, to see you in a coffin night after night?" I complied and used the cot instead, though Régine gave a weak laugh. "I don't mind the coffin," she said. "I like to see Sarah playing a corpse."

As Madame G. now attempted to wrangle my hair into a suitable chignon, I found myself straining to hear the bell at the door until she said, "If you don't sit still, you'll be greeting your new gentleman caller with your tresses loose."

"He's not a gentleman caller," I retorted, more tartly than the situation warranted. "He's a fellow actor from the Comédie. We're to discuss a collaboration for the season."

"Here?" Madame G. eyed me in the mirror. "Not at the theater, as is customary?"

"It's a secret collaboration. And no more questions. I can't hear myself think—" I went still, gazing in horror at the base of Régine's bed. "Where is Clotilde?"

Madame G. paused in her threading of a ribbon through my hair. "I have no idea. She was just there. Perhaps she went into the garden to relieve herself?"

"Dear God." I started to rise as in a simultaneous crescendo I heard pandemonium erupt downstairs: a sudden cry, the crash of something, and then rushing footsteps, followed by Caroline's horrified "Clotilde, *no!*"

I bolted down the staircase, Madame G.'s painstaking attempts at my coiffure gone awry as I burst into the parlor and precisely upon the very scene I'd hoped to avoid.

Mounet-Sully stood with his back against a bookcase. Not fearfully, but with definite caution. One of my pedestals was overturned; the clay bust I'd been working on in my spare time lay shattered on the floor. The pedestal had toppled a birdcage, and my hapless canaries swooped about in panic, for they knew the cats roamed the bookcases, and they refused to land there. I came to a halt, gazing in disbelief at another unexpected sight: a plump man in a linen summer suit, cowering on the settee before the table with my Limoges tea service, his bronzed complexion gone completely ashen.

An overturned platter of petits fours lay a few feet away from him. As did Clotilde, crushing a straw boater between her jaws.

"Alexandre?" I said in disbelief.

Alexandre Dumas *fils*, eldest son of my beloved patron, and a mirror image of his father, with his red-gold curls and protuberant blue-gray eyes—now wide with terror—could barely open his mouth to say, "My hat. Your . . . your lion is eating my hat."

"She's not a lion. Clotilde." I stomped my foot. "Let go of Monsieur Dumas's hat." I had to reach down to pry it from her mouth; she snarled, leaping up to retrieve it until I smacked her on her snout. "Bad girl! Go upstairs at once to Régine."

As Clotilde stalked off, her tail twitching, I regarded the ruined boater in dismay before returning it to Alexandre. "I must buy you a new one." I paused. "Why are you here?"

He righted himself, tugging at his rumpled frock coat. "We had an appointment today. To discuss my play. Don't you remember?"

My expression must have betrayed that I did not, for he pouted. "Sarah, you promised. I adapted the novel for you in Papa's honor."

"Yes. I know," I said, embarrassed by my own forgetfulness.

I didn't meet Jean's gaze until he stepped from the bookcase to murmur, "If this is an inconvenience, I can always return at another time."

"Whatever for?" My laugh sounded high-pitched in my ears. "It's entirely my error. I didn't recall inviting Monsieur Dumas, but you're both here now, are you not?"

"Evidently," he replied. Though he didn't smile, I heard mirth in his voice, which brought a rush of heat into my cheeks.

Dumas peered at Jean. "Are you an actor, Monsieur . . . ?"

"Jean Mounet-Sully." He held out his hand. "Yes, I am an actor. I'm honored to meet you, Monsieur Dumas. I am a great admirer of your father's work. And of yours, naturally."

Having failed to make the introductions, I determined to seize control of whatever dignity remained in the occasion. Turning to Caroline, I hissed, "Fetch a pot of fresh tea and more petits fours. And open those back-parlor doors to let the birds into the house."

"But the cats—" she started to protest.

"Never mind that. The birds know to avoid cats." As there was no hiding the upheaval, I didn't attempt it. I assumed my seat on the settee opposite Dumas and motioned to Jean. "Please, sit. Caroline will bring more tea in a moment."

Ducking to avoid a canary flapping about his head, he uncoiled his long limbs upon the settee, reminding me somewhat of a lion himself.

"I've read the play," I said, turning to Alexandre. "It's sublime."

I was fond of him. Born from one of his father's innumerable liaisons, he'd benefited from my late benefactor's generosity toward all his children, receiving a superior education followed by encouragement when Alexandre expressed the desire to take up the paternal occupation. He'd collaborated with his father on later works; upon Dumas's death, he'd unearthed the play my benefactor had drafted for me, which I, pregnant with Maurice, had never had the chance to perform. He'd converted it into a novel. The publication of his tale of a tragic affair between a courtesan and her lover of means had proved an instant success.

"But I'm afraid it must wait," I went on. "Your father's *Mademoiselle de Belle-Isle* was not well received, so I can't possibly ask to stage your *Dame aux Camélias* this season."

"But the Théâtre du Vaudeville has already expressed interest," he said.

"A pity. Seeing as I'm not under contract there."

"What am I to do? I've spent over a year on the play. I have my family to support."

"Then you must accept the Vaudeville's offer." I reached over to pat his hand, remembering with a pang how his father had saved me twice, at moments when it seemed my life was unsalvageable. "Do not let my obligations impede you. There will be another opportunity for me to play the role."

He looked crestfallen. "Marguerite Gautier was written for you."

"And I will play her. I *want* to play her." I actually didn't, at least not at this time. While the role had all the drama I could desire, his courtesan perishes of consumption, which reflected my sister's circumstances too keenly. "Who else have you in mind?"

"Eugénie Doche," he said, lowering his eyes, as the actress was his current mistress. "But," he hastened to add, "I told her I must ask you first and she understood."

"I'm sure she'll be wonderful." I had to say it, even if it left me with a bitter taste in my mouth. I might not want to play a woman with the same affliction as Régine, but I certainly didn't relish another actress taking the part.

He finished his tea, making conversation with Jean, who asked about the role of the courtesan's suitor. Then Alexandre took his leave with his shredded boater in hand.

"I'm so sorry about the hat," I told him at the door. "And the play. I'm not in the same position at the Française as I was at the Odéon, but that will change."

"I could try to delay." He had a pained note in his voice. "It was

Papa's dream to see you in the role. Before he died, he told me no one else could do her justice."

"I miss your father every day," I whispered, embracing him. "You mustn't delay if you cannot afford it. I don't expect you to wait for me."

When I returned to the parlor, I found Jean still on the settee, with a cat on his lap, purring under his caress. He smiled. "I prefer them this size."

"That one still has its claws," I remarked.

Now that we were alone, I experienced an unsettling reluctance to reveal my intention. As I sat opposite him and his intense gaze focused on me, as it had that night in my dressing room after the premiere of *Ruy Blas* and later in the greenroom at the Comédie, it took all my self-possession to not look away. *What* did he see, to regard me thus? I wasn't naïve; I'd plied my mother's trade long enough to recognize attraction in a man, even if I found his opaque. My aunt and mother had drilled into me that if one couldn't interpret a man, one should turn one's sights on less elusive prey. As this warning crossed my mind, a jolt went through me.

Did I harbor more than professional interest in Mounet-Sully?

"When did you become so handsome?" I heard myself blurt out, my own discomfort prompting me to disturb the impassivity of his gaze.

"I don't think I am." His fingers slid through the purring cat's calico fur.

"You must know that you are. Yet somehow, I never noticed it before."

A smile crept to the corners of his mouth. "You mean at the Odéon?"

"Where else?" I reached for my teacup, aware I was venturing into dangerous waters. It wasn't wise to pursue this approach. I needed a successful play, and I needed him to achieve it. A dalliance between us would only complicate matters.

"I think you must have been too occupied to notice me, even when I noticed you."

"Oh?"

"From the moment I first saw you." He didn't stop caressing the cat nor did he elucidate, but it was there between us; if I invited further intimacy, he would oblige.

"Well." I smiled, thinking I could enjoy this little flirtation as long as I didn't let it get too out of hand. "Sophie Croizette certainly noticed. She recommended you to me, in fact. She believes you'd make a superb Britannicus to my Junie."

I hoped to startle him. The role was a renowned leading part he could never have anticipated only a season into his first contract at the Française; however, yet again to my disconcertment, he appeared unaffected. "I doubt Monsieur Perrin would agree with Sophie Croizette."

"He might if he hears you play the part."

"Maybe you should hear me play it first."

I contemplated him for a moment before I went to my bookcases. Before I could locate my copy of the play amidst the jumbled volumes, he said from behind me, "I know it by heart. I recited it for my exams at the Conservatoire."

As I looked back to him, realizing I'd not asked him a single question about himself, he came to his feet. "I won first prize in tragedy with the role. I'd hoped to play it in its entirety before an audience, but then we went to war. I enlisted to fight the Prussians. When the war ended, over a year had passed and I thought I'd never return to the stage. I had few credentials, so I was making plans to return to my parents' vineyard in Brittany—"

"Brittany! I was raised there myself." I found it a delightful coincidence that he hailed from the same rugged region where I'd once lived as a child.

"Then you can understand why the eldest son of a Calvinist family wasn't supposed to be an actor," he said. "My father railed against my decision to move to Paris and apply to the Conservatoire; he said I'd fail miserably and bring dishonor to our family name."

"Yet you did it anyway. I know all about parental disapproval," I said, surprising myself with my voluntary admission. "My mother also thought me a fool to think I could ever be an actress. She did everything she could to dissuade me."

"Yet you did it anyway." He took a step toward me, imposing in his stature, like a tower of muscled granite. "Why are you doing this? You're the most well-known actress in Paris. Why me, when you could have your choice of any actor at the Comédie?"

Perhaps it was the way he spoke of my fame, with near reverence. Or perhaps it was the unexpected vulnerability I discerned beneath his impressive façade, of a rebellious nature that despite his undeniable advantages had driven him, as it had driven me, to defy his family's expectations. Kindred souls, I thought, as I met his eyes. This was why he looked at me as he did. He had recognized it before I had.

"Because," I said softly, "I don't want any actor at the Comédie."

He shifted back, not as a befuddled boy might, but with the self-restraint of a man who knew he must contain himself. "I should go," he murmured, half-turning away.

"Scene six," I said. "Recite it for me."

He went still for a moment. Then he slowly turned back to me, his large hands pressing to his chest and his face filling with yearning as he pronounced in that great voice which could fill an arena: "'Ah, princess! Do I again behold you? My palpitating heart can scarcely trust the happiness it feels.'" One of his hands reached toward me, as if to release my withheld breath. "'Repeat, dear Junie, all that has befallen thee. Our enemy, deceived, has let us free. Speak then, Junie. Tell me all thy thoughts.'"

I said, "Lower your voice. There's no need to shout the lines." And as he looked taken aback, I averted my eyes from him and whispered my response: "'This place is full of Nero's power. The Emperor is ever present. The very walls have eyes and ears.'"

He stepped so close, I could smell the scent of tobacco on his black velvet waistcoat, the hint of lavender in the pomade that couldn't subdue his thick mass of hair. " 'Such timid circumspection was never wont to interrupt the freedom of our love. Have you forgotten the vows so often sworn, that Nero himself should envy our condition? Banish then, Princess, your ill-founded fears. We still have powerful succor.' "

" 'And I know, my lord, such thoughts are not your own. . . .' " My voice faded as the rest of my dialogue failed me, as I felt the fire of alchemy between us and saw in his sudden immobility that he felt it, too.

In the silence that abruptly enveloped us, which seemed too precious to break, I finally said, "Now do you see why?"

He did not lower his gaze. "I see you could be dangerous to my heart."

In the greenroom, Perrin gathered us to announce the season's assignments. I waited anxiously, perched on the edge of my chair. The moment he spoke my name, I stood. "I have a request," I declared, bringing an immediate glower to Madame Nathalie's face.

"We do not *request* at the Comédie. Do you think us a street troupe, perhaps?"

I ignored her, meeting Perrin's glacial regard. "Mounet-Sully and I would like to recite a scene from *Britannicus* for you, Monsieur Director."

"Recite a scene!" Madame Nathalie shifted her outrage to Perrin. "Will you please inform this—this *pensionnaire*, as she's not shown herself worthy of another designation, that the director assigns the roles and the company complies. *All* of us comply," she said, returning her stare to me. "Even those of us in the position to make our wishes known."

Perrin gave me a razor-thin smile. "And deny ourselves the pleasure of Mademoiselle Bernhardt's recital? By all means, mademoi-selle, proceed."

Jean stood up to join me, appearing, as ever, unperturbed, even as my heart pounded and Madame Nathalie looked ready to launch herself at me like an avenging titan.

Stepping into the center of the room, the company surrounding us in disapproving silence, I didn't fail to note Marie Colombier's sneer as Jean and I commenced the scene we'd rehearsed for two weeks during our brief summer reprieve. Every day, for several hours, we'd practiced until we could have performed it blindfolded, though he'd grumbled about my obsessive attention to every detail. I was determined to impress; to my satisfaction, I now felt the ten-sion in the room thaw as we performed Junie and Britannicus's se-cret reunion before Rachel's sad-eyed portrait, that spark from our first day heightened by my perfectionism. While Jean had an innate gift for tragedy, I'd insisted that he moderate his propensity for en-larging his voice, which diminished the subtlety of the verse, and refrain from speaking directly to the audience, an archaic tradition from the past when actors felt compelled to assert their own identity rather than their character's.

"We no longer have an emperor in the imperial box," I told him, when he protested that Perrin mandated adherence to the custom. "Stepping to the footlights to declaim distracts from the moment. We must *be* our character, not wear the character like a costume."

He grumbled—I'd learned that, true to his Breton blood, he could be combative—but once he performed it as I instructed, the joy on his face was genuine. "I forgot there was an audience," he said, as if it were an unforeseen revelation. "I forgot myself."

"That is how it should be," I replied. "Even if our esteemed di-rector thinks otherwise."

When we finished the scene, with me draped against Jean, I peeked through my downcast lids to see Perrin regarding us with an inscrutable expression.

Madame Nathalie shattered the spell. "In all my years in this house, never have I witnessed such a spectacle. If you think I will reprise a role I've made famous, playing Agrippina to such intolerable mannerisms, let me assure you that I will not."

Perrin stood so still, I feared he must agree with her. Instead, he set the roster of assignments aside. "Madame Nathalie, I intend for you to play Agrippina this season."

As she gasped out her protest, he aimed his next pronouncement at me: "Mademoiselle Bernhardt, are you aware of how we assign roles in this house?"

"Yes." I made myself step away from Jean. "But we agreed on *Britannicus* and I—"

"We do not agree. We do not request. You appear to have forgotten or you choose to ignore the fact that you are not a *sociétaire* in this company. Did I err in thinking your time at the Odéon had improved your disposition?"

"I should be a *sociétaire*," I said, suddenly no longer caring if he dismissed me. I'd had enough of the House of Molière's condescension. "I left the Odéon, where I was already playing lead roles. I had no need to prove myself, but I was grateful for your invitation to remedy my unfortunate past here. Had I known the limitations, I would have declined."

"Have a care, Perrin," gloated Madame Nathalie, having clearly longed for such an outburst from me. "Lest she puts you into an early grave as she did Monsieur de Chilly. I did warn you, did I not? We are not so indebted as to permit this Jewess from an inferior playhouse, who thinks too much of herself, back into our ranks."

I spun toward her, my fist clenching. I heard Jean whisper, "Sarah, no," but it was the flicker of something indecipherable in Perrin's gaze that detained my advance.

"Regardless," he said, "you are part of this company now. And while your methods leave much to be desired, you are perhaps the very attraction we require at this time."

"Would you *indulge* her?" Madame Nathalie heaved herself to her feet. "After she flouts every rule sacrosanct to us, performing in our greenroom as if it were a circus arena?"

He shifted his regard to her. "Madame, this house's receipts are lower than they've ever been. Though it may pain us, indulgence is necessary." He forestalled her tirade as her face turned apoplectic. "If you do not wish to play Agrippina, I will recast the role. But we will stage *Britannicus* this season, with Mademoiselle Bernhardt as Junie."

"Never. We refuse! We own a stake in this company and you cannot move forward without us." She gestured to her fellow *sociétaires*. To my disbelief, and no doubt hers, not one of them lifted their voice in support. Only Samson, her most stalwart ally but also supposedly Marie Colombier's patron, surprised me by muttering, "Nathalie, be sensible. We must feed ourselves. We can no longer afford to quibble over who provides the meal."

She gaped at him, her immense bosom taking in shallow breaths. An unexpected surge of pity came over me, though she didn't deserve it. I was witnessing the end of her era, which I'd unwittingly set into motion.

"You . . . you agree?" she whispered. "You would condone this buffoonery?"

"It's not buffoonery." He glanced at Jean and me in reluctant admiration. "Anyone can see they are the future. We must accept it, if we are to survive."

Madame Nathalie's entire person seemed to cave upon itself. Gripping her cane, she waddled past me. I made myself stand firm as she paused to hiss, "You've not won anything yet. You need my approval to be a *sociétaire*, and you will *never* have it."

I returned her stare. I didn't need her approval; she was only one, and elevation to the status of *sociétaire* didn't require a unanimous vote. All it required was a majority.

After she departed, the rest of the company sat in stunned quiet and Perrin retreated to the *sociétaires* to conduct a hushed discussion; when he looked up at me, I flinched. "Sarah Bernhardt and Mounet-Sully will play Junie and Britannicus. Monsieur Samson shall play Nero and Madame Courvasel has agreed to the role of Agrippina. Rehearsals will commence immediately." He gave an arid smile. "Considering Mademoiselle Bernhardt has already begun to rehearse, I see no reason to delay."

It was a victory, no matter what Madame Nathalie declared, but I was so affected by the confrontation to obtain it that I could only turn in relief to Jean when Perrin said, "Everyone save Mademoiselle Bernhardt is excused."

The company hastened from the room, Marie Colombier casting a malignant look at me. Jean squeezed my arm in encouragement, and then I was left alone with Perrin, who took his time reviewing his roster before he said, "You are . . . what? Twenty-six?"

"Twenty-eight this October," I replied.

"Still young, even for our profession. Surely you must realize that making a foe of a senior *sociétaire* cannot serve your interests."

"Madame Nathalie was my foe before she had reason to be. If I can play the roles I want, so be it."

He gave a dry chuckle. "You are rather confident, after one unremarkable season."

"I did tell you that *Mademoiselle de Belle-Isle* would be a mistake. . . ." My protest faded. "I did not intend it," I added, hating the fact that I felt the need to apologize to him.

"Oh, I think you did. I think you cannot help but intend it. You are disruptive by nature. I was indeed warned by Madame Nathalie and de Chilly himself before his death. Nevertheless," he added, before I could defend myself, "while I do not approve of your methods, as I've stated, nor do I enjoy having my authority being challenged before the company, the *sociétaires* agree."

"Agree?" I braced for the worst.

"We will accept you as a junior *sociétaire*, with a lesser share in our receipts, providing *Britannicus* exceeds expectations." He let his words sink in. "You'd best be certain this is how you wish to proceed and that Mounet-Sully is ready for the challenge. If not, now is the time to admit it. One scene, no matter how impressive, is not an entire play."

"I am certain," I said. "Jean and I . . . we will prove it to you."

"Not to me. Prove it to our patrons."

VI

Rehearsals were terrible. There was no other way to describe it. Samson made every attempt possible to assert his leading status, no doubt incited by his fellow *sociétaires*, so that his pompous diction and penchant for appearing in full costume when there wasn't yet an audience to witness it turned his Nero into an aging matron fretting over a cracked teapot. Nor was Madame Courvasel a convincing Agrippina, unlike Madame Nathalie, who I had to admit had always commanded the stage in her signature role. And Jean, to my disbelief, reverted to declaiming as if he were delivering a lecture, gesticulating toward the empty seats until I flung up my own arms and cried at him, "*Who* are you playing to?"

With our opening a fortnight away, I was in despair. Perrin attended our first dress rehearsal and his tight-lipped grimace impeded my own performance, so that I found myself stalking the stage in a fluster, shrill as a banshee.

At the back door, he waited for me. "Two weeks," he intoned. "If this is what you expect to prove, consider yourself forewarned."

When I reached my flat, I discovered that Régine had suffered a setback, her cough racking her until Madame G. doused her into a stupor with the syrup. "She's dying," wept *ma petite dame* as I stood at my sister's bedside, her thin form barely making an indent under the sheets. I had been so engrossed in my struggle to salvage the disaster *Britannicus* threatened to be, I'd spent most of my time in the theater, staggering home well after midnight to collapse in the spare room. In my absence, Madame G. had resumed her nightly vigil over Régine. Maurice was fretful, too; now in his ninth year, he was old enough to understand his lifelong playmate was very ill, and he'd turned rebellious at school, picking fights with other students and playing the truant, until the head instructor sent me a stern letter stating that unless my son improved his marks and his attitude, he ran the risk of imminent expulsion.

Everything was falling apart. I couldn't stanch my grief as I caressed Régine's feverish brow and told Madame G. we must call again for the physician.

"Why?" She collapsed onto a stool, so frail I feared she'd fall ill herself. "He cannot save her."

I clasped her hand. "We mustn't give up hope. There must be a way. . . ."

"There isn't," she whispered.

I went to Maurice's room. He was asleep, his blankets tousled and arms akimbo, with a trio of cats slumbering by him and Clotilde sprawled on the carpet. Her luminous amber eyes lifted to me as I nestled at his side, shoving the grumbling cats out of the way so I could hold him. My beautiful boy. I fell asleep, clutching him like a talisman. I'd thought of sending him away, in fear for his own health, but Madame G. said it would be unbearably cruel to separate him from my sister, as every day after school, he ran upstairs to read to her. Only then did he seem content, as if reciting stories to her eased his troubled heart.

In the morning, the physician emerged from Régine's room with a grim expression. "I'm afraid there's nothing more we can do, except ensure she's kept as comfortable as possible."

"But the spa," I said. "What if we sent her there?"

He sighed. "It is too late for a spa. I'm very sorry, Mademoiselle Bernhardt."

I had to return to work; it was our week of dress rehearsal. As I performed, I kept swallowing my wail. All of a sudden, none of it mattered. I couldn't feel my character, but perversely, the sorrow I fought to contain inspired my performance, so that when I was done, Perrin declared, "If the rest of this cast can do half as well as Mademoiselle Bernhardt, we may actually be ready to open on our scheduled date."

Jean followed me to my dressing room, a tiny closet of a space into which I'd stuffed as much as I could, including a cot for those nights when I was too weary to return home. He stood on the threshold, watching me shove my makeup tubes into the battered box.

"Is everything all right? You seem distressed."

I whirled to him. "Everything is *not* all right. What on earth has come over you? I championed you for this role. I assured Perrin you were perfect for it, and this is how you repay me? By performing like a younger version of Samson? Is that your plan? To prove you can be as outdated as any *sociétaire* in the hope they'll grant you the pension, too?"

"I had no idea we had a debt." He stepped toward me, even as I raised a hand to ward him off. "Sarah, whatever is troubling you, it must be more than the play."

"Don't." My voice snagged in my throat. "I don't want your pity. I want you to be as you were when we rehearsed alone together. I don't understand how you can be satisfied, when you have so much grandeur within you."

"I . . ." He lowered his gaze. "I want you so much," he whispered.

"What?" I stared at him.

He raised his gaze. The anguish in his expression . . . it quenched my very breath. "I cannot perform because all I can do, all I can think of, is you."

"Don't be ridiculous," I said, even as I recalled Sophie's words: *He must be in love, to follow you around like that.*

"Am I?" He held my stare with that intensity he'd displayed

when I didn't yet know his name. "Can you honestly say you don't feel the same for me?"

"My sister is dying," I whispered. "This is not the time or place to—"

He came at me so swiftly that I couldn't evade him as he seized me, as his large taut body pressed into mine and his mouth was at my throat, the shadow of his beard scalding my skin, his hands everywhere, incinerating my flesh under my dress.

I hadn't felt such an explosion of lust since Kératry. I hadn't realized how much desire I'd kept pent up inside me until he was lowering me to the floor, upon my discarded costume and sandals, until I heard my groan, like an animal in a snare, a desperate combustion of yearning and fury that turned molten with heat.

He rucked my skirts to my waist, ripping at my undergarments; when his fingers found me, I gasped. He thrust himself into me, whispering my name over and over, violating me even as I welcomed it, even as I bucked in climax against him and he spilled his seed inside me, something I'd allowed no man since Kératry to ever do.

We lay panting, our breath mingling in the fraught aftermath. He started to rise, his face contorted in shame. "Forgive me. Sarah, please . . . I didn't mean it. Not like this."

I raked my tangled hair from my face, feeling the bruise of his ardor on my lips.

"Use it," I said, and he froze. "I want to see this same passion on opening night."

I saw him swallow. "Is that all you have to say?"

"For now." I pushed him aside. "We shall see about later."

Opening night. A full house. *Britannicus* was always a draw, its timeless theme of ambition, power, and murderous envy, coupled with its ancient Roman setting, still an attraction for audiences.

Backstage, I kept away from Jean. We'd begun an affair. Or rather, an affair had consumed us. There was no way to avoid it; the moment we found ourselves together, the passion between us was inescapable—and evident to everyone, provoking smirks and whispered asides. He was ferocious in his desire, as if he sought to devour me to my bones. His ardent declarations of love were disconcerting, and if I let myself dwell on them, frightening, as well. The very thing I had vowed to not let get out of hand had erupted past any attempt I might make to contain it. Yet I found him irresistible, and as I'd hoped, our lust ignited his fire onstage, as if bedding me had given him the confidence he needed to fully inhabit his role. I wanted to tell him we should never rely on personal gratification in order to perform, for we'd always suffer disappointment. I refrained. As long as he performed the role as I intended, I couldn't quibble over his source of inspiration. We had to make our first play together an unrivaled success.

Sarcey, Meyer, and a host of other critics flocked to the complimentary orchestra seats that Perrin proudly provided. He may not have relayed equal enthusiasm to me, but we both knew what was at stake. Perrin had lured me from the Odéon to cast me in a role that failed to meet expectations; to prove my engagement still merited attention, he, too, required a success. If Racine's *Britannicus*, a staple of the Comédie's repertoire, did not accomplish it, he'd face a censure he might never overcome, while I'd destroy any chance I had to be a *sociétaire*.

And we had our drawbacks. Samson lumbered about in his heavy sandals with inset lifts, so he could tower over Jean and exert his dominance. Madame Courvasel, arrayed in a veiled tunic voluminous as a pavilion, was beset by nerves, aware she'd inevitably be compared to Madame Nathalie's incomparable embodiment of Agrippina. On their shoulders rested the bulk of the play; to counter their weakness, Jean and I had to overpower them.

As the curtain rose on the first act to an apprehensive applause that weighed on me like lead, I watched Jean stride onto the stage in his red-mantled toga and gilded wreath. As he commenced his monologue, relief flooded me. Here was the actor I'd first admired in that insipid play—magnetic and authoritative, still declaiming too loudly, but refraining from doing so at the audience. He dwarfed Samson in his absurd red Nero wig and lifts; by the end of the first act, the audience's response was fervent. No one could deny they were bearing witness to the emergence of a superb tragedian, whose skill belied his limited experience.

At my cue, I drew down my veil and invoked Junie's longing to escape Nero's seduction. I must hold my own against my lover in the play.

Deafening applause greeted my entrance. Evidently, I hadn't lost my appeal despite my last season, but I couldn't let it affect me. Instead, I chose to improvise, playing Junie not as a craven girl torn between rival brothers, but as a champion for her right to love as she sees fit. I acted out our scene as if I were fighting a duel, forcing Jean to improvise his reaction. I demanded the very best of him, and I felt his palpable rage when he took me in his arms to force Junie to confess her love for him.

By the time the curtain fell, I was spent. Unlike de Chilly, Perrin didn't hover backstage during performances. He perched in the first-tier mezzanine like a hawk, annotating every misspoken line or missed gesture from above.

But the standing ovation as we took our curtain call must have warmed even his sterile heart.

Despite everything, *Britannicus* was the defining event I'd set out to achieve.

VII

'Not since the great Talma, the Théâtre-Français's preeminent interpreter of classical tragedy, has another actor shown such virtuosity.'" Jean brandished the copy of *Le Figaro* with Meyer's final notice of our play, his entire person suffused with satisfaction. The self-congratulatory moment was marred somewhat by his lack of attire, though no man was better suited to it, every muscle coiled under his taut frame, his sculpted thighs and broad chest dusted with dark hair exuding virility.

I lay on his bed, equally unclothed, gratified not only by his lovemaking—every night after our performance, he charged at me like a bull—but also by the fact that we'd concluded the season to such acclaim that my acceptance as a *sociétaire* was a given.

"Before you let his praise go to your head," I remarked, casting a look at his semi-erect manhood and recalling how I, too, had once pranced about in self-indulgent glee with a newspaper notice by my lover's bed, "you should know that Meyer . . ."

"What?" He seized a cigarette from his case on the side table. "You don't think what he says about me is true?"

"I would hope you aspire to more than a dead man's reputation," I said, electing not to inform him that Meyer was clearly infatuated with more than his talent. Why spoil his moment? I'd learned from experience that we players would rather not have our praise marred by sordid truth.

His eyes narrowed. "Are you jealous? He barely mentioned you this time."

"Should I be?" I reached for my pantalettes and chemise, tumbled on the floor by the bed where he'd torn them off. "Bring the notice to Perrin and demand a raise. You've earned it. And once you get it, you need to replace my underthings. This is the sixth petticoat you've ruined in as many days, rutting at me like a beast."

His voice darkened. "Do you ever take anything seriously?"

I paused, looking up at him. I'd also learned from experience that besides his obstinacy, he had this repressed fury inside him, fueled by his need to prove his worth. "I took our play seriously enough. If our notices hadn't reflected as much, I'd be very concerned, indeed."

Pulling on my dress, I turned to the looking glass over his bureau—surprisingly, for such a handsome man, he lacked outward vanity, without much in the way of mirrors in his flat, where I'd insisted we conduct our affair so as to not disrupt my household.

"I suppose this means you'll be leaving me," he said.

I met his stare in the glass. "Why would you say that?" The vulnerability I had first sensed in him was actually a persistent bane. Having defied his family to pursue a player's life, he sought constant reassurance he'd made the right choice, and it seeped into our relationship, his insecurity converted into this unfounded fear of my eventual desertion.

"Because our play is done." His exhale of smoke muffled the resentment in his eyes, but not his tone. "You don't need me to be your Britannicus anymore."

Taking a moment to let my silence smother his ridiculous declaration, I piled up my hair, stabbing the ivory pins through it to keep the knot in place. Only then did I turn back to him. "Jean. Don't you think you're being childish? We are both adults—"

"Childish!" He crushed his cigarette into the ashtray. "I not only aspire to a dead man's repute, but now I'm a child as well? Is that what you think of me?"

"Stop this." My voice sharpened. "You know very well what I think of you. I chose you for the role. Perrin has stated he will cast us next in *Zaïre*. It's a tremendous opportunity for us—"

"And this?" He thrust his arm toward the bed, with a grandiosity reminiscent of his stage persona. "Does any of this mean more than a stage to you?"

I was so taken aback that I didn't know how to respond. My silence was enough.

"I see." He flung on a robe and lit another cigarette, making me wince. The room reeked of tobacco smoke, though it was his only vice. He rarely drank any alcohol, not even wine. "It is what you do."

"What I *do*?" I fought back a surge of sudden anger. "Are you implying that I've used you in some fashion?"

"What else would you call it? All this time together, and not once have you said you love me, though I've said it countless times to you. I also know . . . things."

I was sorely tempted to walk out. But I'd encouraged liberties between us and we now had a lucrative partnership; our onstage pairing had reaped critical adulation and summoned audiences in droves. Every performance of *Britannicus* sold out, with Perrin adding an extra two weeks to our schedule, which caused Samson to bellow in protest and Madame Courvasel to plead exhaustion. With astounding alacrity, Madame Nathalie—practiced opportunist that she was—stepped in to play Agrippina, determined to gain some attention for herself. Not even Samson's overwrought performance could dampen her vengeful empress. Her acting elevated the play, making it the most profitable *Britannicus* in the Comédie's history.

"Yes. Things," he repeated. "About your past."

I had to smile. "I see. Has Marie Colombier been whispering sweet poison in your ear? Perhaps you should violate her next. No doubt she'd welcome it, though Perrin might not."

His cigarette quivered in his fingers. "I told you I was sorry. I never intended it."

"Instead, you intend to insult me." I stalked past him to fetch my cloak.

His hand reached out to detain me. "Sarah," he said, his voice sinking, "forgive me. I can be such a brute. You . . . you make me say and do things that I don't really mean."

I glanced at his hand clutching my sleeve. I wanted to tell him we couldn't go on like this. Not only was it unwise for our professional relationship, but I had no idea what, if anything, I wanted of our personal one. Our passion was real enough, yet he'd been correct in saying what he had, despite his callousness. Love was a risk I couldn't afford; it had too many unforeseen consequences, too many pitfalls and uncertainties.

As I sought the right words to say as much, an urgent knock came at the front door. Jean's flat wasn't spacious—a rented bachelor abode, furnished with the bare minimum, yet I still stubbed my toe on a nearby footstool as I pulled away from him. Hastily fastening his robe about his waist, he went to the door.

His concierge, a rodent-like man who always greeted me with a lascivious sneer, said, "This note arrived for the mademoiselle," as if I didn't deserve to be addressed thus.

"Merci." Jean handed me the note. I'd left his address with Caroline, in case of an emergency; when I read the few lines my maid had dispatched, my knees buckled.

Jean grasped hold of me before I slid to the floor.

"No," I heard myself whisper. "No, please . . ."

He threw on his clothes within minutes, barking at the concierge eavesdropping in ghoulish delight at the door to summon a carriage for us.

"You don't have to," I said, as my entire world crumbled around me.

"I do." He steered me down the staircase into the street. "You need me at your side."

...

She lay so still, so quiet, that for an inchoate moment I thought there must have been a mistake. She was only asleep. How dare they cause me such anguish?

But my mother was already there with Rosine, seated by the bed where Madame G., a wreckage of grief, had draped Régine's wasted form in a tarnished white veil, like a bride on her nuptials. Flowers pulled from our garden were scattered about her body; at the foot of the bed, Clotilde lay with her head mournfully on her paws.

"Must you keep that beast inside the house?" said Julie peevishly, with a sidelong glance at Jean where he stood on the threshold.

I ignored her, moving to the bed. So serene. It seemed impossible for a girl who had never shown an instance of calm. The bones of her skull showed under the envelope of her skin; I pressed my hand to my mouth to stifle my sob.

"When?" I whispered.

"Early this morning," Julie said. "Caroline sent us urgent word. We arrived just in time. It was a mercy that she at least had family with her in her final hour."

As I turned to her, thinking of how Régine had always despised her, Julie added, "We did try to reach you at the theater. We thought you must be rehearsing. . . ." She let her gaze linger again on Jean. "Apparently, you were occupied elsewhere."

"The play closed last night." I wouldn't let her anger me. Whatever she said or did now was of no importance. With Régine gone, the threadbare chain that bound me to my mother had disintegrated. I no longer cared if I ever saw or spoke to her again.

She let out a sigh. "Funerals are so expensive these days. At least we have a casket."

I stared at her, aghast. "No."

"Why ever not? Surely we needn't spend any more than required."

Before I started shouting her out of my house and my life forever, Madame G. interjected weakly, "Régine so loved to see you in it, Sarah. She—" Her voice broke. "She would like it, I think."

"It's old and dirty. The lining is torn. . . ." I couldn't believe I was saying these words. None of this seemed real. It *couldn't* be real.

"Linings can be replaced." Julie glanced at Rosine. My aunt nodded, voiceless, her eyes brimming with tears. "We'll see to it." Gripping her cane, my mother came to her feet, her movements awkward, no longer the polished courtesan who'd sacrificed us to her welfare. "I'll speak with the parish this afternoon. We must veil her today, but with the summer heat upon us, we mustn't delay. Providing there's no other objection?"

"None," I said. "But I will pay for a new coffin." I wanted her gone. I wanted everyone gone so I could be alone with my sister. Then I remembered. "Where is Maurice?"

"Caroline took him to school earlier," said Madame G. "Before it happened. He left a book here to read to her later. He'll be beside himself, the poor boy."

I didn't want my son to see her like this. It would devastate him. Swallowing the bitterness in my throat, I said to Julie, "We must veil her at your flat."

"In my salon?" She regarded me in astonishment. "Absolutely not. Jeanne was to receive callers this evening. I'll postpone, naturally, but I can't guarantee they'll oblige on such short notice. Imagine what they will say, should they arrive to find—"

"Never mind." I turned away from her. "I wish to be alone with her."

She limped from the room, Rosine hastening behind her. Jean stepped aside to let them pass. Madame G. gave me a sundered look, the years of loss she'd kept at bay, with her industriousness and unending devotion, fallen upon her like an unbearable burden. As much as she loved me, Régine had been most like the child she'd never borne. I feared she would never recover from this, that none of us would ever recover.

"Go," I told her. "Attend to that woman. I want the service to be perfect. It's the very least she can do, after how very little she has done."

Madame G. shuffled out. From the doorway, Jean said, "Sarah, she's at peace now. God called her to His side."

He actually believed it; I could hear it in his voice. Rage overcame me. "She was seventeen! *How* could God have wanted such a travesty? All she ever knew was hardship."

"She had you." He didn't step forth to console me, as if he knew I couldn't abide a single touch, that it would destroy the last remnants of my strength, which I had to maintain for the dark days ahead. "She had her sister at her side."

"Not enough." My voice fractured. "I wasn't at her side when she most needed me."

He retreated. I whispered to Clotilde, "Come here," and my puma crept to my side, licking my fingers. That innate animal instinct to heal finally roused my tears; as they streamed down my face, I took my sister's inert hand in mine.

"Forgive me, Régine," I said into the endless silence. "You must forgive me."

I didn't know if she could hear me. I didn't believe she could. When I was a girl, I'd believed in the saints and heaven; now, death seemed to me a chasm without redemption, a senseless whim of fate. But as I stayed beside her and tried to say farewell, I knew the person from whom I most needed forgiveness was the only one who couldn't grant it.

Myself.

VIII

Voltaire's *Zaïre* was indeed a tremendous opportunity, and the one role Provost had assured me during my training at the Conservatoire that I should never play. My old instructor had died, mourned by all of us who'd had the privilege of suffering under his baton, but his advice persisted. Though I'd proven myself at the Comédie and had been elected as junior *sociétaire* with no one dissenting (Madame Nathalie abstained from the vote), taking on the titular role of the Christian slave who falls in love with her captor, the Sultan, the role assigned to Jean, kindled all my insecurities and fears.

I'd always found the prose overwrought and the plot ludicrous, but the play had enjoyed immense success at the Comédie since its premiere in 1732. To capitalize on the attention stirred by my pairing with Jean, Perrin opted to present *Zaïre* in its original costumes and sets, stored in some moldering warehouse. He also refused to allow us a break, setting us to intensive rehearsal, as he'd dredged up a copy of the play with Voltaire's personal staging instructions and he was determined we must adhere to them.

I had no time to grieve for Régine, whom we buried in the Père Lachaise Cemetery. To my surprise, my mother had acquired plots for the entire family years before. Though my sister's absence left a vast hollow in my heart and in my house, where Clotilde went off her food for days, Maurice refused consolation, and Madame G.

started to fade before my very eyes, I had to devote myself to my work. But the grief was always there, like an oil stain underwater, a distortion that was invisible to the eye but obscured clarity.

Jean took it upon himself to rally my spirits. On Sundays, the one day we had free of rehearsal, he organized excursions for Maurice and me, taking us on outings to the countryside surrounding Paris or visits to the Tuileries Zoo, now fully refurbished and a constant source of delight for Maurice, who shared my love of animals.

"Can we get an elephant?" he implored, standing on tiptoe by the paddock where a new pair of the majestic creatures had replaced the much-beloved ones slaughtered for meat during the siege. When I laughed and said we had no room in the flat, he pouted and turned to Jean. "When you're my papa, you'll let me have an elephant, won't you?"

Jean ruffled his hair, smiling, even as the remark caught me off guard. As soon as we returned home, I steered Maurice into my salon.

"Why would you say such a thing to Jean?" I asked him. He was growing so tall and lean, the blood of his father starting to show. "You must know he can't be your papa."

Maurice toed the carpet with his boot. "Why not? You like him, don't you? He likes you. We spend a lot of time with him, so I thought . . ." His voice faded.

"What, my son? What did you think?"

He lifted his gaze to me. "I thought you might wish to marry him. Then I'd have a father and you won't have to worry so much about me anymore."

My heart cracked in my chest. "Oh, my child. I'll always worry about you." I paused, seeing him turn away, as if to deflect a blow. "Do you miss not having a papa?"

That he might have suffered from the lack of a male figure in his life had never occurred to me. We'd never had the conversation; not once had he asked me about his father and, I realized in belated guilt, I'd never thought to broach the subject. I had neglected to recall

how keenly I had felt the absence of my own father in my childhood.

"All the other boys at school have fathers. They say it's not nor-
mal that I don't."

I took him in my arms, pressing his head to my breast. "You have
me," I said, biting back my tears. "Your *maman*. You always have
me. Isn't that enough?"

I felt him nod. "Yes. But I'd like to have a papa someday, too."

I wept myself to sleep that night, distraught by my sorrow for
Régine and my concern over Maurice. Daily rehearsals, in which
Perrin proved as dictatorial as Provost had ever been, didn't help
matters. Perrin was of the mind that his players had no right to decide how we should interpret our characters, insisting we obey Voltaire's staging instructions, never mind that the playwright had been
dead for almost a hundred years, or that I'd shown him I knew how
to please an audience. He ordered me to restrict myself to the performance as ordained, and I suddenly found myself right back
where I had started, locked in the prison of the Comédie's established order, with Perrin criticizing my delivery of Voltaire's lines
until I stormed off the stage. Positioning himself between me and
the exit door, he pronounced, "This is what I want. Zaïre is betrayed
because her father makes her promise to be baptized. In keeping it a
secret, she leads the Sultan to think she's been unfaithful. She must
show this same helplessness when she tries in vain to persuade him
of her innocence."

I wanted to retort that Zaïre was an idiot for not explaining herself, but I was too enraged to speak when I saw Jean nod his agreement from the stage. My rage at his willingness to accept all of
Perrin's directions without debate, when he'd been so full of contra-
diction with me during *Britannicus*, seared off my voice.

"Perrin is wrong about our final scene," I harangued Jean that
night in his flat, where I'd begun to feel almost as trapped as I did at
the theater. "You mustn't yell at her. The Sultan must confront her

without emotion, as he's already convinced of her guilt. Only after he kills her and realizes his error can he show rage. It will make his suicide more realistic."

"Perrin doesn't think so." Jean sat smoking by the window, his hair tumbled across his brow, the twilight beyond the glass etching his handsome profile in shadow. "He's the director. He surely knows the nuances of the play better than we do."

"He's not performing in the play, is he?"

"That doesn't make us more qualified."

"It does to me." I stood. The entire room, suffused with stale smoke and the stale aftermath of our lovemaking, was making me ill. "I don't accept his notion that we're incapable of making decisions for ourselves when it comes to our performance."

"And you don't accept his notion for our costumes or sets, either. Not even the playbill; you had to demand some unknown acquaintance of yours provide the design."

"Mucha is a talented illustrator," I retorted. "What's more, he's a *modern* one. Our playbills are as antiquated as the stage décor. Even the Comédie must adapt to the times."

He ground his cigarette into the windowsill, scattering embers. "You're a *sociétaire*, invested in the company. Surely you want this play to be as successful as Perrin does."

"Being a *sociétaire* doesn't make me his sheep. You've questioned me often enough. Yet if Perrin tells you to lift that finger instead of the other, you obey him as if he was your father," I said, and as soon as I did, I knew it was wrong thing to say.

His eyes narrowed. "I obey him," he said, "because—"

"He can promote you." Though I knew I risked his temper, I didn't care to mind my tongue. "While I'm but the upstart Jewess who used to be a whore."

He rose to his feet, suddenly seeming too large for the room. "Why?" He threw out his arms. "Why must you provoke me and everyone else around you?"

"I don't provoke you any more than you should provoke your-self." I was gripping my bonnet in my hands. I'd not forgotten his physical strength. "I'm simply asking—"

"When?" He took a step toward me. "When does this charade end? When will you finally admit that you've had what you wanted from me, and now you're tired of it?"

"Did I say I was tired of it?" Though I was, exhausted in fact, and now wanted only for it to end. I couldn't abide this incessant quarrel between us.

"You don't need to say it," he said. "I can feel it. Every day, every night that you're with me. You—" His voice broke. "You cannot love me."

I went still. I hadn't expected to contend with this now, yet the relief that suddenly washed over me was irrefutable. "My sister has died. I'm in mourning. I can't focus on anything else."

"I know her death was a tragedy, but you're about to perform one of the greatest roles ever written. Isn't this what you always wanted, the reason for everything you do, to become as acclaimed as Rachel?"

I met his stare. "I detest the play," I said, terrified by my admission and his uncanny ability to pierce my defenses. "I just want time away to rest and be with my son."

"Your son, who's growing up without a father," he muttered.

"And what of it? I grew up without a father. Many children do."

"But Maurice doesn't have to. I would be a father to him, if you and I married." He let out a harsh chuckle, making me think he was mocking me, using my own son's words against me. When I real-ized he wasn't, I said in dismay, "Marry? Are you mad?"

"It's not madness to want to start a family, not where I come from." He met my appalled gaze. "Your son needs a man in his life. Every boy does. And you've achieved more than most women ever do. If you're so unhappy with it, you can stop now. Marry me and I'll—"

"Provide for me, while I birth and raise your brood?" Though I tried to curb it, my voice took on a serrated edge. "Is that what you want? To tuck me away like a prize doll, so you can become the great Mounet-Sully of the Comédie?" My words twisted inside me, sharp as knives. "You don't love me. You love what I have, only you're too much of a hypocrite to admit it."

He gave a sigh. I almost wished he'd lunged at me with his fist raised, for in that single exhale, I heard utter defeat. "If you truly believe that, there is no hope for us. I do love you, more than I thought I could love anyone. But it's not natural. You don't behave as a woman should. It's always a fight with you. A competition. I can't do this anymore."

"Then don't." I stepped to the door, my eyes on him as I reached for the latch.

"Sarah." He didn't move, his shoulders hunched about his neck. "Please . . ."

"No apologies," I whispered. "No regrets." My fingers twisted the doorknob; as it gave way, I felt the corridor outside beckoning me, the cool draft of my imminent escape.

"If you go . . ." He let out a shuddering breath. "You mustn't return until you have an answer for me."

Not until I was on the gaslit street, in the sultry air of the mid-July night, did I start to move faster. Clutching at my skirts, I ran blindly, without destination, toward the river, away from the specters unleashed within me.

When I reached the turgid waters, sluggish and fetid from the heat, I leaned against the bridge railing and finally let it overwhelm me. *It's not natural. You don't behave as a woman should.*

I had fled love, no matter what my reasons might be.

And I had to wonder if there was a deeper truth I sought to flee more.

I wandered the city, losing myself in throngs of pedestrians enjoying the warm night, dressed in light attire, sipping anisette at the cafés and perusing the kiosks lining the banks of the Seine. It had been so long since I'd gone unrecognized among strangers, without vying for attention or applause, that I lost myself in my rare anonymity. After walking for hours until my feet ached, I realized where I'd been heading all along.

At the building, I paused to look up to her salon window. A single lamp burned there, on one of her useless little tables, but as I strained to listen, I didn't detect the rumble of male laughter or tinkle of music from her pianoforte.

Before I lost my nerve, I went inside. The concierge came bustling out from her downstairs flat, wiping her wet hands on her apron. "Yes? May I help you?"

"It's me, Sarah. Don't you remember? Sarah Bernhardt."

Her frown lightened at once. "Mademoiselle Bernhardt! Why, I didn't recognize you at all. Such an honor. It's been some time since you visited. I was so very sorry to hear about your sister Régine. Such a dreadful loss—"

"Yes," I interrupted softly. "Is my mother entertaining tonight?"

"Not that I'm aware of. It's been very quiet of late, come to think of it." A practiced busybody like most concierges, she kept an ongoing tally of every coming and going in the building. "Your aunt Rosine and sister Jeanne did leave earlier in a carriage, to supper and the Opéra, I believe. But not Madame Julie. Shall I announce you?"

"No need. I have my key." I climbed the stairs to her door. Once there, I paused. This was a mistake. Why did I expect to find? When had she ever been a fount of wisdom for me, much less one of consolation or comfort?

Yet I still inserted my key and stepped into the cobweb of my past.

"Who is there?" I heard her say peevishly from beyond the curtain-draped entry to her salon. Even in the dim light of the lamps, patches of mending and frayed bits of fringe were visible on the curtains. The flat felt empty as a tomb, awaiting its dead.

"Is that you, Rosine?" Her voice lifted. "Did Jeanne forget her gloves again? Honestly, I'm beginning to fear for her reason. How can a daughter of mine be so absentminded?"

Moving past the drapes, I found her reclined on her settee in her Chinese stork robe, a cigarette in her hand, its smoke floating about her. It startled me. I hadn't known she'd taken up the vice. Her expression didn't register any surprise. "Sarah. How unexpected." She set her cigarette aside in an ashtray. "Have you come to reproach me for some affront?"

When I didn't respond—I was distracted by taking in the room, those same ponderous landscapes, darkened from years of her suitors' cigars; the porcelain figurines cluttering the mantel and the pianoforte draped in its sun-bleached shawl—she said, "It's rather late for a visit, don't you think?"

It was. Years too late. But I unhooked my cape and draped it over the back of one of her tiny chairs, moving to the window to gaze past the glass, remembering how I'd once tried to fling myself out of it in despair. Then I heard myself say, "Do you ever regret it?"

I didn't look at her. But I heard the crinkle of silk as she shifted upright on her settee. "What an odd question. I was just about to retire. . . ." Her voice faded when I turned around. She regarded me in silence before she said, "Oh dear. Are we in trouble again?"

I almost burst out laughing. She was nothing if not consistent. "Jean has asked me to marry him."

Now, her surprise surfaced. "Has he? Well. I suppose congratulations are in order. That is what one ought to say on such an occasion, is it not?"

I returned her impervious regard. "Do you regret it?" I asked again. "The choices you made. Rosine once said you wanted something different for me. Not this life. Is it true?"

She took up her cigarette, as if she required an object to avoid the moment. "Rosine always did talk too much. She has never learned the value of a confidence."

"It is true?" My voice hardened.

"Does it matter? You never paid me any mind, even as a child."

Before I could erupt, she went on: "Do you question it now? I hardly see the purpose. None of us can undo what's been done."

"Maman," I said, and she flinched. "Just this once. I—I need to know."

She inhaled, her cigarette tip glowing briefly. Exhaling smoke in a plume through her lips, she let the silence between us settle into a chasm.

"We are not unalike," she finally said, "much as you think otherwise. It's probably the reason we've never gotten along. I, too, was once young and ambitious. My father was a traveling merchant who sold spectacles, but I later found out he actually was a petty criminal. I refused to take his name of Bernhardt after he abandoned us. My mother raised me and my five siblings on her own as best she could, but I never wanted the life she prepared for me—an upstanding marriage to a boy of our faith, to bear his children and turn old on the very street where I'd skipped rope as a girl, without any say in the matter. I wanted to experience the world. To discover what it had to offer. I was reckless."

I sank into the nearest chair, holding my breath, as if I might shatter the moment.

"Of course, I didn't anticipate what the world had in store," she went on, her voice placid, as if she spoke of someone else. "We never do. Not your father, certainly. Nor you. After that—well, I finally had my say. Not as I'd envisioned, but at least I had it."

"Would you have stayed in Holland?" I asked, thinking if we'd had the courage to talk like this earlier, we may not have ended up as we were. "Had you known."

"Why? There was nothing for me there." She extinguished her cigarette. "Do you think because I'm alone in this salon, with one of my daughters estranged from me, another in her grave, and the other unhappily following in my footsteps, that I should find cause for regret? As I said, I see no purpose in it. None of us have the luxury of foresight."

"It's only that . . ." I kneaded my hands in my lap. "I have a difficult choice to make now, and I don't know what to do."

She smiled. "Have you come here to seek my advice? You never wanted it before. And as I recall, you never wanted his or my kind of life."

"He said it wasn't natural," I whispered.

"It isn't. Men can never understand why we refuse what they have to offer." She went quiet, her gaze fixed on me. For the first time, I felt as if she saw me, in my entirety, not as her daughter, but as a woman in my own right. She confirmed as much with her next words. "The path you have chosen isn't easy; I know it well. To be a woman alone in this world, when everything you have can be taken from you—it requires great sacrifice. I don't take pleasure in admitting it, but I underestimated what you were capable of. You did what you set out to do: you've made a name for yourself. You earn your own living and you kept your son by your side, though to me, that was the most reckless choice of all. If you doubt it now, you must learn to make peace with it."

"I don't doubt the choices I've made," I said, bristling. "I doubt whether to continue with them."

Her smile widened. "By marrying the first man who asks you? Do you think I lacked for such proposals in my day? My beloved Morny, God rest his soul, couldn't take me as his wife, but he declared his abiding love and offered to keep me entirely to himself. It was very tempting, considering my position in life. In the end, however, I had to decline his offer."

"Why?" I hadn't known this. I had never imagined it. I'd always seen her through the resentment of my childhood, of my abandonment and neglect. To me, she had always seemed like a lovely, heartless piece of stone whom no one could ever love.

"Because when a woman lets herself be kept, be it as a mistress or a wife, she's no longer free. Freedom was my choice. Like you, I had to accept the consequences."

I sat still. Not comfort or consolation, but candor, when I'd least expected it. She did not speak as I rose to retrieve my cape. Yet when I went toward the door, I heard her say, "He would no doubt make a fine husband. So handsome and capable. So assertive. But you'll forget your own strength. It's inevitable when we surrender. We forget who we are."

I wanted to thank her. For her sincerity, cruel as it was.

I did not.

IX

I couldn't return to Jean. I knew what my answer must be, but every time I gathered the courage to tell him, I shied away. It was as if twin antagonists battled inside me, tearing me apart. Yet we had to rehearse together every day, spend hours enacting the passion of Zaïre and her Sultan on the stage, and by the time we neared opening night and I beheld his magnificent embodiment of his forlorn, enraged character, it broke my heart. I could see that our estrangement was agonizing for him, that he didn't know what else to do but funnel his thwarted pride into his work—the very lesson I had sought to instill in him.

The publicity churned out by Perrin sold out the first month in advance, with Mucha's stylized posters of Jean and me in costume reproduced in every newspaper and sold in every souvenir shop. By the time *Zaïre* opened on a sweltering August evening, there weren't enough seats in the house to accommodate every ticketholder. Fake tickets had circulated, with a riot nearly ensuing when management had to step in to verify that only legitimate purchasers were admitted.

The storm of protests as people were turned away at the doors reached all the way backstage; as the curtain rose on the first act, I was overtaken by such a resurgence of my dreaded *trac* that I vomited. I had to discard my soiled sandals in the wings and make my entrance barefoot, to deafening applause.

In the final act, when the Sultan advances on Zaïre with his dagger drawn, I saw the unfeigned rage in Jean's eyes; as he lifted his hand, I seized the blunted wood dagger from him and gouged at my own breast, writhing and exhaling my declaration of innocence as I crumpled at his feet. It was a spontaneous sabotage on my part, a death scene so overwrought it should have left everyone appalled. Instead, I made headlines for my ability to portray romantic death so convincingly, obliging me to continue in that vein, with a month of matinées added to the run. Upon the play's closing, I detested it so much that I vowed never to perform it again as long as I lived.

Despite the record receipts, Perrin was censorious. "Our productions must stand on their own. I don't appreciate unauthorized changes to the established choreography or costumes, regardless of any subsequent acclaim."

As for Jean, he finally accosted me in my dressing room. "Was it necessary? Wasn't it enough to humiliate me offstage or must you see me on my knees before all of Paris?"

"None of your notices mention you on your knees." I brandished a newspaper from my table. "Even Sarcey, who until now reserved his opinion, acknowledges the Comédie has finally engaged an actor capable of assuming all the roles made legendary by our late Talma." My smile felt taut on my lips. "Another comparison to the great ghost. You must be elated. You're becoming as celebrated as me— and in far less time."

His expression darkened. "Is this your answer to my proposal?"

I felt myself falter. There was no avoiding the truth now.

"I have no other," I said quietly. "It would be impossible. We are too different. And too alike. We both want too much to ever be satisfied by each other."

He looked stunned, though it couldn't have come as a surprise. "You're refusing something you will regret," he said, his voice resolute, as if he'd been practicing his response for weeks. "No one will love you as I do. No one will understand you."

"Do you understand?" I met his pained eyes. "Because you want someone who isn't me. If you truly understood, you'd know that."

"You never loved me," he said. "That much I understand."

As he turned on his heel, I had the sudden urge to call him back, to soothe him with endearments and vague promises. He loved me and wanted to make me his wife. Women plotted the course of their entire lives for such a declaration. How could I turn away from something so coveted, when I might never hear it again? But I resisted my weakness, knowing it was my personal bane: my terror of ending up like my mother, fading into obscurity among the detritus of my choices. Instead, I let his footsteps pound down the passageway into silence, and only then did I let myself weep.

Nothing that went on in the theater was private; within days, spurred by Jean's morose expression and my avoidance of him, rumor spread that the Comédie's lead attractions had had an altercation. I couldn't bear the thought of preparing for another season with so much tension between us, and when I caught Marie Colombier whispering my name backstage to another actress, I gave her a cold stare. "If you have something to say," I told her, "please do me the courtesy of saying it to my face."

"Why must you think everything is about you?" she replied as the other actress—a newly hired ingénue—scuttled away at the flick of my hand.

I rounded on Marie. "Enough. You must be suffocating in your own venom by now. Just say what you think of me and be done with it."

"Very well." She drew herself erect. "You are turning this company upside down with your impossible temperament and—" She paused, as if she didn't dare say more.

"And . . . ?" I prompted, without taking my stare from her.

"Perrin doesn't condone personal affairs that interfere with our work," she added primly, as if her own personal affairs were of no consequence.

I could have clawed her eyes out. "What would you know about our work?" I stepped so close, she had to step away against a backdrop. "You've never worked a day in your life, save to further your own interests—backstage."

Her gaze hardened. "At least I know my limitations."

"I should hope so." I turned from her in disgust. "Limitations are all you have."

I went straight to Perrin, barging into his office and, before he could so much as look up from his papers, declaring, "I've been working without respite for two years at this house. I must have some time off, lest you wish to see me at my wits' end."

He gave me a penetrating look. "Our own Mademoiselle Révolte at her wits' end? Perhaps we should charge admission for such an event." Wiping his pince-nez on his sleeve, he added, "It so happens a reprieve is impossible. I intend to stage Racine's *Phaedra* for our next season—"

"*Phaedra*!" My voice lifted even louder in disbelief. "After the demands of *Zaïre*? Is there not a single play written in this century that you find worthy?"

"If you find one, don't hesitate to bring it to me. For the time being, however, you will accept whichever roles I see fit to assign."

I couldn't tell if he'd decided to embark on his own act of sabotage. The classical role of the ancient Greek queen was extremely challenging, considered the culmination in an actress's repertoire, and that he had chosen me for it indicated his trust not only in my public appeal but also in my talent. Phaedra is no innocent wronged by fate; unyielding in her incestuous love for her stepson, Hippolyte, she wreaks mayhem until she kills herself. To embody her, I'd have to devote myself body and soul to the part; and as I wrestled with elation that he'd think me ready for such a task and with despair that it would entail brutal months of rehearsal under his merciless eye, I said, "I cannot possibly play that role until I've had time to rest. I'm an actress, not a mule. I can't keep trudging onto the stage at the call of a bell."

"Is that so?" He gave me a thin smile. "Very well. Seeing as you are in such dire need of rest, you are excused for the season. I will cast another in the part."

"Another?" I went still, appalled by the very thought. I knew of no other actress in the company capable of such a demanding role except Madame Nathalie, and she was too old for it. But as I saw his smile turn smug, a cold bolt of shock went through me. Marie. He intended to cast his paramour as Phaedra. She must have been campaigning behind my back this entire time for a leading role to eclipse the success of my Zaïre.

It almost made me threaten to leave the company permanently, until he said, "I trust you'll enjoy your time away. Unless you now care to reconsider?"

I detested him in that moment, for dangling such a prize only to bait it like a snare. But if he meant to fling Marie into a part that she was utterly incapable of performing, it would only result in ridicule, and be the very comeuppance they both deserved. While I would finally have the time I needed to escape Jean and the theater, to turn my much-needed attention to Maurice, my household, and my languishing *moi*.

"I do not care to reconsider," I informed him, and I left to pack up my things. It wasn't until I was hailing a carriage home that I suddenly wondered if I'd fallen into his trap anyway. What if his intent to cast Marie Colombier as Phaedra wasn't just his means to satisfy her rivalry with me, but an underhanded attempt to prove I wasn't indispensable?

I tried to put the thought out of my mind, even when it gnawed at me as I returned to my neglected sculpture and painting, which had always soothed me. Art demanded as much as love, but once given shape, it never betrayed. It never lost its luster; it remained intact, indifferent to the passage of time even when time or the audience ceased to appreciate it.

After seeing Maurice to school, where he fared no better with his marks, I went into my studio to work, then paid overdue calls to my friends. Clairin had finished my portrait; while I didn't think I bore any resemblance to that boneless creature lounging like an odalisque on a cushion-strewn sofa, with a wolfhound at her feet, the rendition had apparently excited titillating interest at its recent exposition.

"I hear the demoiselles of quality were so taken with it, they now receive their gentleman callers thus," Clairin told me. "You've created a new style: Bernhardt *déshabillé*."

"Thus?" I echoed skeptically. "In a tea dress, peacock fan, and oversized dog?"

From her easel in the corner, Louise Abbéma remarked, "Perhaps not the dog."

I turned to examine her work. She'd changed from the first time I'd met her. Still petite, but now dressed in a male cravat and waistcoat, her dark hair cut short, which surprised me; and she was painting a landscape, which also surprised me—a sun-dappled meadow with a cottage, saccharine as boulevard candy. When I didn't make a comment on it, she did.

"I sell these for the shops. It pays the rent on my studio."

"I didn't mean to imply . . ." My apology faded into a pang as she lifted her dark eyes. All of a sudden, she reminded me of Régine, that same fey quality.

"Of course you did," she said. "I am aware this is not distinguished."

"Her portraiture, however, is," interjected Clairin. "You should let her paint yours."

I suddenly recalled that I'd once offered as much, so I now felt obliged. "As Georges can testify, I'm not an easy subject."

"The best subjects rarely are. Shall we attempt a draft first?"

I drew up a nearby chair, and was looking about for a prop when she said, "It's only a sketch."

The scratch of her charcoal on the paper tacked to her easel lulled me. I found myself drifting into contemplation of how different her occupation was from mine. The bickering and intrigue at the annual expositions were the same as opening nights; critics would always be critics, and the public prone to fickleness; but the act of creation was entirely apart. Unlike acting, painting was an intimate communion between the artist and his or her subject, without tyrannical directors or zealous rivals to undermine its conception.

When I came back to attention, Louise was contemplating me with her soulful gaze. "You seem unhappy," she said. It wasn't a question.

I leaned forward to examine her sketch. My profile, with my hawkish nose and upswept chignon unraveling about my angular cheek—a remarkable yet discomfiting likeness, its absence of flattery almost brazen. "Do I also look so forlorn?" I said.

She gave me a smile that I sensed wasn't meant to reassure. In her masculine attire, and with her little features overpowered by those huge dark eyes, I thought she was perhaps the most intriguing person I'd ever met, whom I'd neglected to properly know.

I also wasn't sure if I liked her depiction of me, which made my decision.

"When should I sit for you?"

"Whenever you like." She took a calling card from her waistcoat. As I nodded awkwardly, wondering how she could exert such an effect on me, she whispered, "We can always add the dog and fancy dress later."

Louise's studio was in Montmartre, in one of the tumbledown buildings on a corkscrew alleyway where the sun sent slivered fingers and artists toiled amidst the fumes of pigment and walnut oil. It wasn't inexpensive to rent space here, despite the decrepit conditions, and when I beheld her garret loft with its drapery crowned by dried flower wreaths, the antique busts, Oriental carpets, and a rosewood pianoforte in a corner, I knew my first impression had been correct.

No amount of paintings of pastoral scenes could have paid for this.

She confirmed as much as she offered me tea and prepared for my sitting. "My family is wealthy. I don't try to hide it, but I don't care to advertise it, either."

"Why not?" The tea was delicious, a jasmine-infused brew. Though she was wearing stovepipe trousers and a waistcoat with a fob chain, reminding me of George Sand, her feminine mannerisms and expertise with a teapot revealed an impeccable, undeniably upper-class upbringing, as if her attire was intended as a mockery. Or a distraction.

"Wealth isn't considered an asset for a female artist," she said. "It reinforces the belief that we paint out of indolence, not from vocation."

"Haven't you exhibited in the Salon?" I regarded the paintings on her studio walls. Clairin hadn't exaggerated; as insipid as her landscapes were, her portraits were bold, all women in various stages of undress, their bare shoulders and shadowy eyes seeming to gaze from the canvas in apathetic seduction, the brushstrokes evanescent, light refracting on skin as if distilled in water, more impressions of spirit than of mortal flesh.

"The selection committee rejected my submission last year. Too risqué, they said. Perhaps this coming year will be different." She slipped on a smock and began to sketch me on a fresh-stretched canvas. Just as I was, sitting on a chair, sipping tea.

"Ah." I decided to tease her. "Is this portrait of mine to be your ploy?"

She paused, regarding me. "Would you mind? The most famous actress in France, painted by another woman: I think they'll not dare deny my submission then."

"I don't mind." In fact, I appreciated her honesty. It was refreshing to hear someone state their intent without pretense or evasion.

"Are you unhappy?" she suddenly said, stepping to me to tilt up my chin. The touch of her fingers was so light, I barely felt it.

"About helping a woman break into the hallowed Salon des Artistes?" I smiled. "I know all too well what it's like to be degraded for our sex and our supposed lack of vocation for our chosen craft."

"That isn't what I asked." She began sketching me with rapid strokes.

I wanted to lower my gaze, but I couldn't. She'd managed to hold me captive. "Yes," I said at length. "I am unhappy these days. I can't say why."

"Can't? Or won't?" She did not cease to work, but the pause between us turned leaden until she said, "Life is never what we think it will be, is it?"

"I lost my sister recently." My voice quavered at the unwitting admission; I hadn't intended to tell her, but something about her— her pensive tranquility, perhaps—had incited my confidence. "She died of consumption."

"How terrible." Louise paused. "Such a common yet dreadful affliction."

I swallowed against the anguish knotting my throat. "I haven't been able to forgive myself for her death. I keep thinking I should have been there for her, more than I was. My career, all the time in the theater . . . Then someone recently asked something of me that would have required me to give it all up. For a time, I thought I should."

She didn't reply at once, taking a step back to survey her work. "You can serve yourself more tea if you like," she said into the silence. "I think I have the pose."

I took up the pot, unsure why I should feel disturbed that she hadn't responded to my confession. Then she said abruptly, "Perhaps that is why I cannot love men. All those expectations . . ."

Now it was my turn to be quiet. It didn't shock me, though such things weren't spoken of openly, and certainly not between those who'd just begun their acquaintance.

She added, "Not that it's any less complicated," and her sudden smile, with a hint of pearly teeth, transformed her somber face into mischievousness. "As you can imagine."

"Women are always expected to sacrifice," I replied. "Even to other women."

She nodded, motioning to me. "What do you think?"

The sketch was in profile, my collar folded like wilting petals about my throat and my gaze distant, as if I were searching for something elusive.

"We can add whatever clothing you like," she said. "I wish to only show your shoulders and head. A portrait of the actress. Is there any particular costume you'd prefer?"

"Hugo's Queen of Spain," I whispered. As I met her eyes, I couldn't evade the fact that from the moment I'd met her, I had felt an inexplicable attraction toward her. But it also made me ashamed, so that I started to look away when she reached out a charcoal-stained fingertip to trace my cheek. "You needn't be so afraid, Sarah."

"I've never . . ." I felt and sounded utterly inept. "I don't know how . . ."

"You do. You simply haven't done it yet," she said.

She was a thread of silk between my fingers; wet paint on smooth canvas, pungent with scent. I'd never known such pleasure. I, who made a living out of grandiose emotions, who'd honed my craft on a trade of erotic enticement, found myself a neophyte in her hands, unable to contain my near-anguished gasp as she brought me to ful-fillment.

I felt as languid as Clairin's portrait, supine on her studio floor as she went to a cabinet to fetch a cigarette. As she stood there, smoke diffusing about her, rimmed in scarlet while the sun slipped past the window behind her, I had a sudden, unsettling memory of Kératry during our first encounter.

"You are very beautiful," she said.

"I am not." I inched up the rumpled shawl upon which we'd lain. Her eyes lost some of their luster at my gesture.

"You needn't regret this, Sarah. I am not a man. I don't expect you to be responsible for me. All I expect is honesty."

I swallowed. I feared I might ruin our newfound intimacy. I didn't want to hurt her; I didn't want to see the same pain and disillusionment on her face as I'd seen on Jean's.

She retrieved her shirt. "Shall I brew us more tea? Or must you leave?"

I sat upright, running a hand through my tangled hair. "I can stay awhile longer."

Huddled over her fragrant tea and copious cigarettes, she coaxed everything out of me. As if a crumbling dam had been breached, I told her of my childhood, of never knowing where I belonged, of my fantasy of a father I'd never met and the reality of a mother I couldn't love. I confessed my struggle to become someone, anyone, other than who I was; I even confided in her about my courtesan past, of my conception of Maurice and my hopes and fears for him, and then, in a halting voice, I finally spoke of Jean.

She listened without any interruption. When I was done, night had fallen outside and urgency overcame me, that need to escape what I myself had created.

Her hand touched mine. Lightly, as when she'd positioned my chin for her sketch.

"Success can bring its own kind of sorrow. As much as you gain, you also lose. You shouldn't dwell on what cannot be, but on what is. You may not see it, but to many of us, you are more than just an actress. You are an inspiration."

I let out a humorless laugh. "If they only knew what I've done."

"It's the achievement that matters. Don't you realize how few of us ever become more than what was intended, how we never question the path set down before us by our mothers and their mothers before them? Women are the most oppressed of beings."

I contemplated this. "My mother did teach me that much, I suppose. She, too, refused to settle for what was expected of her. Yet in the end, she still built her own cage."

"Is that what you fear? That you'll end up in a cage of your own making? Is that why you cannot give yourself to this man who says he loves you and wants to marry you?"

Her words made me flinch. "Is it love? To want to possess someone so completely that they cease to be who they are?"

"Not to me. But then, I've always known I will be alone. My fear isn't solitude. It's not being true to myself."

"You're not alone." I took her hand in mine. "We can be friends, can't we?" I'd not realized until this moment how much I'd longed for another woman with whom to share myself, not carnally, pleasurable as it was, but in a way that, to me, was more intimate and fragile.

"I would like that very much." She lifted my hand to her lips. *"Mon amie."*

X

"Louise!" I burst into her studio with my hat tumbling off my head, the note crunched in my gloved hand. Pausing to catch my breath, I saw her lift her eyebrow in that ironic manner of hers as she stood by her easel, a cigarette between her fingers.

"Two hours late. Again." She sighed. "Sarah, much as I delight in your lack of punctuality, if we wish to see this portrait finished in time for my application—"

I thrust the crumpled note at her. "Look!"

She unfolded it under the light filtering through the overhead louver. She went still. "He relented."

"He had no choice. He's desperate. Marie couldn't do it." I pulled off my hat, feeling the perspiration of this unseasonably hot September day seeping down my temples. "She fell ill under the strain and left him stranded—eight days before opening night!"

I wanted to laugh, for it was exactly what Perrin deserved, but I had a stitch in my side from racing to the studio on foot. The upcoming Paris Exposition had filled the city with visitors, and trying to find a public cab was as futile as it had been after the siege.

"Eight days." Louise widened her eyes at me. "Impossible." She put out her cigarette and went to fetch me a glass of water as I collapsed onto a chair.

"Is it?" I said, when she returned with the glass. "The role of a lifetime. Thousands of visitors here from all over Europe, the first three weeks already sold out. How can I not?"

"The question shouldn't be how you cannot, but *how* can you? Phaedra isn't something you can prepare for in a week. You said so yourself, it's the role of a lifetime."

"I know the part." I gulped down the water. "Perhaps not as well as I should, but enough to perfect it by opening night. And you read Perrin's note; he's practically begging me to return." My words tumbled out in the same reassurances I'd been reciting to myself since his missive arrived at my door. "This could be my only chance to play her as I want. He's in no position to argue. No other actress can do this, as his request proves."

She regarded me in silence before she said, "It might also be a trap."

Her words gave me pause, reminding me of my own suspicions as I'd departed the Comédie for my leave. "How so?"

"Well, you told me that you and he had words because you insisted on a reprieve. He cast Marie in your place, an actress he's been sleeping with and who proved herself not up to the task. Now she's begged off and left him at your mercy. None of it can be to his liking. He will find himself in your debt. But should you fail . . ."

"I won't fail," I said at once. "Perrin knows that."

"Be that as it may, he's not your ally." She made a placating gesture. "I'm only telling you what I think. We did promise to be honest with each other. I could be wrong. He may not intend anything other than to lure you back to work, seeing as you're the only one whom he can depend on to save the play."

I considered the disquieting possibility. Perrin had put Marie's jealousy of me over the best interests of the company; it wasn't far-fetched to assume he'd now seek to turn a disaster of his own making to his advantage. If I failed to do Phaedra justice, I could never again reproach him for whatever roles he assigned.

I flicked my fingers against the glass. "What should I do?"

"I believe you've already decided that," she said, with a wry smile.

I gave it another moment of thought. "He wouldn't dare undermine me if my name is on everyone's lips by opening night. He'll want me to succeed if only for the sake of the receipts. But how . . . ?" And then it suddenly occurred to me. "How else? Extraneous publicity: the one thing he detests."

It was like floating on a cloud, after one suffered through the stomach-churning lurch as the enormous silk-and-canvas contraption ascended in tandem with the alarming hiss of hydrogen gas released from the central canister and the cracking of the untethered ground leads.

In goggles and a leather overcoat slung with so many utensils that he resembled an insane scientist, Nadar worked the rudder and levers to regulate our ascent. I stood by the edge of the wicker gondola, gazing down in amazement as the Tuileries grew smaller, more and more distant, like a theatrical set reduced to infinite perfection.

"It's . . ." I had no words to describe the sensation. Raising my eyes to the vast blue skies expanding around us, feeling the wind tug at the gossamer scarf knotted about my throat and press like a lover against my jodhpurs (I thought male riding attire suitable for the occasion), I wanted to fling out my arms and shout from the sheer intoxication of it.

"Spectacular, is it not?" said Nadar as the balloon made a graceful swerve past the serpentine coil of the Seine toward the countryside. "Just as you imagined it would be?"

"I never imagined this," I breathed, glancing at Louise. I'd badgered her to accompany me, seeing as it had been her idea to rename the balloon *Phaedra. S*he was clutching the gondola's side as if she might topple off at any moment.

"Come, look at this." I beckoned to her. "You must see it."

She grimaced. "I'd rather not."

"Don't lean too much against the side," Nadar warned her. "The extra weight could veer us off course."

She let go with a horrified gasp. "Could we crash?"

He chuckled. "The first hot-air balloon was sent up at Louis XVI's command from Versailles, and it relied on only a primitive straw fire. Its passengers were a duck, a cockerel, and a ewe. It landed within four minutes, without incident."

"Were the animals alive?" Louise was breathless.

"Very much so," said Nadar. "The following year, the Robert brothers flew a hydrogen-propelled dirigible much like this one for six hours from Paris to Beuvry. That's over a hundred kilometers." He gave her a reassuring smile. "Again, without incident. I assure you, it's perfectly safe. I've stationed watches below for our entire trajectory. I'll just take some photographs and we'll descend within an hour or so at most."

"So short a time?" I protested. Louise glared at me.

"An hour is a lifetime," she said, "without solid ground under your feet."

I laughed. "Well, between the two of us, I'm sure we weigh less than a ewe."

She shut her eyes, disregarding the chair bolted to the gondola floor to sink down into a huddle as we soared through low-lying mist. Rain spattered upon us. I couldn't stop gazing at the sights below, everything so minute yet so detailed, every tree like a tiny umbrella, every hamlet a collection of pebbles. There was no sound save for the whisper of the wind and creaking of the ship, as if we soared through a fantastical weightless realm.

Nadar employed a portable camera the size of a small box hoisted on a collapsible tripod, positioning it at various stations to take his pictures. Every time he changed its direction, Louise groaned, for the gondola swayed under his shifting weight.

I implored him to let me look through the camera; to my disappointment, the lens's magnification distorted the view.

"The lithographs won't be like this once I develop the plaques," he explained. "But I can't be sure of what I capture in the moment, which is why I must take as many as I can."

"Don't forget you must take some of me," I reminded him.

As I assumed various poses for the camera, I thought of Maurice, who'd kicked up a fuss when I refused to let him join me. Despite my assurance to Madame G., who declared me insane to undertake this endeavor, I wasn't so certain of its safety as to risk my son. When I tried to explain my reasons for leaving him behind, Maurice pouted. "How will I ever learn to live if you never let me *do* anything?"

The unexpected maturity of his remark took me aback. "By doing what you love," I said. "Read. That's how you can learn everything you need to know about life right now."

Recalling this, I decided I should write a story for him about my adventure. I looked around. "I'll tell the story of that empty chair, which no one will sit upon. A children's tale about a talking chair on a balloon! Louise," I called out, "wouldn't that be splendid?"

She groaned. "Yes. Splendid. Whatever you like."

By the time we landed, a steady rain was falling and a crowd huddled under umbrellas by the site, though the rising wind had pushed us past it, resulting in a jarring leap by the men waiting below to grasp the trailing ropes that Nadar released to anchor us.

Louise emerged wobbling from the gondola, as if she'd survived a storm at sea. As Nadar packed up his gear, I hastily rearranged my disheveled scarf and sauntered toward the journalists and gaping onlookers who'd followed our less-than-graceful descent and now regarded the deflating balloon as though it might explode at any moment.

I carried a basket of foodstuffs I'd packed for the voyage; with Louise on the verge of throwing up and Nadar enthralled by his task, neither had expressed the desire to eat. I was famished, however, my appetite stimulated by the exhilaration and the sight of astonished journalists scribbling in their notebooks as fast as they could. Locating a spot under a nearby oak, with raindrops dripping from the leaves, I set up an impromptu picnic.

I could have hugged Nadar as he joined me with Louise; he'd orchestrated our flight to perfection, each milestone on the route witnessed from below. Heaping smoked cheese on bread and handing it to him (Louise grimaced in revulsion at my offer), I heard the journalists approaching, followed by their eruption of questions:

"Mademoiselle Bernhardt, did you not fear for your life?"

"Nonsense," I declared. "How can we possibly exist if we're always in fear of death?"

"Yet you cannot deny that air flight is quite dangerous?"

"So is living. What other remedy do we have, save to savor our pleasures?"

"Would you do it again?"

"Oh, yes." I glanced at Nadar, who was eating contentedly. "I'd do this every day if I could. You cannot imagine the freedom of it. High above the clouds, unencumbered as a bird."

Louise made a disparaging sound under her breath. "Unencumbered indeed," I heard her mutter. "If the bird could bring a stage up with her on the balloon, she would."

"Why now?" asked another journalist coyly, for while the balloon's deflation may have rendered its painted name invisible, they must have seen it as we descended.

"Why not?" I said. "Must one have a reason to experience modern life's novelties?"

"So this doesn't have anything to do with your new play opening next week?" said the journalist, confirming my suspicion. "Isn't the airship named *Phaedra*?"

"Is it?" I regarded him as if I had no idea.

He gave a knowing snort and began writing. I bit into my sandwich.

Extraneous publicity; I now had a surfeit of it.

XI

Phaedra opened to a standing-room-only house. I'd badgered Perrin into employing a minimal décor, to allow the tragedy to unfold without excessive drapery and distracting backdrops. For my costume, I wore a simple white Grecian tunic with a shroud-like hood, my bared arms devoid of jewelry, lending Phaedra a famished desperation.

The eight harrowing days of twelve-hour rehearsals had taken their toll: I looked and felt as ravenous as my character. But I'd seen in Perrin's impassive expression that regardless of whatever intent he had, I'd thwarted his ploy. I embodied Phaedra in a manner that took even him by surprise, giving her a humanity that defied her evil repute, a woman overwhelmed by illicit desire who must die to atone for it. My death scene brought the house to tears—and no audience before had ever wept for her.

We were summoned for six consecutive curtain calls, the audience shouting out their ovations. Critics penned eulogistic notices, with Jean receiving the most laudatory praise of his career as Hippolyte. He had ascended with stunning alacrity to the pinnacle of success as the Française's anointed lead tragedian, and was indeed now poised to play all the challenging roles that no actor since the late Talma had mastered.

Although we didn't exchange a word offstage, I was as delighted for him as I was for myself. No part had demanded so much of me, but with its accomplishment my future at the Comédie was secured. No longer did I have to toil under Rachel's shadow, especially not after Sarcey declared in his column that upon seeing my portrayal of Phaedra, he'd never suffer another actress in the part and advised all others to retire it from their repertoire.

Perrin extended the run for two months, an exhausting ordeal that left me in a state of near collapse. With the season's end, it was announced that for the first time in more years than anyone could recall, the Comédie would shutter its doors for much-needed repairs in the summer. Even as we scrubbed the greasepaint from our pores, Perrin summoned us to the greenroom to announce that he'd accepted an offer to present the company at the Gaiety Theatre in London for six weeks—an unparalleled achievement for a man who in just five years as managing director had restored the house to its former glory.

I regarded him in disbelief. "London? We don't perform in English."

"English audiences can, and often do, attend plays in French," he replied. "However, having anticipated your reaction, I was going to excuse you from our program, seeing as your fragile constitution can be so easily perturbed."

His allusion to my prior request for a reprieve, spoken with an imperious intonation that nevertheless conveyed biting sarcasm—much as he might revel in our record receipts, he'd not soon forgive me for forcing him into the very situation he'd created—made me rise in fury from my seat. "I've just performed four months of *Phaedra* without missing a single performance!"

He ignored my rebuke. "However, I've been informed that the Gaiety has sold more than half the tickets in advance for our appearance, with His Royal Highness of Wales stating his intent to attend specifically to see you perform. So I fear you must accompany us."

Marie couldn't contain her glower. After having lost the lead, she'd barely staggered through her secondary part as Aricia. Whatever security she still enjoyed in Perrin's bed couldn't alleviate the ugly truth that she'd never amount to more. And whatever friendship we'd once shared had been vanquished by her enmity; by her bitterness at making a bid for a role she could not fulfill, handing me the very success she'd sought for herself. Ironically, her disregard of her limitations had cleared the path for me to become the Comédie's undisputed leading actress.

"I see," I said. For I did.

"I'm relieved," said Perrin. "You now have a respite of a month before we depart. I suggest you use it wisely." He paused, in marked emphasis. "And with discretion. That escapade with the balloon was most ill-advised. I must insist you refrain from such—"

"Intolerable," cut in Madame Nathalie. "The height of vulgarity. This entire city on display for the Exposition, and all anyone could speak of was the Jewess in the balloon. And to put the cherry on the disgrace, she then sees fit to publish some ridiculous fable about a chair."

I turned to her. "The Jewess in the balloon filled this house for the season. And her ridiculous fable is selling by the thousands. Everyone loves it."

"Gustave Flaubert certainly does not," she retorted. "He complained in an editorial in *Le Figaro* that publishers have neglected literature to indulge mere Bernhardt whimsy."

"Then perhaps Flaubert should change his style and write about a table," I said, forcing myself to not give in to the scalding desire to remind her that had it not been for my so-called whimsy, this theater, her sole source of income, would be defunct.

"Mademoiselle Bernhardt." Perrin's voice wrenched my attention back to him. "I've said this before, so I find it tiresome to repeat it: You are a junior *sociétaire*. We have standards to uphold, and such behavior is unacceptable. It will not be tolerated in London."

At the censure in his tone, which I'd suffered too many times already, I looked about the room at my fellow actors—all colleagues who'd benefited from my success and should have spoken up in my

defense. No one said a word. When my gaze fell upon Jean, standing against a wall with his arms crossed at his chest, he averted his
eyes.

Something long-crumbling inside me broke apart. I had thought
my future here secure, but I now understood what that security
would demand of me: utter submission.

"Then I regret that I cannot go to London unless I'm made senior *sociétaire*," I said, coming to my feet. "His Highness of Wales
will have to request a refund for his ticket."

As I marched toward the exit, Madame Nathalie cried out from
behind me, "Over my dead body! *Who* does she think she is? Since
when has this company ever seen such—"

I didn't pause for the rest of her tirade. As far as I was concerned, my time at the House of Molière had come to its inevitable
finale.

I sought refuge in my household, with my Maurice and Madame G.,
and in my painting and sculpture, and the support of my friends.
Meyer laughed uproariously when I told him what had occurred.
"Perrin might keep you waiting until the last minute, but he has a
reputation to uphold. If London wants Sarah Bernhardt, he'll ensure that London gets her."

"I'm not so sure," I said, as Louise motioned at me to tilt my
head. We were in her studio, where she was finishing a new portrait
of me. Her first one had been accepted by the Salon, and since its
exhibition, she'd been inundated with requests from society ladies
who suddenly had to be painted by her. "He was very censorious
over the balloon and my book. . . ." I let out an exasperated breath.
"He's not about to ever let me have my way."

Meyer waved his hand. "Don't underestimate your considerable value, my dear. Balloons and books aside, Perrin knows the
Comédie would never have survived without you. Trust me, he will
comply." He paused, watching Louise paint. "Though I must won-

der if this unfortunate impasse has anything to do with the superb Mounet-Sully?"

I pursed my lips. "No."

He chuckled. "Oh, I think it must be more than no. Much more, in fact."

Louise's head reared up from her easel. "How is it any of your concern?"

Meyer clucked. "Oh my. It seems I'm about to wear out my welcome. I shall depart before she flings her palette at me." Tucking his fob chain into his vest, he kissed my cheeks. "I'll call on you later, *chère* Sarah. You mustn't fret. It's bad for the complexion."

As he sauntered out, Louise spat, "How can you abide him? He's so conniving and—"

"The most important critic in Paris after Sarcey," I reminded her. I let a moment of silence pass. "Jean and I are no longer together. You know that."

"It's not my concern, either." She didn't look at me.

I sighed. "Louise."

She went still.

"What is it?" I knew she cared deeply for me, as I did for her, yet despite our friendship, the one afternoon we'd had together was always between us. I would have done it again, for the comfort of it, but had refrained from offering, as I sensed that what to me would merely be a pleasurable way to pass the time would mean more to her. Though she and Jean couldn't have been more different, in this respect they were more alike than I could admit. Louise would have been appalled to hear herself compared to a jealous man. Still, I lamented my lack of inclination; in many ways, she would have been my ideal lover.

"It's not him," she finally said. Wiping her brush on the palette, she set it aside. She lit a cigarette, running her paint-smeared fingers through her cropped hair. "But . . ."

"But?" I dreaded her next words. I didn't want our intimacy to be marred by an inadvertent admission of neglected need. I didn't think I could bear it; what we had was so perfect precisely because we didn't make claims on each other.

"A man came to see me." From her cabinet, she removed a card. "Asking for you."

I stared at the card. "Edward Jarrett," I read aloud. "I don't know him." I couldn't curb my smile. "Did he actually make the effort to track me here?"

"Evidently. He's an American. An impresario, or so he said. He tried to contact you at the theater and claims he left his card with another actress there, but you never replied. Then he saw my portrait of you at the Salon and—rather apologetically, I must say, for a foreigner—inquired as to the location of my studio, hoping to find you here."

"I never received word from him at the theater. . . ." My voice faded. "That witch."

Louise said dryly, "Marie?"

"Who else? She must have intercepted his missive. Torn up his card." I swallowed my fury. "What did he want? I hope you told him I'm not in the trade anymore."

"He's an impresario, Sarah. Impresarios seek out talent to promote."

It still sounded disreputable to me. "Well, I'm in no need of such. I have a contract." My voice faltered. "Or at least, I think I still do."

"I believe he wishes to offer you a new one—for an overseas tour." She turned back to her easel. "He mentioned various interested parties in America."

"America? I haven't been to England yet!" I laughed. Yes, disreputable, indeed. "I doubt anyone in America even knows who I am."

"He certainly seemed to know." She squeezed out a measure of azure paint from a tube. "Now, shall we proceed? I'm going to paint you wearing a riding habit this time, against a hunting scene. Sarah Bernhardt *à la chasse*. Appropriate for England, wouldn't you agree?"

I had to laugh as I took my pose.

...

Upon saying goodbye to Louise, I elected to walk home rather than endure the frustration of finding a public cab. It was a lovely spring evening, the trees in bloom perfuming the twilight. As I passed bustling cafés where shabby writers argued over coffee-stained sleeve cuffs and heard the rusty clank of grates being yanked down over shop fronts, I pondered my future.

I hadn't expected to ever find myself in this situation. I'd spent so much time and effort trying to achieve recognition as an actress, to overcome the foibles of my past and make my mark, that somehow along the way I'd ceased to enjoy it. I still loved performing more than anything else, but what I'd hoped to accomplish by returning to the Comédie had not turned out as I imagined it.

Success can bring its own kind of loss.

Even more so, it brought tiresome responsibilities, anchoring me like a stone tablet of submission. I didn't doubt Meyer's assertion that Perrin would eventually comply, if only because he couldn't afford to renege on the commitment. Our theater was in dire need of upkeep; we'd been performing with buckets backstage to catch leaks from the moldering roof. In the dead of winter, pipes burst without warning, inundating our dressing rooms. The upholstery on the seating was threadbare and the curtains had faded to a murky hue. London would pay for all of it—if London got what it paid for, which was me.

I'd not paused to consider whether my fame might have extended beyond my native land; the cloistered arena of the theater always made it seem like a world apart, where only the current play, the most recent notice, the latest affair gone awry, or an unwelcome change in the repertoire held any importance. Much as I resented Perrin's stranglehold and dreaded what he'd prepare for me in London, I couldn't deny that I was curious to experience how a foreign audience would receive me. A new venue, with a new public; a new summit to conquer: it was something I craved, without having recognized it.

Descending the slope from Montmartre, the silver twist of the Seine coming into view under the violet-tinged sky, I was so engrossed in my thoughts that I didn't realize I was being followed until all of a sudden I heard the footsteps behind me. Quickening my pace, I didn't look around until he said, somewhat out of breath, "Mademoiselle Bernhardt, if I may?"

I came to a halt. He stood a few steps from me, a spare, tall figure in a charcoal-gray overcoat, a silken top hat in his gloved hands. Not a young man; his hair was streaked with silver and his features were delineated by middle age, with crevices about his mouth and his piercing light blue eyes nested in shadow. It only heightened my mistrust of him, especially as I also noted he must be a man of means, judging by his tailored attire. I'd seen plenty of men like him in my mother's salon; they were always married, with families.

With a hint of reproof, I said, "Is it customary in your country to accost women in the street, Monsieur Jarrett?"

He didn't look abashed that I'd surmised who he was. In heavily accented French, he said, "Certainly not, Mademoiselle Bernhardt. Yet under the circumstances, I had no alternative."

"Oh?" I regarded him with what I hoped was a detached expression.

He moved toward me. "I've been attempting to speak with you for several weeks."

I allowed myself a slight smile. "You might have called on me at my home."

"You're never there." He didn't return my smile. "I did leave my card at the theater for you with a certain Mademoiselle Colombier—"

"Yes, I am aware. I shall have a talk with her."

"She doesn't interest me. You are the one I wished to see. I have a proposition."

It was precisely the statement I'd expected, though the setting— a street meandering from Montmartre with omnibus carriages rattling behind us, crammed with people returning home from work—was not. A gentleman of breeding would have known that.

"So soon?" I had the sudden urge to ruffle his impeccable façade, which I suspected was cultivated to impress, the trappings of a self-made man seeking a liaison to add the finishing touch to his hard-earned status. "In France, we prefer our aperitifs before the main course."

He went still, as if he didn't understand. I nearly laughed aloud. *Mon Dieu*, was such a lack of wit awaiting me abroad?

"An overseas tour," he finally said, and I was impressed that de-spite his eventual comprehension of my innuendo, he elected to ig-nore it. "I have contacts in many theatrical venues abroad, who I believe would pay top dollar for—"

"Top dollar? Is that an actual expression?"

"An American one, yes." He turned his hat in his hands. "Made-moiselle, would you be interested?"

"Perhaps." I looked about us. "There's a charming bistro just down this hill. If you care to dine with me, I might ask to hear more about this . . . proposition of yours." He wasn't unattractive, I de-cided. Since I had no idea whether I still had a place of employment, regardless of Meyer's assertion that Perrin would eventually com-ply, I might require a patron to tide me over while I sought a new theatrical contract. Nothing permanent, of course; and this Ameri-can, which he apparently was, would suffice for the short term.

"Oh, I couldn't." He bowed his head. "I am honored, but . . ."

"Yes?" His reluctance amused me. Must I *woo* him? "Monsieur, you did seek me out."

"I did, but I simply cannot—" He raised his eyes to me. I was startled to see that he appeared sincere; he conveyed none of the feigned reluctance of an inexperienced man on the prowl, who felt he must put up an initial show of propriety. "If I may, however, call upon you at a later time, we can discuss my proposition at leisure."

Sudden doubt curdled in me. I'd grown accustomed to homage from my set: the struggling painters, sculptors, and writers, all of whom moved in the same circle as me and sought to bask in my achievements. But I could never allow myself to forget that those of us who made our living onstage weren't deemed worthy of respectable society; that whenever someone outside our circle offered assistance, it was usually an invitation to a carnal interlude. I may have overcome my tainted past, but it couldn't be erased; I'd grown accustomed to my notoriety. That this dapper man would refuse to dine with me after chasing me down, without seeing fit to offer an explanation, seemed to carry a hypocritical aversion to being seen in public with a former courtesan.

"I'm leaving soon for London, as you surely know," I said tersely. "I'm also under contract at the Comédie-Française."

I started to walk away when he replied, "Yes, but for how long?"

"Pardon me?" I stopped, looking back at him. He stood there, his hat in his hands.

"It is my understanding you're not happy there," he went on, "and Monsieur Perrin, the managing director, is even less happy with you, despite your considerable successes."

"Monsieur Jarrett, it's in very poor taste to inquire into another person's affairs."

"Again, I had no alternative." His lack of apology took me aback. He refused to dine with me yet still didn't disguise his interest. And he'd undertaken the effort to investigate me, which no doubt had proven fortuitous, as Marie Colombier surely hadn't hesitated to regale him with my predicament. It would be in her best interests if I absconded from the Comédie as I had from the Odéon, preferably before London.

As if he sensed my doubt, he said, "I do not fault you for being unhappy. A player like you will never be content under the constraints of a state-sponsored institution. The Comédie is very respectable, but your talents demand more than it can provide."

"You seem to know much about my talents," I said. "While I know nothing of yours."

"I wouldn't say that," he replied. As velvety night fell around us, the street lamps shimmered to light. Pedestrians getting off the omnibus trudged around us, casting ill-tempered glances because we were standing there, impeding their passage, but he didn't move, regarding me as if we were the only two people on the hill. "You do know who I am."

"Monsieur, I know your name. I'm not in the habit of accepting business propositions from strangers. It is a *business* proposition you wish to offer me, I presume?"

A hint of mirth flickered in his eyes, lightening their steely hue. "I fear you may have misunderstood my intentions. Business is indeed all I wish to propose."

As he spoke, I realized with a start that I'd erred in my assessment of him. He was like . . . like Perrin, I thought. Entirely self-assured, only without my director's pompous conceit. "Should you care to make inquiries of me," he added, "you'll find that I maintain offices in London and New York. I'm well regarded in my field and I believe you could be a sensation abroad. We can both reap significant rewards from it."

I took a moment to absorb his remarkable declaration. As I did, I recalled my motto: *Quand même.* Just when I'd decided to step out on my own, despite all odds, fortune had again found me.

"I suppose you have more than your belief to support such an assertion," I said at length. "Since you've clearly made inquiries of me, you must understand that my obligations are such that any overseas tour would pose significant sacrifice."

His mouth twitched; to my delight, he appeared to be restraining a smile. "Would my assurance of a small fortune in compensation for a series of arranged private recitals in London's select drawing rooms suffice as evidence of my support?"

"Private recitals?" I echoed, as if I'd never heard of the concept.

"Yes. There are interested parties who wish to pay to hear you recite outside of the theater. It's often done by players, a time-honored means to supplement their income."

He wasn't speaking of my mother's trade, but he was also suggesting an approach that was equally likely to incite Perrin's wrath.

"It is not done at the Comédie," I said, even as I recalled my

mounting household debts, my frustration with the lack of choice in
my roles, with the staid air of the Française, where even if I was kept
on, I already knew I'd be curtailed, as he put it, at every turn. Earning the retirement pension due as a senior *sociétaire* after twenty
years with the company would extract every last drop of creativity
in my veins, if I managed to survive that long. I couldn't conceive of
it, being relegated to playing overdone classical heroines until I
graduated to Agrippina, resisting in vain my inevitable disillusionment and the encroachment of my decrepitude.

"Nothing in their contract states as much," he said. "I've taken
the liberty of consulting their boilerplate. They may not approve of
the practice in theory, but how their players elect to spend their time
outside the theater is their own affair. Should Monsieur Perrin declare otherwise, he is in the wrong." He clicked open an expensive
gold-plated case, extracting one of his cards. "I only ask that you
consider it. I can ensure that your appearances do not interfere with
the scheduled program at the Gaiety. If there are any concerns, you
may direct them to my office in London. The address is there on my
card."

I pocketed it. "Then I shall consider it."

As he bowed his head again and began to turn away, evidently
unperturbed that we'd just conducted our business in the middle of
a street on the descent from Montmartre, much as any client might
do with a common prostitute, I called out after him, "How much is
a small fortune, exactly?"

He paused, placing his top hat on his head. "Exactly what it
sounds like. Don't lose my card, mademoiselle. I will call upon you
in London. With a contract."

XII

Louise and I sat on the floor of my foyer, surrounded by heaps of my luggage. When Perrin's note had finally arrived, informing me that I'd been elected to senior status, along with the terse reminder that I was due in Calais in a week (he had, of course, delayed contacting me until the last minute), I'd overturned my household in a panic.

I had never performed abroad. I had no idea what to bring, what kind of impression I should strive to make. Should I be sedate and discreet? Or outrageously bohemian? Or both? Madame G. tried to assist me until she wilted in fatigue, ankle-deep among strewn clothing, every bureau and wardrobe ransacked as I picked through articles, holding each up for inspection. "This?" I'd ask, and when she'd nod and say, "Yes, that would be——" I'd fling it aside, saying, "Too banal" or "Too outrageous," and grab up another article. "How about this?"

Eventually, I summoned Louise; I'd insisted she accompany me to England and she had agreed, so she rolled up her sleeves and went to work. "Be yourself. London hired Sarah Bernhardt. You must give them what they paid for."

We chose my extravagant velvet walking coats and skirts, patterned damask shawls and silk shirtwaists, a variety of Doucet evening gowns, my signature scarves, and a plethora of eccentric hats.

She then went through and discarded several of my choices: "Not the bat," she said, plucking the hat from my hands. "No one in London wants to see Sarah Bernhardt with a dead creature on her head."

"But everyone in Paris loves my bat," I said. "My photograph in it has sold nearly as well as my children's book."

"In England, they have an old bat on the throne. I should think that is enough."

Once we were done, nourished on pâté sandwiches Caroline delivered at regular intervals, along with pots of hot tea, Louise slumped onto the floor, disheveled from our day-long effort. She lit a cigarette, her back against a trunk and legs splayed out before in her striped stovepipe trousers.

I eyed her. "I hope you're planning on packing a dress for yourself."

"Why?" She blew out smoke. "London isn't paying to see me." Taking up the last of the sandwiches, she said, "Is Maurice still upset he's not going?"

I sighed. "Madame Guérard will look after him. He failed most of his courses this year, so he must take a remedial summer term. Naturally, he's not speaking to me at the moment."

"Sarah, must he?" Louise bit into the bread, with her cigarette still hanging from her lip. "You do realize no matter how well he does in school he'll never be accepted into one of our *grandes écoles*. He lacks the pedigree."

"Pedigree doesn't pay for tuition. Money is still money, even to a *grande école*. I stand to earn plenty of it in England."

Louise gave me an amused look. "You've clearly never been to a *grande école*." She paused. "I assume this means you agreed to Monsieur Jarrett's proposition. I did wonder at the heightened concern over your apparel, as you'll presumably be in costume at the Gaiety."

"I haven't agreed yet," I retorted, my very defensiveness betraying my interest. "He said he would call on me in London. I did, however, consult with Duquesnel about him," I admitted, as her eyes widened in surprise. "As you can imagine, he wasn't amused to hear from me after my defection, but he assured me that Monsieur Jarrett is exactly what he claims—a well-regarded and successful impresario."

She chuckled. "That sounds like acceptance to me. Perrin will have an apoplexy. Strong-armed into naming you a senior *sociétaire* and now you're off to entertain British aristocrats in their drawing rooms. Not his idea of a foreign engagement by the Comédie."

I shrugged, though I didn't feel as nonchalant as I feigned. "Jarrett assured me it's not forbidden by my contract. He claims if Perrin says otherwise, he's in the wrong, as other notable players have done it—which I suppose is true enough."

"Has anyone paid to hear Madame Nathalie declaim over the soufflé, I wonder?" mused Louise, making me laugh aloud.

"Perhaps not," I said, "but she doesn't have this menagerie to support."

Louise drew on her cigarette. "Well. London should be very interesting."

I gave her a grateful smile. "I'm so pleased you've agreed to come with me."

"Agreed?" She scoffed. "You gave me no choice. But as you say, money is money. And I intend to profit, too. All those proper English ladies with nothing to do can commission me to paint their portraits while you recite and eat their beefsteaks."

The Channel crossing wasn't arduous, despite the dire warnings of unpredictable tempests and savage currents. It was almost pleasant, this short passage over water, though predictably Louise was confined to our cabin with seasickness, and had to be tended by Caroline, as my friend moaned that she was in imminent peril of being buried alive by my luggage as the ferry dipped and rolled.

The rest of the company fared no better; all save Jean were sickly pale and unsteady on their feet by the time we reached Folkestone. To my surprise, a crowd of photographers, journalists, and admirers had assembled to welcome us.

Hurrying onto the deck in my ankle-length brown velvet overcoat with its oversized ivory buttons and leopard-fur collar, my enormous hat festooned with rosettes and swaths of tulle, I heard the distant cries—"Hurray for Bernhardt!"—and I clapped my hands in eagerness to finally be arriving on foreign shores to such unexpected hospitality.

Perrin detained my excited stride toward the gangplank. He was dressed in a somber suit with a bowler hat, like an undertaker about to retrieve a corpse, rather than the overseer of an historic engagement by the Comédie. In his gloved hands he held a newspaper, which he thrust before my distracted gaze. "What, may I ask, is *this*?"

"A sodden newspaper." I started to march past him when he snarled, "*Look* at it."

I paused, turning from his icy expression to the others, assembled in the foreground like sentinels of doom. Jean was handsome as ever in a black cashmere overcoat, his thick mane cascading about his chiseled, moody face. His intense stare caused me to lower my eyes to the article Perrin had circled in irate red ink:

Drawing Room Comedies of Mlle Sarah Bernhardt,
under the management of Mr. Edward Jarrett:

The *répertoire* of Mlle Sarah Bernhardt is composed of comedies, sketches, one-act plays and monologues, written especially for her and other artistes of the Comédie-Française. These comedies are played without accessories or scenery, and can be adapted for *matinées* and *soirées* of the best society. For details and conditions, interested parties should please communicate with Mr. Edward Jarrett, Secretary of Mlle Bernhardt, at His Majesty's Theatre.

Looking up at Perrin, I saw such antipathy that I thought for a moment he'd refuse to let me disembark. I was speechless in that moment, too, for in my rush to prepare for the voyage, I hadn't glanced at a single newspaper, though, as Perrin confirmed, it wouldn't have done me any good. "In the London *Times*." The paper crunched in his fist. "An *advertisement* for the extracurricular services of a senior member of this company on the very eve of our arrival."

I forced out a smile. "I understand others have done the same."

"They most certainly have not," he retorted. "Not under my management."

"Is it forbidden?" I assumed ingenuousness, for the last thing I wanted at this hour was an altercation with him. "Are we not allowed to do as we wish in our spare time?"

"Mademoiselle Bernhardt." The constrained fury in his voice turned my name into an indictment. "You knew very well how this would appear, as well as my sentiments regarding it. I'll not have our engagement in London disturbed by more of your unseemly antics. It may not be stated in our contract, but rest assured, I *do* forbid it."

"Then, as the advertisement says, you must address your concerns to Mr. Jarrett." I stepped past him, feeling his stare, and those of the others, boring into my back as I sauntered to the gangplank and flung out my arms to the waiting crowd.

There was even a band, with discordant trumpets and cymbals. Bouquets of carnations were deposited in my arms as I paraded to the boat train with the company trudging behind me, and hordes of strangers with wind-chafed cheeks shoved playbills and shreds of paper at me, begging for my signature.

Naturally, I had to stop, smile, and sign. A stout woman in a preposterous bonnet gasped in my face in broken French, "I saw you in Paris as Zaïre, Mademoiselle Bernhardt! I wept. I barely understood the play, but I didn't care. I wept like a babe at her death."

"How charming." I scrawled my name across her playbill. She clutched it to her chest as if she'd received a benediction.

"What next?" snarled Marie Colombier. "Marble busts and champagne?"

Before I mounted the train, a booming voice called out, "Incomparable One!" I turned to gaze into the crowd. A long-limbed youth in a bold purple-collared frock coat was shoving his way toward me, waving a clutch of white lilies—my favorite flower—in his hands. *"Vive l'Incomparable!"* he cried, and he tossed the lilies into the air, their sculpted petals showering about me as the crowd took up his chant in their atrocious accent.

The youth regarded me in adoration through heavy-lidded green eyes, his elongated Germanic features under a tousle of wavy brown hair; in response to my amused smile, he bellowed in perfect French: "Remember me. I'm your devoted slave and poet, Oscar Wilde!"

Once in the train, I collapsed onto my seat. Louise eyed me. "I expect you're going to find many interested parties for your drawing room comedies and monologues," she remarked, as I twitched aside the curtain at the window to catch another glimpse of that strange young poet who'd thrown lilies into the air like confetti. I'd found the gesture too extravagant, a waste of fragile beauty, but also very romantic and decidedly continental.

"I had no idea the English could be so impulsive," I said, turning from the window in disappointment when I failed to spot him.

Louise snorted. "They're not. Perhaps you are about to change them."

London was beset by rain and smothered in an acrid fog that made my eyes burn. At Victoria Station, there was no band or cheering crowds. There was a soiled red carpet, but not for us, as we were informed by the stolid employees of the Gaiety Theatre sent to escort the company to the hotel. The carpet had been laid out for

Their Royal Highnesses of Wales, who'd just departed on a trip to France, of all places.

"Departed?" I echoed in dismay, before Perrin could utter a word. "But we've only just arrived. Won't Their Royal Highnesses be attending our premiere?"

"I'm afraid not. His Grace the Duke of Connaught will attend in their absence," replied one of the escorts, as if I had any concept who this duke was. "But Their Highnesses will return in time to see you perform, Mademoiselle Bernhardt. His Highness Prince Edward made himself clear on that account."

More unpleasant surprises were in store. The company had rooms in the assigned hotel, but Mr. Hollingshead, managing director of the Gaiety, had rented me a furnished private residence in Chester Square, at Mr. Jarrett's expense.

"Why should *she* have a residence?" Marie turned in outrage to Perrin. She'd adopted Madame Nathalie's deprecation for the trip, as Madame, citing her advanced age and inability to digest foreign food, had refused to join us. To emphasize her displeasure, she'd also announced her retirement.

Perrin had to swallow his own outrage. "We are a company," he said, to no one in particular, as the employees of the Gaiety could hardly be blamed. "I don't see why such a separation is necessary." But it was unthinkable to refuse the offer, so he and the others had to proceed to the hotel while Caroline, Louise, and I took a hansom to Chester Square, a fashionable district with a gated green that did not relieve the abrupt plunge in my spirits.

Caroline set herself to helping the waiting staff unpack and set our belongings in place as I drifted through the lavish townhouse, which, despite all the visible comforts of home, felt alien and oppressive to me. All of a sudden, with a longing akin to despair, I missed the chaos of my own house, of my Maurice, Madame G., and our animals.

Pausing in a sumptuous parlor where vases of roses overflowed every table and sideboard, bearing *bonne chance* notes from my friends in Paris and invitations from English admirers I'd never heard of—except for Sir Henry Irving, Britain's foremost actor, who wrote that he was arranging a private soirée for me, where I'd not be required to recite a single word—the weight of what I'd undertaken fell upon me, every bouquet and good luck note like an omen of impending doom.

"What if they hate me?" I turned to Louise, who dangled an unlit cigarette in her hand, as if she wondered whether it was permissible in England to smoke indoors.

"Hate you? You heard your devoted poet. You are their Incomparable One. You could go onstage and do nothing, and they'll applaud as if you recited Racine's entire oeuvre."

"No." I reached for her hand. "What if I cannot deliver what they expect? It's too much; they expect too much of me. You saw Perrin's expression at the station, he'd dispatch me back to Paris this instant if he could. It's obvious no one will be coming to the Gaiety to see the company."

"And that surprises you?" She waved her hand impatiently. "Sarah, just do what you do best: perform. Judging by what I've seen today, you haven't forgotten how."

Monsieur Jarrett arrived that evening, wearing an extremely well-tailored gray wool suit, his silvery hair slicked to his scalp. As he removed his overcoat and opened his satchel, I started to rebuke him over his cavalier assumption that I'd agree to his terms, until he showed me the three-page list of those requesting my presence in their drawing rooms.

"Impossible," I said, perusing in disbelief the over forty unfamiliar names with unfamiliar yet impressive titles. "How can I perform my scheduled program and all this?"

"I did promise you a small fortune. All of London is eager to receive you. It's very unusual for a player to be welcomed thus by society. Your name precedes you, but players here are only starting to gain acceptance, thanks to His Highness of Wales's passion for the theater—"

"His passion for actresses, you mean," I said. "I'm aware of his predilection."

"Be that as it may, these invitations represent the highest echelon of British society. You'd do well to accept every one, if you wish to pursue your current course."

"My current course?" I set the list aside. "Whatever course might that be?"

He gave me one of his rare smiles; I'd begun to deduce he did not smile often, unless there was significant profit involved. "To leave the Française, of course," he said in his matter-of-fact way, another trait I found disconcerting.

"I never said anything about leaving," I exclaimed, as taken aback by his presumption as by his perceptiveness, for I hadn't admitted as much to myself.

"You don't need to. I was informed of your reception at Folkestone."

"For which I can assume we have you to thank. Not to mention the advertisement in the *Times*, followed by this mansion for me and the hotel for them."

"I assure you, the reception in Folkestone wasn't my doing. This house, on the other hand, is necessary. You have important engagements to fulfill that require privacy." He took out a sheaf of paper and pen. "You are destined to become the most celebrated actress of our age. Monsieur Perrin will not abide it. The only idol he can tolerate is one he creates, and she must be beholden forever to the Comédie. It's a matter of survival for him. Is that agreeable to you?"

I regarded the pen and paper he extended between us. "Yet if I sign this . . ."

"You'll be taking charge of your future. I will manage everything; it's what the terms of this contract and my commensurate fees dictate."

"Why me?" I searched his face. He was one of the few men whose emotions eluded me, making me uncomfortable, even if I was certain he wasn't a liar or fraud.

"Because there is no other like you." His voice softened. "You cannot bring yourself to believe it yet, but you will in time. Should we fail to find mutual accord, I will not oblige you. You are free to void our contract."

As I still hesitated, he added, "I can make you very wealthy. You can provide for everyone in your family. For your son. You can perform whatever you like, however you like. Institutions like the Comédie will always serve a purpose, but not for you."

Before I could persuade myself otherwise, I took the pen and signed in furtive haste, as if I were engaging in a shameful act, knowing Perrin would indeed never abide it.

This time, as he let the ink dry, Jarrett's smile was almost warm. "I promise, we are about to embark on an extremely lucrative partnership, Mademoiselle Bernhardt."

Opening night at the Gaiety made a mockery of the theater's name; it had all the solemnity one might expect from the Comédie-Française, punctuated by Perrin's demand that the bust of Molière, which he'd had transported in a felt-lined crate, be placed onstage opposite one of Shakespeare, with the entire company assembled between the deified dead lions in full costume from our various roles.

The company dean began the evening by reciting an interminable poem composed especially for the event, after which, amidst a leaden silence broken only by the ruffling of fans and playbills—it was sweltering inside the theater, June in England apparently consisting of ceaseless damp and rain—the first performance commenced.

I fled into my dressing room, as much to avoid the cold regard of my fellow players—Marie had wasted no time inciting resentment over my preferential treatment—as to evade the polite boredom emanating from our British audience. Perrin had assigned me the scene from *Phaedra* when she accosts her stepson; as I touched up my white ceruse makeup while Samson delivered a monologue on-stage from Voltaire's *Brutus*, in its original archaic French, I felt *le trac* rising to choke me.

As always, when I'd either pinned too much hope on a role or had too little confidence, it surged in me like a curse, constricting my throat until I could barely draw in any air, much less draw a full breath.

I was still fighting back my nausea as I took my place in the wings for my entrance; I'd been scheduled for the second hour, giving enough time to build anticipation for my entrance and for me to succumb to terror. Wild thoughts of dashing from the Gaiety into the night, of walking all the way to Folkestone to board the first ferry back to France, tumbled through my mind. I'd rather be accused of irresponsible temperamentality than confront what by now must be an exhausted and thoroughly perplexed audience, subjected to Samson's funereal intonation as he recited a role written for an actor thirty years younger than he was, arrayed in a musty costume a hundred years older than anyone alive.

It was a calamity. I knew it as surely as I was biting back the urge to vomit. We were going to be yawned out of London on our very first night.

Then Jean stepped to my side. Since the end of our affair, he had maintained an impenetrable distance. His fingers now grazed my bare arm, so warm against my chilled flesh, and he murmured, "You mustn't let them dissuade you."

I almost burst into tears. "How can I not? Can't you feel it? We are boring them to death. They don't understand a word of what we're reciting, and—"

"I'm not referring to the audience." His hand tightened on my arm.

I braved a look at him, afraid of what I might find. His refusal to acknowledge my presence all these months, after the volcanic passion we'd shared, had hurt me more than I'd dared admit. How could anyone love me as much as he'd claimed, then despise me with equal intensity? Though I understood his feelings were twin sides of the same coin, other than Marie and Madame Nathalie, I thought he must yearn most to see me brought as low as he thought I had brought him when I refused his proposal.

Instead, I found only stoic determination on his face.

"Everyone is here to see you," he said. "Remember what you once told me: We must never disappoint. No matter what, we must give our best performance."

"Jean . . ." I whispered.

He released me. "Show them who you are."

I followed him out, blinded by the footlights—Perrin had opted for glaring realism instead of muting the flames for mystery—drifting like a whisper in my white robe. Another mistake, I thought; I should have chosen any other color than one that reduced me to spectral fragility. I felt as if I might disintegrate into a pile of evanescent cloth as the scene began.

My tongue stumbled over lines I'd recited hundreds of times before. I heard my voice crack, and though I tried to focus on Jean, to absorb his Hippolyte's revulsion at Phaedra's frantic avowal and play into it, he grew indistinct, his own lines issuing with a power that seemed to batter the eaves, chipping at my eroding composure.

I didn't feel myself faint. Darkness simply overcame me, and the last thing I heard were the gasps of the audience as the curtain fell. When I came to, Jean was holding me in his arms. He was smiling. Acid surged in my throat. He'd had his revenge at last.

"Up, up!" hissed Perrin, for tonight he'd planted himself backstage like an avenging conductor. "To your feet at once."

As the company hastened to their places in line of precedence, headed by Samson in his sweat-drenched ancien régime costume, Jean supported me around the waist.

The curtain lifted for our call. Blinking in the glare, it was only then that I realized beyond that wall of light, the audience was standing, their applause ricocheting in my ears.

"Sarah! Sarah!"

My name. They were crying out my name.

ACT VI

1879–1880

::

Entrepreneur

Slow down? Rest? With all eternity before me?

—SARAH BERNHARDT

I

"'It would require some ingenuity to give an idea of the intensity, the ecstasy, the *insanity*, as some people might say, of the curiosity and enthusiasm provoked by Mademoiselle Bernhardt.'" Upon translating the notice in his fluent French, my devoted poet flung the London *Times* aside in a gesture as flamboyant as the one he'd made in Folkestone. "Utter tripe. How can any respectable newspaper publish a man with such a limited vocabulary? He's turned the performance of a lifetime into a rheumatic complaint. My poem to you is far more in keeping with your incandescent spirit."

I smiled at him from my divan, reclined over scones, tea, and flattery, unopened offers to dinner and other ventures piled up on my side table.

"Your poem is certainly more in keeping with how I prefer to see myself," I said, enjoying his self-indulgent scowl. His long-limbed body, which should have been clumsy yet he managed to make supple, was arrayed in an emerald-green velvet frock coat; the red-satin-lined opera cape he had worn here in midday was tossed over a chair.

Oscar Wilde had not awaited my invitation. He'd been in the audience at the Gaiety on opening night; even as critical praise was heaped upon me for a performance that had been a disaster—my missed lines not seen as missed at all because who cared what I said in French, my stumbling delivery interpreted as the epitome of Phaedra's delusion, my swooning at the end deemed the most devastating example of Gallic tragedy that Britain had ever witnessed, rather than the Gallic talent's horror at her own ineptitude—my poet elected to ignore the prerequisites and storm my house with armfuls of lilies (this time, I insisted on a vase), avowing eternal homage at my feet.

Louise took one look at him, rolled her eyes, and trudged upstairs to paint.

Oscar now exhaled an exasperated breath. "Yet the *Times* somehow saw fit to publish my poem on their editorial page and allotted that tedious American an entire column."

"Henry James is a rather famous American, is he not?" I said. "I understand he's published several novels." Not that I could cite a single title, let alone claim I'd read one.

Oscar sniffed. "I'm a far better writer." Humility was anathema to him, which I could appreciate. I also had no illusion that his homage toward me was altruistic; a journalist by trade, he aspired to wide recognition, cleverly befriending the most influential in current cultural and artistic circles. He'd already informed me that once he completed work on his first novel, he intended to write a play for me, a sordid recounting of Salome. He'd created plenty of sordid scandal already from what I had heard, though not yet past his thirtieth year, with his defiance of expected attire and his scathing opinion pieces on the arts, published in the newspapers, skewering anyone who failed to meet his standards—which was nearly everyone.

Oh yes, he was decidedly continental. He spoke several languages, had lived in Paris for a time, and even traveled to America. Not at all what a British gentleman ought to be.

All of which I found delightful.

"Come." I beckoned him. "Stop pouting and help me sort through these impossible invitations. I don't have the faintest idea who any of these people are."

With elfin-like glee, he tore into the pile. "Frightful bores. Except for Miss Terry and Henry Irving, everyone here promises to put your incomparable self into a stupor. They've been dousing Mayfair in conversational laudanum for centuries."

"Yes, but Mr. Jarrett insists. He says these are my incomparable entrées into the highest echelons of tedium. So, whom shall I allow to put me into a stupor first?"

He gave a dramatic pause, his finger tugging at his lips as if he were pondering. I knew he wasn't considering anything other than his own interests, as he confirmed: "If you must accept every one of these engagements, you'll need a proper British escort, who can also act as your translator. Your command of our language is beyond appalling."

I passed my gaze over him.

"I can be proper," he said at my unvoiced insinuation. "More proper, in any event, than your Mr. Jarrett from the United States. A foreign *impresario*." He enunciated the word with an exaggerated shudder. "My lady Dudley has invited you to tea and a jaunt in Hyde Park; she would never permit a man of such low station, from a former colony no less, to mount one of her purebred mares."

"But she'd allow *you*?" I couldn't repress my smile. I was certain she'd rather not, but the thought of appearing with him in his velvets in elite drawing rooms was irresistible. If I must undertake this exercise in pursuit of my present course, I needn't be *too* bored.

"If you say nothing in advance," he said, "how can she refuse?" As he spoke, he opened one of the larger thick cream-paper envelopes. He went still. "HRH Prince Edward of Wales requests Mademoiselle Sarah Bernhardt's attendance at—" He let out an uproarious laugh. "Our quim-whisker prince has invited you to a midnight supper at *la maison de Rothschild*."

"Is that what he's called?" I'd heard plenty of salacious talk about Bertie of Wales, but not this particular nickname.

Oscar set his hand on his hip. "It's what I call him. Must I explain?"

I smiled. "I believe I understand."

"Even if his long-suffering spouse, Princess Alexandra, does not. Nor his venerable forever-in-mourning mama, our beloved and most tedious Majesty, Queen Victoria."

"Will she be there?" The possibility startled me. "The queen herself . . . what on earth does one wear to such an occasion?"

Oscar waved the embossed invitation about him as if to dispel an offensive odor. "Her Majesty will most certainly *not* be there. You may have enchanted London, but you're still an actress. But everyone else who is anyone will attend—which is why you must bring me with you. Or I shall chastise you in my next article for your heinous disregard of our English dressmakers." His eyes narrowed at my silence. "Or do you fear I might embarrass you before His Royal Highness?"

"I hardly care." I laughed. Embarrassment in England seemed rather improbable, considering how everyone thought my premiere at the Gaiety had been superb.

"I will ensure you are received as your incandescent spirit deserves," he declared, with the grandiosity of an imperial official. "You must therefore reply at once that Mademoiselle Bernhardt would be honored to accept His Highness's invitation. And allow me to see to your attire. I know my royals. Moderation is a fatal thing. To them, nothing succeeds like excess."

In between my performances at the Gaiety and recitals in exclusive abodes, Oscar lured me to Charles Frederick Worth's establishment in London. My poet had an unerring eye for fashion, and utter disregard for its cost. After ordering an entirely unsuitable custommade white silk suit with trousers for working in my studio, which caused a fuss—"White silk, to *paint* in?" exclaimed Mr. Worth—I was obliged to then order several day dresses, as well as an evening gown for my dinner at the Rothschild estate, though I thought Worth's gowns fussy and unimaginative. When I mentioned this to Oscar, he laughed. "You've just described England. Seeing as there's nothing fussy or unimaginative about you, you will lend his dresses the qualities they so sorely lack."

I also ordered a gown in dark blue silk for Louise, obliging her to attend a fitting, which didn't please her in the slightest.

Oscar indeed proved to be the ideal companion. His fluency in French and English helped me navigate the interminable receptions I had to attend, followed by the recitals I was obliged to deliver. He was amusing without harboring ulterior motives—whatever motives he had, he stated out loud—though he reveled in exciting attention with his wit, which bordered on the insulting without ever quite being so. Most of the ladies naturally flocked to his charm, while most of the gentlemen regarded him askance, as if they weren't sure whether to let him alone or hunt him down like one of their foxes.

"He's quite impossible," remarked the actress Ellen Terry, at the soirée that she and her lover Sir Henry Irving arranged in my honor. She spoke fluent French, to my relief, as I had made no effort to learn any English. "How ever did you come across him, Sarah?"

An auburn-haired woman with enviable cheekbones and an English-rose complexion, she seemed bred for afternoon tea. Not at all what I expected of an actress who'd become the most renowned in London for her Lady Macbeth, but I soon discovered her persona was deceiving, for like all of us who toiled on the stage, she had an avid ear and tongue for gossip.

"He found me," I said. "He bathed me in lilies. He wouldn't take no for an answer."

She leaned to me. "You might have a care, Sarah, where he is concerned. He has a reputation. Greek affairs—rather the scandal, as I recall."

I smiled, watching Oscar saunter through the room, bestowing his feline smile, his fingers stroking his wineglass stem as if he were transmitting a secret code. "I admire him for it. He refuses to be anything but himself."

"Be that as it may, he is still married, with a child," said Ellen, without any perceptible judgment that I could discern. She was merely stating a fact.

"Is it so unusual here?" I asked. "Surely not. Men like him abound in Paris, particularly in our profession."

"London isn't Paris, as you have seen. We still have censorship laws here, restricting what we can perform. You need only look at the turmoil you've created, with all these claims that you parade about in trousers in the company of a decadent Irish dilettante and a female painter of equally uncertain disposition, smoking cigars on your terrace at Chester Square and fencing at midnight on the green."

I burst out laughing. "That's absurd! I don't smoke. And I don't know how to fence, though perhaps I should learn."

She smiled. "Evidently, you also don't read our periodicals."

"They're in English," I reminded her.

"Ah. But they're reporting much the same in France." She paused, her smile faltering as she took in my expression. "Sarah, didn't you know? I regret to tell you this, but in Paris, they're saying you are unpatriotic for consorting with foreigners, among other unsavory accusations."

"Unsavory?" I suddenly felt drenched in ice. "Such as . . . ?"

She let out a sigh. "I don't wish to spoil our evening. Suffice to say, we don't believe a word of it. It's not considered avarice here to recite in private, given our paltry theatrical earnings. None of us prefers to starve for our art."

I had to nod, even as anger simmered inside me. I'd paid no attention to what was being printed about me, unless Oscar mentioned it, as he often did, bringing me excerpts of the notices from my latest performance at the Gaiety so we could revel in "the execrable prose of writers who should only be permitted to review a washerwoman's hose." We'd laughed over the hyperbole, reading it aloud as if it were a comedic play, but he'd never cited any criticism, though he must have seen it, since he scoured the newspapers on a daily basis for items to exploit.

Ellen reached for my hand. "You mustn't pay it any mind. You're a sensation, invited to dine by His Highness. It's envy. We don't want to admit that men like Oscar Wilde exist nor that we harbor resentment for those who aren't British, but as we both know, men like Oscar do exist and many here resent the French. It's always been thus: You have Voltaire and Hugo. We have Shakespeare and Byron. A constant battle to prove who is superior."

"You also have an empire," I retorted. "We lost ours."

She laughed. "Indeed. We still have that much in our favor."

I came to my feet. I'd chosen one of my Doucet gowns for tonight—stark black velvet, with a high gauze neckline and Chinese-silk scallops down the side and about its frothy hem, with elbow-length leather gloves and my untidy chignon to highlight its unusual design. No woman wore anything like it, as I'd noted by the appraising looks when I'd first entered the townhouse, where Sir Henry had gathered the luminaries of the British stage to meet me.

Now, all eyes turned again to me as I called out, "My poet!" and Oscar bounded to me with a grin that betrayed he'd imbued enough wine to be primed for mischief. "Shall we recite for this marvelous assembly?" I said, my voice loud enough to carry.

Sir Henry immediately protested. "Sarah, it's not necessary. You are our guest tonight. You must be exhausted from the Gaiety and all the recitals you've already—"

"I wish to do so." I cast a warm smile in his direction. He was very handsome, with his thick, well-groomed beard and expressive features. And like Ellen, he had no pretension despite his success; they suited each other perfectly. "I'm so moved by this occasion."

As Sir Henry stepped forth to accompany me, I said, "Oscar and I shall perform a scene and poem, a recital in dual languages to celebrate friendship between our nations."

Oscar clasped my hand in his, his voice lowering as he said to me, "Which poem?"

"The one you composed for me," I replied. "I shall recite from *Zaïre*, when she's unjustly accused of betrayal."

Once Oscar had declaimed his English verses in a voice made for the stage (he would have made a magnificent actor), I delivered in French my plea of innocence. We'd never rehearsed together, though we'd had plenty of practice with my notices; and it was, in my opinion, the best performance I'd given thus far in England. When we were finished, the silence in the drawing room was taut. Then Ellen began to applaud; at her cue, the others followed suit, even as Henry Irving's pained look betrayed that he knew what had motivated my impromptu delivery.

Oscar executed a sweeping bow. "Ladies and gentlemen," he declared, his voice thick with emotion, "I give unto you the Incomparable Sarah Bernhardt."

I did not curtsy. I made no gesture of obeisance. I kept my gaze fixed on these people who must have already read what I hadn't. Let everyone here report that Mademoiselle Bernhardt refused to display anything but supreme confidence in her abilities.

While I plotted my revenge.

"Who is it?" I stood before Jarrett in his office, my newly purchased copies of *Le Monde* and *Figaro* flung onto his desk. "*Who* is telling such intolerable lies about me?"

To his credit, Jarrett didn't immediately try to placate me. But then, he'd never seen me in a temper before and his French was somewhat limited, so he may have needed a moment to digest my outrage.

Then he said, "Sarah, this isn't unexpected. Your name at the Gaiety is the company's sole draw; when you're not on the playbill, their receipts drop by half." He paused. "You also cannot be unaware that Mr. Wilde is not considered a suitable companion."

"He suits *me*." I'd already confronted my poet earlier, demanding to know why he'd kept such vicious rumors from me; breaking into tears, Oscar swore he only sought to protect me. "How dare they judge me on the company I keep? And how dare my own countrymen denounce me for doing what every actress in my position has done? You told me that these recitals would not impede. How is this *not* impeding?"

"It is only impeding your standing in Paris." He raised a hand to stifle my outrage. "Sarah, I have it on good authority that Sarcey is responsible for the criticism. I had a luncheon with Mr. Hollingshead of the Gaiety last week and he expressed disappointment in the

Comédie. Perrin's choice of repertoire is antiquated; were it not for you, their engagement would be a disaster. Sarcey has come to London to support the Comédie. He's offering paid lectures and writing in his column on the superiority of French theater—"

"He's always been enamored of the superiority of his own opinion," I cut in. "Like every critic."

"Well, his opinion isn't doing you any favors. He knows your recitals are garnering more profit than the Comédie stands to earn in their entire run here. It's precisely what Ellen Terry told you: they are envious of your success and seek to tarnish it."

I couldn't believe what I was hearing. "How can calling me a traitor and a Jewish opportunist," I seethed, quoting one of the vile commentaries in *Le Monde* that I'd made myself read, "tarnish anything but the very company that hired me, which I now represent as a senior *sociétaire*?"

He sighed. "In my experience, envy rarely conforms to reason."

I thrust my hand into my bag, yanking out a sheet of paper. "I've written a rebuttal. I want it transmitted to the newspapers, both here and in Paris. Oscar has done me the favor of translating it into English."

He lowered his eyes to my letter, tear-stained by Oscar, who'd taken my dictation as I'd stormed about my residence parlor. "I will not let myself be defamed," I added.

To my surprise, he gave assent. I'd expected more of an argument.

"Very well," he said. "But might I suggest a delay until after your dinner with His Highness?"

"Why?" At this point, I wasn't sure if I cared to dine with the prince or anyone else.

"Because his influence can do more to stifle this controversy than any rebuttal. Should the Prince of Wales come out in your defense, all of London will be yours."

"I thought London was already mine. And that's why they envy me."

He actually had the temerity to smile. "With Bertie of Wales in the royal box at the Gaiety, you can be assured of unquestioned vindication."

When I descended the staircase of my residence on the evening of the Rothschild dinner, Oscar arched his eyebrow at me from the foyer. He wore black tails and his opera cape; behind me, encased in her new Worth dress, Louise yanked at the bodice's low cut and grumbled, "Am I required to display my entire bosom to His Highness?"

"I have it on excellent authority that His Highness would prefer it," said Oscar. He kept his gaze on me. "I see no such worries on your account. Did your new gown not fit?"

"Like a shroud." I swept past him to the waiting carriage in my ivory-lace Doucet, as high-necked and unembellished as the gown I'd worn to Henry Irving's soirée. "The Rothschilds are French. This gown is French. I am French."

Oscar gave a resounding clap of his hands. *"Vive la France!"*

Louise scowled at him. "Must you behave as if everything is a farce?"

"Isn't it?" he replied.

The Rothschilds' London townhouse was a mansion, replete with stained-glass windows that might have adorned the Sainte-Chapelle. Carriages lined the entire roadway to the entry, where footmen escorted guests into the gaslit three-story house.

"How garish," muttered Louise under her breath.

"Chin up," I told her. "Smile. Tonight, we are in France."

She might have scoffed had we been alone. She'd declared my pillorying in the newspapers meaningless, with her habitual indifference. She truly had no care for what anyone said or thought, but then she came from money, and those with money often didn't need to care.

As for me, I didn't know what to expect. By now articles of my alleged misdeeds were a daily event, each story more ludicrous than the last. I'd submitted to Jarrett's request to delay my rebuttal, but the hasty cancellation of several of my recitals warned us both that Sarcey's pen was accomplishing its venomous work. In retaliation, I'd canceled a Saturday matinée at the Gaiety, claiming illness. Perrin had to replace me with Marie and the attendees swarmed the ticket office to demand refunds. He sent me a curt note that any further absences would not be tolerated. I wanted to submit my resignation from the Comédie, having had enough of Perrin and threats, but Jarrett once more forestalled me. This was not the time for such a move, he advised.

The Rothschilds were devoted patrons of the theater, who'd donated to my ward during the siege, and were as oblivious to petty journalistic vendettas as any immensely wealthy family could be. But not immune, I told myself, as we entered their vast drawing room, where the assembly partook of wine and canapés before dinner. And tonight, I needed their support. Like everything I did, and much of what I'd never done, this evening could end up reported in the newspapers; I couldn't fathom how they managed it, but journalists seemed to possess a vermin-like ability to infiltrate any occasion.

The sudden lull in the conversation as I paused on the threshold sent a shudder through me. With my honed instinct for an audience, I sensed a quality of hesitation, as if everyone was waiting for someone else to dictate their reaction to my arrival.

The women wore their hair in ringlets, their variety of Worth creations exposing bejeweled throats and bared shoulders. From what I could see, I'd once more succeeded in being the only one with a collar to my chin. And no jewels, which was also deliberate. The Rothschild women had jewelry unsurpassed by most queens. It was pointless to try to outshine them, not that any other lady present seemed to share my opinion.

Baron Ferdinand de Rothschild materialized from among the

crowd. An older, bald man with a trim beard and soulful gaze, slim and immaculate in his monochromatic evening wear, he greeted me with a gentility that brought tears to my eyes. He and his wife had attended my performances at the Odéon—I knew because they'd always sent a congratulatory bouquet of yellow roses backstage—but until now, we'd not met in person. Their world of international banking and staggering art collections was as inaccessible to me as mine of greasepaint and squabbles over stage lighting was to them. Yet despite the vast social divide between us, we shared a common bond: they, too, were of Jewish blood.

"Mademoiselle Bernhardt," said the baron, kissing my hand. "It is my great pleasure to welcome you to my home. We are such admirers of your unparalleled gifts."

"Monsieur le Baron." I inclined my head, feeling tendrils of my hair already escaping the pins holding my chignon in place.

"His Grace the Duc d'Aumale has expressed eagerness to meet you." The baron cupped my elbow, steering me with the lifelong expertise of a consummate host past the drawing room into an adjoining scarlet-damask library. The hue of the wallpaper made me think of the linings of Oscar's frock coats; glancing behind me, I saw I'd effectively been separated from Louise and my poet.

The smile on my lips felt strained. I didn't know who this duke was or why he'd be so eager to meet me, but as the baron made a slight motion toward the fireplace, I saw two men seated before it in winged armchairs. The firelight cast their faces in shifting shadows; as I wondered which one was the admiring duke, one of them came to his feet.

I recognized him at once. His official portrait hung in the royal box at the Gaiety. In person, however, he was smaller, more rotund, of average height, dressed in a simple black tie and gray evening jacket, his egg-like pate at odds with his bushy mustachios and forked beard. He had sharp blue eyes that were startlingly youthful for someone who otherwise appeared much older. Those eyes, I thought as he neared, were his sole attraction. He didn't require more. Eyes that appeared capable of removing one's dress with a single glance, coupled with the inviolate power of his rank.

"Mademoiselle, you are here at last," said Prince Edward of Wales. "We'd begun to wonder if you were going to leave us famished and in perpetual suspense."

I began to curtsy, but the narrow fit of my gown—without excessive petticoats or underpinnings—constrained me. For a mortifying instant, I found myself crouched before the heir to the British throne with my knees half-bent, clumsy as a newborn foal.

Bertie of Wales gave a throaty laugh. "Charming, as I'd supposed. Shall we?" He held out his arm. Through his sleeve, I could feel the strength in his flesh. Not muscular, but hardy—a man who enjoyed his physical pursuits. "I had dinner delayed to accommodate your tardiness." He cast a sidelong glance at me. "I hope you like venison. I shot it myself at Windsor. Especially for you."

I had to smile. "I'm afraid I no longer eat meat, Your Royal Highness. A peculiarity of mine."

"Is that so? Well, let us hope they serve plenty of fish, too, yes?" He patted my hand on his arm. "And you must call me Bertie. No 'royal highness' here tonight. Consider me just another of your legions of admirers."

I suddenly remembered. "What of my lord the duke?" I asked, shifting my gaze to the other figure slumped in the armchair.

"Fast asleep." Bertie leaned to me, his mustachios prickling my ear. "No head for spirits, I'm afraid. And deaf as a stone. He'll regret it later. I will not."

At dinner, he consumed his slaughtered deer with gusto, along with copious glasses of Rothschild's vintage wine. He told me that while he loved the theater, he detested books.

"I've never understood the purpose of turning the pages of someone else's story," he declared. "I prefer to make my own stories." He went on to regale me with tales of his travels, fascinating me with his hunts in India on elephants and making me think of Maurice's love for those majestic creatures. The prince also surprised me by being fully versed in my own adventures during the Prussian war—"Such a barbarous display of Teutonic rapacity," he growled. When I explained that I'd lost my appetite for meat after the wholesale slaughter during the siege of every living creature in Paris, he nodded as if he understood my unusual abstention, though it didn't deter him from ladling his plate with slabs of his freshly shot venison. He made no mention of his absent wife. Neither did I.

After the ten-course dinner, during which he monopolized my attention and most of the conversation, he announced that he wished to smoke and bade me accompany him back to the library. The other guests leapt to their feet, bowing and scraping back chairs in their haste to accommodate him.

"Such a gaggle of nobodies," he groused as we entered the library to find the somnolent duke exactly as we'd left him. Bertie snapped open a cigarette case and extended it to me. I nearly demurred before I took one and allowed him to light it for me. I let the aromatic smoke drift uninhaled from my lips as he poured two cognacs.

"Some might say I'm a nobody," I remarked.

"You?" He let out a guffaw. His face was flushed; he had eaten and drunk more than I'd ever seen a man consume in a single sitting and still remain upright. "The Incomparable One. Isn't that how your friend the poet has christened you?"

I sipped the cognac he handed me. "I thought you didn't like to read," I said.

"Books. I don't like to read books. Newspapers are shorter, if no less arduous."

I smiled. "Oscar has a propensity for exaggeration."

"No." He regarded me. "He's very peculiar, but he's no fool. He knows an exceptional woman when he sees one." I saw a smile tease under his mustachios. "I understand that in addition to performing on the stage, you also like to paint and sculpt."

"Whenever I can find the time——"

"I'd like to see your works." His smile widened. All of a sudden, he resembled an overgrown cherub. It was nearly impossible to believe that this man with too much wine on his breath stood to inherit one of the largest empires in the world. Had I not known, I'd have thought him one of those enterprising charlatans who ran a boulevard theater; he had the same ability to make one believe his charm was exclusive, despite the inescapable fact that his charm was as promiscuous as his appetites.

"I'm afraid I didn't bring any of my artworks with me," I demurred.

"Then you must send for them. We shall mount an exhibition here, patronized by me." He chortled. "You will sell every piece, I assure you. And," he said, bringing his voice to a confidential hush, though the duke was snoring and we were otherwise alone, "it'll put a well-deserved bridle on those insufferable wagging tongues. If they must resort to gossip, let them do so with a smattering of truth."

I downed my cognac. Its fiery spear coiled about my heart.

"How can I ever repay such generosity?" I met his stare. "A private recital, perhaps?"

"I'll hear you recite on closing night at the Gaiety." He drank his tumbler, setting it aside. "I had another type of private performance in mind." He held out his arm again. "Shall we return to the wolves? We don't want them resorting to gossip too soon."

I accepted his escort into the drawing room. He was right, of course. If they were going to spread slander about me, let it be slander that I initiated.

III

Jarrett made the arrangements to bring my paintings and sculptures from Paris; he also undertook the task of communicating with the prince's secretary to determine the venue and list of invitees. Seeing as my artworks were coming to England, I saw no reason not to send for Maurice and Madame G., as well. My son hadn't completed his summer term, but in her correspondence, *ma petite dame* conveyed he was unlikely to pass his failed courses. All he did was mope about the house, the dogs at his heels, saying he missed me.

Under the prince's patronage, one hundred invitees were agreed upon; on the night of the exhibition, more than two hundred showed up, alerted by newspaper articles highlighting that Mademoiselle Bernhardt had made HRH of Wales's acquaintance at a private dinner organized by a foreign banking dynasty. The innuendo was hardly subtle, given Bertie's well-publicized affection for foreigners and actresses, so I elected to capitalize on it.

In addition to having French champagne served at the Piccadilly art gallery, I paired an ebony ivory-handled walking stick with my Worth suit of white silk, adorned by a large tulle bow at my throat. I made certain to greet everyone personally, to make amusing conversation and provide anecdotes about the inspiration for my works, none of which were true. But high society expected art to have a raison d'être, and only Prime Minister Gladstone, a longtime ally of the prince, deduced I was playing everyone present for a fool.

Decidedly attractive even in his seventieth year, with piercing, agate-colored eyes and a well-tuned, melodious voice, the prime minister was also extremely erudite, engaging me in spirited conversation ranging from the moral lessons we could derive from *Phaedra* to our shared opposition to capital punishment, as he was renowned for his liberal notions.

"If I were queen," I told him, "I'd put an immediate end to such savagery."

He gave me an indulgent smile. "I fear you'd not last long on our throne."

"No doubt," I replied. "But imagine how few heads would roll in my brief reign."

When Bertie arrived with his princess, he bestirred the guests to a sudden rush to purchase my works. Alexandra of Wales greeted me with the polished opacity that only those born to royalty could display, but women have an unerring instinct for betrayal, and I felt a pang of remorse when I glimpsed the wound behind her glacial poise, her constant awareness that her husband was an incorrigible voluptuary. Whenever Bertie pointed out a piece he favored, within minutes said piece was acquired by a sycophant eager to curry his favor.

"A very successful exhibition," said Princess Alexandra, as she and Bertie prepared to depart. "What shall you do with the proceeds, Mademoiselle Bernhardt?"

"Put it toward my son Maurice's tuition," I replied carelessly.

Her practiced smile slipped. "I wasn't aware you were married."

Bertie regarded me with an insouciant smile, as if he was daring me to lie.

"I am not, Your Highness." I leaned to her. "My son was *un petit accident d'amour*."

Alexandra did not display a visible reaction, which I had to admire, even as the court ladies flanking her released a united gasp of dismay.

On the carriage ride back to Chester Square, Louise said dryly, "You now seem determined to prove that everything they report about you is true."

"What else should I do?" I retorted. "Don one of their funereal gowns and *bon marché* bonnets, while dragging a penitential cross to the Gaiety?"

She burst out laughing. "Finally. *This* is the Incomparable One I know and love."

I was overjoyed to have Maurice with me, to hear him race about the house jabbering in French, startling the English staff, and earning Caroline's reprimand for taking to the staircase banister as if it were a toboggan.

"Maman," he said to me, "why don't we have any animals here? I miss Clotilde."

Our pets had remained in Paris in the care of my maids, seeing as my stay in London was nearing its end. But upon my son's dejection, I asked Jarrett where I might acquire additions for my menagerie. He located a gentleman in Liverpool who kept an exotic zoo and offered to receive me. Maurice fell in love with a young cheetah he named Sylvie. I fell in love with four iridescent African chameleons and a pair of majestic lions, though after some deliberation, I conceded the lions were too imposing to ship back home. Instead, I settled on an Irish wolfhound as large as a pony and docile as a puppy, resembling the one Clairin had depicted in my portrait. Hiring an entire train carriage to convey them—and expending my exhibition proceeds—I arrived in Chester Square with the chameleons clinging to my skirts, having munched on hand-fed leaves on my lap during the trip.

Maurice's cheetah strained at her tether. She was scarcely out of cubhood, lean and strong; at the sight of her, Madame G. shrieked in terror and fled into the house.

My son frowned. "Sylvie won't hurt anyone, will she?"

"No," I said, "but she must be very hungry by now. Come."

Putting my chameleons in a cage and handing it to Caroline, I strode into the gated private green of the neighborhood with the wolfhound, Sylvie tugging at her leash. As squirrels scampered in panic up the trees, the wolfhound bayed and I told Maurice to unclip Sylvie's tether. She pounced with a speed that left us breathless. Faster than our eyes could follow her, she sprang onto a branch to seize an unfortunate squirrel in her jaws, devouring the poor creature whole.

Maurice went wide-eyed. "She *was* hungry," he said in amazement.

"Indeed. We must take care she doesn't try to eat Madame Guérard."

Maurice let out an uproarious laugh; about the green, the windows of neighboring houses flung open, heads poking out to determine what the clamor was about. When they saw Sylvie slinking to us at Maurice's insistent call, her snout bloodstained, an eruption of fearful outrage obliged us to hasten back into my residence. The police were notified.

The very next day, every newspaper was flooded with declarations that Mademoiselle Bernhardt kept wild animals about her, which she let loose on the streets to hunt. I was fined a hefty sum for my transgression and warned to keep my pets under strict restraint.

I thought it a fitting conclusion to my British sojourn.

On closing night at the Gaiety, I performed scenes with Jean from *Zaïre*, followed by my regal monologue from Hugo's *Ruy Blas*. The notices were unanimous; no one, exulted the London *Times*, "can argue that Mlle Bernhardt is our era's most accomplished player, even if her private life isn't at all what one is accustomed to."

Bertie fulfilled his promise to the last, leading the house in a standing ovation with his princess at his side. He flooded my dressing room with roses.

As I was packing up my belongings for my return to Paris, Oscar came to say goodbye. His despondent expression made me chuckle.

"Now, now." I cupped his chin. "None of that. We shall see each other again in Paris, yes? I insist you come visit. And don't forget you have that play to write for me."

I almost added that he would also find plenty of like-minded gentlemen in Paris to entertain him. Meyer would find him irresistible and take him to all the places where those of their persuasion gathered. I did not say it, though, because while I knew his secret, Oscar himself hadn't told me, so I had no wish to pry into his private affairs unless he allowed it.

While he made the effort to be cheerful and helped me pack, remarking that he thought it ill-advised that I hadn't brought my bat hat with me and worn it to my meeting with the prince, the English maid entered my bedroom with an envelope. "This was just delivered for the mademoiselle," she told Oscar, who, to my amusement, displayed that he shared none of my compunction regarding privacy as he ripped the envelope open himself.

He let out a laugh, laced with the gusto that had made me adore him. "No need for my translation services here," he said, handing the note to me. "It's written in perfect French. And from an exalted admirer, I might add."

Looking at the handwritten note, I read:

You have conquered this isle. Alas, we failed to conquer the wagging tongues.

I looked up to see Oscar smiling. "Will you miss him?" he asked.

"Not as much as I will miss you," I replied.

IV

I was overjoyed to return to Paris, to be home among my pets and things. I soon discovered not everyone in Paris was overjoyed to have me back.

Invitations from friends were piled in my foyer; along with cascades of flowers and, I discovered, an anonymous note in an envelope. No postmark, indicating whoever had written it had delivered it personally—a fact that curdled my blood when I read it:

> *My poor skeleton, you'd do well to not show your horrible Jewish nose at the opening ceremony. I fear it would serve as a target for all the potatoes being cooked especially for you in Paris. Have notices put in the papers to the effect that you are spitting blood and stay in bed to ponder the consequences of your excessive publicity.*

I stood in my salon, the note like a stain in my fingers. The handwriting was scrawled, almost crude, but its threat was unmistakable. I knew exactly which ceremony it referred to, as I informed Perrin when I went at once to the theater to show it to him.

"Our annual tribute to Molière," I said, trying in vain to keep the anger from my voice. "Someone is planning a crime against us."

Perrin made a moue of revulsion. "Against *you*. This is the result of your outrages in London. You have placed this entire company in an intolerable position because of your outrageous lack of sensibility."

"Your receipts from London show a profit only because of my outrages," I reminded him, realizing I should have expected a confrontation. He had restrained the full weight of his disapproval while in London, no doubt to ensure I did not call in sick twice, but now his expression turned as remorseless as autumn's encroachment over the city.

"And you think it makes you invincible? Though it would be unprecedented in this company's history, I am prepared to petition our governing committee to withdraw your senior status. In fact, the committee has already called on me to do so, given your aversion to behaving as you ought. You shall never work here again, nor will you receive the pension due on your retirement, which may come about much sooner than you suppose."

"Do so." I didn't falter as I met his stony regard. Here it was at last, the dénouement that had been brewing between us since my return to the Comédie. When I turned and started to walk out of his office, with pride in what I'd accomplished and overwhelming relief to finally be freed of the burden, I heard him menace from behind me, "Until you are officially released, however, you will comply to the terms of our contract. You will attend our tribute as scheduled. I'll not have a rabble-rouser put a halt to our proceedings. I expect you to be there, with your lines memorized, so think carefully before you defy me."

I didn't dignify him with a look, but as soon as I departed the theater, I raced to the nearest wire office to send an urgent telegram to London, requesting Jarrett's advice. By the time his response arrived, I was prepared to defy not only Perrin, but all of Paris itself. Jarrett's reply only made me angrier, for he counseled that I must attend the tribute and put my trust in him to see to my future arrangements. What those arrangements entailed he did not elucidate, so on the date of the tribute, I joined the company for the ritual, which this year doubled as a welcoming reception for the Comédie's return from a "vastly successful run in London," as heralded by Sarcey, though no one who'd read the British coverage of our time in England could have doubted the success was solely mine.

In pairs, the actors advanced to set the fronds at the foot of Molière's plinth. I was partnered with Jean; when our turn came, I held out my hand to detain him and stalked alone to the front of the stage, my frond in hand. The select audience of journalists and patrons of the house—many of them also members of the governing committee, who'd called for my removal—was indistinct, yet I felt their stunned reaction as I stood before them with my shoulders squared, as if braced for an execution. I stared out at them in absolute silence, daring them to lambaste me.

Without warning, they came to their feet in unison, with a fervent burst of applause.

Tears filled my eyes. Only once they had exhausted themselves did I turn back to the bust to set down my frond. As I returned to the company, Jean gave me a knowing smile.

Given my reception by the very house that Perrin claimed had sought to revoke my senior status, he didn't dare follow through on his threat. Instead, he set me to the ordeal of a demanding 1879–80 season, culminating in my role as the queen in Hugo's *Ruy Blas*. Hugo himself attended the celebration for the fiftieth anniversary of his historical drama, where the playwright Coppée, who'd attained his own fame following the debut of his *Le Passant*, composed a poem in Hugo's honor. I recited it before my past lover with fiery conviction, and Hugo declared to all present, "Sarah Bernhardt is our crown jewel. Without her luminescence, we would languish in a dark past that no longer exists."

He sat me at his side at dinner, where we laughed and whispered to each other.

Perrin may have been stymied, but he wasn't about to be dissuaded. The tension between us grew so strained, we could scarcely abide to be in the same room together. For the spring season—I insisted on an extended Christmas respite to celebrate the holidays with my son—he informed me that I would play the lead in Émile Augier's *L'Aventurière*, a ridiculous play with nothing to commend it.

"Absolutely not," I said. "I know of a marvelous play written in this century: Dumas fils's *La Dame aux Camélias*. It just ended its run at the Vaudeville, where it enjoyed monumental success."

"I am aware," he replied dryly. "With Eugénie Doche reaping accolades as the consumptive courtesan."

"A part written for me—" I started to say.

Perrin snorted. "We still have a reputation to uphold, much as you wish to tear it down. That play is an embarrassment, an unsavory romanticization of an immoral trade." He eyed me as he spoke, deliberate in his condemnation of my own tenure in said trade. "I will close our doors permanently before I ever allow such a travesty on our stage."

In that instant, I made my decision. Jarrett had advised me not to risk further contention with Perrin, but it was glaringly obvious that I had to leave the Comédie, lest he and I come to blows. I must now take matters into my own hands.

On opening night, I sashayed onto the stage as the titular adventuress and overplayed every line like "a vulgar tart in a Zola novel," as Sarcey hissed in his notice. It was precisely the denigration I'd hoped for. Citing Perrin's disregard of my value to the company, I submitted my resignation from the Comédie. Before anyone could mount a protest, I sent copies of my resignation letter to every newspaper in Paris.

Jarrett hurried across the Channel to see me. "Why?" he asked, standing in my salon in his sopping hat and overcoat, the skies dumping rains such as had not been seen since the year of my pregnancy with Maurice. "If you'd only waited awhile longer—"

I thrust my most recent notices at him. "Look at these. From Hugo's crown jewel, I've descended to the status of a vulgar tart because of Perrin's dreadful play. You said if we failed to find mutual accord, I was free to leave. Now I have done so."

Removing his hat, he passed a hand through his damp hair before he said, "Be that as it may, you voided your contract and made your complaints with the Comédie public. After such a break, Perrin will ensure that no other company dares hire you."

I paused. "Are you saying my career is over?" All of a sudden, I had a sharp pang of regret over my own brashness. I'd thrown caution aside, all the years of toil and sacrifice to become who I was. I hadn't stopped to consider whether anyone would hire me after this, though I suspected Duquesnel would be more than eager, providing I agreed to an iron-clad contract that would require my beheading should I defect again.

Jarrett replied, "What I'm saying is you have closed the door to any future employment with an established theater company."

My throat constricted. "But you were the one who told me no established company could satisfy me. And I want nothing more to do with rules and limitations. I want to perform whatever I like, however I like—as you promised," I added, as he lapsed into one of his indecipherable silences.

At length, he sighed. "Are you certain this is how you wish to proceed?"

"Yes." I gave an emphatic nod. The truth was, I'd left myself with no other alternative. "Is it possible? Or must I go begging in the streets?"

When his smile surfaced, I almost wept. "As I said, if you'd only waited, I would have informed you it's not only possible, but imminent. The Gaiety has requested your return to London for an exclusive six-week engagement next year. I'm also in the process of negotiating an extensive overseas tour for you in the United States."

I went still. "Exclusive? How . . . ?"

"By establishing your own company." From his briefcase, he took out a ledger, opening it before me on the table. "Here is the sum total of the proceeds from your recitals in London, minus my commission." He tapped a number in the column that widened my eyes. "Even with your considerable extravagances," he said, glancing at my chameleons in their cage, "you've earned quite enough to do as you please."

"All this?" I was incredulous. "It's far more than a small fortune."

His smile widened. "Indeed. Shall I cable the Gaiety with our agreement?"

I could have hugged him. Instead, I sank onto my couch. "Yes," I whispered.

Quand même.

1896

I stand in the wings, dressed in Marguerite Gautier's mother-of pearl satin gown, my dyed hair piled about a diadem of camellias, opera-length gloves sheathing my arms.

It is the premiere of *La Dame aux Camélias* at le Théâtre de la Renaissance. Beyond the curtain, I can hear the audience settling into their seats like a restless sea, the papery crackle of handbills and slice of ebony-and-lace fans cutting the air. I've made this role one of my signature parts, performing it hundreds of times from Moscow to Chicago, even though in London I risked arrest, as British censorship laws had branded the play immoral.

I've traveled the world with my character Marguerite, traversing the vastness of America on my specially appointed train to perform in tents on windswept plains where the blood of slaughtered tribes still drenched the soil; on grandiose stages in gargantuan cities; and on decrepit platforms in tumbleweed towns. Everywhere I've gone, Marguerite's doomed love has elicited tears. Regardless of whether my audience understands Dumas's verse, they weep anyway, stirred to emotion by her self-sacrificing dance into death.

But never in Paris. Until tonight.

As I await the curtain's rise, I see those who have gone before me. My sister Régine, flittering among the coiled ropes like a sprite. Jeanne, dead before her thirtieth year of an opium overdose. My mother, Julie, laid to rest in her prepurchased tomb after years of languishing in an empty salon, drifting past me with a censorious glance. And my aunt Rosine, the last of my maternal family to depart, fretful in the shadows.

Ma petite dame is here in spirit, too. I feel her close as I always have, her palm at my brow, gauging my temperature and suggesting a cup of hot cocoa to warm my blood. I lost her to pneumonia on a bitter winter night that shattered my heart.

And the living. Jean is in the audience, having sent me an enormous bouquet of congratulatory roses, competing as is his wont with Bertie of Wales, not yet king of Great Britain, as his ancient mother clings to her throne. Duquesnel stalks backstage; still debonair, he's organized several of my international tours under Jarrett's patronage and continues to champion me, our grievances forgiven. Louise sits in the front row, with her sketchpad at the ready. She wants to paint me as Marguerite, though Mucha has already immortalized me in his lavish, swirling posters.

I am fifty-two years old, but my past is never far from my present.

How will the city of my birth receive me?

"Maman, it's time." Maurice comes up beside me. So handsome now, so tall like his father, with my coppery hair darkened by Kératry's hue. He is my most precious achievement, this son I chose to keep despite everything aligned against us. He has become a playwright, a producer, and an aspiring director; he has always dreamed of managing our own theater, and so I've given him the lease on the Renaissance.

He kisses my cheek. "*Merde*, Maman. Remember who you are."

After the hammer blows preceding the curtain's rise, the orchestra strikes up the refrain. No matter how long I've been on the stage, opening nights are always the same. The sudden hush, taut as cloth about to rip. The sensation of nothing under my feet, as if I'm again taking flight in Nadar's balloon. The constriction of my throat as the claw of *le trac* uncoils, a curse that has never fully deserted me.

Tonight, however, there's also something else.

Fear.

The French public and critics have always been unpredictable, as liable to condemn as to praise me. How will they react to this tragedy that echoes my now-obscure past, my own fraught beginnings as a courtesan and the demise of my younger sister of the same disease? How will they compare me to those who've performed this role before me, the loyal actresses who never strayed to foreign shores in search of fortune and acclaim? Yet it is *my* role, first conceived of for me by my beloved Dumas, long gone now, but growing ever more famous, his works a fount of inspiration for hundreds of writers seeking to emulate him. Marguerite is his gift to me. She is mine; she has always been mine.

I glide forth for the first act, my practiced steps exuberant as a waltz.

Behind the music, the silence is oppressive, a sound in and of itself. I almost falter. I see myself as if from above: the unwanted child separated from her dog. The devout schoolgirl yearning to take the veil. The struggling ingénue, felled by mistrust in her own talent. The lead actress of the Odéon, in her lithe hose and page-boy cut. Mademoiselle Révolte of the Comédie, letting a cheetah loose to hunt in a London park.

It does not matter how I'm received. I have made my mark. No one can take that away from me. Regardless of what is said of me tonight, I will always be Sarah Bernhardt.

As I pause on the stage, my hand set on my hip in Marguerite's provocative stance, the sudden roar of applause overwhelms me. The orchestra is forced to stop. Gazing upon hundreds of strangers and friends as they come to their feet, I hear their enthusiastic cry:

"Sarah! Sarah! *Notre divine* Sarah!"

I am home. I am adored. And, yes, I am finally divine.

Curtain Call: Afterword

Sarah Bernhardt performed for the rest of her life to worldwide acclaim, success, and failure. She often toured for months on end, with her first North American tour covering 157 engagements in 51 cities. She refused to perform in Germany because of the annexation of French territory after the Franco-Prussian War, but she went on tour throughout most of Europe and Russia. In Kiev, anti-Semitic crowds hurled stones at her; in Saint Petersburg, Tsar Alexander III broke court protocol to bow to her. She counted several royals among her admirers, among them Edward VII of Great Britain, Alfonso XII of Spain, and Emperor Franz Joseph I of Austria.

In 1882, she met a Greek diplomat-turned-actor, known by his stage name of Jacques Damala. He was eleven years younger than she; Sarah fell in love and made him her leading man. Upon their wedding in London, she told friends she had done it because "marriage was the only thing" she'd never experienced. Damala's lesser talent, however, caused him to envy and humiliate his famous wife. He became a morphine addict, expending her money on his vice and mistresses until she confronted him. He left her only to eventually return, penniless and ailing. Always forgiving, Sarah took him back and performed with him until he proved himself unworthy of her trust. In 1889, he suffered a near-fatal overdose. She nursed him until his death at the age of thirty-four. Sarah sculpted his bust for his tomb in Athens. To the end of her life, she signed all of her official documents as his widow.

Her unwilling rivalry with Marie Colombier became an international scandal when Colombier, who'd gone on tour with her at Sarah's behest, published in 1884 a fictitious work about an ambitious actress that made no attempt to hide its resemblance to Sarah's life. Enraged, Sarah assaulted Colombier backstage with an umbrella, prompting a slew of caricatures and gleeful headlines. For Sarah, it was the final betrayal; she filed suit against Marie for "gross indecency" and the book was withdrawn after selling thousands of copies in ninety-two printings. Marie's acting career faded, but she continued to publish novels, as well as volumes of her memoirs, before her death in 1910 at the age of sixty-six.

In contrast, Sarah's friendship with Louise Abbéma endured for the rest of their lives. Louise's prolific accomplishments as a painter, sculptor, designer, and printmaker earned her the Palmes Académiques in 1887 and the nomination as "Official Painter of the Third Republic." She was awarded a medal at the 1900 Universal Exposition and made a chevalier of the Order of the Légion d'honneur in 1906. She died in 1927, at the age of seventy-three.

Oscar Wilde eventually wrote his *Salomé* in French for Sarah. Rehearsals for its 1892 debut in London were brought to a halt because it was illegal in England to depict biblical characters onstage. Sarah was forty-eight years old at the time. Three years later, Wilde was convicted of sodomy and imprisoned for two years. Upon his release, he left England, wandering through Italy until he ended up destitute in Paris, where he died at the age of forty-six.

Sarah never performed the role he had created for her.

Her later years were replete with financial catastrophes and extended tours to recoup her losses. She made several returns to the United States and South America, where her popularity ensured immense profit. Tireless despite her advancing age, she performed for years while suffering pain in her right leg, which she'd injured in a fall from a stage in Brazil in 1905. She finally had to have her leg amputated in 1915 after gangrene set in; she had just turned seventy. Never one to wallow in a setback, Sarah took the loss in stride.

In 1907, she was awarded the Légion d'honneur for her work as a theater director, not as an actress. The acting award depended on the recipient's moral character, and Sarah was deemed unfit due to her numerous love affairs and controversial roles. Regardless of the criticism leveled against her, French journalists often depicted her as the heroic embodiment of patriotism, and she remained beloved in her native country.

Sarah was one of the first actresses to star in motion pictures. For her film debut, she performed a scene from her famous London stage production as Hamlet. Her son, Maurice, made a phonograph recording, making the film one of our first sound movies. In 1908, she filmed *La Tosca*, which has sadly been lost. She also filmed her signature role as *La Dame aux Camélias*, a financial and critical success. In 1912, she filmed scenes from a play about Queen Elizabeth I, in which she performed the role of the Earl of Essex; the hand-tinted print made it one of history's first colorized films. Sarah's ability to embody both male and female roles, coupled with her fascination with emerging media, exemplified her pioneering spirit and fearless quest for challenge, as well as her lifelong disdain for time-honored tradition.

She also starred in two documentaries, including one about her daily life. Many years before reality television became an entertainment staple, Sarah was the first celebrity to invite the public into her home. In 1914, she made a propaganda film to encourage the United States to enter World War I.

Sarah's memoir *Ma Double Vie* (*My Double Life*) was published in 1907. While given to dramatic license, her writing exudes her charismatic flair. She authored six other books, among them her children's story of the talking chair and a treatise on the art of the theater. She continued to sculpt and paint throughout her life, holding exhibitions at the Paris Salon and in London, New York, and Philadelphia. Many of her artworks are still on display in museums in France, England, and the United States.

She also performed in her self-named theater in Paris, which was managed by Maurice until he died in 1928 at the age of sixty-three, five years after his mother. During the German occupation in the Second World War, the Nazis renamed her theater the Théâtre de la Cité because of her Jewish ancestry. Known today as the Théâtre de la Ville, its façade bears a plaque honoring Sarah's contributions.

In the weeks before her death on March 26, 1923, Sarah was preparing for another motion picture. She passed away from kidney failure before filming began, at the age of seventy-eight. Laid to rest with the honors of a dignitary in the Père Lachaise Cemetery, she was mourned worldwide. In 1960, she was given a star on the Hollywood Walk of Fame.

Much of Sarah Bernhardt's oeuvre is still performed today, while other of her signature roles have become less known. *Zaïre* inspired several operas. *La Tosca* and *La Dame aux Camélias*, known popularly as *Camille*, were both made into operas by Puccini and Verdi, respectively. Verdi's opera, titled *La Traviata*, renamed Marguerite Gautier as Violetta Valéry. Since its premiere in 1853, it has remained one of our most beloved operas. *La Dame aux Camélias* has also been adapted for nineteen films, with the titular character played by Sarah herself, as well as María Félix, Theda Bara, Greta Garbo, and Isabelle Hubbert, and by Teresa Stratas in a sumptuous rendition of the operatic version, directed by Franco Zeffirelli. Sarah's monumental role as Phaedra continues to be a staple in classical theater.

Although extant fragments of her filmed performances appear mannered by today's standards, Sarah's naturalistic approach to acting was considered nothing short of revolutionary, enrapturing audiences accustomed to artificiality on the stage. As a standard-bearer for women's rights before the movement had a name, her daring entrepreneurship challenged systemic control over an artist's career, as did her single motherhood, which defied social ostracization by her willing admission that she had borne her son out of wedlock. Despite her conversion to Catholicism, she always took pride in her Jewish blood and never denied it.

At the height of her fame, Sarah was earning a higher salary than her male counterparts, demanding to be paid what she was worth; she recognized her value and upheld it, anticipating our contemporary movement for equal pay and inclusion for women. During her international tours, she performed in both high-end theaters and on improvised stages in way stations along her travels, determined to make the theater accessible to everyone. Sarah detested elitism; to her, acting was an art form, and the public's ability to enjoy it shouldn't be reserved solely for the well-to-do.

Her searing talent and ambition, coupled with her eccentricity and joie de vivre, have cemented her legacy and her lasting influence on history and the world of acting.

I relied on many sources to research this novel. While the list below is not intended as a full bibliography, it comprises the works I consulted most often to portray Sarah and her world:

Agate, May. *Madame Sarah*. London: Benjamin Blom, 1969.

Baring, Maurice. *Sarah Bernhardt*. London: D. Appleton–Century, 1934.

Brandon, Ruth. *Being Divine*. London: Secker & Warburg, 1991.

Gold, Arthur, and Robert Fizdale. *The Divine Sarah*. New York: Alfred A. Knopf, 1991.

Gottlieb, Robert. *Sarah*. New Haven: Yale University Press, 2010.

Hough, Richard. *Edward and Alexandra*. New York: St. Martin's Press, 1992.

Ockman, Carol, and Kenneth E. Silver. *Sarah Bernhardt: The Art of High Drama*. New Haven: Yale University Press, 2006.

Richardson, Joanna. *Sarah Bernhardt and Her World*. New York: G. P. Putnam's Sons, 1977.

Skinner, Cornelia Otis. *Madame Sarah*. New York: Houghton Mifflin, 1966.

Weber, Eugen. *France, Fin de Siècle*. Cambridge: Harvard University Press, 1986.

Acknowledgments

As I was revising this novel, my beautiful aunt Meme, whom I adored while growing up in Spain, passed away of lung cancer. Whenever I smell night jasmine, I think of her, as it festooned her home during my childhood. Despite many challenges in her life, Meme always had a warm smile and a loving heart for others. My aunt had always wanted to be a writer; I dedicate this novel to her indelible memory.

I also lost my ex-feral feline companion, Mommy Cat, whom I'd rescued from a park seven years ago along with her son, Boy. She died of the same ailment as Sarah. Mommy's gentle spirit and noble courage in the face of adversity will never be forgotten. She was deeply loved and she is deeply missed.

My interest in Sarah Bernhardt first began in Spain, with my maternal grandmother, Pilar Beinart, a theatrical actress who chided me for my dramatic tendencies with the adage "Don't be a Bernhardt." I later learned that "being a Bernhardt" was a popular admonishment of Jewish mothers everywhere. My mother's father, Tomás Blanco, was also a successful film and television actor, so I was naturally drawn to Sarah Bernhardt's appeal because of my familial connection to the performing arts.

Documentation about Sarah Bernhardt is plentiful, but can be contrary. Her memoir is more fictional than autobiographical—she was notorious for embellishing the truth, especially about herself—and even her birthday is subject to debate, as her personal records were destroyed in a fire at the Hôtel de Ville. The identity of her son

Maurice's father has also never been established. While I've strived to stay faithful to the facts and documented personalities, I admit to certain liberties, such as shifts in time or place to facilitate the narrative, as well as the omission of certain people and events to maintain a cohesive pacing. My insight into these characters is my personal interpretation, based on what is known. Any errors I may have made are inadvertent.

My intent wasn't to depict Sarah's life in its entirety, as that would require two volumes or more, but rather to create a fictional portrait—based as closely as possible on the facts—of her rise to fame as one of the era's most exceptional figures.

As always, I thank my husband, who supports my preoccupation while in the throes of my work. My cat, Boy, reminds me that innocence and love are cherished gifts. My agent, Jennifer Weltz, is my literary advocate and champion. She and her staff at the Jean V. Naggar Agency never cease to try to ease the tribulations of being a professional novelist.

My editor, Susanna Porter, was the first to take a chance on me, and remains gracious and insightful in her ongoing support. My assistant editor, Emily Hartley, and copy editor Deborah Dwyer also contributed to this novel in many ways. I'm privileged to have Ballantine Books as my publisher in our very challenging marketplace.

I owe special thanks to booksellers everywhere who continue to invite me to speak at events and recommend my books.

Most of all, I thank you, my reader. Your purchases of my novels, comments on social media, emails, and appearances at my events help me to continue to pursue this oft-lonely profession. I hope I can continue to entertain you for many years to come.

Sarah's love of animals is a motif that I share with many of my leading characters. Please do whatever you can to help save our beleaguered planet and the unique species that depend on its survival. We must never cease fighting for every animal's right to live and thrive; without them, our Mother Earth will be a desolate place.

Thank you!

THE FIRST ACTRESS

A NOVEL OF
SARAH BERNHARDT

C. W. Gortner

A Book Club Guide

The Trailblazing Sarah Bernhardt

By C. W. Gortner

Pursuing a character with whom I can spend more than a year writing about, and who wants me to do it, isn't always easy. There have been times when my enthusiasm has been met with disdain and refusal to cooperate; she simply doesn't want me meddling in her affairs, obliging me to apologize and slink away in defeat.

Other times, as with Sarah Bernhardt, I find myself regaled by a candor that exceeds even my vivid imagination. When this happens, when the barrier between past and present dissolves to reveal how much has changed and how much has not, I find my nirvana. Because for me, historical fiction is more than entertainment. At its heart, it's a doorway to our shared humanity, to the struggles and triumphs of those before us; it offers a common experience that transcends time. Sarah herself famously said, "Life begets life. Energy creates energy. It is by spending oneself that one becomes rich."

She certainly spent her energy without regret. While Sarah isn't as well known today as she should be, which is why I wanted to write about her, stories about intrepid women abound in historical fiction. Sarah stands apart, not only for her defiance of society, but because she didn't see it as defiance. She was a feminist before the concept was coined. A single mother before it was acceptable. A champion for equal pay when women had few employment options and fewer rights. An independent artist who believed art should be accessible to everyone, at a time when the theater was deemed either a venue for rabble or a pantheon for classic posturing. And she did all of this without anticipating the impact she would make.

Why is she important to us? She was an actress, after all, albeit the most celebrated of her era. She didn't invent a miracle drug or protect an endangered species. It can be argued that she was just trying to get her way and didn't accomplish anything of serious merit. And that might be true, if we disregard the profound influence she had on her profession. What we see today in film—the naturalistic approach in acting—is Sarah's legacy. Before her, acting was stiffly narcissistic, the quest for fame grounded in the actor's oversized personality. No actor before Sarah cared about how well they portrayed their characters as much as they craved to be known for their own name. This isn't new; the most successful actors are always those whose fame can fill the seats. But talent has become integral to success, and that's due to Sarah. Yes, she wanted to succeed and was willing to go to extreme lengths to achieve it, but in her era, ambition in a woman was a threat. No respectable lady sought public recognition, as it was strictly a man's purview. Sarah turned the tables on this notion. She believed she deserved to be recognized for her talent and paid commensurately for it. Her demand for equality among her peers echoes in our twenty-first century, where women continue to receive less recognition and lower salaries than their male counterparts.

The outrageous antics Sarah displays in my novel, like reciting poetry from a coffin, her air balloon publicity stunt, and rescuing a puma, are factual. She was eccentric by nature, driven by the lack of love in her childhood to bestow her affection on those who could love her unconditionally in return—first, her menagerie of animals, and later, her only child. She could be flighty and extravagant, as well as selfish. I didn't omit her less attractive traits because to craft a living being on the page, a writer must depict their entirety; only then can we understand *why* they became who they were. I believe Sarah's adulthood showed the emotional aftermath of her upbringing: money was to be earned and spent lavishly because she never had it growing up. Family must be supported regardless of how difficult the relationships might be, but also kept at bay lest they swallow her whole. And work—her true fulfillment in life—must be sacrosanct, because only through work could she retain her independence. She was never given choices as a child, so for her, work was her choice. It was her escape and redemption.

It's important to honor those upon whose shoulders we stand, the courageous and flawed, whose efforts helped make the world better for future generations. If nothing else, Sarah Bernhardt accomplished this. She proved women could become well-paid professionals. She proved women could raise children on their own. She proved artists could throw off the shackles of corporate oversight and create art on their own terms. These are great achievements in any era, but for the nineteenth century, they were unprecedented. She wasn't the only successful woman of her time; she was, however, the most notorious.

She might have laughed to hear herself defined as a trailblazer. She would have replied that she was only doing what she had to do, to be true to who she was. And this alone warrants respect. Being true to ourselves is a goal most of us strive for but rarely attain. Sarah wasn't afraid of who she was. She was afraid of not being true to it.

I hope you've enjoyed her journey as much as I enjoyed writing it. Every character I create holds a special place in my heart, even if I often don't agree with them. Sarah is one I would have truly liked to befriend. And through *The First Actress*, I feel as if I did.

Questions and Topics for Discussion

1. Sarah's schoolmate says of Sarah's mother, "To live as you please and make your own fortune: it's a freedom that of all women, only a courtesan enjoys." Considering the times, do you agree with that sentiment? What options seem available to women? What kind of women role models does Sarah have in her life?

2. Discuss Sarah's faith and her draw to Catholicism. Why do you think she wants to be baptized? What do you think of Mère Sophie?

3. Mère Sophie suggests that *quand même*—despite the odds—should be Sarah's motto. How many examples of *quand même* in Sarah's life can you pull from the book?

4. Discuss Sarah's relationship with her mother. Why do you think it is so complicated? What does each represent for the other? How does her mother shape—directly or indirectly—Sophie's life and choices?

5. Mère Sophie reminds a young Sarah to "choose the life you want." Do you think, by the book's end, Sarah has done that?

6. Why do you think Sarah feels such a pull to the stage? Have you had a similar experience with something in your life?

7. Name the people in Sarah's life who seem to have had a hand in her fate. Do you think her success is based on her talent alone? Or do you think she was fortunate to have help?

8. Why do you think Sarah is determined to have her child? What kind of a mother do you think she becomes?

9. Do you think Sarah is a woman ahead of her time? Discuss her impact on culture—in her art, in Parisian society, and even in Hollywood.

PHOTO: © STEPHANIE MOHAN

C. W. GORTNER holds an MFA in writing, with an emphasis on historical studies, from the New College of California. He is the internationally acclaimed and bestselling author of *The Romanov Empress, Mademoiselle Chanel, The Queen's Vow, The Confessions of Catherine de Medici, The Last Queen, The Vatican Princess,* and *Marlene,* among other books. He lives in Northern California. To learn more about his work and to schedule a book group chat with him, please visit his website.

cwgortner.com
Facebook and Twitter: @CWGortner
Pinterest.com/cwgortner

ABOUT THE TYPE

This book was set in Fournier, a typeface named for Pierre-Simon Fournier (1712–68), the youngest son of a French printing family. He started out engraving woodblocks and large capitals, then moved on to fonts of type. In 1736 he began his own foundry and made several important contributions in the field of type design; he is said to have cut 147 alphabets of his own creation. Fournier is probably best remembered as the designer of St. Augustine Ordinaire, a face that served as the model for the Monotype Corporation's Fournier, which was released in 1925.

RANDOM HOUSE BOOK CLUB

Because Stories Are Better Shared

Discover

Exciting new books that spark conversation every week.

Connect

With authors on tour—or in your living room. (Request an Author Chat for your book club!)

Discuss

Stories that move you with fellow book lovers on Facebook, on Goodreads, or at in-person meet-ups.

Enhance

Your reading experience with discussion prompts, digital book club kits, and more, available on our website.

Join our online book club community!

f g randomhousebookclub.com

RANDOM HOUSE